Lynda Page was born and brought up in Leicester. The eldest of four daughters, she left home at seventeen and has had a wide variety of office jobs. She lives in a village near Leicester. Her previous novels, *Evie*, *Annie*, *Josie*, *Peggie*, *And One For Luck*, *Just By Chance* and *At The Toss Of A Sixpence*, are also available from Headline.

Praise for Lynda Page:

'In Lynda Page, we have an author who writes with skill and style; her characters are strongly drawn and thoroughly believable and her settings are just that little bit different . . . it keeps the reader enthralled from start to finish' *Hull Daily Mail*

'Lynda Page creates strong characters and is a clever and careful storyteller . . . She has the stamina not to alienate you as a reader and to keep the story going on a constant flow of purpose and energy . . . A great writer who gives an authentic voice to Leicester . . . A formidable talent' *LE1*

Any Old Iron

Lynda Page

HEADLINE

First published in 1998
by HEADLINE BOOK PUBLISHING

First published in paperback in 1999
by HEADLINE BOOK PUBLISHING

10 9 8 7 6 5 4 3

ISBN 0 7472 5505 9

Typeset by
Letterpart Limited, Reigate, Surrey

Printed and bound in Great Britain by
Caledonian International Book Manufacturing Ltd, Glasgow

HEADLINE BOOK PUBLISHING
A division of Hodder Headline PLC
338 Euston Road
London NW1 3BH

For Dave King.
A very special man.
With my love.

ACKNOWLEDGEMENTS

Roger and Jackie Goode, for your invaluable reminiscences of your family's history in the rag and bone trade.

Eric and Barbara Vardy from The Bookmark, Syston, Leicestershire. Who needs publicity when I have enthusiasts like 'yerselves'? Thank you for all your hard work in selling my books.

With extra special thanks to my boss, John Owen. I have worked with some wonderful bosses but you have to be the best. By the way, you owe me three cigarettes, hundreds of packets of Victory Vs, and it's your turn to make the coffee!

Chapter One

'Help me! Fer God's sake, Mickey, help me, I'm slip-ping.' Blind panic filled Frank McCallan as he clawed frantically at the slimy capping tiles on the summit of the church roof, his thin-soled boots desperately seeking a foothold on the slippery lead roofing. 'Mickey,' he pleaded. 'Mickey . . . MICKEY!' A hand grabbed his shoulder and he gasped with relief as he was roughly pulled just high enough to snatch hold of the capping. He took several deep breaths, fighting to calm himself. 'Ta, Mickey, ta. Oh, God, I thought me end 'ad come that time.'

Mickey McCallan leaned towards his father, eyes ablaze with anger. 'You were in no danger,' he hissed.

'I wa', Mickey. Yer saw me. I wa' . . .'

'You got the wind up, Dad, that's what yer done. Yer panicked. I knew this'd happen, that's why I told yer not ter come. This ain't the kinda place fer the likes of you.'

Frank recoiled from his son's words, eyes filled with humiliation as they met Mickey's. 'There wa' no need ter say that. No need ter mek me feel any more useless than I already do.'

Righting himself, Mickey eased his position astride the tiles, sniffing disdainfully. Before the war had arrived to wreak its havoc, the love and respect he had held for his father had known no bounds. But not now. Despite being told what Frank had suffered, Mickey could not

1

make allowances. The war had been over for three years and, to him, that was surely more than time enough to quash bad memories, heal wounds and get on with living. The man on the roof with him was nothing like the strong proud father who had gone away. This man was weak, one easily intimidated and manipulated. An unexpected show of character from him was merely annoying now.

'I only speak the truth. You ain't fit for this kinda lark, Dad, and the sooner you realise that the better for all of us. I could have asked Rod. I know it would have meant splitting the profit with him, but sooner that than what nearly happened. You could have killed yerself, or worse than that – got us both caught.'

The last accusation was spat out harshly and Frank gasped with horror to realise that his son was more concerned for his own safety than for his father's life.

'What's going on? Dad . . . Mickey . . . what's happening?'

Both men gazed down to the shadowy figure thirty feet below, half concealed behind a gravestone.

'Keep yer voice down, Kelly,' Mickey hissed harshly. 'Someone might hear yer. Dad just had one of his turns, that's all. But it's all right now. You just keep yer eyes peeled and stop concerning yerself about what's going on up here.'

'I never had a turn, Mickey! You know I never. I just lost me footing, that's all. It's that dark I can hardly see what I'm doing.'

Mickey grunted. 'Let's just get on with this, Dad. I don't relish the thought of being caught while we argue the toss.'

A shivering Kelly, heart pounding painfully, stared worriedly upwards, scanning her eyes across the roof. Something had happened, but whatever it was seemed to have righted itself, thank goodness. The thought of Dad tackling such a precarious undertaking suddenly scared her witless, especially in his present state of mind. And she felt guilty too, for it was only due to her pleading with her brother that their father was here now. Hopes of restoring a little of his pride had far outweighed worries for his safety when this job was being planned several nights before.

'Just let Dad take part, Mickey,' Kelly had begged then. 'He needs to feel part of things. It'll be the end of him if yer don't.'

Her brother had shaken his head grimly. 'But what if he . . .?'

'What if he does!' she had erupted. 'You'll be there to help him. It ain't his fault his nerves are gone. The bloody war did that. Can you imagine what it must have bin like for him, watching his mates die in that prisoner-of-war camp? Having no medicine and hardly any food. They were treated worse than dogs by them Jerries. No wonder Dad won't speak about it. And he ain't the only one. Remember, Mickey, we're lucky 'cos our dad got off much lighter than most. He could have lost his life. Now we're his family. We're supposed to help him. You know what the doctor said: the support and love of his family'll do more for him than any medicine can.'

'I don't think the doctor had in mind stealing lead sheeting off church roofs when he prescribed that!'

'Mickey!'

'Oh, for God's sake, Kelly. You talk about love and support. I've supported me dad for two years while he recovered his health. Then he was lucky enough to get his old job back and within two weeks he lost it for having a . . .'

'He never had a turn! He lost his temper,' she snapped, defiantly tossing her mane of near jet black hair, her vivid blue eyes sparkling angrily. 'And I defy any sane man not to have lost his temper in the same

3

situation. None of them get on with Mr Smith. Calls himself an Inspector, saying he's got the men's best interests at heart . . . what a load of balderdash! That man hasn't a decent bone in his body. Dad was three minutes late. Three minutes, that's all, and Smiggy gave him the sack without so much as a by your leave.' Her pretty face twisted bitterly. 'Smiggy didn't go to war, did he? Oh, no, he was one of the lucky ones needed here. So he didn't come back home after five years of fighting fer king and country, having suffered God knows what, to find . . .'

'Okay, okay, Kelly. Give over, will yer? You ain't telling me n'ote I don't already know.'

Hands planted firmly on her hips, she looked him in the eye. 'I'll only shut up if yer let Dad take part. Please, Mickey. I'll give my share to you if yer do.'

Her brother didn't need to deliberate. Hard cash was always a deciding factor with him. 'Okay then.'

'I knew if n'ote else it would be money that swayed yer.'

He grinned. 'Yer thought right then. But if 'ote goes wrong, you're responsible.'

Now, as she watched the shadowy figures going about their illicit business on the roof, Kelly felt sick to her stomach. If anything happened to her father she would never forgive herself.

'Have yer checked the cart?' she heard Mickey whisper urgently. 'All we need is for that to be nicked.'

She froze. No, she hadn't. It was part of her job to make sure the borrowed window cleaner's barrow, still housing its buckets, ladders and tarpaulin cover under which the stolen rolls of lead would be hidden, was still where they'd left it, parked by the side of the church wall. Sammy the Shammy would have plenty to say if his cart was lost and it would be more than a five-bob rental he'd be wanting from them then. Barrows, ladders and

4

buckets didn't come cheap even if the buckets were rusty, the ladders not far off rotten and the barrow itself only holding together by a miracle.

Her ears pricked as footsteps crunched against gravel. All worries for her father and the barrow instantly vanished as she swung into action. All the McCallans had their parts to play. This was her responsibility and if she didn't give the performance of a lifetime, the consequences were unthinkable.

A dispirited Reverend Billings was deep in thought as he unlatched the iron gate to the churchyard and passed through. He was a tall man, thin and sharp-featured with a shock of greying hair. Despite his severe appearance, though, he was kindly in nature and much liked by his parishioners. He came from a long line of ministers, the dedicated kind who devoted their lives to the Good Lord's work.

The young Algernon Billings had been expected to follow in the family tradition and had been happy to do so at the age of twenty-four, finding great satisfaction and fulfilment in his duties. That was until the last couple of years when he had realised retirement was approaching. One night, feeling thoroughly drained, he had arrived home extremely late to find his aged housekeeper had forgotten to light the gas oven to keep his meal hot and the fire was nearly out. As he sat and forced down the congealed cold mutton and watery vegetables, he'd thought back over his lifetime's achievement.

The journey over the years had taken only minutes. All in all his uneventful life amounted to forty-five years of preaching sermons, mostly to people who didn't understand half he said; and in being polite to the odd wealthy parishioner he encountered, most of whose benevolent gestures were undertaken, he felt, only in order to pave their way to the hereafter. Apart from that, the vast majority of his time and strength had been poured into trying to lift the spirits of the desperately deprived to whom he ministered. His efforts, he knew, may have helped to muster just a little hope within these poor unfortunates, but he had done nothing by way of altering for the better their wretched circumstances.

How could he? These people needed money. It was the one and only thing that could give them all they needed. And it was the one thing Algernon Billings couldn't provide. He was as poor as a church mouse himself. All he had to look forward to was passing his remaining years in a home for retired clergy. His only consolation was the thought that maybe it would not be as draughty and cold as the mausoleum of a Vicarage he had lived in for the past thirty-five years. And, of course, the food might be a little more palatable.

He sighed heavily as he rounded a bend in the path, instinctively ducking to avoid a stray branch of laurel from an overgrown hedge. He had endured the company of several needy families tonight, ones whose living conditions he found inhumane and general health so poor he pondered deeply how they were still amongst the living. Their lack of hygiene was so dire he hadn't even been able to force himself to accept the usual offering of a cup of milkless weak tea, something that was a great sacrifice to these people.

As he strode along the path he sighed again, long and deep, shaking his head. It was dreadful to think that in 1948, after living through such atrocities as the war had brought, and despite the advent of modern technology and great steps forward such as the instigation of the much needed Health Service, people still suffered such terrible poverty. It wasn't right. After witnessing all that he had throughout his ministry, much to his own bewilderment and shame, the Reverend Billings found he was beginning to question the workings of the Lord.

The plight of the poor was not all he had on his mind tonight, however. Recently there had been a spate of robberies in the area and he was worried about his church. Usually it was the verger's job to do the rounds last thing but like the Reverend Billings's housekeeper, Mrs Mottle, Albert Flowers was getting far too old to do his job properly and very shortly the man would have to be retired. But unlike Algernon Billings, Albert Flowers would not have the luxury of the home for retired clergy to look forward to. It would be the workhouse for him. If Algernon's own stipend was by no means plentiful, Albert's was a pittance. The thought of having simultaneously to retire both loyal employees grieved the Reverend Billings deeply but he knew the deed could not be put off much longer.

Suddenly he halted abruptly and listened closely. He could hear someone crying.

'Who's there?' he called sharply.

The crying became louder and he jumped with shock as a figure leaped from behind a gravestone, launched itself at speed down the path and threw itself upon him.

'Oh, yer reverence, yer reverence! 'Elp me – please 'elp me!' Kelly raised tear-filled, pleading eyes to his. ''Ave they gone?'

Algernon prised her fingers from his arm and held her away from him. 'They? Who's they?'

'Them lot. The ones that chased me. Big boys they were with chains. Thick ones. Threatened me they did. I were really scared.'

He glanced hurriedly around, ears pricked. 'Well, whoever they were it seems they've gone now.' His eyes settled on the shabby creature before him, trying to discern the face beneath the pulled down woollen hat and curtain of dark straggly hair. 'Chased by hooligans

7

or not, you shouldn't be out at this time of night,' he scolded. 'How old are you?'

Head bowed, Kelly studied her feet. 'Twel . . . thirteen. Fourteen next week.'

Algernon frowned, taken aback. 'Oh, I thought you were older somehow.'

'I'm big fer me age,' she blustered. 'Me mam sez I were born older than me years. She breeds 'em big. You should see me brother. Six foot two and built like a . . .' She stopped herself from saying 'like a brick shit house', remembering just in time whose company she was in. 'An Irish navvy,' she continued. 'If our Mickey had been around tonight, them lads wouldn't have dared come near me.' Oh, damn, she thought. She had said her brother's name. She hoped that fact had not registered with the minister, especially when he discovered the lead of his church roof missing the next time it rained.

'Huh! Pity he wasn't then. Anyway, I'd get yourself straight off home and let this be a lesson to you, young lady.'

Kelly's face puckered in distress. 'Can't yer take me, yer reverence? Please? I'm still worried they could be waiting somewhere. Please? Even just halfway?'

Algernon ran a weary hand across his brow. 'What's your address?'

'Near the Fosse Road.' She grimaced again. First her brother's real name, and now an address close to where she actually lived. She was getting sloppy. She really would have to watch her mouth.

Algernon frowned thoughtfully. Fosse Road was a good twenty minutes walk away from Highcross Street where his church was situated. Then he thought of his dinner, hopefully still hot inside the oven. But how could he refuse his help to one of the Lord's children? Then another thought struck him. Only that very morning he had been asked by one of his parishioners to visit a very

8

sick lady on Tewkesbury Street, and that was in the vicinity of Fosse Road. It was out of his own parish, though. Normally he would have passed on the request to that area's minister . . . He sighed. Maybe he was meant to go. The Lord sometimes chose mysterious ways of showing His hand. Reverend Billings smiled down at Kelly. 'I'll just keep you a moment while I check the church doors are secure.'

He made to walk away and her mind raced frantically. It would not do for him to go any closer to the church; her father and brother could be discovered. She grabbed hold of his coat. 'Er . . . er . . . they're locked. I tried, see. I pushed and shoved really hard. They're definitely locked. I . . . I wa' looking for somewhere to hide.' Burying her face in her hands, she let out a loud wail of anguish. 'Oh, don't leave me 'ere, yer reverence. This graveyard's giving me the willies.'

Algernon turned back. 'Oh, hush, child. Don't take on so.' Compassion for this poor girl flooded through him and he took hold of her arm. 'If you say the doors are locked, then I'll take your word for it. Come on, let's get you home.'

As he guided her back down the path Kelly hid a smile of relief.

Chapter Two

Panting hard, Kelly flattened herself against the rough red bricks of the dark alleyway. She shook her head. At nineteen, she thought critically, she was getting far too old to pass herself off as a young girl. Even the kindly Reverend Billings had looked suspicious when she had lied about her age. And besides, the tight strapping binding her shapely breasts restricted her breathing to such an extent she had had to fight for every bit of breath as, feeling they were a safe enough distance from the church, she had without warning kicked up her heels and run off as fast as she could, leaving the poor man staring after her completely flummoxed.

She felt a twinge of guilt regarding the Reverend Billings. As he had guided her down a warren of bitterly cold, grim streets, he had asked all sorts of questions about her home life, his sole intent, she knew without doubt, being to ascertain whether he could offer any help to ease their burdens. The guilt she felt was for the lies she had told him – something she had not, in all the time she had been a part of the 'family business', ever experienced before. She wondered uneasily why she should now.

It must be something to do with the clergyman himself. He had not been like the others she had encountered: brusque and more interested in what would be offered him by way of refreshment once he saw her safely home than genuine concern for her welfare. This minister of the faith had been different. He had been genuinely concerned about her and her family. Still, she thought, he must meet all sorts in his job. What the McCallans did was undertaken out of necessity, and there were many people who did far worse than they. It was a way of life. And the McCallans had never taken anything from those who could not afford to replace it. Churches were rich. They could afford to lose a few rolls of roofing material.

Her guilt suddenly evaporated as more worrying emotions filled her, principally fear for her father. She prayed – which under the circumstances she knew to be hypocritical – that nothing untoward had happened to him, and gnawed her bottom lip anxiously. Mickey was right, blast him, and she should have listened. Her father really was in no fit state to be clambering about on church roofs. In future his role would have to be restricted to safer tasks. The bit of profit they made from their illicit activities was not worth either the injury her father might suffer or her own anxiety over his welfare, which she felt sure was behind her sloppiness tonight.

Hurriedly righting herself and making sure she kept in the shadows close to the wall, she scurried down the winding alleyway until she reached her own back gate and slipped inside, then on into the tiny shabby kitchen of the rundown two up, two down terraced house where the McCallan family lived. She tiptoed the several steps across the bare, dark kitchen and on into the passage, not wanting to make a noise in case her mother was sleeping.

She need not have worried. As she entered the bare-boarded passageway, with its peeling dingy cream and brown paint, she heard a low hum of voices coming from the back room. She placed her ear against the door, wondering who her mother's caller was, and frowned. Whoever it was, it was a man which struck her as strange. Her mother's callers were usually from among the neighbouring women. Regardless, she dare not investigate until she had changed her clothes and, more importantly, freed herself from her painful bindings.

Ten minutes later, Kelly studied herself in the length of chipped mirror glass propped up against the wall – which was proving difficult as the silvering on the back was badly pitted. A smile lit her face. Gone was the dishevelled youngster in sagging grey socks, worn baggy brown coat and moth-eaten hat. Staring back was a pleasant-faced, shapely nineteen-year-old woman.

Her smile slowly faded as her eyes ran critically over her clothes and she vehemently wished that the faded second-hand ecru 'A' line skirt with its strategically placed pocket hiding a repair, and the plain jumper she had knitted with wool unravelled from an old cardigan bought for a shilling from the second-hand stall in the market, were more fashionable. But it was pointless wasting her life in longing, she thought, as she straightened her skirt. Any money brought into this house had far more important uses than buying fashionable clothes.

Her straggly black hair was now brushed and pinned up into a becoming french pleat, and tiny imitation pearl clip-on earrings given to her by her brother at Christmas adorned her ears. No doubt he had acquired them at a good price from some hard up soul on his bin round, but that did not matter to Kelly who had been grateful to receive them.

She smiled broadly as she gave her appearance a final check. It wasn't surprising that vicar had stared when she had lied about her age. No doubt he had never encountered such a well-developed nearly fourteen year

13

old in all his years of preaching.

She was just about to go downstairs when she heard a noise coming from the yard and rushed to the window, pulling aside the tatty paper blind with her heart soaring in thankfulness. Her father and brother had returned safely and were busy stashing their ill-gotten gains inside the old outhouse ready for Mickey to take down to the rag and bone yard where he would haggle over a price for them. Although, she thought, as she let the blind drop back and headed for the door, haggle was not really the word to use. You either accepted the pittance offered or you didn't make a sale. It was as simple as that. Just who exactly were the thieves, when all was said and done? she thought as she headed down the stairs.

Her eyes went straight to her mother as she entered the front room and as usual her heart filled with a deep, agonising sadness. Flora McCallan was dying, ravaged by a vicious growth in her stomach, an evil, relentless disease that had transformed this once striking, proud woman into a grey, shrunken shadow of herself.

For Kelly daily to watch the illness do its worst, unable to prevent the inevitable, was unbearable, but like the rest of the family she put on a brave front for the sake of the woman she loved, doing her crying and venting her anger and remorse well away from this room.

Despite intense pain, Flora McCallan smiled at the sight of her beloved daughter. ''Ello, me duck,' she greeted her. 'Mrs Brady – yer know, the lady who visits the sick – asked the Reverend to pop in and see me. Weren't that nice of 'er?' Her faded blue, pain-filled eyes went to the man seated in a chair next to the bed, his back to Kelly. 'And nice of you too, Minister, considering I ain't never set foot inside your church before.'

He turned to acknowledge her and how Kelly managed to stop herself from crying out in shock was a mystery to her. For there, hand outstretched in greeting,

14

was the kindly vicar, the very one she had distracted an hour previously in order for her father and brother to strip his church of its roofing.

Despite being shocked rigid, she automatically stepped forward and accepted the proffered hand. 'Please to meet yer,' she said, her voice pitched high.

Her mother eyed her worriedly. 'Is there summat wrong, Kelly?'

'Eh?' She cleared her throat. 'Oh, no. I think I've got a bit of a cold coming, that's all, and it's causing me voice to go funny. I'll, er . . . leave you to your chat. Would you like a cuppa, Vicar?'

He smiled in gratitude. 'That would be much appreciated, thank you.' His eyes lingered on her. There was something familiar about this young woman but he couldn't quite place it. 'Have we met before?'

'Eh? Oh, no, definitely not.'

'Are you sure?'

''Course. I ain't bin near a church for years,' she lied. 'I'm not much for religion. That finished for me with what went on in the war. I can't for the life of me see how, if there is a God who's supposed to be so loving, He could have allowed all that to happen.' She turned and made for the door, seized with a strong compulsion to get out of this room. 'I'll see about the tea.'

Flora eyed Algernon shame-faced. 'I apologise for me daughter, Reverend. I'm sure she meant no disrespect.'

He patted her bony hand. 'Don't concern yourself, Mrs McCallan. There's many who think just the same as she does. I find it refreshing to meet someone who speaks their mind, and I must congratulate you on having such a lovely young daughter.' He smiled reassuringly. 'Besides, your faith more than compensates for your daughter's lack of it.' And, he thought, who could blame the daughter for those feelings in such circumstances as these?

Flora relaxed back on her pillow and smiled, eyes filling with tenderness. 'Yes, I've been blessed. If I don't have much else I've the love of me family.'

As soon as Kelly left the front room she rushed straight for the back door and out into the yard. 'Mickey,' she hissed urgently. 'Mickey, he's here! Sitting wi' Mam.'

He poked his head around the rotten door of the shed. 'What yer babbling on about? Who's here?'

'Him, that vicar. The one whose church we've just robbed.'

He shot out of the shed. 'Eh? Kelly, I hope you're having me on?'

'No, no, honest I ain't. I got the shock of me life when I saw him sitting there, I can tell yer.'

Mickey glared at her accusingly and grabbed her arm, gripping it tightly. 'You led him here. Yer must have done.'

'Give over, Mickey. You know how careful I am. Let go of me arm, yer hurting me.'

His grip tightened and his eyes narrowed menacingly. 'I'll do more than hurt yer arm if I find out summat you've done put him on to us . . .'

'Put him on to us? For God's sake, Mickey, he couldn't possibly have a clue yet about us pinching that lead. Him being here is a coincidence. One of his parishioners asked him to call on Mam. You never gave me a chance to tell yer that before you went for me jugular. I only came ter warn yer, that's all.' Her eyes narrowed and she glared back at him. 'Now let go of me arm before I put me shoe against yer shin.'

He pushed her from him. He knew his spirited sister would do exactly as she threatened and the shoes she was wearing were not the soft leather the wealthy wore, but hard, serviceable ones. The one thing he admired about Kelly was her strength of character. Mickey knew

16

he could intimidate and charm most people he came across, but not his sister. Secretly he admired her for that. Running his fingers through his tangled black curls, he grimaced. 'I don't like the sound of this, our sis. Summat ain't adding up. Seems a funny coincidence to me.'

'Yeah, I agree. But I can assure you that's all it is – a coincidence.' She pressed her lips together. She hoped she was right. She dared not divulge to Mickey that the clergyman had commented on her familiarity, or worse still tell him about her slip of the tongue earlier in the evening – not once but twice.

'Damn, this is all I need! Some do-gooding vicar poking his nose in. I'd better get rid of the stuff tonight, just in case,' her brother reluctantly decided. 'It's the last thing I want to do. You never get a decent price as it is, but even less when it's obvious you're trying to get shot of it quick. Thank God I ain't took Sammy's cart back yet.'

'Well, at least this time you ain't got my share to pay out.'

Mickey eyed her for a second then a slow grin split his face. 'Yeah, that's right. You agreed I'd have yours if I took Dad along. Oh, well, that ain't so bad then.'

Kelly scowled. Her brother's selfish streak never ceased to amaze her. Still, at least the thought of extra money in his pocket seemed to have restored some of his good humour. 'I'd better get back,' she muttered. 'I'm supposed to be making a cuppa and I ain't put the kettle on yet. Don't forget to warn our dad so he don't blurt out nothing he shouldn't.'

'Oh, Christ, I forgot about him. I'll keep him busy out here. I'll need him anyway to help shift the stuff. You just go and get rid of that vicar, and make sure you hurry up about it. Give us the nod when the coast is clear.'

17

'Mickey, a' you coming back to give me a hand?' Frank McCallan called softly from inside the shed. 'I can't manage it on me own. It weighs a ton and me back's about breaking.'

Just then the yard gate opened and a man entered. He smiled briefly at Kelly, giving her a friendly wink before addressing her brother. 'Yer back then. How'd it all go?' he asked eagerly.

'Keep yer voice down,' Mickey snapped. 'We've problems but Kelly's just about to sort it. Ain't yer, Kelly?' he directed her aggressively.

'I'll do me best,' she responded sharply. 'But I can't exactly shove him out in case Mam asks questions.'

'Shove who out?' the newcomer asked.

Mickey grabbed his arm. 'Come and give us a hand in the shed and I'll explain.'

As Kelly hurried back her thoughts were torn between anxiety about getting rid of their visitor without arousing suspicion and her feelings for the young man who had just arrived.

Rodney Collins was indeed an arresting sight for any warm-blooded female. An inch off six foot in height, he was broad-shouldered and slim-hipped, with a thatch of unruly corn-coloured hair and startling green eyes in a ruggedly handsome face. Kelly knew she was lucky to have him.

She had met Rodney through Mickey. She had been fifteen, slowly blossoming from girl to woman, still unsure of herself and awkward, despite several admirers whom she giggled over with her friends. Until the night Mickey had casually told her he had arranged a foursome for the following Friday night, she had been unaware of the existence of the good-looking youth who worked alongside him. Mickey fancied Rodney's sister and saw this as a way of getting acquainted with her.

Kelly was not used to proper dating and the thought

18

of going out with a stranger frightened her witless. Mickey scathingly dismissed her fears and demanded she go. She flatly refused. He ordered, then bullied, then blackmailed, making up a blatant lie to tell their mother if she did not go. Kelly knew she had no choice in the matter and reluctantly relented.

The instant she set eyes on Rod outside the picture house as he strode up with his sister, Glenda, she fell in love and on looking back, often wondered how she'd got through that first night, so tongue tied was she. But, greatly to her surprise, Rodney asked her out again. Their dates were casual at first, gradually settling into a cosy routine over four years. After two years of going out, when he asked her to get engaged she was delighted but, like everyone else, not exactly surprised. The match seemed inevitable somehow. They became engaged in name only, he had no spare money to buy her a ring but was saving like mad. Two years on, he was still saving. But Kelly was not bothered. She had Rodney, they loved each other, and a ring was unimportant.

The only blight on their relationship, she felt, was the fact that at times Rodney seemed more interested in her brother than he did in her. Mickey and Rodney were friends, she could not deny that, and had been before she had come on to the scene, but all the same she sometimes wondered if his relationship with her was just a convenient way to ensure Rodney had easy access to her brother.

Like now, for instance, the way he had given her a hurried wink of acknowledgement then gone straight to Mickey – an avuncular wink not unlike ones she received from the ticket collector on the bus or their friendly coalman.

Annoyed, she spun on her heel and went back inside the kitchen, checked the kettle for water, then slammed it on the stove and lit the gas ring beneath. As she

19

grabbed two cups, mindful to make sure she gave the Vicar the one with the fewest cracks, a knock sounded on the back door and a woman of her own age entered.

Mickey's fiancee, Glenda Collins, was a female version of her brother, extremely pretty where he was handsome. For a woman who could surely have her pick of men, it seemed Glenda was content to love Mickey to such an extent that she was blind to any bad traits in his character.

Mickey was Kelly's brother. As such she loved him and had no option but to put up with him. Why the likes of Glenda did was beyond her, for most of the time he showed a lack of consideration and attentiveness which was marked and seemed to be worsening. But then, just when Kelly was sure that this time her brother had gone too far, he would fix Glenda with a devastating smile that would have turned the strongest woman's legs to jelly. Rod might be handsome but Kelly knew that her brother possessed a charm and charisma that were impossible to ignore. He was fully aware of this, of course, and never failed to press home his advantage.

'There's a lot of swearing coming from the shed,' Glenda said, stripping off her coat.

'Keep yer voice down,' Kelly whispered urgently, pressing a finger to her lips. 'We've got problems.'

Glenda's green eyes widened. 'Problems? What d'yer mean? N'ote went wrong tonight, did it?' She frowned worriedly. 'My Mickey's all right, ain't he?'

'Mickey's fine. It depends what yer mean by wrong.' Kelly sighed heavily as she poured milk into the cups. 'They got the roofing off okay. That's what all the swearing's about. They were trying to force it into the shed 'til our Mickey can get rid of it. But now they're taking it back out.'

Glenda stared at her. 'Why?'

''Cos the Vicar of the church we robbed just happens

to be sitting here at this minute, talking to me mam. So Mickey thought it best to get rid of the lead tonight, just in case.'

Glenda's jaw dropped. 'What! But how come . . .'

'He reckoned one of his parishioners asked him to call. Oh, Glenda, I'm just hoping it's a coincidence,' Kelly whispered worriedly. She caught hold of her friend's arm and pulled her close. 'Don't dare breathe a word to our Mickey but the vicar sorta recognised me. Well, he asked if we'd met. I nearly passed out, I can tell yer.'

'What did yer say?'

'I lied to me back teeth, telling him I hadn't bin near a church for years.' A mischievous smile crossed her face. 'Which, considering the circumstances . . .'

Glenda clasped her hand to her mouth to stifle giggles. 'Oh, Kelly, you'll never get to heaven the rate you're going.'

'Glenda, my place in hell was booked the moment I was old enough to help our Mickey.'

'Well, if it is hell you end up in, there's many'll be accompanying yer. If we didn't help ourselves no one else would.'

'Yeah, I agree, but it still don't make what we do right, does it?'

Glenda eyed her in surprise. 'Changed yer tune a bit, ain't yer? You never seemed bothered about the rights and wrongs before. In fact, I'd go as far as ter say you were just as keen as Mickey.'

'That's going too far, Glenda. I've done what I've done because I had ter and for no other reason. And our Mickey has always been the instigator of any of our jobs, as you very well know.'

'Well, someone has to be in charge,' the other girl replied defensively. 'And there's no one better than my Mickey.'

Kelly frowned in annoyance. 'You'd better watch it, gel,' she said, wagging a finger. 'You're talking like a gangster's moll.'

'And you watch too many American films at the pictures. Gangster's moll indeed,' scoffed Glenda. 'I'm only trying to point out that it's Mickey's jobs that are practically keeping you all, 'cos yer dad certainly ain't bringing in any money and the bit you earn ain't much to speak of neither.'

Kelly's face darkened. 'The money situation in our house is none of your business, Glenda, and I'll thank you to keep your thoughts to yerself.'

'I happen to be engaged to your brother so I reckon what goes on in this house *is* my business.' She flashed the diamond ring on her finger. It was only a minute solitaire but more than Kelly possessed and so Glenda felt superior. 'If my Mickey didn't have to fork out so much, we could afford to get married. I'm sure if he tried harder yer dad could get some sort of job and put an effort into keeping it.'

Kelly's eyes sparked and her voice lowered dangerously. 'You leave my dad out of this,' she warned. 'You should count yerself lucky your own dad got out of going to war and didn't have to go through what mine did. We're lucky to have him back, and whether he ever gets another job or not we're grateful to have him with us. And if that means me and Mickey have ter stay at home and support him for the rest of our lives, then that's what we'll do.'

Kelly abruptly turned her back on Glenda, fighting to stop herself from telling her friend that she gravely suspected Mickey would have found some other excuse for not getting married had Dad not provided him with a convenient one. Kelly knew that Mickey had only bought that ring in an unusual moment of weakness, mortally tired of being dragged by all the jewellers' shop windows whenever Glenda could coax him to go shopping. She did not know either that although the ring itself was by no means valuable, it had been acquired for a fraction of its worth from one of Mickey's mates on the bin round who had bought it for an engagement that had not materialised, and was afterwards glad to be rid of the painful reminder.

Glenda gulped, suddenly realising she had gone too far and should not have voiced her feelings.

Leaning against the sink, she folded her arms under her shapely bosom. 'I'm sorry, Kelly, I didn't mean any of that. I get frustrated sometimes. I just feel somehow that me and Mickey will never walk up the aisle, and I want that so much.'

Taking a deep, calming breath, Kelly turned to face her. 'I know you do, Glenda. But you should have realised by now that Mickey won't get married 'til he's good and ready. My brother ain't the type to be pushed into anything.'

'Who's pushing?' the other girl retorted sharply.

'You are. You're always dropping hints. If yer don't watch it our Mickey'll retaliate and then you'll never get yer wish. And will yer keep your bloody voice down?' warned Kelly. 'Remember that vicar is still with me mother.'

Glenda frowned. Deep down she knew Kelly spoke the truth and quickly decided she'd be more careful in future. The thought of losing Mickey for any reason was unbearable. 'What's up with you tonight, gel? I ain't never heard you speak like this before.'

'I'm just doing what you are, Glenda, speaking me mind.' Kelly turned her back again and busied herself with the tea. Memories from earlier in the evening flooded back. She felt sure that something had happened up on the church roof and would have liked nothing more than to have discussed this with Glenda, obtained her opinion. She would not do so, though. Whatever had happened was family business, and therefore not to be discussed with anyone but immediate family. And poor Glenda, however hard she tried, was not yet one of them.

Forcing a smile, Kelly turned back to her friend. 'I don't know what's up with me tonight. I spouted off to the Vicar when I should have done what I've just told you and kept me thoughts to meself. But I was so shocked by finding him here. D'yer know, I ain't never felt like this before, Glenda.' She shrugged her shoulders. 'Maybe I'm having a brain storm or summat. Maybe I'm feeling guilty. That Vicar is a nice old geezer, seemed really concerned about me. I just feel bad that it was his church we picked on to rob. It's all right for you, you don't get involved like I do.'

She sighed. 'Oh, why couldn't he have just been a nasty old sod like others we've done it to then I wouldn't be feeling like this? I'd much prefer it if Mickey stuck to pinching from factories and building sites. I know it sounds daft, but that don't seem so bad somehow.' She looked towards the stove and frowned at the kettle. 'Why hasn't that thing boiled? Oh, blast, the gas has gone and I've no money. Have you a shilling I can borrow?'

'A bob? Kelly, it's Thursday. I don't get paid 'til tomorrow so how the hell do yer think I've got a shilling to spare?'

'Sorry, I weren't thinking. Nip out and tell our Mickey to cough up. I know he's got some money. He always has.'

Hand on the door knob, Glenda paused. 'Here's you feeling guilty for robbing the church and you ain't got a shilling for the gas. I bet that Vicar doesn't have ter worry about where the next penny's coming from. Everyone knows churches are loaded.'

Kelly smiled wanly. 'Yer right. Why should I be

worrying? Hurry up and tackle our Mickey, though, 'cos if I don't mek this tea and get shot of the vicar soon he'll murder me.'

'I'll go out the back way if it's all the same to you, Miss McCallan. I can cut through the jitty and be on the main Fosse Road in half the time it would take if I went by the main streets.'

Kelly eyed their visitor in alarm. And risk running straight into Mickey, Dad and Rod, catching them red-handed with the lead? Oh, no, she wasn't having that. 'Sorry, Reverend, Mam wouldn't be happy if I showed you out the back. Besides, our yard is so full of junk, you'd likely go a cropper.'

'But . . .'

'Please, Reverend, she has this superstition that you go out the same way you come in. I wouldn't like an ill wind to befall you. And neither would I like to upset me mam, 'cos she's bound to ask me.'

'Oh, well, I see. Front it is then.'

As Algernon stepped into the street he turned and took Kelly's hand, patting it sympathetically. 'Thank you for the tea, my dear.'

'My pleasure, Vicar. Now, if you'll excuse me, I must get Mam settled down for the night.'

'Yes, of course. Look, er . . . if there's anything I can do . . .'

'Like what, Reverend? Perform miracles, do yer? 'Cos that's the only thing that'll save my mam.' Kelly grimaced in shame. 'I'm sorry, I didn't mean . . .'

He patted her hand again. 'I know, I know. Watching our loved ones suffer is no easy thing to do.' He eyed her meaningfully. 'I did take note of what you said earlier but turning to the Lord can have its rewards, you know. If you should find yourself near a church, go in and say a prayer. You'll be amazed by how different you'll feel.'

25

'Really, Reverend,' she said matter-of-factly. 'No disrespect, but I meant what I said about my feelings on religion and it would take a miracle to change them. I admire people like yerself who put all their trust and faith in some man they have never seen in the flesh nor are ever likely to. Me – I prefer to stand face to face with whoever I'm dealing with. Look them in the eye, so to speak. Now, if yer don't mind, I must get on. Thank you again for calling. I could tell me mam much appreciated your visit.'

Algernon mentally shook himself, realising he was being dismissed. Despite that, he found he sympathised deeply with many of Kelly's words. He had heard them all before, of course, from atheists and sceptics, but somehow this young woman brought fresh feeling to them. Maybe it was his own frame of mind, his own recent questioning of the workings of the Saviour that were primarily responsible.

He smiled distractedly at her. 'Goodbye.'

She sighed with relief as she shut the door and rushed down the passage. 'I thought he was never going to go,' she said, arriving in the kitchen. 'He's gone, Glenda. Go and tell our Mickey, will yer, while I see to Mam. The quicker we get shut of that lead sheeting the better as far as I'm concerned. The whole night's been jinxed, if yer ask me.'

Algernon had just turned on to the main Fosse Road when he realised with annoyance that he had left his gloves behind. He chided himself for being so careless. He would have to go back for them. The gloves were old and worn but the only ones he possessed and much needed in weather like this. As he began to retrace his steps he smiled. There was no silly superstition in force now to stop him cutting through the jitty and entering the McCallan house by the back access.

As he rounded a curve in the jitty and the yard gate came into view he stopped abruptly as it opened and a head popped out, glancing rapidly up and down. Then three men emerged. Across each man's shoulder lay a length of something which must have been extremely heavy judging by the way they were struggling under its weight. Whatever it was they were carrying was then loaded on to a cart parked by the side of the wall. Although the light was bad, it looked to Algernon like a window cleaner's cart. He frowned. What on earth were these men loading at this hour of night? And, more to the point, why were they acting so suspiciously?

'Thank the Lord we never took the barrow back, Mickey,' he heard one of the men say.

'Keep yer voice down,' came a hissed reply.

Algernon waited until they had disappeared around the corner before continuing on his way.

Chapter Three

Kelly sat down on the chair by the bed in the front room and gently took her mother's hand. 'Anything else I can get yer, Mam? Another cuppa?'

Tired, pain-filled eyes settled on her. 'No, thanks, love.'

She gazed at her mother in concern, rubbing her own hand affectionately over the back of Flora's bony one. 'That Reverend's tired you out, ain't he?'

Her mother nodded. 'A little, but then it was good of him to take the trouble to call when I'm sure he's a lot else he could have been doing. I'm always grateful for visitors whatever the time, you know that. I like to have contact with the outside world.' She eyed her daughter questioningly and asked unexpectedly, 'Is yer dad all right, Kelly?'

She gulped guiltily. Her father's losing his job had been kept from Flora. Instead Frank went out each morning and wandered the streets until homecoming time. It was a strain for all of them, but they had agreed that they could not further tax Flora's health with this new worry. Although Frank's health had improved they all knew that getting another job was not going to be easy for him. Kelly just hoped something would turn up soon. It didn't matter what, just something to restore her father's self-respect as well as bring in some much needed money.

'He's fine, Mam.' With difficulty she smiled reassuringly. 'Yer know the doctor said his recovery would take time. He's doing really well. He ain't had a turn for a while now, so stop worrying.' She gnawed her bottom lip, hoping that whatever had transpired on the roof tonight had not been associated with her father's illness.

Flora sighed with relief. 'No, he hasn't, has he? But it's strange, he doesn't speak much about his work. He always used to be full of the capers that he and the lads got up to. Now he doesn't mention anything.' She sighed. 'Oh, I'm being silly, I know. I just worry for him, love. He's been through such a lot, and then to come back and find me like this. Well . . .'

Kelly squeezed her hand. 'Eh, come on, yer can stop this train of thought, Mam. Anyway lots of things have changed since he came back. I don't think they're allowed to get up to any larks any more. Smiggy keeps his beady eyes peeled all the time. Our Mickey was only saying the other day he thought Smiggy paid some of the lads to sneak on their mates.' Kelly hoped her lie worked, but then realised it could be true. It wouldn't surprise her in the least if the Inspector did just that.

'Does he?' Flora exclaimed. 'But he knows as well as anyone the men make up their wages on the bits and pieces they pick up.' She frowned worriedly. 'Oh, dear, if he's put a stop to it, how we gonna manage?'

'I shouldn't worry, Mam. The men have his measure and will find a way to outsmart him, never fear.'

Flora sighed heavily. 'I hope so, love. That Smiggy's no heart. In my opinion he shouldn't be in charge of men. Anyway, did yer dad say he'd be long? Only I'm just hoping I can stay awake 'til he comes in. I don't feel right if I don't say me goodnights.'

Kelly chose her words carefully. Her mother was oblivious of any of the McCallans' illicit activities. As far as she was aware the bits and pieces Mickey picked up on the bin round were the only extra resources they received. In an environment where supplementing wages by any means was the norm, Flora had striven hard to instil in her children a respect for honesty and they knew she would be horrified to learn the truth, no matter how badly the extra money was needed. 'I shouldn't imagine he will be. I think being's you had a visitor they decided to pop out for a quick half.'

'Ah, well, yer dad won't be long then. He's never been a boozer, thank goodness.' She paused and studied her daughter for a moment. 'You and Rodney, yer both all right, ain't you?'

''Course we are, Mam. Why d'you ask?'

'Just checking, me love. A mother's interest, that's all. I'm so glad that at least . . .' She stopped herself just in time from saying that at least she had lived to see the man Kelly had chosen, even though she knew she would not be alive to see her beloved daughter walk down the aisle. She knew Kelly knew it too, but to voice it would only grieve them both further. The awkward moment was saved by a loud knock reverberating on the door. 'Oh, is that someone at the back?'

Seconds later Glenda poked her head around the door. 'The Vicar forgot his gloves.' Smiling, she entered, retrieved the worn gloves from the floor by the chair Kelly was sitting on and departed.

Flora sighed. 'She's got her faults, that girl, but I can't help but like her. If our Mickey doesn't start treating her a bit better, I expect she'll start looking elsewhere.'

'I don't think so, Mam. Glenda worships the ground our Mickey walks on.' Although, thought Kelly, I'm not so sure he feels the same way. She decided it was best to say nothing. Her mother had enough to cope with. 'There's one thing I do know, though, and that's that it'll never be the love match you and our dad had. That's been a match made in heaven, ain't it, Mam?'

Flora's face softened tenderly. 'Yes, it has. I've bin lucky with yer dad. There's not many been as fortunate in feelings as we have.' Her eyes grew misty as memories flooded back and her voice became husky. 'I fell in love with your dad the moment I clapped eyes on him, leaning up against the factory wall smoking a fag with his workmates. I can still see it as clear as if it were yesterday.'

Kelly settled back in her chair. Her mother liked nothing better than to reminisce. She had not much future left to her, so looking back and revisiting the past was now her only pleasure. Kelly had heard the stories many times but was more than happy to let Flora ramble on, conscious that it afforded her mother several precious minutes in which she was able, for the most part, to forget her pain and fear.

'Yer dad said that was when he fell in love with me,' Flora continued. 'Though God knows how. I must have looked a sight, dressed in me working togs, me hair scraped under a cap, stinking of fish glue from me job in the shoe factory. Mind you, he didn't look that much better. A bin man's clothing ain't exactly Burton's shop window, but there was something about him, something different. I can't put me finger on it, but it was there.

'He winked at me, Kelly, and such a cheeky wink it was. Me friend Alice was appalled. She grabbed me arm and dragged me past. "He's a bin man, Flora, and looks like a gypsy ter me." "I'd say Irish meself with that head of black hair," I replied. Alice's mouth dropped wide enough to get a tram through. "And that's worse! What would yer mam and dad say if you turned up with an Irish navvy in tow? Or one of gypsy origins, come ter that?" "Alice," I said, "he winked at me, not asked me to marry him." 'Course, it weren't long after that, Kelly, that he did. From the start we both knew we were meant for each other and couldn't see the sense in waiting, even though I was only seventeen and yer dad a year older.

'Courting in those days was hardly more than a walk round the streets sharing a bag of chips, and a cuddle up the entry when it got dark. If we wanted to go to the pictures or music hall we had to save like mad. My wages were pennies, yer dad's weren't much better. By the time we'd paid our dues there was hardly 'ote left for much else. Times were harder then than they are now, if that's possible, but we had our love and that were enough for me and yer dad. And Alice was wrong. Me mam and dad took to him straight away. And what mam and dad wouldn't have, eh?'

Kelly smiled distractedly. She barely remembered her grandparents, both of them having died when she was just a little girl, but had vague recollections of them as being warm-hearted people, never having much themselves but very giving – the sort of caring, loving parents who would readily accept their only daughter's choice of husband as long as she was happy. And, Kelly reflected, her father had made her mother very happy. Their lives together had been fraught with difficulties, at times they'd had barely two halfpennies to rub together. A bin man's wages, even enhanced by the bits and pieces her father had managed to salvage and sell, would never amount to a fat wage, but nevertheless their mutual respect, regard, and obvious love for each other had given them the strength to see all their hardships through.

And they hadn't done too badly compared to some. The house they lived in was hardly a palace. Neither was it in the best of areas nor the items inside worth much, but what they had was all theirs. Many times during the past harsh winters there had been no money for extra fuel and they had all had to huddle together in Flora and Frank's bed, under an assortment of threadbare blankets and coats in order to keep warm. But the rent- and tally-man had always been paid, and Flora had made sure there was always some sort of meal on the table.

They had managed, just. But then the war had come, and if they had thought they had faced hardship before, nothing had prepared them for that. What a terrible time it had been! It had changed all their lives.

Frank had done his duty and signed up, never for one moment envisaging that he would not see his beloved family for over five long years or what hardships they would suffer during his absence. A soldier's allotment was hardly enough to pay the rent, let alone feed and clothe his family. So like thousands of others Flora had taken factory work, dividing her time between her family and her job, constantly worrying for her husband's safety and her children's welfare while all the time being exhorted to work longer hours. This she had done without complaint until her health began to suffer so noticeably that it was obvious she could no longer keep up the punishing regime.

But despite poor health she still had two children to feed. Money had to be found from somewhere. So Flora had scraped a living by other means – a few hours in the corner shop; washing and sewing and the caring of children for women who were earning good money in the factories. Inevitably it had meant she worked harder than she had done previously, and for less money. To try and compensate she went without herself.

Pouring all of her meagre resources into the care of her son and daughter, Flora skimped on food; she went cold of an evening when they had gone to bed by letting the fire go out in order to save fuel; and the odd spare copper for clothing had been spent on the children's, despite her own being almost threadbare and no protection against the bitter winter winds.

Kelly had always believed that it was then, when her

mother was at her lowest, that the disease had struck and begun to gain its stranglehold on her.

And it was during this time, she reflected, that a change had come over her brother. She couldn't pinpoint exactly when this change had happened as it hadn't at first been glaringly obvious. She had been, after all, a young girl of about ten – a sister who naturally looked up to her elder brother. Far too much had been going on in her own life, with her own friends and all the war had brought, for her to take much notice of him.

But a change had come about. It seemed that Mickey was suddenly no longer a carefree young boy, the brother who relentlessly teased her when he was not playing football or cricket with his mates in the street. He became moody and very secretive, and, most startling of all, began to have money in his pocket. Not much, the odd penny or threepence, but still a cause for surprise given their precarious finances. It appeared that her mother did not notice. But Kelly did and eventually she confronted him.

His angry response had frightened her, and his threats against her should she breathe a word were terrifying, but his explanation made a kind of sense despite Kelly's knowing deep down that it was wrong. Mickey stole. And the reason he did so, he insisted, was to help their mother. And besides, how could what he did be classed as real stealing when it was done in order to ease their mother's burden?

Kelly's young mind could see a kind of sense in that and it wasn't long before she was joining him in what became a regular occurrence. Just the odd item from a corner shop; vegetables snatched from allotments; washing from lines – anything they could sell on for a few coppers which would then be given to their mother, telling her it was payment for errands run for grateful people in the area. Flora's delighted response was all Kelly needed to spur her on. As time passed this petty pilfering became a way of life. The pennies made a difference and were quickly depended upon.

At fourteen, Mickey reluctantly followed in his father's footsteps and joined the Leicester Corporation refuse gangs. It was either that or learn a trade in a factory, and he felt he had had enough of learning. But from the very first morning he detested his chosen profession. He hated traipsing the streets in all weathers; the collection of heavy bins full of other people's stinking rubbish; the stigma that was attached to what others saw as a lowly occupation. But above all he resented the meagre wages. The job's only saving grace was that money could be made on the side. And at that Mickey was a natural.

But as time passed a few extra coppers were not enough. He wanted more. Much more. It was only a matter of time before he had progressed to stealing lead from church roofs; building materials from sites; anything moveable from factory yards. And when necessary, whether she liked it or not, Kelly was expected to play her part.

She frowned. Her brother, she knew from experience, would some time soon become dissatisfied, and when that happened what would he turn to next?

Her own role had changed from those early days. Mickey no longer expected her to take part in the actual stealing of the goods; it was her job merely to stand guard and warn of any dangers. But nevertheless she believed her part in the proceedings was just as bad, she was just as involved, and if caught, God forbid, her sentence would be just as heavy. But if they stopped, how would they live, especially now her father seemed incapable of keeping a job? And they still had to cover his wage so as not to arouse her mother's suspicions.

Kelly jumped as she realised Flora was addressing her. 'Sorry, Mam?'

'What were yer thinking about? You were miles away?'

'Oh, er . . . Just life, Mam, just life.' She forced a smile. 'So, what were yer saying?'

'Asking if you remembered the day yer dad returned from the war. Oh, what a joyous day that was.'

'I do remember it well, Mam, and it was a great day.' But little did they know, she thought, how badly he had been affected by it all. Thankfully he had all his limbs but his mind . . . no, that would never be the same.

Showing the same strength of love she had displayed towards her children, and despite her own failing health, Flora had tirelessly nursed her husband night after night, the months stretching to over two years, through terrible dreams, bouts of screaming and shaking, weeks on end of depression in which he would not leave the house. All this she endured without complaint. Flora had been thankful just to have her husband back alive, completely convinced that given time, with her love and care, he would heal. She had not foreseen that she herself might not be around to see that cure completed.

Kelly sighed sadly. Her mother must have loved them all very deeply to have acted so unselfishly in all she had done. Her life-threatening illness was so unfair. And that Vicar had dared to tell her to put her faith in God! What God could do this? Strike down such a wonderful woman in the prime of her life, and leave behind people who loved and would miss her dreadfully. Hard as she tried to avoid it, her eyes filled with tears.

'Kelly.'

She gulped, sniffed and fought to control her emotions. 'Yes, Mam?' she said lightly.

'Don't, Kelly.'

'Don't what?'

'Don't be sad for me, love. I know what's going

through your mind and I know yer angry for what's happened to me. But I don't want you to be. What's happened has happened. No one has the power to change things.'

'Oh, Mam, I . . .'

'Kelly, dry those eyes. Remember, me darlin', I've bin one of the lucky ones. I've had much more than most women and that's love and happiness, Kelly. For my part, I'd sooner have had them than a miserable life and lived 'til I were ninety.' She paused to take several laboured breaths. 'Oh, Kelly, none of us know when our time will be up. That's why we've got to make the most of what we're given. Some people live to ripe old ages, some go young. My lot is ter go young.' She smiled and for a brief second Kelly saw a flash of just how lovely her mother used to be. 'I never did like the idea of getting to an age when me face looked like a mouldy apple! Yer dad wouldn't fancy me looking like that, now would he?'

Kelly sniffed again and smiled. 'Dad would fancy you whatever you looked like.'

Flora nodded. 'Yer right, he would. But then, that's love for yer. And the most I hope for you, Kelly, is that you experience love like I have. It carries yer through anything.' Trying to hide the effort it cost her, she patted her daughter's hand. 'Yer know, I think I will have that cuppa, if you wouldn't mind?'

'I don't mind, Mam, I don't mind at all. While I wait for the kettle to boil, I'll put the clothes into soak for tomorrow.' She rose to her feet. 'Back in a jiffy.'

As she reached the door Flora called out to her. 'Kelly . . .'

She turned and smiled. 'Yes, Mam?'

'I love you, Kelly.'

'I know, Mam,' the girl whispered. 'And I love you too.'

Flora lay back against her pillow and stared distractedly at the ceiling. At nineteen her daughter should not be concerned with putting washing into soak, she should be out enjoying herself. She should also have a full-time job, not the few hours she did at the corner shop, earning a pittance. And when she wasn't working she had hardly any time for herself because not only did she have an invalid and her father and brother to care for but also a household.

Momentarily Flora closed her eyes, sucking in her breath as a wave of severe pain flowed through her. It was becoming worse by the day, increasing in intensity and severity, becoming hardly bearable. To keep this knowledge from her family would soon become impossible. What would she do then? How would she cope, knowing the further distress she was causing them? 'Oh, God,' she sighed wearily, 'why did you have to do this to me when I have so much to live for? How much longer do I have to wait for the blessed release of death?' Because, she thought, that's all I'm doing now.

She knew there would be no reprieve for her, no miracles. The illness had too strong a hold. The thought of leaving her beloved family was unbearable, but what good was she to them now? She could do none of the things a mother did for her children, none of the things a woman did for the man she loved. Even the effort of drinking a cup of tea sapped all her energy.

Her illness was causing suffering for those she loved. Better for them all that her death came soon, that she didn't linger much longer. Then her beloved family could get on with their lives.

Not for the first time, she contemplated the only solution. But it saddened her greatly to know she had been reduced to such thoughts.

She heard the sound of Kelly returning and, pushing aside her despair, she fixed a smile on her face.

Chapter Four

'Is that you, Frank?'

He jumped at the sound of his wife's feeble voice. He had been sitting in the darkness by her bed, her limp hand clasped gently in his, lost in thought for several hours.

With a great effort Flora tried to raise herself. 'A' you all right, Frank? Turn the light on so I can see yer.'

He froze. The last thing he wanted was for Flora to witness the state he was in. He had been crying and she would know it at a glance.

For Frank the fear of losing his beloved wife was far worse than anything he had been through or was ever likely to. It was selfish of him, he knew, but he would rather keep her here, with all her pain and suffering, than have her gone from him. He could not visualise life without her, couldn't bring himself to. 'No,' he whispered hoarsely, 'let's just sit here for a bit with it off, me darlin'.'

Flora sank back against the pillows, knowing exactly the emotions her husband was experiencing. 'Yes, let's do that. I like lying here with you in the dark.' Then you can't see what my illness has done to me, she thought. You can picture me as I used to be.

There was silence between them for several moments.

'Are our kids all right, Frank?' Flora whispered. 'Only I worry so much for 'em. Mickey keeps things from me,

I know he does. And our Kelly. Oh, Frank, our daughter's got responsibilities a girl of her age shouldn't have. She should go out more and enjoy herself, 'specially now she and Rodney are engaged. She'll lose him if she doesn't spend more time with him.'

'Eh, stop talking like this, Flora. Our Kelly's fine. She enjoys running the house. Right little mother hen she is.' He gently squeezed her hand. 'Teks after her mother, she does. If she wanted to go out, she would. You know our Kelly. She ain't backwards in coming forwards.'

'And I'm glad of it.' Flora paused. 'Frank . . . Mickey ain't doing anything he shouldn't, is he?'

He drew breath sharply. 'What meks you ask that, love?'

'I don't know. Just a mother's feelings, I expect.'

He grimaced. When he had gone away to war his son had been just a boy. Five years had done much to change him. Even in the dreadful state of mind in which Frank had returned, he could not fail to notice, so dramatic was it. There was a hardness about Mickey, a single-mindedness that worried Frank. And it was all his fault! If he hadn't had to leave his family to fend for themselves, Mickey would not have had to grow up so fast, taking on responsibilities a lad of his age should not have had to shoulder. But what Mickey was doing now was not from any necessity. He had no family to care for. Frank had no doubt what drove his son now was pure greed.

But then, how could he blame him? The foundations of that greed had been nurtured by a longing to get away from these mean, poverty-ridden streets, to build a better way of life. Hadn't he himself, like every young man of Mickey's age, longed to do just that? But what concerned him now was how far his son was prepared to go to satisfy those desires.

A feeling of revulsion overcame him. Revulsion for his

42

own part in Mickey's recent activities. By joining in it was as if he had condoned what his son did. He had been selfish, blinded by a desire to feel useful again and a vain hope of seeing pride, rather than pity, in his son's eyes.

He had been a fool to have looked for either.

Like his wife, Frank felt that stealing in any way was wrong. Somewhere someone felt the loss and usually theft hit those who could ill afford it. Neither was the small amount they made worth the worry of discovery and the guilt suffered.

But even more worrying for Frank was his daughter's involvement. Mickey should never have roped her in, expecting her to do her bit. If he or Mickey were caught, then it was only right they should receive punishment. But not his daughter.

Frank's head drooped in shame. He had gone away to war the head of his household. On his return, if he was honest, he'd been glad to find his son had taken over that role, ill equipped in his own fragile mental state to cope with any responsibilities. But now two years had passed, years in which, with the help of his family, his health was almost restored. But regardless it was too late. Mickey had been his own master for far too long ever to acknowledge a need for parental guidance. Frank knew that even to try would invoke his son's hostility.

As much as he wanted to regain his status he had not at this moment the fight in him, nor the courage, nor the energy to tackle his son. Nor had he the mental agility necessary to try to make Mickey see reason and put a stop to his illegal activities before it was all too late. Frank knew he should try but there was something far more important to him before which everything else paled into insignificance: his beloved wife was dying.

43

Taking a deep breath, he slowly raised his head. 'You mustn't worry, me darlin',' he reassured her. 'If our Mickey was up to 'ote he shouldn't be,' he lied, 'I'd know and put a stop to it, now wouldn't I?'

Flora eyed him tenderly. 'Yes, yer would, Frank. I should know better than even to be thinking it.'

They lapsed into silence again.

Flora was acutely aware, despite the pain, of the comforting feeling of Frank's hand in hers and a surge of longing for him to climb into bed beside her and begin his gentle lovemaking filled her being. How she missed not having him lie next to her each night, feeling his closeness, the security his presence had always afforded her. But it was no good wishing for one more night together. Even holding his hand now took all her strength and caused her pain. Holding him in her arms was something she could not hope to achieve again.

Frank's eyes were fixed unblinkingly on a dark corner of the cracked ceiling. He was filled with unbearable sadness. Lying so close to him was the woman he loved, the woman with whom he had shared his life, the mother of his children, the light of his life. And that light was about to go out very soon. What was he going to do without her? How as he going to face each day without looking into her lovely face, seeing the merry twinkle in her pale blue eyes? If only he could die with her, then they could face together whatever lay in the hereafter. That was the way it should be. They had always been so close he knew that Flora, wherever it was she was going, would be lost without him. And he would become nothing without her.

What he would give to lie next to her just once more, hold her in his arms, feel the closeness of her. But that was an impossible wish. Just holding his hand, he knew, caused his beloved wife such pain.

As with her daughter, Flora suddenly felt her husband's distress. 'Frank,' she whispered. 'Frank.'

'Mmmm? What? Sorry, I was just, just . . .'

'I know, Frank, I know. You . . . you were wishing this was just a nightmare. But it ain't, Frank.' Her voice lowered to barely a whisper. 'I'm going to die. I am, Frank. And there's nothing anyone can do ter stop that.'

Momentarily forgetting the pain it caused her, he gripped her hand. 'Don't,' he pleaded. 'Please, Flora, don't speak like this.'

'I have ter, Frank. We have ter face this, and I'd sooner face it together than alone.'

'Alone! Oh, Flora, you ain't alone. I know it's hard for me to accept. I just . . . Oh, Flora, I just can't see me life without yer.'

'I know. Me and you, well . . . we were meant, weren't we? But when I go, Frank, I don't want you to mourn me. I won't rest easy if I know yer mourning me.'

'Oh, Flora,' he groaned despairingly. 'How can I not? You've bin everything to me. Everything.'

She shut her eyes tightly and sighed. 'And you me, Frank. And you me. But you have the rest of yer life ter live. I want you ter be happy. What we've had . . . well . . . people would give their eye teeth for that. We've bin lucky, much luckier than most. Keep that in your heart, Frank, when I'm not here. I know it'll be hard, but you have ter do that. Just remember the good times, and we had many of those.'

He smiled wanly. 'Yes, we have, ain't we?' His eyes glazed over. 'I remember all the picnics. Miles we used ter walk to find a spot near water where there was nobody else. All we had ter eat was bread and lard and a can of cold tea. But bloody marvellous they were, those picnics. Watching the kids running barefoot through the grass . . . me and Mickey fishing, you and our Kelly picking daisies to mek chains.'

She smiled. 'And I remember when me and Kelly were cornered by a bunch of cows, and you and our Mickey had to save us.'

Frank grinned. 'They were harmless, Flora.'

'Not to me and Kelly they weren't.'

Sadness washed through him again and his whole body sagged as memories of their life together flooded in. A trickle of tears fell down his face. 'Oh, Flora,' he uttered. 'Why? Why did it have ter be you?'

'Frank, don't,' she begged. 'Please.' She shut her eyes tightly as his pain filled her. They couldn't go on like this; she couldn't go on like this, day after day, living with the uncertainty of whether it would be her last, worrying if there were things left unsaid, witnessing and sensing their pain as well as her own. She suddenly knew the time had come. The deed could not be put off any longer. With a great effort she gripped his hand. 'Frank, listen ter me.' She drew breath, fighting to muster all her courage, knowing that what she was about to ask was unforgivable but, regardless, something she felt she no longer had any choice over. 'I . . . I want you to end this suffering. Not just for me, but for all our sakes.'

He sniffed, wiped his hand under his nose and stared at her blankly. 'What?'

'Yer did hear me right, Frank,' she whispered. 'Please do it. Please put an end to it.'

'But . . . but I don't understand?'

'I think you do, Frank. All you have ter do is put a pillow over me face while I'm sleeping. I won't feel any pain. It'll just be like I've gone ter sleep and not woken up. It'll be a blessed release.' Her voice faltered. 'Not just for me, Frank, but for all of us.'

His mouth dropped open. 'Flora, how could yer? How could yer ask me to do that? You know how much I love yer . . .'

'Do it 'cos yer love me, Frank. Put me out of this misery. Please,' she begged. 'Please find it in yerself.'

Dumbstruck, he just sat and stared at her.

They were so engrossed in each other that neither had heard the back door open some minutes earlier, neither had felt the presence of someone else standing listening at the door.

Chapter Five

Kelly turned and smiled at her father as he entered the kitchen at five-thirty the next morning.

'Oh, yer up,' he said as though shocked to see her.

''Course I'm up. I'm always up, Dad.' She stared at him hard, taking in the mane of iron grey hair her mother still saw as jet black, the deep lines etched on his once handsome face, the stoop of his shoulders, the pain and sadness filling his grey eyes. 'Didn't yer sleep?' she asked in concern.

He shook his head. 'Not much.' How could he have slept with the burden of what was racing through his mind?

'Sitting with Mam most of the night, were yer?'

His answer came slowly. ''Til she fell asleep. I have ter mek the best of the time we've got left.'

Kelly sighed. 'I know, Dad, I know. Cuppa? I've just mashed.'

He smiled appreciatively. 'I could murder one.'

She poured him a mugful and handed it to him. 'I'm just about to tek one through for Mam.'

'I'll do that,' he said quickly.

She eyed him in surprise. She always saw to her mother first thing. 'As you wish, Dad.'

'It's just . . . it's just, well . . . yer mam was a bit down last night. It's my fault. We were reminiscing, yer see, and she got very maudlin. I shouldn't have allowed that. I should have . . .'

49

Kelly rushed to him and placed her hand on his arm. 'Come on, Dad, don't feel bad. Mam likes nothing more than to remember the past. If it's fault you're laying, it's mine too, 'cos we were going over the past earlier on. Come on, tek her tea through while I dish up yer breakfast.'

He nodded. 'Not much fer me, love. I ain't that hungry.'

She turned back towards the stove. She didn't like to tell him there wasn't much. 'Fried bread and an egg. I'm sure you can manage that, Dad. And give our Mickey a shout. He's late down this morning which isn't like him.'

She had just raised the fish slice in order to lift his egg when there was a crash of shattering pottery followed by a blood-curdling scream. Dropping the slice, she rushed towards the door and on into the makeshift bedroom.

'What . . .?' Her voice died away at the sight of her father slumped by her mother's bed. He was clasping her limp hand in his own.

'It's yer mam, Kelly,' he said brokenly. 'She's gone. Oh, Kelly, she's left us.'

'Oh, no,' she gasped. 'Oh, no.' Trancelike she moved towards the bed and knelt down beside him, staring into the peaceful face of her beloved mother, a lump forming in her throat. 'Oh, Mam,' she whispered, taking hold of her father's arm for support. 'Oh, Mam.'

'So yer did it then, Dad?'

The voice was harsh, cruel, and Kelly spun around to see Mickey framed in the doorway. She rose awkwardly and took several steps towards him, her face creased in bewilderment. 'What did yer say?'

'You heard, Kelly. He did it.' He advanced into the room, eyes glinting with hatred. 'You killed her!' he spat accusingly.

Dropping Flora's hand, Frank rose and turned to face his son. 'How dare you?'

50

Horrified, Kelly rushed towards Mickey and grabbed both his arms. 'Fer God's sake, Mickey, what's got into you?'

He pushed Kelly from him, eyes still fixed on his father. 'Don't deny it, Dad. I heard you last night. I heard you agree . . .'

'Agree? Agree to what?' Kelly broke in.

Face set in stupefied horror, Frank stared at him. 'Mickey, now listen ter me . . .'

His son, face filled with hatred, punched his fist in the air. 'No, I won't listen to yer. I know what I heard. Mam asked you to end it for her and you did it. Go on, admit it.'

'Mickey!'

'Keep outta this, Kelly. This is between me and him.' He faced his father and folded his arms. 'Admit it,' he shouted.

Astounded, Frank stared at him for several long moments then raised his chin defiantly and said, 'I can't believe a son of mine is accusing me of this. You know how much I loved yer mother.' A sudden gush of tears rushed down his face. With head bowed and shoulders slumped, he walked past them and out of the room.

Kelly glared up at her brother. 'Dad's right, Mickey. How could you? Mam's hardly cold . . .'

'Leave it, Kelly,' he answered icily. 'I know what I heard. She asked him to end it for her. Put her and us out of misery. And this morning she's dead. Don't that seem strange to you? Oh, he killed her all right. I know he did.'

She grabbed hold of his arm, gripping it tightly. 'I don't care what you heard. Dad would never harm Mam. Never, do you hear?'

'Well, if he didn't then why didn't he deny it? Go on, explain that?'

Kelly's mouth snapped firmly shut. Could it possibly

51

be true? Had Dad ended her mother's suffering? The thought was too dreadful. But it would explain his actions this morning. Had he known her mother was already dead and wanted to spare her the trauma of finding the body? Oh, God, her mind screamed. It wasn't true. It couldn't be. The dreadful pain of her mother's death was bad enough without having to endure that knowledge as well. Eyes filling with tears, she turned and fled from the room.

Chapter Six

Later that morning a shocked and dismayed Reverend Billings stared upwards.

'Mindless cretins what done it. N'ote but mindless cretins.'

Algernon sighed heavily. 'Albert, I would have said myself that a lot of thought had gone into stealing the lead from the roof. So whoever did this was anything but mindless. Clever more like it. And brave. You'd have to be brave to tackle something like that.' He sadly shook his head. 'I suppose it was only a matter of time before my church was targeted.'

'Want castrating the lot of 'em, if yer ask me.'

'That'll do, Albert,' Algernon snapped disapprovingly. He turned his gaze upwards once more. 'I suppose I will have to inform the Bishop and he isn't going to be pleased. Having a roof releaded isn't cheap these days.'

'Church can afford it.'

'What was that, Albert?'

'Er . . . nothing,' the verger muttered. 'So what d'yer want me ter do, yer reverence?'

'Not a lot we can do. I'm just glad you noticed before it rained on the congregation. Well done for spotting it.'

Albert smiled, pleased with himself, although spotting the missing lead hadn't been that hard as the mess the robbers had left behind was clearly evident on the slab path below. He grimaced at the sight. On top of everything else that was another job he would have to fit in. 'I'll get back to me grave then, will I?' he grumbled.

'Pardon? Oh, yes, yes. I nearly forgot, I have a funeral at eleven.' Algernon consulted his watch. 'It's almost ten. Have you much left to dig?'

Albert sucked in his cheeks, plunging his gnarled muddy hands into the pockets of his ancient corduroy jacket. 'Couple of foot give or take. An hour should do it.'

'Well, please make sure it does. I wouldn't want the funeral party arriving and you to be still digging away. They'll be suffering enough distress without that.'

Albert touched the peak of his flat cap. 'Right yer are, Reverend.'

Clasping his hands as though in prayer, Algernon turned his gaze back to the roof. How on earth was he going to find the money to get the repairs done? A vision of endless jumble sales, coffee mornings and whist drives flashed before him. He did not relish the thought. He rubbed his chin, thinking that whoever had risked his life stealing the lead obviously had a head for heights. And, he mused, it must have taken more than one to do the job. Lead sheeting was very heavy. No, it must have taken two of them, maybe even three.

A recent memory momentarily flashed to mind but as quickly disappeared.

He consulted his watch again and gasped. Better get a move on or the mourners would be arriving before *he* was ready for them.

Chapter Seven

It was half-day closing and, taking a break from her laborious chores, Kelly sighed miserably as she placed her elbows on the worn pine table, rested her chin in her hands and stared absently around the tiny kitchen. She faced several dilemmas and wasn't sure what to do about any of them.

It was six weeks since her mother's death and the atmosphere in the shabby house was strained to breaking point. Her brother would not shift from his belief that Dad had ended their mother's suffering and had hardly spoken a word to him since his astounding accusation on the morning of her death. Kelly herself refused even to consider her father could contemplate such an action, let alone carry it out, but what she found totally confusing was the fact that he refused either to deny or discuss the accusation in any shape or form.

Since his wife's death he had taken to sitting for long periods in her makeshift bedroom – which he had refused to have touched in any way – staring into space, or else embarking on aimless long walks. Kelly had no idea where he went. He hardly ate, picking at whatever was placed before him no matter how appetising she strove to make the meals. He was wasting away before her eyes and she couldn't seem to halt that process.

Her own grief over the loss of her mother was worse than she could ever have imagined so how her father felt was beyond her. Flora had been his wife, he had loved her totally, his whole existence centred around her. Now his reason for living had been cruelly cut short, Kelly feared he felt that life held no purpose for him now and saw death as the only release. If only, she vehemently wished, something would happen to give him back a sense of purpose. Just something small that would help to start the process.

It would go some way, she thought, if Mickey would come to his senses. She would have to try again to convince him that his accusation, based purely on something he had overheard, was due to a misunderstanding. Grief-stricken at his mother's death, he needed to blame someone. Whether he would listen to her and retract his accusation was doubtful. Her brother's behaviour had become almost unbearable since their mother had died: cold, abrupt, sometimes downright hostile.

Again she attributed his attitude to grief, but how long could she put up with this state of affairs? And reasoning with him would be almost impossible. He barely spent any time in the house these days. He came home from work, washed and changed, gobbled down whatever food she had prepared and immediately went out, always returning after she had gone to bed. They hardly exchanged half a dozen words. But she would have to make him talk to her and sort something out because she did not know how much longer she could go on living in this atmosphere, watching two people she loved dearly at each other's throats. And it wasn't as though she did not have problems herself.

While Kelly had been caring for her mother, her own affairs had been put aside. Now she could no longer ignore some pressing problems, but how she would tackle them was another matter.

She was nineteen, thought herself reasonably intelligent considering the scant education she had received, but had never held a proper full-time job. She had left school at fourteen like most girls of her background and started an apprenticeship in a local factory. She had hated every moment. She found she had no talent for machining whatsoever, which the management had soon worked out, and she had been given no alternative but to leave and find other employment or take the lowly job offered her there as the factory runabout.

Deeply worried that she may well have no other talents, and concerned about the problems at home, Kelly decided to take the job as it was better than nothing.

She had been no more than a badly paid skivvy at the beck and call of all those senior to her, which was practically the whole workforce, and wasn't sorry when in due course she had been forced to leave for a job with fewer hours so she could care for her mother and take over the running of the household. Working for Ada Adcock four hours a day proved much pleasanter but the pay was hardly enough for her to pay a contribution towards her keep, let alone to buy the things a young woman of her age wanted: clothes, makeup, new nylons, magazines, funds to go out with friends. A record player now . . . she craved one of those so she could listen to the type of music that she liked instead of what came over the old, crackling wireless set her father had picked up and mended just before he had gone off to war.

Mickey had come home once armed with a pile of 78s he said he had found stacked beside a dustbin and besides recordings of Dame Nelly Melba and Caruso she had found to her delight the music of Glenn Miller and several other big American dance bands, Frank Sinatra and Ella Fitzgerald. If she had had the money and something to play them on – even the ancient player she had come across in the second-hand shop with its huge protruding trumpet – she could have haggled with

Mickey to buy them, but she hadn't. So a record player and records, like everything else she craved, was just wishful thinking.

A better paid job was her answer, but apart from learning to add up quickly and accurately, give correct change and be pleasant to customers, working her few hours for Ada Adcock had afforded her no real grounding for better paid employment. Mrs Adcock saw to all the ordering and bookwork.

So what was she equipped to do? Kelly suddenly realised with a sense of distaste that all she was proficient in was the art of stealing. Was taking what belonged to others and hoping she had been clever enough not to be caught going to be her whole way of life? Because that was the way it seemed to be shaping. How could it not be when she was surrounded by people whose lives continually revolved around what job they were planning next and who, more to the point, actually seemed to enjoy what they were doing?

A knock reverberated down the bare-boarded passageway and she jumped, wondering who would be calling at this time on a Wednesday afternoon. Since her mother had died callers to their house, apart from ones wanting money, had dwindled to practically none.

She opened the door and was surprised to find a tiny, grubby, shabbily dressed old lady standing on the pavement staring up at her expectantly. She was clutching a large, bulging, tattered brown handbag to her chest. Kelly immediately noticed the old woman was in some distress.

'Can I help yer?' she asked.

'I hope so, me duck. Does Mickey the dustman live 'ere?'

Always cautious, Kelly folded her arms and defensively asked, 'Why?'

The old lady's face puckered worriedly. 'Oh, I 'ope 'e

does. Please say 'e does. I've 'ad 'ell of a job to find him. Traipsed the streets I have, knocking doors. 'E done me a favour, see. Nice lad is Mickey. He's done it before, only this time . . .'

'What kind of favour?'

'Oh, bought some bits from me. Not worth anything but Mickey 'elped me out of a hole. Had no money fer the gas see and the Pru man was due ter call for his shilling. Mickey didn't really want to take the bits off me hands, but being the kinda chap 'e is he agreed. And I wa' bloody grateful. Only . . .'

'Only what?'

'Well, there was a little vase. Mickey said it was cheap rubbish and give me a tanner for it. Only it wa' me mother's. Only thing I'd got left of hers and it's preyed on me mind since. I can't sleep knowing I parted with it.' She thrust her hand in a pocket of her coat, rummaged for something then held it out towards Kelly. 'Here's a tanner. D'yer think I could 'ave me vase back?'

The old lady's plight touched Kelly. She herself had been without money for the gas on so many occasions. If Mickey had not been able to help out then she had resorted to using the piece of tin cut in the shape of a shilling which the kindly gas man would deduct from the total when dishing out their rebate. Many families resorted to similar actions; maybe this old lady was unaware of such tricks.

Kelly sympathised with her strongly. She herself could never part with anything that had belonged to her mother. She would sooner starve or freeze to death than do that. She smiled at the old lady. 'I don't see why not. If I can find it that is. Mickey might already have got rid of it. Wait here, I'll go and have a look.'

The woman beamed a grateful toothless grin. 'Oh, ta, me duck, ta.'

Kelly returned several minutes later. 'Is this it?' she

asked, holding out the ornament she had found in a box under Mickey's bed, along with several other items, mostly trinkets of brass or copper worth not much more than a shilling or two.

'Yes, that's it,' the visitor cried in relief.

As she handed it over in exchange for the sixpence, Kelly examined the ornament. 'It's very pretty.'

'It is. Me mam used ter work as a maid for a woman in a large house up Belgrave Road.' She clutched the vase protectively to her skinny chest. 'The mistress gave it to her as a wedding present. I should never 'ave parted wi' it.'

'Well, yer've got it back, that's the main thing.'

'Yes, I 'ave, ain't I? Maybe I'll sleep better ternight. Thanks, me duck. Thanks so much. You'll tell Mickey I'm sorry, won't yer? But maybe I've done him a favour, 'cos he reckoned he'd be stuck wi' it.'

Kelly thoughtfully watched the old woman shuffle away down the street, then shutting the door behind her returned to her seat at the table, their visitor's sorry state uppermost in her mind. She didn't want to end up like that, and she would if she didn't do something about it now.

The thought of starting a career from scratch when girls of her age would usually be finishing their training did not appeal. It wasn't the thought of finding something suitable that bothered her. After all, there must be something she could learn to be good at. Neither was it the learning.

What worried her was the meagre wages she would receive while training. How would she manage when she and Mickey were the only ones bringing anything in? As she knew by his manner, her brother already begrudged every penny he had to hand over to support the household. He sorely resented the fact that his own father was not making any contribution. If she got a job now maybe

60

that grievance would be partly alleviated. She decided to buy the *Leicester Mercury* later and scan the job columns, see what was on offer. It would be a start.

That problem dealt with as far as it could be for the present, her thoughts strayed to Rod. She sighed loudly, staring dreamily into space. She loved her fiancé deeply, couldn't imagine life without him, was looking forward to the day they got married. She visualised the kind of dress she hoped to wear, the church decked out with flowers, all the guests laughing and joking. And sighed again. Would that day ever come? she thought. Rod still could not afford an engagement ring let alone find the money for a wedding. A contribution from the parents on either side was out of the question.

Maybe, though, once she got a job, if she was careful with her wage, she might be able to start putting money aside herself. Not much, but even a little would help. A lot depended on her getting a full-time job and the sooner that came about the better.

Her thoughts went deeper and she frowned. What would married life with Rod be like? Her frown stayed fixed on her face. She hadn't actually thought about that before, her mind usually travelling no further than the wedding itself. Was being physically attracted to someone enough to sustain a marriage? Rod, after all, liked to spend a lot of time with his friends, sometimes to the extent that she hardly saw him for two or three days except when he called in to see Mickey, find out what he was up to. Would all this change when they married? Would they begin to share common interests, do more things together, talk even, like her parents had done? What was married life really all about?

She shuddered. More to the point, why was she suddenly thinking like this?

Totally confused, she shut her eyes and groaned. So many problems needing urgent attention. If only she had

61

someone to talk to openly and ask an opinion of, someone she could trust. It was a pity, she thought, that she could not consult Glenda about this. But how could she when it was her friend's own brother she was worrying about?

She jumped for the second time that afternoon as someone knocked on the back door and rose to open it. She smiled warmly at the visitor. 'Hello, Alec.'

He returned her smile. 'Hello, Kelly. I just wondered if yer dad were in?'

She shook her head. 'No, he ain't. I don't know when he'll be back either. Did yer just call for a chat with him? I expect he'll be sorry he's missed yer. He don't get many visitors now and I know seeing you would have done him good.'

She had known Alec Alderman practically all her life. Her own father and his, having been on the same gang on the bin rounds, had become friends. Although five years older than Kelly, as a growing boy Alec had been a frequent visitor to their house on family visits and vice versa, and while the elders entertained themselves playing cards or chatting over a jug of beer fetched from the pub, the younger members would play snakes and ladders, ludo or whatever took their fancy. Until, that was, the war had disrupted everything. Alec's father hadn't been so lucky as her own. He had died in battle. His wife had never got over it and now lived with her brother's family in Sussex.

Kelly had always liked Alec. He was a very likeable sort of man. He couldn't be considered handsome but he was passable. He was a little over six foot tall, with a head of thick dark hair and twinkling blue eyes. He was slim, bordering on the thin side, always looking as though he needed a good feed, when in fact his appetite was perfectly healthy. But it wasn't his physical attributes that principally drew people to Alec, so much as his

62

good-heartedness. Unlike most of the men Kelly was acquainted with, Alec possessed a very caring and considerate nature without in any way demeaning his masculinity, and that quality in him had not waned in the slightest as he had entered adulthood.

When young, he was the only boy Kelly had known who would happily run errands for neighbours and not accept payment, despite his great need of money. He still did so now. The elderly or infirm or anyone in need knew that if Alec was on their bin round and they required help, they only had to ask. If it was in his power the job would be done, whatever it was. Pity, she thought, that Mickey wasn't more like him.

'Do yer want to come in and wait for him?' she asked. 'I could mash you a cuppa.'

He grimaced thoughtfully. 'I really do need ter get home. I've got hold of a couple of old wireless sets I'm trying to repair and hopefully sell, 'cos we could do with the money, and Norma's wanting me to make a start on the bedroom.'

Kelly frowned. 'I thought you decorated that house from top to bottom just before you got married? That was only three years ago.'

'I did. But Norma's not keen on the colour now. She's set her heart on the new forget-me-not blue.'

'Then Norma's a lucky woman! Most men would tell her to be happy with what's she's got.'

For a moment Kelly envied Alec and Norma. The pair were devoted to each other. They had been childhood sweethearts and no one had been surprised when they'd announced their forthcoming marriage. Norma had made a lovely bride and the expression on both their faces throughout the service told everyone exactly how they felt about each other. They had moved into a little rented terraced house next-door to Norma's widowed mother and Alec had done a grand job of decorating throughout before they had moved in. They appeared the perfect couple. Yes, Kelly thought, if Rod and she ever achieved a fraction of what this couple shared between them then she would have no complaints.

'If time spent redecorating a bedroom makes Norma happy, then it's time well spent to me. Anyway, I really would like ter see yer dad, Kelly. So I'll hang on a few minutes,' he added. 'But I'd better wait out here. I'm still in me working togs.'

She looked him up and down and grinned, taking in the typical bin man's attire of a workworn donkey jacket with scraped and scuffed leather patches on shoulders and elbows, and bib and brace overalls that swamped his thin frame, tied tightly around the bottom in case of encountering rats, which the men frequently did. 'Alec, I'm used to dirty, smelly bin men. Come on in,' she ordered. 'If yer that bothered, I'll put newspaper on the chair before you sit down.' She turned and eyed him quizzically as he pulled a chair out from the table and perched on the edge of it. 'Anyway, what did yer want to see me dad about?'

'About a job I've heard of.'

Her eyes lit up excitedly. 'A job? Oh, Alec, what kinda job? On the bins, is it?'

'No.' He didn't like to tell her that Frank would never be allowed to work on the bin rounds again. The vindictive Ernest Smith had seen to that. 'It's for a road sweeper. It's a comedown to what he's used ter, but . . .'

'It's a job,' she cut in. 'Oh, Alec, d'yer think he'll stand a chance?'

'As good as any, I reckon. The gaffer in charge is a decent bloke. He had a rough time of it during the war so I think he'll be sympathetic towards yer dad.'

Kelly had trouble containing her emotions. 'Oh, Alec, I think this could be the miracle he needs.'

'Well, don't get too excited, Kelly, just in case,' he warned.

'No, I won't.' Her eyes sparkled brightly. 'But I'll keep everything crossed all the same.'

Alec smiled, finding her enthusiasm infectious but managing to keep his own feelings in check. Kelly had been through enough just lately and he did not like the thought of causing her unnecessary disappointment. 'Just get yer dad down, boots blacked, to the Corpo office first thing tomorrow. Tell him to ask for Bill Bundy.'

'I will, Alec, I will. I'll black his boots meself. Oh, you more than deserve that cuppa. I wish I had a biscuit to give yer.'

'A cuppa will be fine, ta.'

Alec watched her as she busied herself mashing the tea. Right from being a young lad he had taken to Kelly. He had always admired the way she had stood her ground with her domineering brother, but that aside he had enjoyed her company and watched her change with pleasure from pretty child into an attractive woman. She was easy to talk to and possessed an intelligence superior to most other women he encountered. Kelly had the ability to make something of herself, he thought. It was only the events around her that had held her back. Maybe now the tragedy of her mother's illness and death was behind her, she would see her way to go forward. He hoped so. He felt Kelly had a lot to give.

Mind you, he thought ruefully, what chance had she got with her choice of future spouse? His dislike of Rodney Collins was nearly as great as the one he harboured for Mickey McCallan, and he had more than enough reason to have those feelings. Like Mickey, Rod also was doing things that Alec did not agree with and if the rumours were true, recently the pair were getting into things that could cost them dearly if caught. For

Frank and Kelly's sake he hoped that what he had heard was just rumour and no more, although he had suspected for a while that Mickey coerced his sister into joining in with many of his illicit activities. If this were true then Alec felt it was inexcusable of Mickey, whatever reasons he may give for doing so. To Alec, money should be earned honestly or not at all.

As she placed two mugs of steaming tea on the table he eyed her with concern. 'How are you in yerself, Kelly? How yer coping?'

The question was only to be expected coming from Alec but all the same her eyes flashed briefly in surprise. Apart from at the funeral where everyone had expressed their sympathy, no one had asked her how she was truly feeling. 'I'm all right,' she said lightly. 'Thanks for asking.'

Folding his arms, he leaned on the table, looking straight into her eyes. 'It's me yer talking to, Kelly. I asked how yer were?'

She met his gaze, sighing heavily. 'I'm just about coping, Alec, ta. It ain't easy. I loved me mother and miss her dreadfully. I didn't think it would be this hard. After all, we were expecting it.'

'I don't think anything prepares you fer death, Kelly. I'll never stop missing me dad. I know my mother never will either. In time you feel less grief-stricken, though.'

She smiled wanly. 'So people say. But you have to live through that time, don't you?'

It wasn't a question but a statement and Alec nodded.

'You'll get through it,' he said with conviction. 'How's Frank? Is he any better since the last time I saw him?'

She shook her head sadly. 'Not really. Me mam were his life. He won't let us sort out the front room. Still won't let us touch anything. He just sits in there for hours or disappears on long walks. Where he goes is anyone's guess. It's worrying me, Alec. That's why I'm so excited about this job. But then, to be honest, I'm also bothered what will happen if he doesn't get it. If he got knocked back again, I'm worried it could be the finish of him.'

'Kelly, there are some things you can't control. Yer dad's got to handle his grief in the only way he knows how. Like you, he needs time. All you can do is be there to help him.'

Kelly smiled fondly at her childhood friend. 'Yer a good man, Alec. Pity you're already married and I'm engaged,' she said, a twinkle in her eye, 'or I'd have made a play for you meself.'

He grinned. 'Well, when Norma and Rod decide they've had enough of us, I'll be straight round.'

'Well, I'll wait forever then, won't I? 'Cos Norma's never gonna part with you.'

'And if Rod's any sense he'll not let you out of his sight neither.' He scraped back his chair and rose. 'I should be getting home. I'll drop by later in the week and see how Frank got on. Thanks fer the tea, Kelly.' He gave her a cheeky wink. 'I can live in hope I'll get a biscuit next time, eh?'

'Live in hope is about all you'll do, 'cos unless our fortunes take a miraculous turn for the better it'll just be tea – and weak tea at that.' She followed him to the door. 'Oh, I never got a chance to thank yer for coming to the funeral. I did appreciate it and I know Dad did too. It couldn't have been easy for yer.'

Getting the time off had been anything but easy. Unless it was for immediate family, no official leave was given for such occasions. He had only been able to come after his mates on the round had risked their own jobs by covering for him. Alec knew Kelly would be fully aware of this. There wasn't much she didn't know or under-stand about the Corporation bin rounds. 'Nothing would have stopped me paying my respects, Kelly. I liked your mother. She was a lovely woman. One of a kind.'

She nodded, appreciative of his comments. 'She liked you too, Alec,' she whispered, and swallowed hard against the lump forming in her throat. 'Give my best ter Norma.'

'I will, ta.'

He opened the door and stepped through it, coming face to face with Mickey.

He scowled his recognition. 'What you doing here?'

'Mickey!' Kelly scolded her brother.

'I'm only asking a question,' he spat. 'So what's brought you here, Alec?'

'I see your manners ain't changed. Still as nasty as ever,' he retaliated, a glint in his eye. 'For your information, I came to see your father about a job that might interest him.'

'Huh! Well, yer wasted yer time then, didn't yer?' Mickey snarled, stepping past Alec and Kelly and on into the kitchen. 'Ain't you heard? Me dad's unemployable,' he called after him.

Kelly gasped in shock. 'There's no need fer that, Mickey,' she cried. 'Alec's trying to do us a favour. He didn't have ter waste precious time by coming round here. He could have left us ter hear about the job by chance.' She took hold of their visitor's arm and ushered him down the yard. 'I apologise for me brother, Alec. Just tek no notice.'

He pulled her to a halt and turned her to face him. 'It's hard to ignore a statement like that, Kelly. The bad feeling between me and Mickey is one thing but I ain't never heard him speak out like that about a member of his own family, 'specially his father. What's gone on?'

She gulped. 'Nothing. Nothing's gone on,' she protested. 'Mickey's took me mam's death hard, that's all.'

Alec was not convinced. 'There's more to it than that, Kelly.'

She averted her gaze, pretending to study the line of wet washing flapping in the cold breeze. Alec was too old a family friend to fob off with a light excuse but as great as her desire was to confide in him and ask his advice on how to handle the situation between Mickey and her father, she felt it was a terrible thing to divulge to anyone. And there was also the risk that he could think there was some foundation to the accusation and she would not chance that.

She brought her attention back to him. 'They had an argument, that's all, over summat stupid. It'll blow over given time.' She eyed him questioningly. 'Anyway, Alec, I've never known what went on between you and our Mickey. One minute you were bosom buddies, the next arch enemies. So what did happen?'

He took a deep breath. 'Summat and nothing. It's that long ago I've forgotten what it was now.'

'So how come I don't believe yer?' she said sharply. For a moment she eyed him curiously. Boys of whatever age were always having fights and misunderstandings, but within a short space of time all would be forgotten and they would be back together in the thick of it as if nothing had happened. All Kelly did know for sure was that whatever had happened between her brother and Alec must have been very serious to have caused such an irrevocable breach. She sighed. Whatever it was, he wasn't going to tell her. He never had been one for gossip. 'Come on,' she said good-naturedly, 'get off home, else we'll have Norma round brandishing her rolling pin.'

Alec laughed. 'Now that's one thing you'll never catch Norma with. She doesn't like cooking.'

Nor do I much but I still have to do it, thought Kelly. 'Oh, you still have yer meals with Norma's mam then, do yer?'

He nodded. 'Makes sense really. Gives Mrs Quick something to occupy her and make her feel useful, and the bit we pay her helps eke out her war widow's pension. And to be honest, by the time Norma comes home she's too tired to cook a meal.'

'Still doing well at Woolies, is she?'

He nodded proudly. 'Yes, she is. She loves her job. Did I tell you she's in charge of the cosmetics counter?'

'Yes, you did, several times when you were here last. Now get off home, will yer?'

As soon as Alec had latched the back gate behind him, Kelly marched back into the kitchen, temper high. Mickey was standing, stripped to the waist, washing the day's grime from him. For all his faults, one good thing about her brother was that he was meticulous about his personal hygiene. Every inch of him would be scrubbed as soon as he came home, regardless of any other commitments.

Hands on hips, Kelly glared at him. 'Did yer have ter be so rude?'

Body glistening from a thin layer of lather, he nonchalantly turned his head and stared back at her. 'What?'

'Don't "what" me, you heard. You were downright rude to Alec and there was no need. By the time we heard of this job through word of mouth it might have bin too late for Dad to apply.'

Mickey reached for the piece of towelling hanging from a nail in the wall by the stone sink and began to dry himself. 'And do you think that really matters? He ain't going to get this job so I don't know why yer even bothering to tell him about it.'

'Mickey, stop it. Dad's got as good a chance as any. And stop calling him he. This is yer father we're talking about.'

Angrily he threw the towel in a heap on the floor. 'I can call him what I bleddy well like, but "Dad" I won't

70

and you know me reasons. Now if you wanna waste yer time, that's your choice. Just don't involve me in it. Let's change the subject, shall we, 'cos this conversation is grating on me. What's for me dinner?'

Kelly's mouth snapped shut. She had been hoping to try and broach the subject of what she still saw as Mickey's false allegation against their father but knew without a doubt that anything she said now would be an utter waste of time. Mickey was adamant in his belief. Maybe if she left the subject for a while he might calm down. She could only hope. But regardless she was still smarting about his attitude towards Alec. 'Get yer own bloody dinner,' she blurted angrily. 'I ain't cooking tonight. I don't feel like it.'

He leaped across and grabbed her arm, pulling her close. 'You listen here. I'm the only one bringing any decent money into this house. The pittance you earn ain't worth mentioning. So whether you feel like it or not you'll cook my dinner or I'll stick me boot up yer arse!'

She wrenched herself free. 'You try it and see what yer get.'

He glowered dangerously. 'Don't push yer luck, Kelly. Just think of the consequences should I stop handing over as much as I do. Now I'll ask yer again, what's for me dinner?'

Deeply reluctant to give in, she snapped, 'Egg and chips.'

'We had egg and chips last night.'

'Well, we've got it again tonight unless you want ter fork out for something more to yer taste,' she said sarcastically.

'I want two eggs.'

'You'll get one like the rest of us.'

'I'm warning yer, Kelly.'

'You can warn as much as you like but I've only three eggs 'til pay day and if you expect me to give up mine then you've another think coming.' She reached up and grabbed the chip pan from the shelf above the stove and slammed it down on top. 'Now if yer want me to get yer dinner, you'd better move out the way. This kitchen ain't big enough for the two of us.'

A broad smirk of satisfaction on his face, he grabbed up the newspaper he had discarded on the table earlier and headed for the living room. 'Oh, by the way,' he called back, 'keep yerself free Friday night.'

'What for?' she shouted.

'Wadda you think?'

She sighed heavily and gnawed her bottom lip anxiously, then after several moments followed him through. Mickey was sprawled back in the worn moquette armchair, long legs stretched out, feet crossed on the hearth with its chipped tiles. He lowered the newspaper when he realised she was standing in the doorway and nonchalantly met her gaze. 'What?' he demanded.

Kelly took two steps forward. 'About Friday . . .'

'What about it? You know the drill. We don't need to go over it. And before you say 'ote, he ain't having anything to do with it, so don't bother asking. Rod's helping this time.'

She frowned. 'He never mentioned it to me.'

'Expect him to tell you everything, do yer?'

'No, not everything, but I thought he would have mentioned something like this.' She took a breath and advanced several steps, clasping her hands nervously, not looking forward to her brother's probable reaction to what she had to say. 'Mickey, I . . . I don't think it's a good idea for me to be involved the way I am any more.'

He eyed her sharply. 'Wadda yer mean?' he demanded.

'Look at me, Mickey. I mean, look at me. I'm too big now to pass for a young kid. I can't get away with it any more. It's a wonder that vicar didn't twig on the last job

72

we did. I can tell yer, he looked at me really strangely when I said I was thirteen.'

'Well, there's a simple answer to that one.'

'Is there? What?'

'Just act yer own age. You can still disguise yerself. Wear an old coat and a scarf round yer head. That should be enough.'

She tutted crossly. 'The only coat I possess is old. Look, Mickey, I ain't happy about doing that.'

In an instant the newspaper was flung down and he shot out of the chair and grabbed hold of her arm, squeezing it tightly. 'I don't give a toss whether you're happy or not. I've made arrangements and I expect you ter do yer bit. We can't risk it without you. Someone's got to be the lookout and waylay anyone coming too close. Now I'm going upstairs for a few minutes and I want me dinner on the table when I come down, 'cos I've got an appointment at six.'

'Who with?'

'Never you mind.' He tapped the side of his nose. 'A man about a dog.'

She watched as he headed out of the room and listened to the thump of his feet as he pounded up the stairs. She sighed in defeat. Whether she liked it or not she was part of the 'family business' and it seemed that while Mickey still needed her he was not going to let her relinquish her duties.

As she cut chunks of potatoes into chips she heard the sound of his feet heading down the stairs again and turned to see him framed in the kitchen doorway, his expression thunderous.

'Have you taken anything out of the box under my bed?'

She shook her head. 'No. Oh . . . yes, I did.' She related the story of the old lady's vase. 'The tanner's on the mantelpiece.'

73

'You gave it back!' he erupted. 'Whatever possessed you to do that?'

She frowned. 'I told yer. She was upset 'cos it were her mam's. I don't know why you're so angry. What would you have made on it? A shilling. That's only a tanner profit. Surely sixpence ain't gonna break yer?'

'That vase were worth at least ten bob, maybe a pound.'

She stared at him, stunned. 'But you told that old lady it were worthless?'

He pushed his face close to hers. 'It's called business, Kelly.'

She looked horrified. 'You call it business, fleecing a poor old lady who hadn't two ha'pennies to her name? How could your conscience let you do that?' Her eyes flashed and her lips tightened. 'Or haven't you got one?' she accused.

His face darkened. 'How d'yer think people get rich? Not by having a conscience. That woman agreed the sale. She was grateful to me. So that's fair in my book. Now I've lost money through you. If you ever dare do anything like that again, I'll skin yer alive.'

Astounded by his reasoning she stared at him and with a sense of shock suddenly realised she did not like what she saw. Her brother had become a stranger to her. And if he could do this to an old lady, what else was he capable of? Sudden fear swept through her at a vision of stern policemen, iron bars on windows, and filling her ears the sound of metal doors slamming and huge keys turning in locks. She shivered violently. It was like a premonition, a dire warning of what could lie in store. A sense of utter doom settled on her and she knew she could not go on with this state of affairs any longer.

'I don't want no part of this no more, Mickey,' she blurted out. 'I'm gonna get a decent job. Earn me money honestly.'

74

He grunted disbelievingly. 'What? And what kinda job you going after then? Boss of the Bank of England?'

'Stop being sarky. I'll try for anything and see what comes up. I know I'll have to start at the bottom but I don't care.' She sighed loudly. 'Look, what we're doing can't go on forever. I tell yer, Mickey, it's just sheer luck we ain't bin caught. Even you've got to admit that. I don't know about you, but I don't fancy spending years in jail.'

He stared at her for several long moments. 'Yer've gone chicken, that's what yer've done.' A knowing look suddenly crossed his face and he grabbed her roughly by her arm, digging in his nails deeply. 'Has this got anything to do with that bastard Alderman by any chance? Has he put ideas into your head?'

Instinctively retaliating to his attack, she kicked out her leg and brought it hard against his shin. He yelped, released his grip and bent down to rub his smarting leg.

'Will yer stop doing that, Mickey?' she shouted. 'Me arms are covered in bruises.' Her eyes flashed a warning. 'I ain't scared of you, you know that, so just stop it.'

He pulled up his trouser leg and examined his shin. 'You've bloody cut me,' he complained.

'Good. Now listen ter me and listen good. Alec has nothing to do with this. I don't talk about family business, you know that. It's what you've done to this old lady that's made up me mind, and I tell yer, Mickey, my mind's made up good and proper and you ain't gonna change it. We've had more than a good run for our money and if you've any sense you'll stop yer thieving now.'

'What we've done has never bothered you before.'

'I didn't know you robbed old ladies before, did I? As far as I was concerned we took from those we thought could afford to lose it 'cos we were desperate.'

'Our need ain't changed, Kelly.'

'No, maybe not, but the way you go about things has.' Another worrying thought suddenly occurred to her. 'Does Rod know everything that you do?'

'My business, I think.' He smirked at her. 'If you pull out, Kelly, you'll get nothing more from me apart from the normal board and lodging, and that's a promise. Then what you gonna do when you find you ain't enough money to pay yer way?'

She gulped. 'I'll manage like others do. If Dad gets this job . . .'

'Oh, quit babbling about him getting a job,' Mickey erupted. 'That ain't gonna happen in a million years.'

Her mouth opened before she gave herself time to think and she blurted out, 'Well, I'll support the both of us then.'

He stared at her, long and hard. 'If that's the way you want it,' he snarled.

'It is,' she replied firmly, turning her back on him to face the stove.

He spun abruptly on his heel and stormed from the kitchen.

As she lit the gas under the chip pan the enormity of what she had just committed herself to almost overcame her and her shoulders sagged with worry. Despite this feeling, though, she knew her decision had been the right one, and felt tremendously relieved about it. She had made a commitment to support herself and her father, knowing Mickey meant every word of his threat not to pay out any more than the normal amount for board and lodging. But what was done was done, and somehow, though God knows how, she would stand by her decision. If she retracted she would be under her brother's thumb for ever.

Chapter Eight

Later that evening the Reverend Algernon Billings stood wearily shaking hands with his departing congregation. 'Good-night, Mrs Smith. Good-night, Mrs Allen, I hope your son gets over the measles soon. Let me know if there's anything I can do. Mr Bunson, yes, I'll call and see your wife as soon as I can. Possibly tomorrow evening after service. It's nice to see you, Mrs Timpkins. How are you?'

'Lovely service, Reverend, and I'm very well, ta very much. You were right, yer know.'

He frowned. 'Was I? Good-night, Mrs Mundin. And how's that?'

'The Lord does answer prayers. I prayed like bloody hell to get me vase back and I did. He's not a bad lad, yer know. I've heard what people say, but he's done me a few good turns when I've needed them most.'

Algernon's bushy eyebrows rose. 'The Lord?'

'No, Mickey.'

'Mickey?'

'The lad that bought me vase. He's a dustman by trade but buys and sells on the side. They all do it, yer know, in one way or another.' She frowned thoughtfully. 'In fact, Mickey might be able to help regarding the lead for the roofing.' She winked secretively. 'He knows people, yer know. He told me. "Lily," he said, "there's n'ote I can't get and n'ote I can't sell so you tell people to try me first." He might be able to get you a good deal then yer won't have ter raise so much doing bring and buys. You'll find him at number ten Tewkesbury Street. I'm not supposed to know that but that's where the Lord came in. He's the one that guided me there. Mind you,' she said, shaking her head ruefully, 'He didn't mek it easy for me. Traipsed the streets for hours I did, knocked on just about every door 'til I landed the right one. I must be off now, Reverend. I promised to pop in on Mrs Amos on me way home. She's a poor old soul. Can't get out at all now. Maybe you could visit her sometime?'

'Er . . . yes. Yes, of course I will.'

Algernon watched thoughtfully as she scuttled away. Mickey . . . now where had he heard that name before? And not just once. A vision of the night the lead was stolen flashed to mind. He briefly remembered the shabby young girl who had waylaid him. She had mentioned a brother called Mickey, he felt sure she had. Then came a brief mental image of three men weighed down by a roll of something extremely heavy emerging from the back gate of the house he had visited and where he had left his gloves. The address had been number ten Tewkesbury Street. He frowned, deeply puzzled. The daughter of the poor woman who was dying was adamant they had never met before, but somehow she had seemed familiar. He sighed loudly. Was this all just a coincidence or, more to the point, was his memory playing tricks?

The congregation now all departed, he made his way back inside the church, picked up the box strategically placed to collect donations for the roof fund and shook it. He sighed. A few coppers, maybe one or two shillings. At this rate it would take years to collect enough. But then, what else could he expect? His congregation was mostly made up of people who, if they were lucky, could afford second-hand shoes once a year.

He replaced the box and frowned in annoyance. It wasn't fair that some mindless persons, for whatever reason, should feel they had the right to take what belonged to others, seemingly with no thought for the consequences. It wasn't right that his congregation should suffer as a result.

His thoughts were interrupted by a presence at his side. 'Ah, Albert. Can you make sure the church is secure, please, then you can get off home.'

'I always mek sure it's locked up,' the verger mumbled under his breath.

'What was that, Albert?'

'Er . . . nothing, yer reverence.'

'Oh, just a moment. Do you happen to know of anyone by the name of Mickey? He's a dustman but buys and sells on the side.'

Albert frowned. 'Can't say as I do. I know plenty that buy and sell but no one called Mickey. Why, what yer needing?'

'Oh, nothing.' Algernon sighed forlornly. But I would like my church roofing back if this Mickey's the one that took it or knows who did, he thought.

Chapter Nine

'Road sweeper? Oh, I dunno, Kelly. It's being on the bins I'm used ter. All I've ever done. I dunno about road sweeping.'

'Come on, Dad,' she coaxed. 'I think it sounds a grand job. All that fresh air, and as long as you do what's asked, no one breathing down yer neck.'

'Mmmm, I still dunno though. I don't know what yer mam'd say to me road sweeping.'

She leaned forward in her chair and placed her hand tenderly over his. 'Whatever you did Mam would have been chuffed for yer, yer know that.'

He sighed longingly. 'Yes, she would have backed me in 'ote, would yer mam.' He raised tear-filled eyes. 'I miss her so much, Kelly. So very, very much.'

'I know you do, Dad. She loved you more than anything. I believe she's watching over us, you most of all, and I think she'd be willing you to try for this job.'

'D'yer think so?'

'I'm positive. Anyway going to enquire about it can't do any harm, can it? If you don't like the sound of it, you don't have to take it. Alec said Mr Bundy was a good man. He was in the war too. Had it bad according to Alec. And he said, because of that, Mr Bundy would be understanding about you.'

Frank scratched his chin. 'Alec said that, did he?'

Smiling, she nodded encouragement.

'Well . . .' He paused thoughtfully. 'Alec is a good lad, and if he took the trouble to come and tell me about this job then he must think I stand a good chance.' He eyed her gravely. 'But I still don't know if I'm up to it, Kelly.'

''Course yer up to it. And I think road sweeping sounds much better than emptying bins.'

'Yer do?'

'Yeah, I do. You've got none of the heavy lifting for one thing. Just think about it, Dad.' Giving his hand a reassuring pat, she got to her feet. 'I'll rub the iron over your shirt and trousers. Just in case you do decide to go. Now come on, eat your dinner before it gets cold.'

He stared absently down at his plate. 'I can't eat two eggs, me duck, and you've given me too many chips. Why don't you have some?'

'I've already had mine. I couldn't eat another thing.' That was a lie. The few chips she had eaten had done little to fill her but she did not want her father to know he was eating her dinner as well as his own. She felt that at this moment he needed the nourishment more than she did. 'I don't want to throw good food away, so eat up,' she ordered.

He sighed with resignation. 'All right, love, I'll do me best.'

'Stop it, Rod! Stop doing that.'

'Ah, come on, Kelly, just a little feel. There's n'ote wrong in that. We are engaged.'

'Engaged, not married. So keep yer hands to yerself!'

A disgruntled Rod released Kelly from his embrace and flopped back on the grassy bank of the canal. 'What's up with you tonight?' he grumbled. 'Yer like a bear with a sore head.'

She straightened her blouse and settled her eyes on the rippling murky waters in the canal. 'Nothing's up with me. I've just got a lot on me mind.'

'We've all got things on our mind, Kelly, you ain't no different from anyone else, so why don't you lighten up a bit?' He made a grab for her again. 'Come on, give us a kiss,' he coaxed.

She pushed him from her and jumped up. 'That's all you think of, Rodney Collins. The minute we're alone yer hands are all over me.'

'Well, it's only natural. I love yer, don't I?' he said gruffly.

She stared down at him. 'Do you? I mean, really love me?' she questioned.

Leaning up on one elbow, he stared at her quizzically. 'I said so, didn't I? Look, just what is up with you?'

She opened her mouth, then snapped it quickly shut. She would have liked nothing more than to have a good talk with Rod, about anything and everything, but it would be a waste of time. He would not understand her fears for her father or her concern over getting a job. He would only listen to her if she talked about football or anything to do with Mickey. But then, that was her Rod. She loved him despite it all. She smiled at him and shrugged her shoulders. 'I dunno what's wrong. I'm just a bit tired, I think.' She jumped up and brushed down her skirt. 'I'd better get going. It's getting late.'

Idly he rose to join her. 'I'll walk back with you and see if Mickey's around. He might fancy coming for a pint.'

'Mickey's bin down the pub since seven.' She frowned. 'You know, sometimes I feel you think more of me brother than you do of me.'

'Oh, yer do talk rubbish sometimes, Kelly. Mickey's me mate, 'course I wanna see him, but that don't mean I wanna marry him, now does it?'

She laughed. 'I should bloody hope not!' She grabbed his hand. 'Come on, if yer promise to behave yerself, I might let you kiss me good-night.'

Chapter Ten

Kelly straightened her father's collar and dusted several specks from the shoulders of his shabby black jacket. She stood back, smiling admiringly. 'You look grand, Dad. They'd be fools not to take you on.' He shuffled his feet uneasily and she knew he was on the verge of making excuses not to go. 'Tell yer what, I'll get me coat and walk with you to the depot offices. Give you some moral support, eh?'

He gulped. 'There's no need, Kelly. I know the way.'

'I could do with the walk, Dad. I don't mind, honest.'

Before he could say anything else she had grabbed her brown coat from the back of the kitchen door and pulled it on, then wrapped a long knitted scarf several times around her neck. She took his arm. 'Come on, sooner we get this over with, sooner we can get back and have a nice cuppa tea.'

She talked incessantly all the way, about anything, to stop Frank from voicing his excuses. Outside the iron gates to the depot she stopped and turned to face him, a broad smile on her face to hide her own deep fears. Her father had to get this job, he just had to. 'Off you go then, Dad. I'll sit on the wall and wait for you.'

He glanced nervously around him. 'Er . . . there's no need to do that, Kelly love. I can find me own way back.'

She looked deep into the eyes of this once proud man, one who before his recent traumas would never have been nervous of facing any man, for any reason. 'It's no bother, Dad. I've n'ote else to do at the moment.' She thought of the pile of dirty linen in the wash house and the pots that still needed washing; the fact that she started her own job at one o'clock and Ada Adcock did not take kindly to lateness; and of her need to visit the dole office and see what full-time work was on offer. But she knew that if she got her father settled, a load would be lifted from her and hopefully everything else would somehow fall into place. 'Go on then,' she urged.

Frank sighed, smiled half-heartedly and slowly made his way through the gates.

Settling herself on the low brick wall across the road she watched, with a thumping heart as he disappeared through a door marked GENERAL OFFICE. Kelly waited, trying to keep her thoughts away from what was going on inside by watching what was going on around her.

The Corporation depot site on St Saviour's Road where the carts – or fish fryers as they were commonly called, due to the fact that the back of the vehicles resembled the fryers used by chip shops – were emptied was large and for over ten minutes Kelly watched all the comings and goings. After a while her concentration wandered and she spotted a line of metal boxes with lids fixed on to a frame with two wheels and a push handle. Secured to one side was a wide-headed brush. They were not dissimilar to the kind of contraption the 'okey pokey' man pushed around the streets delivering his ice cream, only these collected rubbish. Kelly clasped her hands tightly. Hopefully, her father would be in charge of one of these very shortly.

Finding nothing of further interest in the depot yard she turned her attention to what was going on in the street. Further down the road was a school and she could hear the sound of children playing. The row of shops nearby was doing a brisk trade, especially the pawn shop. That shop, out of all, Kelly mused, seemed to be the best patronised. It wasn't just the McCallan family, she thought, who frequented such places. This area of Leicester was populated by people as poor as the ones in her district.

Every few moments she would glance across at the depot, desperately hoping to see her father emerge, shaking hands with Mr Bundy, sealing his offer of a job. But there was still no sign. The ten minutes turned into twenty, the twenty into forty. Kelly began to fidget uncomfortably. Finally, unable to control her impatience any longer, she jumped up and ran over to the railings and peered through. As she looked around for any sign of her father a worrying thought struck her. She had watched him enter the office door but, knowing his frame of mind, had he slipped out again without her noticing? Her heart pounded. 'Oh, no, Dad,' she mouthed. 'Please don't say that's what you've done.'

A surge of fear filled her. It could be a long time, if ever, before her father got another opportunity like this. Worry and curiosity overwhelmed her and before she could stop herself she had run over the road, gone through the gates, tapped on the door marked OFFICE and entered.

The area was not large and was sparsely furnished, the cream- and green-painted walls chipped and scuffed. Three well-worn high-backed chairs were placed against one wall and in the one next to it was an inset with sliding, meshed glass doors, painted on which was the word ENQUIRIES. There was no sign of her father.

Wringing her hands, she stood nervously wondering what to do. The outer door burst open abruptly and a man of medium height, balding and with the beginnings of a paunch, charged through. On spotting Kelly he stopped short and through his round glasses eyed her enquiringly. 'Are you being seen to?' he asked.

'Oh, er . . . well . . . I'm looking for me dad, Frank McCallan.'

'Your father? And he works here, does he?'

'I'm hoping he does.' Kelly's shoulders sagged and before she could stop herself her overwhelming fears all tumbled out. 'He's come for an interview for a road sweeper, you see, and I'm worried.'

'Worried?'

'Yes, that Mr Bundy – he's the man me dad's come to see – won't understand and won't give him a chance at the job. And me dad would be so good at the job, I know he would.'

'What won't Mr Bundy understand?'

'What me dad's been through. He suffered really badly in the war. Saw his mates blown to pieces then ended up a prisoner of war. Then he came home to find me mam dying . . .' She was babbling and knew it but couldn't seem to stop herself. 'And he did love me mam, and I know what it was like for me let alone me dad watching her die. And on top of all that he lost his job.'

'Oh, how come?'

'For being three minutes late. Me dad's been on the bins all his life. Proud of his job he was. It took him two years to get well enough to work again and he was thrilled to get his old job back. It wasn't his fault he lost it.' She wrung her hands at the memory. 'Yer see, me mam was really bad one morning and me dad stayed with her while I fetched the doctor. He tried to explain to Smiggy – that's Mr Smith the bin Inspector – but he wouldn't have none of it. Late was late and late meant you got the sack.'

'Oh, I see.'

'Me dad's a good man, mister, he just needs this chance. I'm worried he won't explain himself properly which'll mean he won't get the job. I don't even know if he's still here. Is there another way out?'

'There is, but you have to go through the offices first. Look, why don't you sit down and I'll see if I can find out what's happening.'

Kelly glanced across the line of chairs, then faced the man again. 'I shouldn't even be here. Me dad's got little enough self-respect as it is without him thinking I'm checking up on him. I'd better go. I was sitting on the wall opposite. I'll go back and wait there for a bit longer. If there's still no sign, I'll just have to go home.' She grimaced guiltily. 'Look, I'm sorry for babbling on. What must yer think of me?'

The man smiled kindly and patted her on the shoulder. 'I'm sure everything will turn out for the best.'

She forced herself to smile back. A few seconds later she was perched on the wall outside, her eyes fixed rigidly on the door marked GENERAL OFFICE.

Bill Bundy made his way around the cluttered desk inside his tiny office and sat down on the uncomfortable wooden chair that Leicester Corporation had provided several decades before. He looked at the nervous man seated before him. 'Sorry to have kept you waiting. I had to go off site to sort a problem. I see Mrs Williams gave you a cuppa.'

'Er . . . yes. Yes, she did. Very nice woman.'

'Yes, she is. Now what can I do for you?'

Frank took a deep breath. If it hadn't been for Mrs Williams's continual insistence that Bill Bundy should not be much longer he would never have managed the fifty-minute wait. He was still confused as to why she should have acted in such a way. Mere workers like himself were never treated with such courtesy, that was reserved purely for the bosses. 'Well, er . . . I heard there might be a job going for a road sweeper?'

'And you think you can do the job, do you, Frank?'

'Well . . .'

'Right, be here Monday morning seven-thirty sharp. I'll give you a try. Say two weeks. That suit you?'

Frank's mouth fell open. 'Pardon?'

'I'll do some jiggling and you can have the round that covers the bottom of the Hinckley and King Richard's Road. Not far from where you live.' Bill rose and gathered several files scattered across his desk. 'Can you find your way out, only I'm already late for a meeting?'

'Er . . . yes. Yes . . . thank you. Thank you, Mr Bundy, thank you.'

On seeing her father approaching Kelly jumped up and ran over to join him, the confused look on his face filling her with worry.

'Dad?' she said questioningly, taking his arm.

He stared at her blankly for several long moments until finally he blurted, 'I got it, Kelly. I got the job. I'm on two weeks trial.'

Her heart leaped from utter joy. 'Oh, Dad, Dad!' was all she could manage.

They had nearly reached home when he suddenly stopped short.

'What is it, Dad?' she asked, concerned.

'He knew me name.'

'Who knew yer name?'

'Mr Bundy. He called me Frank and he knew where I lived. Said he'd sort out a round nearby. And for the life of me I can't remember telling him any of that.'

Later that afternoon, as Alec was just finishing his shift, Bill Bundy, who was crossing the yard, spotted him and strode over. 'I saw your friend, Alec, and I've put him on two weeks trial.'

Alec smiled gratefully. 'Thanks, Mr Bundy.'

'No thanks needed, lad. The least I can do to try and repay you for all you did for my family during the war.

90

Many a time they'd have gone cold if it wasn't for the bags of slack you got for them, not to mention all the other bits and pieces. Anyway, I trust your judgement and if you say Frank McCallan deserves a trial then enough said.' He laughed. 'He came highly recommended and not just by you.'

'Oh?'

'His daughter.'

'Kelly? But how . . .'

'No time to go into it now, Alec, but let's say if his daughter is anything to go by then Frank will do fine. You were right though when you said I would have to have patience with him. I only had to look at him to witness what the man's been through. His suffering is written all over him. But I'll give him a fair trial, don't worry.'

'Thanks again, Mr Bundy. I'm sure this is all he needs to get him back on his feet.'

Twenty minutes later Alec was standing in the McCallans' kitchen. 'How did it go then, Kelly?'

'You can ask him yerself,' she replied, smiling. 'Dad,' she called. 'Dad, Alec is here.'

Frank appeared and there was a look in his eye Alec had not seen for a long time. It was one of hope.

'You look like a man who's heard something good.'

'I have, Alec. I can't believe it. Start Monday. I can't thank you enough for tekking the trouble to come to tell me about it.'

'My pleasure, Frank. That's what friends are for.' He turned towards the door. 'I'd best get off. I still ain't finished the bedroom yet, nor managed to make a start on fixing those wireless sets.'

'Oh, but you'll stay for a cuppa, Alec. I promised you a cuppa, remember. Although,' Kelly smiled apologetically, 'I can't manage the biscuit.'

'Another time, Kelly. I really must get home.'

She closed the door after him, feeling acutely disappointed that he had left so hurriedly. It would have been nice to have had a chat with Alec over a cup of tea.

She was soon to be interrupted again by the arrival of Glenda, who, judging by the look on her face had something on her mind.

'Is Mickey in, Kelly?'

Her tone was sharp and Kelly frowned. 'You know it's too early for our Mickey. And to be honest, the mood he's in lately the longer he stays out the better as far as I'm concerned.' She eyed her friendly quizzically. 'It's early for you too, ain't it?'

'I didn't feel well.' Glenda pulled a chair out from under the table and plonked herself down. 'I had a hell of a job convincing the forelady but in the end she sent me home. Is there any tea going?'

'Help yerself. So, what's the matter?'

Glenda leaned back and grabbed hold of a mug from the draining board. 'Nothing. Well, not nothing exactly but I ain't sick.'

'You'll get the sack, you will, pulling stunts like that.'

Having poured herself a mug of stewed tea, Glenda raised it to her lips. 'At this moment I don't care.'

'Yer don't? Look, Glenda, what is it?'

'Well . . .'

'Well what?'

She put down the mug. 'Oh, Kelly, it's Mickey. I think there's summat up.'

Kelly frowned, confused. 'Up? In what way?'

'It's . . .' She shrugged her shoulders. 'It's just how he is with me.' Tears filled her eyes. 'I . . . I think he's gone off me.'

Kelly's eyebrows rose. 'What makes yer think that?'

'Well, for one thing I've hardly seen him over the past two weeks. He's not took me out or anything.'

'Well, yer know what a skinflint he is. Probably ain't

got any money. You're saving to get married, remember.' Though Kelly thought that if her brother was saving any money, she doubted it would be towards a wedding. And she doubted if Mickey's finances were really a problem; he always had something, legitimately gained or otherwise.

'Has he got someone else, Kelly?'

'Eh? Oh, it's no good asking me that. Me and Mickey ain't exactly on good terms at the moment. I'd be the last to know anything like that.' She slid her arm around Glenda's shoulders and squeezed her reassuringly. 'I'm sure it's all in your imagination, Glenda. You know what our Mickey's like, you've bin engaged to him long enough. He has these moods. He's just having one now, that's all. If you're serious about marrying him you'll have to get used to them,' Kelly warned.

Glenda sniffed. 'I suppose yer right.'

'Look, why don't you go and doll yerself up and pop back later? Let him see what he's missing. He should be in about fourish as normal. Though I'd leave it a bit later than that, 'til he's had his wash. You know he's not very sociable 'til he's had his wash. In fact,' she added as an afterthought, 'maybe you'd better leave it 'til he's had his dinner.'

Glenda smiled. 'Yeah, I will. Ta, Kelly.'

'Oh, by the way,' she said excitedly, 'Dad got a job.'

'Oh, did he?' came the distracted reply. 'That's nice.'

As Glenda made her way home a thought struck her. It was Thursday and about this time the round Mickey was on this week would still be collecting near Latimer Street, off the Hinckley Road. She would take a walk up there and see if she could see him. What she would say to him she did not know, and she knew he'd be angry with her for turning up, but she felt compelled to go all the same.

By the time she arrived the gang had finished collecting and were preparing to finish for the night. She could not see Mickey. She hesitated, wondering whether to approach one of his colleagues and enquire after him when a door opening nearby caught her attention. Emerging from the door was Mickey and standing on the doorstep was a woman. Though attractive, the woman was at least thirty. She was wearing a tight skirt and low-cut blouse, her ample chest spilling out over the top. Her hair was bleached blonde. She leaned forward and whispered something in Mickey's ear, at which he laughed.

'Thanks for the tea then, Mrs Ridley,' he said loudly as he walked away to join his gang milling around the 'fish fryer'.

'My pleasure,' she called. 'See you soon.'

There was such suggestiveness in her voice that a distraught Glenda darted inside an entry, sick with fear that Mickey would spot her and with conviction that her instincts had been right. Although she did not want to believe it, her woman's intuition screamed at her that it was much more than tea Mickey had received from Mrs Ridley that afternoon.

Chapter Eleven

Kelly was humming to herself as she tackled the washing, pummelling patched winceyette sheets with the dolly in the copper. Normally she hated this task, vehemently wishing that a proper washing machine, like those she had seen in the electric shop window, one with an agitator and a motorised mangle, could be bought instead of the laborious twice or sometimes thrice-weekly ritual of the overnight soaking of the more soiled items, then the time-consuming boiling up in the copper.

But none of it bothered her today. She was happy. She had stood on the doorstep and waved her father off for his first day at work. She had paid extra special attention to his meat paste sandwiches and put two heaped spoons of sugar into his jam jar of tea. She had brushed aside his apprehension, putting it down to the normal nerves felt by anyone on their first day in a job. He would be fine, she kept telling herself, and this was the final step towards his recovery. She couldn't wait to see his face when he came home bearing his first wage packet for several months, when he'd thought he would never earn again.

The only blight on this wonderful event had been Mickey's attitude. When Kelly had relayed the news to him – realising afterwards she should not have been so cocky about it – her brother's reaction had been to smirk and snarl out that it was his opinion this job wouldn't last for long, a week at the most, so she could wipe the smug expression off her face. Regardless, she had not let Mickey's attitude bother her. Dad would make him eat his words, she herself had every faith that he would.

After hanging out the washing, wondering if she was wasting her time as the sky threatened rain, she turned back to the kitchen to tackle the breakfast dishes, prepare the vegetable soup for dinner, then tidy herself and get off to her job, telling herself that if she didn't get a move on she would be late. Then she spotted the brown paper bag holding her father's sandwiches, still lying on the corner of the table. He had forgotten them.

She stared at them for a moment, wondering what to do but knowing she would have to go and try to find him. She could not let him go all day without anything inside him. The rest of the chores would have to wait. If she hurried and had luck on her side she would find her father, hand over his lunch and still get back in time to start her shift in the shop.

It took far longer to find him than she anticipated. She had not expected him to be hiding. It was only by sheer chance that she happened to recognise the edge of the cart sticking out from the entrance to an alleyway. She went in and was shocked rigid to see her father squatting down, his back against a wall, head buried between his bent knees.

All sorts of fears racing through her, she knelt down beside him, placed a hand gently on his arm and asked, 'What's up, Dad?'

When he did not reply she gently shook him and repeated her question.

Slowly he raised his head and eyed her blankly. Suddenly huge tears filled his eyes and gushed down his cheeks. 'Oh, Kelly, Kelly, I can't do it, I can't!'

'Why not, Dad, why? What's happened?'

'N'ote,' he choked. 'N'ote's happened. It's just me. I just ain't got the heart for it. It's all crowding in on me and everywhere I look I see yer mam. I just can't bear it wi'out her, Kelly. There don't seem no reason to it all no more.'

Deep distress filled her. 'That's not true, Dad. There is a reason. In fact, plenty of reasons.'

'Tell me one, Kelly?'

She gulped. 'You're alive for one,' she whispered.

He turned from her and buried his face in his hands. 'Alive,' he uttered. 'No, I ain't, Kelly. I'm dead inside and I don't want to go on living. I don't deserve to go on living.'

Her heart began pounding painfully. Had Mickey been right all along? Was her father about to confess to ending her mother's life? She shuddered violently, shutting her eyes, willing herself not to ask the question but knowing she had to. 'Why, Dad? Why d'yer feel you don't deserve to go on living?'

'Because . . . Oh, Kelly, because it's my fault yer mam's dead. All my fault.'

'And . . . and how is it your fault?'

Slowly he raised his head, face ashen and eyes puffy and red-rimmed from crying. ''Cos I've never amounted to anything, Kelly. All I ever was, was a bloody dustman on a dustman's pay which hardly went anywhere. I couldn't afford to give yer mam anything except the bare basics in life. And if I hadn't have gone off ter war she wouldn't have had to work her fingers to the bone and go wi'out so much, then maybe she might not have got ill. Then I couldn't even keep me job, could I? *That's* why it's all my fault. I should have done more for her. Provided better for her. If anyone should have got ill and died it should have bin me.'

Shocked, Kelly breathed in sharply and gently took his hand. 'Mam never saw any of it like that, Dad. She loved you and wouldn't have changed anything. I know that 'cos she was forever telling me. You were a dustman when she fell in love with you and married you. She knew what yer pay was. So I don't see how you can blame yerself for that. And as for having to go off to war, you had no choice in that. If it's anyone's fault it's that madman Hitler's.' She paused for breath then resumed: 'And as for losing yer job, Dad, you were late because you stayed with Mam while I fetched the doctor. If that Smiggy had even a bit of common decency he would never have sacked yer.' She paused, eyeing him tenderly. 'If Mam had known about it, I know and so do you if yer honest that she never would have blamed you. Dad, listen to me. Mam died 'cos she was ill. If the doctor couldn't save her, how could you have? Now you've got to stop blaming yerself. She wouldn't rest if she knew you were acting like this.'

He stared at her and his eyes narrowed angrily. 'Acting?' he spat. 'Is that what yer think I'm doing, putting on an act so everyone'll feel sorry fer me? How could you know how I feel? How could anyone know what I'm going through?' He thrust her hand from him, turned his back to her and buried his head between his knees once more. 'Go away, Kelly. Leave me alone. I don't need you or anyone.'

She gasped, horrified, and suddenly all the patience drained from her. If he wasn't going to try and help himself it was pointless dishing out any more sympathy. Jumping up, she placed her hands on her hips, her face set harshly. 'All right, Dad, I'll leave yer to wallow if that's what you want. But I'll tell you this: I miss Mam too. She was my mother and I loved her as much as you did. But I can't just give up. If I did that then her whole reason for living would have bin pointless. If it's what'll make you happy, why don't you throw yerself in the canal? Or there's always the gas oven – but make sure you put a shilling in first.' She held up the paper bag containing his sandwiches. 'You won't be wanting these, so I'll have 'em.' She turned on her heel then, ready to leave him where he sat.

'Kelly?'

She stopped and turned back. Her father was standing now and staring after her, looking ashamed. 'I'm sorry, Kelly,' he muttered.

She rushed over and threw her arms around him. 'No, I'm sorry, Dad. I should never have spoken to you in such a way.'

'Yes, yer should have. Yer right, I've bin feeling sorry for meself. Wallowing in self-pity.'

'You've every right, Dad,' she whispered softly.

He sighed. 'Maybe. But it's about time I stopped. Men ain't supposed to act like this, are they? We're supposed to be strong. Carry on as normal.'

She shook her head. 'Whoever made that rule was talking out the top of their head. Everyone, whether it's a man or a woman or a kiddy, needs time to sort themselves out when they've had troubles.'

'And I've had plenty of time, ain't I, Kelly?'

'You've had some time, Dad, not plenty considering what you've gone through. And you'll probably still have relapses. But I'm here to help yer.'

He pulled away from her, holding her at arm's length and gazing at her lovingly. 'I'm a lucky man, ain't I?'

'That's 'cos yer worth it. I'm the lucky one, having a dad like you.'

He sighed heavily. 'It's a pity . . .'

She instinctively knew what he was about to say. 'One thing at a time, Dad. Concentrate on this job first, get your confidence back, then you can tackle our Mickey. You'll be strong enough to deal with him then.'

'Yes, yer right. One thing at a time. But I will have to put matters right between us. And I'll do it, I promise.'

'Everything all right?'

Startled, they both turned to see Bill Bundy standing by the cart. When Kelly caught her breath in surprise, Frank eyed her swiftly before turning his attention back to his boss.

'Er . . . yes, Mr Bundy, everything's fine. Kelly just brought me me sandwiches.'

Bill smiled. 'So keen to get to work this morning you forgot 'em, is that it?'

Frank nodded. 'Yes, that's right, Mr Bundy. Very keen I wa'.'

'Glad to hear it. I just thought I'd come and see how you were getting on. Any problems?'

'No, not that I know of.'

'Good. Well, I'll leave you to it.' He edged by the cart and before he turned the corner called back to Frank. 'I just had a look down a couple of the streets I asked you to tackle and you've done a good job. Keep it up.' He smiled and nodded his head at Kelly. 'Nice to meet you, Miss McCallan.'

When he had gone Frank turned to Kelly. 'You nearly had a heart attack when you seen me boss. Why?'

Kelly swallowed hard. How would her father react if he knew how she had poured out all her fears to a total stranger on the morning of his interview, only to find out now that the total stranger was in fact her father's potential employer. But wasn't it nice, she thought, of Mr Bundy not to let out that secret? 'Oh, er . . . I just thought my being here would get yer into trouble. He seems a nice man, does your boss.' She eyed her father tenderly. 'Now will you be all right, Dad, only I must dash 'cos I'm really late for me shift at the shop?'

He gave her a hug. 'You get on your way, me darlin'. I'm fine now. Honest I am.'

She eyed him closely. 'You sure, Dad?'

He smiled. 'I'm sure. Thanks, Kelly.'

She gave his arm a reassuring pat, kissed him on the cheek, then turned and rushed off, calling, 'I'll see you tonight.'

Frank watched thoughtfully as she disappeared around the corner. How close he had come to giving up. It wasn't easy learning to live without his beloved wife, but Kelly was right: he was alive and should be thankful for that. Flora had not had that choice. And for the sake of her memory and of all they had meant to each other he felt he should try to live out the rest of his days as happily as he could, in the hope that once his time came he would join her again and they would be together forever in eternity. In his dark times, and he had no doubt he would still suffer those, he would have to keep reminding himself of that.

He owed so much to his daughter. Kelly had been stalwart during her mother's illness, and again while coping with his grief, and not once had he heard her complain. He should be striving now to make her life easier.

As he grabbed hold of the cart a sense of pride filled him, something he had not experienced for a long time. It felt hugely satisfying to know that he was once again able to contribute towards their daily living, and if he didn't get on with it he wouldn't be able to because he would surely lose this precious job.

At fifteen minutes past one o'clock a breathless Kelly ran through the door of the corner shop. 'I'm sorry, Mrs Adcock,' she blurted. 'I got caught up with things and didn't realise the time. I'll make it up by staying late.' She had reached the long dark wooden counter before she realised her employer had someone with her.

'Kelly, this is me sister, Mrs Freeby. You remember me telling you about her?'

'Oh, yes.' Kelly smiled. 'Pleased to meet yer, Mrs Freeby.'

A big, hard-faced woman of about sixty, with sparse short grey hair parted down the middle and gripped behind her ears, nodded a greeting.

'Paying a visit?' Kelly asked politely, moving behind the counter and grabbing her apron from one of the cluttered shelves underneath.

Engrossed in her task, she missed the looks exchanged between Mrs Adcock and her sister.

'Why don't you go in the back and make us a cuppa, Mona?' Ada addressed her sister. 'I'm sure Kelly could do with one.'

Straightening her apron, she smiled. 'I could murder one, ta.'

The shop door clanged and a tall thin woman entered, her head wrapped in a scarf turban-style. She was dragging behind her a scruffy boy of about four with a runny nose. Kelly turned her attention to them. 'Afternoon, Mrs Shish. What can I get yer?'

'A loaf. And a fresh loaf, mind. Don't want palming off with yes'day's.'

'All our bread is fresh daily, Mrs Shish. Any left from yesterday is marked down by a tanner and clearly labelled.'

'Is it? A tanner, eh? Well, gimme one of yes'day's then. I'll wet it and heat it in the oven. My lot won't know the difference.'

'I want some sweets,' her son demanded.

Mrs Shish raised her hand and brought it down hard against the side of his head. 'Yer've had yer ration fer this week, so shuddup moaning!'

'I ain't,' the boy wailed. 'You sold the coupons.'

He was belted again, harder this time. 'Shuddup, I said. And I want three pounda spuds,' she addressed Kelly, ignoring her son's loud wailing and Kelly's

102

answering shudder. 'And mind you pick out good ones. The last lot were near all rotten.' In the same breath she said, 'I see your dad's working. Seen him pushing a cart down the Hinckley Road. Bit of a come down for 'im, ain't it, road sweeping?'

Kelly fought to reply politely. Mrs Shish was after all a customer. She smiled sweetly as she bent down to weigh out the potatoes on the large iron scales. 'Don't know how you can see it like that. Road sweepers are more or less their own bosses and they don't have to lug heavy bins full of stinking rubbish or have ter cover for any of the gang who don't pull their weight.' She straightened up and tipped the potatoes into Mrs Shish's bag. 'It's my opinion my dad's landed on his feet getting this job,' she said proudly. 'And he was hand picked, just like your spuds. You won't find any bad in that lot, you have my word.'

Mrs Shish's mouth tightened in annoyance.

'That'll be three and six, please,' said Kelly.

The woman held out a bag which clanked. 'Dozen pop bottles fer return. Tek the shilling off me bill. I'll settle up the rest I owe on Friday,' she snapped, grabbing her son by the scruff of his neck and dragging him out of the shop.

'The day she settles up, I can retire,' Ada said scathingly from behind the counter where she was weighing half pounds of sugar into blue paper bags. 'And tek no notice of what she said ter yer, Kelly. She's just jealous. Her Hubert's bin after a job as a sweeper for years 'cos he hates it on the bins, but it's common knowledge what a shirker he is so he's got no chance. In fact he's lucky to keep the job that he's got and May Shish knows it.'

Kelly eyed Ada thoughtfully as she made her way back around the counter to mark May Shish's dues in the book. 'Yer know, it's suddenly just struck me that most of the men in this street work on the bins.'

'Ah, well, that's the way of many communities. Most sons follow their fathers. It's the mark of the working class and has bin since time began.' She suddenly looked uncomfortable. 'Look, Kelly, I need to talk to yer.'

Her eyes flashed worriedly. 'Oh, er . . . if it's about me being late, Mrs Adcock, it won't happen again, I promise.'

'No, it's not about that. It's about me sister.'

Kelly frowned. 'Oh?'

'Our Mona's not had it easy since Mr Freeby passed on.' Ada grimaced. 'Mind you, it's my opinion that passing on was the best day's work he ever done. He never gave her an easy time of it. But, regardless, she's struggling to make ends meet and as I've got the shop, and being a widow meself . . . well, it's common sense really, in't it?'

Kelly frowned confused. 'What is, Mrs Adcock?'

'That she should come and live here wi' me and help me run the shop. Be best all round really. I mean, Kelly, this ain't no future for the likes of you, now is it? It was always just to make do while yer cared for yer mam. Well, you'll be wanting a proper job now, won't yer?'

Kelly gasped. 'Are you asking me to leave, is that it, Mrs Adcock?'

Ada sighed. 'Well, I suppose I am. Only not right this minute. Mona ain't coming for a couple of weeks. It's warning I'm giving yer. But you do understand, don't yer?'

Reeling from the shock, Kelly nodded absently. 'Yes, 'course I understand.' With an effort she plastered a smile on her face. 'I was thinking along the lines of full-time work meself. This is the push I need.'

Ada smiled, relieved. 'Well, there you are then. Best all round, I'd say. Shall we say two weeks? That should give you plenty of time to get something else.'

104

'Yes, two weeks should be plenty.' Kelly spoke distractedly, hoping that it would be. 'The Lord giveth with one hand and taketh away with the other,' she uttered. 'And people wonder why I ain't religious!'

'What was that?'

'Oh, nothing, Mrs Adcock, nothing at all.'

The doorbell clanged and a young woman entered. 'Ten Woodbines,' she said as she approached the counter. 'And a box of Swans. Why, if it ain't Kelly McCallan! I didn't know you worked here.'

Kelly gazed at the young woman in surprise. 'Hello, Jean. What brings you back to these parts?'

'Oh, I'm just visiting me granny. I've got a flat now, yer know, on the Fosse Road. Look, er . . . I heard about yer mam. I am sorry. I did mean to come round but you know how it is.'

'Yes, I understand.'

'So what you doing with yerself? Apart from working here that is.'

'Oh, this and that.'

'Still seeing Rod?'

'Yes.'

'Not married then?'

'No, not yet. Do you still see the other girls?'

'Yes, most of 'em. Phyllis got married. Got a youngster now and another on the way. But I still knock around with Babs and Audrey. In fact, we're all getting together tonight. Going down the Palais. Eh, why don't you come with us? Come on, why don't yer? It'd be like old times, the four of us together.'

Kelly eyed her thoughtfully. The offer did sound inviting. She couldn't remember the last time she had gone dancing, and the girls were fun. But then, how could she go? She had hardly anything suitable to wear, and nor did she have the money. 'Thanks fer asking but maybe another time.'

'I'll not tek no for an answer, Kelly McCallan.' Jean stared her boldly in the eye. 'You look to me like a gel who could do with a good night out with some old friends.'

'Well, I do like the sound of it, but . . .'

'But what?' Jean interjected. A thought suddenly struck her. 'If it's what Rod'll say that you're worried about, don't be. Take it from me, fellas need keeping on their toes or they start tekking yer for granted.'

Though she felt it should have, what Rod would say hadn't even entered Kelly's mind, though she doubted he'd be pleased if she announced she was going out with old girlfriends, especially to the Palais. 'Oh, no, it's not that, Jean.'

'Well, what then?'

'Well . . . actually I haven't any money, and to be truthful, I've n'ote suitable to wear neither.'

Jean laughed. 'Oh, is that all that's stopping yer? Well, I'll sort you out with both. And don't look at me like that – I've told you, I won't tek no for an answer. Call it a gesture for old times' sake.' She grabbed a paper bag, snatched up a pencil lying by the till and scribbled something down which she handed to Kelly. 'Here's me address. Be there about seven. Now,' she said, laughing, 'am I going to get me fags and matches or do I have to go somewhere else?'

Chapter Twelve

'So then, Mickey, what's next?'

Placing two brimming pints of bitter on the small table between them in the packed Empire public house, Rod sat down opposite Mickey and eyed him eagerly.

'Eh?'

'Next,' Rod repeated. 'What you lining up for us next? I don't know about you but I could do with some cash right now. I'm broke.'

Mickey picked up his pint. 'You should learn to tek more care of your money.' He eyed his friend scathingly. 'That suit musta cost a packet,' he said, taking a large gulp.

Rod beamed proudly, fingering one lapel. 'Yeah, d'yer like it? Burton's best. Ten bob down and the rest on the never-never. Well, I've got to look the part, ain't I?' he justified himself.

'The part for what?'

Rod shrugged his shoulders. 'Well, yer know – the part.'

Taking a sup of his pint, Mickey narrowed his eyes. 'I hope you don't mean to impress the women? You're engaged to my sister, remember.'

''Course it ain't. I bought the suit to impress folk when we went out on business. Well,' he added hurriedly, 'I don't want ter let you down, do I, when you let me come along?'

Rod did not comment on the fact that Mickey frequently strayed though engaged to Rod's sister, and nor did he mention that the suit Mickey was wearing looked far more expensive than his own. Certain thoughts were best left unspoken. It did not pay to cross Mickey in any shape or form. 'So, have yer 'ote planned?' he asked again.

Mickey scowled. 'Keep your fucking voice down, will yer? And if I've 'ote planned, that's my business. I'll tell you when I'm good and ready. But don't bank on anything for the time being. Actually it might pay yer not to rely on me so much in the future.'

Rod frowned in bewilderment. 'Why not, Mickey?'

''Cos I said not, that's why.' He smiled a winning but secretive smile. 'Let's just say I'm aiming ter branch out.' He glanced at the clock on the far wall, downed his pint and rose. 'I godda go.'

Rod gulped back his own pint and jumped up to join him. 'Where we going then?'

'I said *I'd* godda go, not you too.'

Rod's face dropped. 'Yer don't want me to come with yer then?'

'If I wanted you to I'd have said, now wouldn't I?'

'But I always go everywhere with yer, Mickey.'

'Not this time yer don't.'

'But . . .' Grasping at straws Rod blurted, 'But I'm family.'

'Hardly! You might be engaged to me sister but that doesn't make you family. Not yet. See yer.'

Rod slowly sank back down in his seat, watching Mickey as he pushed through the crowd and disappeared out of the door. Where was he off to that was such a secret? Mickey always told him everything, or so Rod had thought. He stared down at his empty glass. Just what was Mickey up to? And why didn't it include Rod any more? He felt distinctly unsettled. The thought of Mickey moving on without him worried him. He had always thought that wherever his friend went, he would be right there with him. But now he saw he might have been mistaken.

He grimaced worriedly. If Mickey left him behind, what would become of him? His job on the bins would only ever provide a bare living, not at all the kind he had begun to anticipate for himself. Besides, he had grown used to having extra cash in his pocket and needed it more than ever now he had bought this suit, not to mention some shoes and two shirts.

'Hello, Rod, on yer own tonight? No Mickey?'

He looked up to see Johnny Riddle sliding on to the seat Mickey had not long vacated.

'Yeah,' he replied. 'Mickey's . . . er . . .' He did not like to admit that the man they held in awe had abandoned him. He did not feel that would do his own credibility any good. 'He's tekking our Glenda out.'

'Is he? Oh, funny that, 'cos I've just seen him catching a bus into town and he was on his own.'

Rod studied the dregs in the bottom of his glass. Now why would Mickey be going into town? But regardless he could not let Johnny see that this information had shaken him. He liked everyone to think that he was Mickey's sole confidant and ally. 'A bit of business to see to then he's taking Glenda out,' he replied casually, passing it off. 'So what you up to?'

'I'm just waiting for the rest of the lads to show then we're off down the Palais. Why don't you come?'

Rod paused thoughtfully. He should really take Kelly out. He hadn't taken her anywhere for quite a while. They could go to the club. There was a live band and the usual game of bingo. But then, by the time she got herself ready the evening would be nearly over. He'd take her out next week. He nodded. 'Yeah, don't mind if I do.'

★ ★ ★

'Fancy a dance?'

Kelly turned to find a man at her elbow. He was tall, good-looking and smartly dressed in a petrol blue suit. 'Well, er . . .' she replied, wondering whether it was the right thing to do when she was supposed to be an engaged woman. She felt a nudge in her ribs.

'Go on,' Jean hissed in her ear. 'I told yer, yer look good in me skirt and blouse, and that makeup's done wonders. This proves it. Now get on that floor and enjoy yerself.'

'Yeah, go on, he's a cracker,' whispered Babs, and Audrey nodded enviously.

Kelly beamed. Why not? she thought. She did feel good. Wearing the low-cut blouse, which showed just the top of her cleavage, had worried her at first. She'd found it daring compared with her usual buttoned up to the neck style. The skirt was full and swung as she walked; Jean insisted the cut flattered her well-shaped legs which now sported a new pair of nylons with seams up the back. These had been donated again by Jean who had stared aghast at the ones Kelly had been going to wear, hoping no one saw the ladder. Also the two gin and oranges she had drunk had done a power of good to her confidence.

Kelly addressed the man, still patiently awaiting her answer. 'I don't mind if I do,' she said carelessly, hoping she didn't reveal her nervousness as it was a long time since a man had asked her to dance – and that included Rod.

The Palais was heaving with bodies and finding a space on the dance floor between couples jiving to the band's rendition of 'Chattanooga Choo Choo' was not easy, but her escort somehow managed and before she knew it he had taken her in his arms. 'Come here often?' he shouted in her ear.

'Er . . . I haven't been for a while,' she responded equally as loudly.

He smiled, showing a row of even white teeth as he swung her around. 'Must be my lucky night then. Me name's Bob.'

'Kelly,' she replied as she spun back into his arms.

Across the wide expanse of the floor Rod was smooching closely with a pretty woman whose name he did not know, but she looked and smelled good and running through his mind were thoughts of whether she would be accommodating at the end of the evening . . . Just then something caught his eye and he frowned, pulling back from the woman in his arms to get a better view.

'What's wrong?' she asked.

'Eh! Oh, nothing, nothing,' he insisted, pulling her close to him again. As they slowly turned his eyes busily scanned the milling crowd, and suddenly he grimaced. He was right. It had been Kelly he had spotted. Without a thought for his partner he released his hold on her and stormed through the dancers. Reaching Kelly, he grabbed her shoulder and spun her around. 'What the hell are you playing at?' he demanded.

She gasped in surprise. 'Oh . . . Rod.'

'What's going on?' Bob asked.

'And you can piss off,' Rod spat, positioning himself between Bob and his girlfriend. 'I asked what yer doing here, Kelly?'

She glanced apologetically over Rod's shoulder at Bob. 'This is . . . er . . . my friend, Rod.'

'Friend!' he hissed angrily, and spun round to face Bob. 'I'm her bloody fiancé. Now, I said, piss off.' He unceremoniously grabbed hold of Kelly's arm and dragged her to the side of the dance floor then turned her to face him. 'Well?'

'I'm just having a dance with me mates, that's all.'

'Mates? What mates?'

'Jean, Babs and Audrey. You remember them. I used to pal about with them before me mam got ill.'

'Oh, them mates,' he said scathingly. His eyes scanned her possessively. 'What's that muck on yer face, and just where did you get those clothes?'

'Jean lent them to me.'

'And I take it you never looked in the mirror before you came out? You look like a tart!'

She gasped in shock.

'Mind you,' he continued, 'wadda you expect from a friend that'd drop her drawers for 'ote in trousers. And the other two ain't much better. How could you even think of coming out with them?'

'That's not true, Rod! How can you speak about my friends like that? They like a good time, having a drink and a dance. There's no harm in that. And I *don't* look like a tart.' She eyed him sharply. 'Why, you're jealous.'

Which was just what Rod was feeling. In truth, he thought Kelly looked lovely and was seeing her with new eyes tonight. But the last thing he was about to do was admit to his feelings. 'I ain't,' he argued.

'I don't believe you. You're jealous 'cos I was dancing with another man. And before you say anything, I was only dancing and there's n'ote wrong in that.' She folded her arms under her shapely bosom, eyeing him questioningly. 'Anyway, what are you doing here? And that's a new suit, ain't it?'

Rod thought rapidly. 'I've had this suit for ages and it's one of the fellows' stag night. I'd forgotten all about it 'til Johnny Riddle mentioned it in the Empire. I wasn't really enjoying meself and was just about to go home when I saw you,' he lied. Suddenly he spotted the woman he had ditched making her way towards them. She didn't look happy. He pulled Kelly out of sight behind a pillar. 'Get yer coat,' he ordered.

'What?'

112

'You heard. I'm tekking you home.'

'But I don't want to go home, I'm enjoying myself.'

He grabbed hold of her arm and pulled her close. 'Just do as yer told, Kelly.'

'Can't I say good-night to me friends?' The look on his face gave her her answer. She sighed reluctantly. What had started off as a very enjoyable evening had suddenly soured. But then, Rod was after all her fiancé, and ring or no ring she was still an engaged woman. In the light of that she supposed she really should not have come out without him.

As a subdued Kelly stood in the queue to retrieve her coat, across town in a seedy, smoke-filled snooker hall, two men sat opposite each other in a shadowy corner.

'So you're Mickey McCallan?'

Mickey puffed out his chest importantly. 'That's me. What can I do fer you, Mr Greenbaum?'

Chewing the end of a fat cigar, Isaac Greenbaum scrutinised him for several long moments. 'Cocky bugger, ain't yer?' he said, blowing a waft of foul-smelling smoke into his face. 'That attitude'll get you nowhere, sonny. You ain't dealing with your poxy little mates now.'

Mickey shuffled uncomfortably in his seat. He had taken an instant dislike to the exceptionally tall, extremely thin but immaculately dressed Isaac Greenbaum when introduced by one of his henchmen only minutes before. But, regardless, Greenbaum was his first real chance to further his career and so liking did not come into it.

He had been taken aback when, several nights ago, while propping up the bar of the Empire, a dubious-looking man had approached him, taken him aside and told him that Mr Greenbaum requested his presence. Mickey had known immediately this was not a request to be refused. Mr Greenbaum was a well-known 'spiv', or to those who knew his real line of business, 'a fixer'. Quite what he 'fixed' Mickey was hazy about and he was still unsure as to why exactly the man wanted to see him. Hopefully Greenbaum would not keep him on tenterhooks for much longer.

'Sorry, Mr Greenbaum,' he forced himself to say humbly. 'You'll soon see I can be useful to you. Very useful.'

Isaac Greenbaum pulled the cigar out of his mouth and studied it closely before glancing dismissively at Mickey. 'Oh? And how's a tuppenny ha'penny dustbin man gonna prove himself any good to me?'

'I know people . . .'

'Just shut it, McCallan. Stop trying to play the big man, you ain't with your mates now. The people you know ain't worth mentioning. This is the real world and if you intend to be part of it you'd better start growing up – fast. My trade's a far cry from the petty bits and pieces you buy and sell.' He grinned. 'See, I know all about you. I've done my homework.' He leaned forward. 'I even know how many women you've been knocking off. But you could do better than that slut who lives in Latimer Street. I hope you don't go in for any careless talk when you're on the job?'

Determined that Greenbaum would not witness any shock at the extent of his knowledge, Mickey nonchalantly shook his head. 'Wadda yer take me for?' he said casually.

'Still wet behind the ears and with a hell of a lot to learn despite all you're doing to try and impress me. I'm taking a risk with you, lad. But I think you've got potential.'

Greenbaum leaned back in his hard wooden chair, crossing his long thin legs, and through a billow of smoke eyed Mickey through narrowed eyes. 'So, Mickey McCallan, how would you like to earn five hundred nicker?'

This time Mickey was unable to control himself. Wide-eyed, he asked, 'Five hundred, did you say? Well . . . er . . . I'd be interested. Yeah. Who wouldn't?' He eyed the man before him questioningly. 'Doing what exactly?'

'Torching a factory.'

He scratched his neck, trying not to show his shock but quickly seeing that he should have realised such a sum would not be earned by any petty means. 'Insurance job, eh?' he said, trying to sound knowledgeable.

'You got it. Can you handle it?'

Mickey's mind raced frantically. He had never tackled anything like this before but setting fire to a factory couldn't be as hard as stripping lead from roofs. And the pay was astronomical. What he could do with five hundred pounds! He could buy a car, several suits, and still have change to supply several pubs' clientele with beer all night. 'I could do it,' he said casually. 'For that kinda money.'

'Thought you might.'

'If you don't mind me asking – why me?'

'Good question, boy. I've heard your name mentioned once or twice and as I could do with some new blood, I thought I'd give you the once over. And you ain't got a record. Police won't be knocking on your door the next day. Which is the way my clients like it.'

'I see. And have I passed the test?'

Isaac gave a secret smile. 'The test is torching the factory. Make a success of it and you'll pass. If not . . .'

'I'll make a success of it, Mr Greenbaum, you have my word.' For five hundred pounds he'd have been willing to set fire to the Charles Street police station. And although he still did not have a clue as to how he would pull the job off, Mickey asked, 'So when d'yer want it done?'

'Don't be impatient, lad. I'll let you know all in good

time. Until then, you keep yer head down and yer nose clean. That means you do nothing. No other little jobs, no getting into trouble. Understand?'

Mickey nodded. 'Understood. But . . . er . . . when you mentioned other little jobs, yer didn't mean me buying and selling?'

'Were you not listening to me, lad? I said *nothing*. And when I say nothing, I mean it.'

Mickey frowned. 'That's all well and good, Mr Greenbaum, but a man has to live. How am I supposed to get through in the meantime?'

By the look on Isaac's face he knew he had overstepped the mark and for a fleeting moment thought worriedly that he'd scuppered his chances. But suddenly his fear melted away and his eyes bulged at the sight of a buxom, bleached blonde, an extremely tight red satin dress barely covering her ample curves, appearing at Isaac's side. She draped her arm around his shoulders, bent over and whispered something in his ear. He nodded, slapped her backside and said, 'I'll be up in a minute. Tell him to wait.'

Eyes transfixed on her voluptuous cleavage, Mickey did not realise that Isaac was laughing at him until he said: 'Put yer tongue away, lad.' Hand on the woman's backside, he pushed her forward. 'Vera, meet Mickey McCallan.'

Acutely embarrassed, Mickey accepted her outstretched hand, fully aware that Isaac was making a fool of him. The woman's display of total indifference only added to his discomfort. Women usually found him irresistible but all Vera's charms were kept for the likes of Isaac Greenbaum. She saw Mickey as a nobody, not worthy of any attention. Rage boiled inside him. He would show them! He would show them all. Women like her would be drooling all over him then, begging for a look . . .

'Off yer go then, Vera,' Isaac ordered, slapping her backside once more. He grinned wickedly across at Mickey. 'The likes of that whore are two a penny. Play yer cards right, boy, and you'll be spoiled for choice. Now . . .' He delved in his inside pocket, pulled out a fat wad of notes and peeled off several which he shoved in Mickey's face. 'This is a down payment.' Mickey went to grab at it but Isaac pulled back his hand so the notes were just out of reach and flapped them invitingly. 'A bit of advice: don't go flashing this about. And a word of warning: if the job ain't successful, I'll want it back, all of it.' His tone was menacing.

'The job'll be done, Mr Greenbaum.'

Isaac stood up. 'I'll be in touch. Now get out of here,' he ordered as he turned and left.

Several streets away from the snooker club Mickey could no longer contain himself. Thrusting his arm upwards he made a fist and punched the air. 'Yes,' he cried, then glowered at a passer-by. 'What the fuck you looking at?'

Jauntily striding forward, his hands deep inside his trouser pockets, one still firmly clasped around the fifty pounds up front payment, his face split into a wide grin. God, was he happy! This was just the break he had been looking for. Five hundred pounds for setting fire to a factory. Easy money. And he'd make sure there'd be more where that came from. This was only the beginning.

Shortly, if he played things right, he'd be able to walk away from his stinking, filthy job, something he had been wanting to do since the day he had started it. And as a parting gesture he'd tell Smiggy just what he thought of him. He stopped abruptly as a thought struck him. In fact, he could do that tomorrow. He had fifty pounds in his pocket! More than he'd earn in a month of Sundays. If he was careful enough to keep him going until he got the rest.

Strutting now, he continued on his journey. At long last his dreams had come true. He was entering the big league, going to mix with people who owned big houses, flash cars, had women like Vera draped on their arm. He was on his way up and nothing was going to stop him.

As he headed along the dark alleyway running down the back of his house, so preoccupied was he with his exciting thoughts he did not see the lone figure standing by the wall.

'Is your name Mickey?'

Hand raised to lift the latch, he jumped. 'Eh!' Dropping his hand, he turned round. 'Who wants to know?'

'Well, I do really.'

Mickey stepped closer and scanned the figure, then sniffed disdainfully. 'If it's me mam yer've come ter see then you're too late, Vicar. She's dead and the rest of us are beyond saving. So I'd get off and do your do-gooding elsewhere if I were you 'cos yer wasting yer time here.' He turned back and placed his hand on the latch again.

Algernon inhaled sharply at this savage mode of address but was undeterred from his mission. 'I'm sorry to hear about your mother. Mrs McCallan was a very fine woman. But if your name is Mickey, then it's you I've come to see.'

He dropped his hand again and turned to face the clergyman. 'Oh! And if I am this Mickey, then what would a man of the cloth be needing with me?'

Algernon swallowed hard. He came across all sorts of different personalities in his line of work and it was part of his job not to let personal feelings intervene. But faced with this young man's attitude he found it very hard to keep those feelings in check.

He had not known what to expect when he had made the decision to investigate the theft of his lead roofing. Not given a thought as to what he might be getting into. Just knew that he had to do something to lift the financial burden of the replacement from his parishioners when any monies raised could, he felt, be put to far better use.

He clasped his hands before him and took a deep breath. 'Well, it's the matter of some . . .' He hurriedly decided he had better be careful about making an accusation just in case he was wrong. 'Some lead has gone missing from my church roof. I was told that Mickey might know something about it.'

Mickey stiffened. 'Oh, and what makes yer think I'd know anything?'

'So you are Mickey?'

He flushed, angry with himself for his slip. 'Me name happens to be Mickey, but I'm not necessarily the one you're after.'

'Well,' began Algernon, more bravely than he felt, 'I happen to think you *are* the one I'm looking for. And I also think you know exactly what happened to the roofing from my church.'

'Oh, yer do, do yer?'

'Yes. And I would like it back or . . .'

'Or what, Vicar?'

'Well, I'll go to the police and see what they have to say about it.'

Mickey froze at the mention of the police, Greenbaum's warning coming rapidly to mind. 'Now you look here, Vicar, I don't take kindly to threats like that.'

'And I don't like my parishioners suffering from others' misdeeds. Now I am not making empty threats. I will go to the police with my evidence.'

Mickey's heart thumped. 'What evidence?' he said slowly.

Algernon paused momentarily. He was about to make an accusation that may not be true, there could be another explanation, but he decided he had gone this far so he may as well continue. 'I saw you and two other men coming out of this very gate carrying rolls of something heavy. It was the night I visited Mrs McCallan. I came back because I happened to have left my gloves behind. And it was that same night the lead went missing.'

Throwing back his head, Mickey laughed. 'And you call that evidence? For your information they were . . . rolls of lino we were shifting for a neighbour.' He turned back to the gate. 'Now if you'll excuse me, I think I've wasted enough time on this claptrap.'

'All right, we'll just see what the police have to say then. If you're innocent you shouldn't have much trouble proving it.'

Algernon turned and began to walk away.

Mickey's heart raced frantically, all his dreams of wealth and prosperity suddenly evaporating before the prospect of being questioned by the police. Isaac Greenbaum had been quite clear in his warning. 'Er . . . just a minute, Vicar. Let's not be hasty. What exactly is it yer after?'

Algernon retraced his steps. 'Just the replacement of the roofing, that's all. Nothing more, nothing less.'

'Well . . . er . . . I can mek some enquiries for yer, see what I turn up and let yer know.'

'I'm afraid enquiries are no good, Mr McCallan. Enquiries won't keep my parishioners dry and March is renowned for its rain.'

Mickey fought a strong urge to place his hands around the man's neck and throttle the breath out of him. What on earth was he to do? He could not replace the roofing. The lead from that particular church was down the scrapyard, parted with for two pounds – a fraction of its worth. And neither could he strip another church and replace it with that. Not if he wanted to keep alive his chance of improvement, because it would just be his luck to get caught. He took a deep breath. In the circumstances there was only one thing he could do, and with the amount of money he had in his pocket he could afford to be generous. 'I ain't admitting ter n'ote, you understand, but I'm a charitable man so how about I make a donation to your roof fund?'

Algernon eyed him warily. 'A donation? How much of a donation?'

'Fi— ten pounds.'

Algernon's bushy eyebrows rose in surprise. Ten pounds was a substantial amount of money for someone who lived in these streets. He knew then that he had found his man. 'Oh, I don't think so, Mr McCallan. As I said, I'll settle in full or not at all.'

Mickey's face turned purple with anger. 'Well, how much will the f—' he just stopped himself in time '. . . the roof cost to replace?'

Algernon had the upper hand and he knew it. 'Well now, let me see.' He paused for effect. 'I've had several quotes and the lowest was for forty pounds.'

'How much!' exclaimed Mickey in disbelief.

'Well, lead roofing is expensive, and then there's the labour.'

Mickey had no choice and he knew it. A surge of anger flooded through him as his newfound wealth disappeared along with the prospect of giving up his job. He thrust his hand into his pocket, pulled out the wad of notes, reluctantly peeled off the required amount and thrust them at Algernon. 'There's the bleddy money,' he spat, his face dark. 'And remember, Vicar, I am in no way admitting to any guilt in this matter. As I said, I'm a charitable man. Understood?'

After staring at the notes in his hand in utter amazement, Algernon folded them and put them securely in his inside pocket. 'Oh, perfectly, Mr McCallan. Your generosity is most appreciated. I'll say good-night. And may God go with you.'

Mickey was too incensed to reply. Grabbing the latch, he thrust open the gate and stormed through. He kicked it shut behind him, causing the rotting wood to bounce dangerously on its rusty hinges.

Chapter Thirteen

'It's nice to see you, Alec. Come on in.'

Stepping into the kitchen he sat down in the chair Kelly indicated. 'I was out doing an errand and as I was passing thought I'd enquire how your dad was getting on?'

She poured him a mug of tea and sat down opposite, placing her elbows on the table and cradling her own mug in her hands. 'Dad's getting on just fine. He's really making progress. I'm not saying it's easy for him, but this job is behind it. It's given him a purpose. He's even started doing his allotment again. That's where he is now. I'll be glad of the veggies, I can tell yer. Save a bob or two on the housekeeping.'

He smiled, pleased. 'I'm glad he's getting himself together. And how about you?'

'Me? Oh, I'm fine, on top of the world.' She sighed and eyed him sheepishly. 'Actually, I'm not all right. I've lost me job.'

He looked astounded. 'Ada's never given you the sack?'

'No, she ain't sacked me. Her sister's come to live here and is going to help her run the shop, so she won't be needing me.'

'Oh, I see. So what are you doing about it?'

'Well, I've scanned the paper and there ain't much chance of earning decent money unless you're skilled. I could try for a training position but it's the pay while yer learning – it's hardly anything for a woman of my age to live on.' She took a deep breath. 'I could get an unskilled job on a production line or summat similar, but I'd be pulling me hair out within no time. It's no good telling me needs must, Alec. I detest factory work. I did it once, remember, and I was no good.'

'That was machining. There's plenty of other factories. What about the new Walker's crisp factory that's just opened? I'm sure they'll be looking for people.'

'I can't travel all the way to Thurmaston. It'd take me all day just to get there and back. Anyway, factories are all the same to me, whatever they make. I can't stand 'em.'

'Me neither. What about another shop? Have yer tried any on Beatrice Road?'

She shook her head. 'Getting another job in a corner shop is gonna be hard 'cos they're usually run by families, so I don't see any point in trying there. I did try three of the big stores in town: Lewis's, Marshall and Snelgrove's, and Lea's.'

'And?'

'Marshall and Snelgrove's turned their noses up at me. I suspect I don't talk proper enough for them. Lea's have nothing at the moment and told me to try again later. But I was offered a junior position in the shoe department at Lewis's, paying two pounds seven and six a week. After my training period I can earn commission but there are five other assistants and I can't serve unless they're all busy. It goes in order of seniority, you see.'

'Stupid idea.'

'I agree but that's how the system works. It was all explained to me at me interview.'

'Are you going to take it?'

'I don't see that I have much choice.' Kelly sighed heavily. 'I quite enjoy working for Mrs Adcock. You get to know the people that come in, and what they buy, and you have a chance to pass the time of day. I don't think I really want to work in a department store, not as an underdog to all those other assistants. They looked a right snotty lot and the manager of the department seemed a right tartar.'

He eyed her searchingly. 'What would you really like to do, Kelly?'

She shrugged her shoulders. 'That's just it. I don't know.'

'Have you thought about office work?'

She laughed. 'I wouldn't know where to begin in an office, Alec. So there's no point in even thinking of it. No, it looks like Lewis's. I've reckoned it out and by the time I'm ninety I might just have reached the position of Senior Assistant, 'cos the way I see it the only way you get promoted is if someone leaves to get married or else dies.'

'Kelly!' he scolded, laughing. 'But then, from what you've told me, I suppose you could be right.' He paused thoughtfully. 'Look, it's just a thought but would you like me to have a word with Norma, ask her if anything's going at Woolies? She can maybe put a word in for you.'

Kelly's eyes lit up. 'Oh, Alec, would yer? Woolies can't be as bad as Lewis's, can it?'

'Norma likes it. As you know, she's got on very well. She's been promoted twice since she started there. I'll have a word when she comes home.'

'I'd appreciate that, Alec. I think somehow I'm more suited to the likes of Woolies than Lewis's, don't you?'

He stared hard at her. 'Don't bring yerself down, Kelly. You're good enough to work anywhere.' He leaned across the table and laid his hand reassuringly on top of hers. 'I think you're just a little scared at the thought of change. But you'll be fine, Kelly. Think of all the people you'll get to meet, and you'll make new friends 'cos there always a good social life when you work in a big shop.' He withdrew his hand and leaned back. 'You never know what this'll lead to.'

She stared at him thoughtfully. Alec was right. This job could be a turning point in her life. It could open all sorts of doors. And she did like the sound of a social life. Due to her home circumstances, a social life was something she hadn't had for a long time. Suddenly a flicker of excitement stirred in her stomach and for the first time in an age she felt enthusiasm rise within her. 'Yer right, Alec,' she said, smiling. 'I didn't realise I was feeling scared. I should grab at this chance and see where it leads me. Thanks, you've made me feel much better.'

'That's the spirit, gel.' He finished off his tea. 'I must be getting back. I only popped out to get a box of matches to light the gas mantles. It'll be getting dark soon and I won't be able to see what I'm doing. I can't understand why the landlord won't get the electric laid on. It ain't half so dirty as gas. Still, beggars can't be choosers, eh?'

'It's all down to money, Alec. They won't make no improvements that'll cost. And putting things right after the electric men have done their worst costs, don't it?'

He nodded. 'And I suppose it'd be another excuse to raise the rent.' He rose. 'That tea were grand, Kelly, thanks. I hope I haven't interrupted your Saturday afternoon?'

'It was nice ter see you. I was only sitting here on me own. Mickey and Rod are at the football.' She grimaced. 'And I hope our Mickey comes home in a better mood. He's bin in a foul one these past few days.' She gave a wry smile. 'To be honest, I can't remember the last time he was in a good one.'

Alec declined to reply. He hadn't a good word to say

about Mickey but respected the fact that he was Kelly's brother. 'I'd better be off before you sling me out for outstaying me welcome.'

She stood, stepped across to the back door and opened it. 'That's one thing you'd never do, Alec. You won't forget to ask Norma about any vacancies, will you?'

He smiled, eyes tender. 'How could I when it's for you?'

A warm glow filled Kelly as she closed the door after him. What a lovely man he was, and how lucky she was to have him as a friend.

Only moments after Alec had gone her Saturday afternoon was interrupted again by a tapping on the door. It opened immediately and Glenda came through. One look at her stricken face was all Kelly needed to tell her that something was seriously wrong.

'What on earth's the matter, Glenda?'

'Oh, Kelly,' was all she managed before she burst into a torrent of tears.

'Sit down, gel,' Kelly ordered, jumping up and grabbing hold of the teapot. 'I'll pour you a cuppa.' Pushing a mug of tea before her friend, she eyed her worriedly. 'Has someone died?' she asked tentatively.

Glenda blew loudly into her already sodden handkerchief and dabbed her eyes. 'No, it ain't n'ote like that.'

'Well, what is it then?'

She raised her head. 'I'm late, Kelly.'

'Late? Late for what? Oh!' Eyes wide, her mouth dropping open, Kelly realised what she meant. 'That kind of late. Oh, my God, Glenda, a' yer sure?'

Miserably she nodded. 'As sure as I can be. Oh, Kelly, what am I gonna do?'

Slowly she sank down on the chair opposite. 'Does our Mickey know?' she asked, wondering if this was the reason for his foul mood of late.

Glenda shook her head. 'No one knows but you.'

Utterly shocked by this news, Kelly ran her fingers through her hair. 'You're sure? You are *sure?*' she re-affirmed.

'I'm positive, Kelly. For God's sake, d'yer think I'd be in this state if I wasn't?'

'I'm sorry, I just can't believe it.'

'Neither can I. Me mam and dad are gonna kill me, 'specially me dad. He's gonna hit the roof.'

That's nothing to what my brother will do, Kelly thought, and sighed despairingly. 'Well, the first thing I think you've got to do is tell our Mickey.'

'Oh, Kelly, what d'you think he'll say?'

She had a good idea but vehemently hoped she was wrong. 'How do I know? I ain't a fortune teller. Look, I'm sorry, I didn't mean to snap but this news is the last I expected to hear. I mean, I never thought for a minute you and our Mickey were . . . were . . .'

'Having sex,' Glenda interrupted. 'It's about time you grew up, Kelly. You don't keep men like Mickey and Rod by playing little Miss Innocent.'

'And look what playing grown ups has done for you, Glenda! In the circumstances I won't take your advice, if yer don't mind. I'll save meself for me wedding night and if Rod doesn't like it then he knows that he can do.' Kelly shook her head. 'Our Mickey ain't gonna be happy about this. But still, he's as much to blame as you so he's just gonna have to get used to the idea that he's going to be a father, and the sooner you tell him the better. Then you'll have ter tell yer parents, but with him by yer side that shouldn't be so bad.'

Glenda eyed her through red, tear-filled eyes. 'You think he will be on my side?'

'He'll have no choice.'

Glenda studied the contents of her mug for some moments. 'He'll marry me now, won't he?'

Kelly stared at her. The words had been more of a statement than a question and she found that a bit strange.

Rod's sister lifted her head and stared hard at Kelly. 'He will marry me, won't he, now I'm expecting?' she said again.

'He'll have to, whether he wants to or not. Your father will see to that.'

Glenda gnawed her bottom lip anxiously, a look of fear crossing her face. 'I ain't looking forward to telling Dad but I think the worst thing will be telling Mickey. Will you be there with me when I do?'

Kelly stared at her, the very thought filling her with dread. 'Oh, I don't think that's a good idea. This is personal, between you and our Mickey.'

'Oh, Kelly, please,' she pleaded. 'Please, I can't face him on me own.'

Kelly's reply was interrupted by the sound of the back gate being unlatched then slamming shut and the clattering of footsteps down the path. The back door swung open and Mickey and Rod entered. The expressions on both girls' faces immediately registered and Mickey asked, 'What's up with you two? Has someone died?'

'Yeah,' Rod echoed, shutting the door behind him. 'What's happened?'

Hurriedly Kelly rose and stepped across to the stove, grabbing the kettle. 'You'd better sit down, our Mickey. Glenda's got summat to tell yer.'

'Can't it wait 'til I've had me tea? I'm starving.'

'No, it can't.'

Sighing, he turned to face his girlfriend. 'Well, what is it?' he demanded.

She flashed her eyes pleadingly at Kelly, seeking her support.

'Just tell him,' Kelly urged.

Glenda sniffed loudly, took a shuddering breath and

129

bowed her head. 'I'm . . . I'm having a baby, Mickey.'

Face draining of colour, he stared at her, stunned. 'What?'

Anticipating the forthcoming storm Kelly sprang to the side of her friend and placed an arm protectively around her shoulders. 'You heard her, Mickey. She's pregnant.'

Rod stood gawping, the shock rendering him speechless.

'No,' Mickey uttered. 'No, I don't believe it.' He looked from Kelly to Glenda then back to his sister. 'It's a joke, innit? Come on, say it's a joke?'

'It's no joke, Mickey,' she replied more calmly than she felt. 'How can you even think we'd stoop to joking about such a thing?'

Mouth wide in shock, he stared at Glenda for several long moments then his face turned thunderous. 'How could you let this happen?' he shouted. 'Why, you stupid . . .'

'That's enough, Mickey,' snapped Kelly. 'You're as much to blame as she is. You're gonna be a father, so you'd better get used to the idea.'

Clenching his fists, he turned away and paced the small room again and again. 'But I don't wanna be a dad. Not yet. I ain't ready.'

'I don't expect Glenda's ready to become a mother but she's got no choice either.'

'Oh, but she has. She could . . .'

'Mickey McCallan, don't you dare even think such a thing,' Kelly cried.

Glenda looked horrified. 'You weren't gonna suggest I get rid of it, Mickey? How could you? This is our baby – ours. We're engaged to be married and we'd have had kids sooner or later, so what's wrong with now?'

He stared at her. 'Married!'

130

Her face paled alarmingly. 'You are going ter marry me, ain't yer?'

'Not right now I'm not. Fer God's sake, Glenda, be realistic. Weddings and babies cost money and I don't know about you but I ain't got none.' A vision of the ten pounds in his pocket flashed to mind, all he had left from the fifty pounds up front payment. Apart from a pound or two made previously from his illicit activities and hidden behind a piece of skirting board in his bedroom, it was all he possessed in the world – and all he was likely to for the time being until the factory job came off. What money he had was his and something he did not intend squandering on any wedding, not even his own. Not if he could help it.

She frowned, bewildered. 'No money? But I thought you'd bin saving?'

'How much d'yer think I can save from me wages? I don't get that much.'

'Yes, but there's yer other . . .'

'Ah,' he erupted. 'The other, has finished, ain't it, Kelly. She's decided she wants no part of it no more. So you can stop planning on me earning anything from that.'

'Eh, don't you go blaming me! I only stopped recently and me dropping out ain't gonna hinder you. You'll soon come up with other ways of doing things, I'm positive of that.' Kelly wagged a finger at him. 'And what about what you made before? We all know you got the biggest share.'

His mouth tightened angrily. 'And quite right I should. I was the brains behind it.' He leaned towards her, his eyes flashing a warning. 'And what I do with my money is my business. Anyway, it's spent, gone.'

'On what?' Glenda asked sharply.

'On what?' he mimicked. 'What d'yer think paid for yer nights out and presents?'

'You ain't took me out for ages. You said you couldn't afford it, being's you were saving towards our wedding. And as for presents . . .'

'That's enough,' he hissed at them both. 'Who d'yer both think you are, the Spanish Inquisition?'

'Oh, I'm sorry, Mickey,' Glenda cried remorsefully. 'I didn't mean to have a go at yer, only I'm so worried. But look, I understand if we can't afford a big wedding. The register office will do, and I know everyone'll help out with things for the baby.'

Kelly glared at Glenda, fighting an urge to tell her to stop humbling herself like this. This baby was Mickey's doing as well as hers and as such he should honour his obligations and marry her without being begged to do so.

'I'll tek no one's charity or cast-offs,' Mickey grunted. 'I've already had a bellyful of that for most of me life. When I get married I'll pay fer it out me own pocket or not at all.'

'Well, you'd better find some money then, and quick, because once Nev Collins finds out about Glenda's condition, he'll make sure you wed,' Kelly announced.

At the mention of Glenda's father Mickey stared at his sister, his chest tightening painfully as realisation struck home. He was trapped and even his calculating brain could not envisage a way out of this one.

Groaning in despair, he sat down on the nearest chair and sank his head into his hands, his mind racing frantically. Even before his plan to improve his lot had begun to bear fruit, the last thing he had planned on was getting married. A baby had not figured in his scheme of things at all. He liked Glenda, liked her a lot, but although in a moment of uncharacteristic weakness he had bought her a ring to stop her nagging, he had not intended actually walking up the aisle with her for a few years to come. If ever, in fact.

He rubbed his hand over the stubble on his chin. But Kelly was right. Once Nev Collins was informed of his daughter's condition, choice would not even figure. Nev Collins's temper was legendary and he was one of the very few men who could frighten Mickey. A solidly built man of forty-three, steel-hard muscles forged from years of lifting heavy dustbins, he was not afraid to use his fists and beat a man to a pulp for what he saw as just cause – which when he had a drink inside him was just about anything his fuddled mind would fix on. A pregnant daughter and reluctant fiancé would be reason enough for murder in Nev Collins's eyes.

Mickey had no choice but to agree to this marriage if he valued his life. He would also have to agree to it if he wanted to keep alive his association with Isaac Greenbaum, and that counted with him more than anything. Any hint of scandal swept round these streets quicker than fire through dry paper. Hearing his name on everyone's lips would not please Isaac, and he was a man of his word, Mickey had no doubt about that.

He shut his eyes tightly. Why now? he wanted to scream. Why now when things were beginning to happen for me? First that bloody Vicar, now this. What else could possibly go wrong? As these tormenting thoughts beset him, from the cooler part of his brain clearer ones suddenly began to emerge and for several minutes, while the others waited with trepidation for his next response, he mulled them over.

Maybe, he thought, it was not as bad as it seemed. He had managed to resolve the problem with the Vicar, albeit it had cost him dearly. As for this marriage – well, that would not be allowed to hamper his plans either. Glenda could have her baby, and Glenda could look after it. The whole thing would be an encumbrance but one he could walk away from when the time was right. Right now time was what he needed. Time to get his future off the ground by ingratiating himself with Isaac Greenbaum, learning all he could about the ways of the underworld, getting some real money in his pocket. Then and only then would he be in a position to do exactly what he wanted. And what he dearly wanted was a life far removed from the one he was living now. One where he'd have power, money, and his pick of beautiful women.

Although the thought did not sit well with him, he knew the best thing he could do right now was play along and keep everyone sweet.

He lifted his head and eyed the three of them in turn. 'I don't have much choice in this, do I?' he said in a self-pitying tone.

Kelly shook her head. 'No, I don't see as you do.'

'So you will marry me then, Mickey?' Glenda cried as she jumped up and shot around the table to throw her arms around his neck. 'Oh, Mickey, Mickey!' she wept. 'And you'll come with me to tell me mam and dad?'

Sighing, he nodded. 'Yeah, I suppose.'

Kelly sighed with relief. 'Well, I suppose this calls for a celebration. Anyone fancy a cuppa tea?'

Mickey opened his mouth to voice his own thoughts on whether it was a celebration or not, but quickly clamped it shut, suddenly remembering his plan. 'I need summat stronger than tea, I need a pint.' He scraped back his chair. 'A' you coming, Rod?'

'Er . . . I'll follow yer down, Mickey. There's just summat I want to speak to Kelly about first.'

'Suit yerself,' he growled as he yanked open the back door, strode through and slammed it shut behind him.

Thoughtfully Kelly stared at the closed door. Something was not right. She knew her brother well and he had agreed to the marriage far too easily to her mind. Oh, he had ranted and raved at first, acted in his usual self-centred manner, but as she had watched him wrestle with the problem she had seen something come over him, something she couldn't quite fathom . . . Her brother was devious and cunning and the way he had just acted was not true to form.

She jumped as she realised Glenda was speaking to her.

'Sorry, what did yer say?'

'I said, I hope Mickey doesn't have too much to drink 'cos I'm wanting him to come and break the news to me parents tonight.'

Kelly tutted, shaking her head. 'Glenda, I think you've done extremely well to get him to agree to marry you so easily without . . .'

'What d'yer mean by "so easily"?'

'Exactly what I said. Easily. I don't know about you but I was expecting World War Three and us having to drag him up the aisle, kicking and screaming.'

Glenda sniffed. 'I suppose yer right,' she said grudgingly.

'I *am* right. Now if I were you I wouldn't push him any more for the time being. He said he'll go and tackle your parents with you. Just give it a couple of days to let this all sink in before you mention it again. 'Course it's up to you, but that's my advice.'

'Yeah . . . maybe yer right.'

Kelly went over to the chair Mickey had just vacated and sat down. She turned her attention to Rod. 'What did you want ter speak to me about?'

He eyed her blankly. 'Eh?'

'You told Mickey you had something to say to me,' she repeated, a mite agitated.

'Oh, yeah. Yeah, I did.'

Rod fixed his eyes on her. When the news of his sister's pregnancy was broken, like the others he'd been shocked. He loved Glenda and this situation was dreadful. She could have been the talk of the neighbourhood, maybe even ostracised. He had witnessed how other girls in her position had been treated. The ones who had not been thrown out at once had been shunned by the local women, branded a harlot, while the men either jeered or pursued them, considering them easy game. But Glenda would be spared all that, thank God. Mickey was going to marry her. And that thought had given him the answer to his own pressing problem. Marriage.

Married to Kelly he would become Mickey's brother-in-law. Family. And as a family member he would automatically be included in all Mickey's schemes. And wherever Mickey was heading, Rod would be right there with him. Because Mickey was going places, he was sure of that.

Like Mickey he was not quite ready to marry yet, the ties and responsibilities frightened him. But he did love Kelly and they were eventually going to marry, so why not now? Get it over and done with. And once married she would not shun his advances any more, which meant he need not go elsewhere to satisfy his sexual needs. The more he pondered the idea, the more it made sense. All he had to do was convince Kelly.

Leaning across the table, he took her hand. 'Why don't we get married too, Kelly? How d'yer fancy a double wedding?'

She looked stunned. 'What?'

'Well, it makes sense, don't it?'

'Sense?'

'Oh, Kelly!' Glenda clasped her hands in delight. 'It's a wonderful idea. I mean, apart from what fun it'll be, it'll work out much cheaper. Say you will? Please say you will?'

Her mind whirled. It might sound a good idea but she wasn't sure whether she was ready to get married right now just because it made sense, sounded fun, and most certainly not because it would be cheaper. She wanted to get married because Rod loved her, wanted to share his life with her. If only he'd said that instead of 'it makes sense'. She looked him in the eye. 'I'll have ter think about it,' she said sharply.

'What's there to think about?' he said, hurt. 'I thought you wanted to get married?'

'Well . . . I do, but I want a wedding of my own.'

'And it'll be years before we can afford that, unless a miracle happens,' he said sulkily. 'Glenda's right, Kelly. A double wedding'll suit us all.'

'Yeah, come on, Kelly,' she coaxed. 'We could have the reception here. If we do the catering ourselves we can keep the costs down.'

'Me and Mickey'll get the booze.'

Kelly eyed him sharply. 'Seems you both have it all worked out. But has either of you given a thought to where we're all going to live?'

Rod grimaced for a moment then his face cleared. 'Why, here! Makes sense, don't it, 'til we can all afford to rent places of our own. Soon as we're married we'll get our names down on the Council list. We'll probably get one of them houses on the estate they're building in Braunstone. I know yer dad won't mind putting up with us in the meantime. I expect he'll be glad of the company. We'll pay him board a' course. And you needn't bother with a job now. You'll be able to look after us all. I mean, it makes sense for Glenda to keep on her job as long as possible 'cos she earns more money than you will, and she'll need yer when the baby comes, won't she?'

Kelly was flabbergasted. 'But I was looking forward to working full-time, Rod! And what if I don't want to stay at home skivvying for you lot?'

'Eh, no wife of mine is going ter work. I put me foot down there. A man needs looking after. He needs his dinner on the table and his shirts ironed. That's only to be expected, ain't it?'

137

She clamped her lips tightly shut. Yes, she thought, despite the fact that many women went out to work, most men still expected those things from a wife. Even her father, whom she considered to be very fair-minded, had automatically expected Kelly to provide those services when her mother had become unable. But it seemed she had always been looking after other people. After her talk with Alec she was actually looking forward to starting a job and experiencing all the unknown things she hoped it would bring with it. If she married Rod none of that would happen, he had made that clear enough.

'I know what's up with you,' Glenda piped up.

'You do?'

'Yeah, it's nerves, that's all. You love me brother, don't yer?'

'Yes, 'course I do.'

'Then that's all it is. Nerves.' Her face lit up. 'Oh, it'll be great, you just wait and see. Me married to Mickey, you to our Rod. Think of all the things we can do together . . .'

Such as? Kelly wanted to ask. Apart from going down the club every Saturday night? Her head bowed, she studied the grain of the old pine table as she sensed their eyes boring into her, felt the pressure they were putting on her, forcing her to agree to their plans.

Watching her with concern, Rod suddenly felt afraid. Kelly was going to turn him down, he felt sure she was. He would not get another God-given chance like this to consolidate his position with Mickey. His mind raced frantically. He had to think of something to sway her. Suddenly he knew what it was.

He leaned forward and clasped her hand. 'Kelly, I don't know what's gone off between yer dad and Mickey, but us all getting married and this baby are bound to bring 'em back together. Well, stands to reason. Things like this always do, don't they?'

She lifted her head and stared at him.

'Rod's right, Kelly. Even I can tell that whatever happened, it's summat bad. I asked Mickey meself and he all but bit me head off. I know you'd give anything to get them talking again. This is bound to do it,' Glenda said persuasively.

Kelly sighed. They were right. She would do anything to bring that about and if her agreeing to this wedding and giving up her plans to work did the trick then it was a sacrifice she would have to make as nothing else she had done seemed to have worked.

Slowly she nodded her head. 'Okay.'

Rod sighed with relief. 'You'll marry me then?'

She nodded. 'Yes, I'll marry yer, Rod.'

As Rod left his sister at the door to their house in order to walk the short distance to the Empire to join Mickey, he hesitated, looking at her quizzically. 'What you up to, our Glenda?'

'Eh! Wadda you mean by that remark?'

He dug his hands into his pockets and stared at her. 'Just what I said. Wadda you up to? Come on, sis, I know you. By rights you should be falling to pieces. Yer not though, are yer? You look as though yer've won the pools.'

'No, I don't,' she snapped. 'Inside I'm wetting meself. I'm just trying to act normal so as not to get Mam and Dad's suspicions up. Yer know our mam, Rod, she only has to look at our faces to know that summat's up and I don't want to be asked any questions 'til me and Mickey face 'em together.'

'Huh,' he grunted, unconvinced. 'If you say so.'

'I *do* say so.'

Glenda watched thoughtfully as he turned away from her and strode off down the street. She smiled, a secretive smile. All had gone according to plan. There had been a couple of worrying moments, but it had worked out better than she had dared hope.

Very soon she would get her heart's desire and that was to be Mrs Mickey McCallan.

There was no baby. That was a lie she had concocted as she had lain in her bed, nearly bursting her brain in the search for a ploy to bring about this wedding. She'd had to do something. She had witnessed with horror Mickey's mounting indifference to her, moving towards the inevitable ending of their relationship. That was something she could not bear. Mickey was all she had ever dreamed of in a man. Not only was he breathtakingly good-looking, just like Laurence Olivier in *Wuthering Heights*, he also excited her beyond reason. Just to catch a glimpse of him each day saw her through; anything else she classed as a bonus. Life without Mickey was unthinkable to her.

Catching him with that woman in Latimer Street had convinced her that if she did not do something, and soon, he would be lost to her forever. And it had to be something he could not argue with, leaving him no chance to worm his way free. Pregnancy was her answer. Pregnant, he would have no choice but to marry her. Even if he resisted at first, she knew her father would make sure he gave in. And she had been right. The mention of Nev Collins's name had put the fear of God into Mickey.

Glenda was no fool though. She knew that even married to him she would never possess him; no woman would ever be stupid enough to think she could own a man like Mickey. He would always do exactly as he wanted; married or otherwise he would still have his dalliances but she would have his name and as such be the one to whom he would eventually return, because she would never let him go. And for the sake of acquiring her dearest wish she was prepared to make sacrifices. All she had to do, which was exactly what she was doing now, was turn a blind eye and pretend it wasn't happening. She would gladly live like that rather than face the alternative: life without Mickey.

As she pushed her key into the lock of her parents' house, turned it and opened the door, her smile broadened. The worst part in all of this charade had been the peeling of that mound of strong onions to make her cry, but it had paid off handsomely.

Chapter Fourteen

Kelly stared down at a plate of limp paste sandwiches. There were cheese and pickle, too, and sardine; a length of square pork pie; three assorted jellies, two of which were not quite set; two plates of fairy and queen cakes; and, Mrs Collins's contribution to the affair, a crudely iced wedding cake whose fruit had sunk in the middle. Hardly the kind of offerings she had envisaged handed round at her wedding when she had lain in her bed of a night, dreaming of the event.

Nor in her dreams had she been wearing a beige costume hurriedly run up on Mrs Connor's ancient treadle sewing machine, the fabric being the cheapest she could find, the cotton not quite matching. 'Oh, but it won't matter, me duck,' Mrs Connor had twittered, 'no one will see it.' But it did matter to Kelly. Mattered a great deal.

She sighed. It had all happened so quickly. Just two weeks from agreeing to get married to the actual ceremony, all the time swept along as though on a tidal wave, unable to escape.

Her eyes rested on the thin gold band around her finger, a declaration of Rod's love, his commitment to cherish her for the rest of her life. But somehow she wasn't convinced by the outward token. Maybe it had something to do with the way he had grabbed it from the best man and rammed it on her finger, his manner that of a man in a rush to get the deed over with, perhaps worried she would change her mind.

She thought back over the ceremony itself. The register office had been grim, impersonal, its only adornment a vase of near dead flowers on the registrar's table. The man himself, small in stature with a pinched face, a balding head and tiny round pebble glasses, had worn a shiny brown suit. As he had conducted the service Kelly had been unable to drag her eyes away from a badly sewn patch with threads of cotton hanging from his sleeve. She would have thought a man in his position would have dressed himself a little better, considering the occasion he was presiding over and the importance of it to his clients.

The whole service had seemed rushed, the registrar's glance flashing continually to the clock on the wall, as though he was worried his dinner would grow cold. It seemed to Kelly that no sooner had she arrived, a single woman, and been ushered inside, than she was being ushered out again a married one, with no time to savour a moment of what was supposed to be her happiest day.

But then the whole day had been like that. From the moment she had risen from her bed, bleary-eyed and fuddled from lack of sleep, Glenda had not given her a moment to gather her thoughts. Kelly had even wondered if her future sister-in-law had sensed her apprehension and purposely seen to it that she did not have a chance to reconsider for fear she would change her mind and put the double wedding in jeopardy.

Her eyes strayed across to her new husband and his father, Neville, standing alongside Mickey and a few male friends and neighbours, dispensing glasses of beer from a barrel standing on a trestle table across the room. None of them would need much more before they were drunk, which seemed to be their aim. As soon as they had arrived back from the register office all the men had gathered around the barrel and hardly one had left it since.

For a moment she studied Rod. The grin splitting his face, albeit inebriated, was a happy one. At least he seemed to be content with this state of affairs. Her glance strayed to Mickey next. Not so her brother. His grin mirrored Rod's and his jokes were coming thick and fast, but to Kelly there was a falseness about him. She knew he was putting on an act.

She turned her head and looked across at her father, by himself in a corner on the opposite side of the room. Her heart went out to him. Sitting stiffly in a borrowed high-backed chair, one hand clutching a plate of untouched food, the other a glass of beer, he looked lost and alone, despite the fact that Mrs Collins sat perched beside him, chattering on incessantly about nothing of interest. Kelly knew her father wasn't listening.

She sighed deeply again. The mending of the relationship between Mickey and his father that Rod and Glenda had prophesied had not materialised after all. If anything it had worsened. If Mickey had had his way, her father would not have attended any part of the wedding. But there Kelly had put her foot down. He was her father too, and whether Mickey liked it or not he would be at her wedding.

She had to give Frank his due. Despite Mickey's attitude, and for the sake of his daughter, he had endeavoured to begin to heal the rift on several occasions but Mickey remained as unapproachable and obnoxious as ever. Kelly had tried herself and met with the same response. With all that was going on, she'd decided it was best to give up for the moment. Maybe time would be the thing to do it.

'You all right, me duck? Only yer look like yer at a funeral, not yer own wedding.'

Kelly jumped. 'Oh, yes, thanks, Mrs Collins.' In her

preoccupied state she had not noticed her mother-in-law come across to join her. In all the time Kelly had known Rod's mother she had never felt quite at ease with the woman. She was nice enough, Kelly supposed, had always appeared to welcome her whenever she had paid a visit to their house to see Rod, but since their intention eventually to marry had been announced, Vivien Collins had become increasingly frosty towards her.

She was a tall woman, on the thin side, and despite not needing them always wore a pair of whalebone stays with which she was constantly fiddling. According to Glenda they had belonged to her own long-dead mother and Vivien wore them out of respect, although to Kelly that seemed more like a punishment than an act of respect, and laughingly she had asked Glenda if she would be expected to carry on the tradition. Her sister-in-law's reply had been peppered with many expletives, but in short her answer had been 'no'.

Now Vivien stood next to Kelly, one hand balancing a plate piled with sandwiches and a glass of cheap Cyprus sherry, the other fumbling unsuccessfully discreetly to adjust the contraption under her navy and white spotted dress, the one she always wore to weddings and funerals. It reeked of mothballs, as did her husband's black suit, but in honour of her children's weddings she had gone to the expense of buying a black felt hat complete with spray of plastic cherries from the church jumble sale, arguing the price down from a shilling to sixpence.

Fighting a desire to ask her new mother-in-law if, just for once, she wouldn't be more comfortable if she took her stays off, Kelly turned to face her. 'I was just wondering if we were going to have enough food. We didn't take into account people dropping by.'

'Now yer married yer'll soon learn, gel, that when there's any food on the go you'll get visits from people you thought had passed on years ago. Don't worry about

146

running out, we can always pop to Ada's and get a loaf and another couple of jars of paste.' Vivien glanced around the room. 'Going well, innit, considering?'

'Mmmm,' Kelly murmured, glancing around too. Considering everything, she supposed it was. Everyone, those she knew and those she didn't, looked as though they were enjoying themselves anyway.

'I woulda loved a church do meself,' Vivien Collins mused wistfully. 'Our Glenda would 'ave looked a picture in a proper wedding dress, she would. But then, I suppose, in the circumstances . . .' She looked across at her daughter holding court from the middle of the sagging settee, surrounded by several well-wishers. 'I have ter say, though, she does look 'appy, don't she?'

Kelly nodded. Glenda looked more than happy, she looked radiant. And in the fashionable pale blue fitted dress and matching coat she wore, her hair freshly permed and styled, she could have stepped out of the pages of a woman's magazine. Kelly felt ashamed of the envious feeling she could not suppress. Thanks to Glenda's having a good job she had been able to find the money to buy her special outfit, and her mother and friends in the factory where she worked had all rallied round and come up with the coupons needed.

'Her dad's took this very well,' Vivien rattled on. 'Our Glenda's always been his favourite out of the two of 'em.' Her voice lowered emotionally. 'With me it was always me son. I never thought my Rodney would get married, I always thought I'd have him to look after.' She glanced at Kelly, a resigned smile on her thin face. 'But I suppose he could 'ave done a lot worse than you. And I mean that as a compliment, gel.'

So that was it, thought Kelly. That was why Vivien had become so aloof towards her. She had seen Kelly as a threat, another woman coming between her and her son. Kelly realised it wasn't personal against her; Vivien would have acted the same with any woman Rod brought home. She made a decision to do her best to make sure he visited his mother regularly, maybe had the odd meal with her. That way hopefully she would not feel that she was being pushed out of his life entirely.

'To be honest,' her mother-in-law confided, 'I thought Mr Collins was gonna commit murders. But I was wrong, thank God.' She exhaled loudly. 'Oh, but I was worried for a minute or two! When Glenda broke the news, by the look on his face, I thought he'd have a heart attack. It was Mickey that did it.'

Frowning Kelly turned her full attention to her. 'Did what?'

'Smoothed things over. "Don't you worry, Mr Collins," he said, "I love your daughter and we were gonna marry anyway. This baby's just happened sooner rather than later. Can I call yer Dad now I'm gonna be family?" 'Course, that did it for Neville. "Yer can, son." And before yer could blink an eye the pair of them had gone off down the pub. They could hardly stand when they came back. Oh, I can tell yer, I breathed a sigh of relief and so did Glenda.' She lowered her voice. ''Cos, yer know, Mr Collins has got a bit of a temper . . .'

'Bit of a temper' was a gross understatement, Kelly thought. A more apt description of a roused Mr Collins was 'raving lunatic'. But at the moment this thought was not uppermost in her mind. Mickey had asked a man like Neville Collins if he could call him Dad – when all the time he refused to address his own father as such. How could he be so callous?

'Talking of dads,' Vivien Collins twittered on, 'what's going on between Mickey and Mr McCallan?'

'Going on? Er . . . nothing,' Kelly replied.

'Oh, pull the other one!' huffed Vivien. 'A deaf and dumb man couldn't fail to notice the atmosphere between them two. Eh, it ain't 'ote ter do with yer both marrying into the Collins family, is it? Yer dad think we ain't good enough, is that it?'

'No, it's not, Mrs Collins. My dad's not like that. He wouldn't care who we married so long as we were happy. He's . . . well, he's still grieving over me mother. He's missing her, that's all, and our Mickey thinks he should be over it.'

'Oh, I see. Well, he'll miss Flora for a long time yet.' She turned, tilted her head and looked hard at Frank. 'He's not a bad-looking man, wouldn't have any trouble finding someone else. In fact, my sister Betty's a widow. Mmmm,' she mused, thoughtfully. 'It's a pity she couldn't manage to come today. I could have introduced them.'

Kelly fought to control her outrage at this flippant remark. Her mother was hardly cold in her grave and Vivien was hitching Dad up with someone else. 'If yer'll excuse me, Mrs Collins, I'll just pass these sandwiches round.'

'Oh, yes, all right,' she replied distractedly. 'Oh, just a minute before yer go. I've bin thinking.'

'Oh?'

'Well, pardon me for saying so . . . mind you, I can say what I like now, being's we're family . . . but, well, yer can't help but notice this house is a bit lacking and what with my Rod and Glenda moving in, I'll have a rummage round our place and select a few bits. Might help liven the place up, mek it more homely. If I remember right we've a standard lamp somewhere that'd go nicely in that corner, and I've a few bits of brass that'd brighten up the hearth.'

Kelly tightened her lips. There was no spare space in the Collins house as every nook and cranny, even the outside lavatory, was crammed with odds and ends Neville Collins had picked up over the years on his bin round. Only unlike most other bin men, who repaired the pieces and then sold them for a few coppers, Neville never actually got around to it. He was a hoarder, a 'that might come in useful' sort of man. Or else, to Kelly's mind, plain lazy. With a little work some of the bits she had seen when paying visits could have been sold on quite easily. Instead they sat gathering dust while Mr Collins was down the pub, leaving his wife to worry over how to make ends meet.

It was doubtful whether the standard lamp she was referring to would be in a workable state and it would certainly be minus its shade, but even that was irrelevant because Vivien had obviously forgotten that the lamp needed electricity to make it work and as yet these houses were not laid on. The brass items would be dented or have bits missing from them. Kelly wanted none of the things, but did not want to hurt the woman's feelings by an outright refusal.

'That's very good of you, Mrs Collins, but I wouldn't like to . . .'

'It's my pleasure,' she cut in, patting Kelly's arm. 'And it'd be my way of saying thank you for your dad agreeing to have you all live here 'til yer get places of yer own. Now off you go and pass them sandwiches round. I'm gonna have some of that jelly before it all goes. Oh, it's a pity yer never thought to mek some custard to go with it. Jelly ain't the same wi'out custard.'

Offering the sandwiches as she made her way round the room, Kelly eventually reached her father and sat down in the vacant chair beside him. 'Can I get you anything else, Dad?'

'Eh? Oh, no, me duck, ta. I ain't touched this yet.' He turned in his chair to give her his full attention. 'I just want to tell yer how beautiful yer look. I'm really proud of you, gel. I only wish yer mother was here to see this day.'

She blinked back tears. 'Yes, so do I, Dad. So do I. Dad?'

He frowned. 'What's on yer mind?'

'I just want to thank yer for agreeing that we can all live here for the time being. It's not going to be easy for you, is it?'

He smiled wanly. 'Because of the bad feeling between me and Mickey, yer mean? Don't worry, Kelly. I've managed to keep the peace up ter now, I can manage a bit longer.'

'Dad . . .'

'Kelly, I don't want to talk about it, there's a good gel, especially not on yer wedding day.'

It would be wrong to broach such a subject on a day like today. But then, she knew that no matter what day it was, this was a subject he would always clam up on. Her opinion still had not changed, though. Her father could not have done what her brother accused him of. She just wanted to hear him explain his side of things.

'You all living here seemed the most sensible thing,' Frank said, changing the subject. 'We'll be cramped but there's more room here than at the Collinses. You can't swing a cat in their place. I don't know how they can live with all that junk cluttering up the rooms. God knows why Neville Collins doesn't do something with it all. He could make a bit of cash with just a bit of effort.'

He sniffed disdainfully. 'Mind you, the bloke has always been a lazy so and so. Years ago I used to be on the same round as him and he never pulled his weight. He was the last to arrive and the first to leave, and the rest of the gang were always covering for him when he sloped off somewhere. From what I can gather he ain't changed much.' He glanced across at the gathering by the beer barrel. 'Apart from Neville, it looks ter me like our Mickey is hell-bent on getting his share today too.'

'And Rod,' said Kelly, making to rise. 'Maybe I should go and say something.'

He grabbed her arm, pulling her back down. 'I wouldn't, Kelly. Any woman'd be a fool to try and come between a man and his beer, especially on his wedding day and in front of his mates.'

She nodded. Her father was right. She would just have to hope that what appeared at the moment to be good-natured banter did not turn nasty, especially as Neville Collins was present.

'A' you happy, our Kelly?'

She turned and eyed her father in surprise. 'Sorry, Dad?'

'I asked if you were happy?'

She laid a hand on his arm. ''Course I'm happy. Why do you ask?'

'Oh . . . you look a bit . . . disappointed.'

'Do I?' She stared at him thoughtfully. He was right. She *was* disappointed. Disappointed that this wedding had come about so hurriedly and that she'd felt pressured into going along with things. Disappointed that she had not been able to afford a proper church wedding, a white dress, and a nice reception in a posh hotel where she could have invited all the friends she would have wished to share her day with.

But what did any of that matter really?

A simple affair made sense all round, and it was far more than many couples had managed during the war. The main thing was she had just married the man she loved. How selfish of her to be feeling disappointed when she should be jumping for joy. As for Rod's clumsy behaviour at the register office . . . he had been nervous, that was all. Suddenly her heart jolted as a thought struck her. She might not have had the outfit she wanted and nor was there any money to spare for a honeymoon, but she had managed to buy herself a skimpy black nylon nightdress from the market, and the thought of that brought the colour to her cheeks.

It's about time, she scolded herself, that I accept matters and buck up my ideas. This day is the beginning of my future, and if I carry on moping the way I am then I'm hardly going to get off to a very good start.

She glanced across at her new husband and a warm glow filled her being. She turned back to her father, smiling brightly. 'I ain't disappointed, Dad. Not at all I ain't. I'm happy. Very happy.'

He patted her hand and rose to his feet. 'That's all I wanted to hear.'

'Where yer going?'

'If yer don't mind, I thought I'd get changed and go and do a couple of hours up the allotment.'

'Oh, but surely . . .' Then the reason behind his decision struck. Her father was making himself scarce in case his presence should cause trouble with Mickey. And she knew he would stay away until he felt it safe to return. He was doing this for her, so it wouldn't ruin her day.

A surge of deep love and admiration for this man filled her. Since the morning she had been reduced to giving him a piece of her mind he had made great efforts to improve his outlook. She knew he would always grieve for her mother, but he was coping well with his feelings and trying to live his life the best way he could. One day maybe he would manage to sort out this problem with Mickey. She could only hope so, because she knew, although he did not say so, that it was causing her father deep distress. She took his hand. 'Can I pack you up some sandwiches?'

He nodded. 'That'd be appreciated.'

A couple of hours later the wedding party was still in full swing. More well-wishers had popped in and with the help of two willing neighbours, Kelly had managed to rustle up more food and had the kettle continually boiling for hot water to keep a constant supply of tea and clean crockery.

A tap came on the back door. It opened and a head popped round.

'Alec,' she exclaimed delightedly. 'Come in.'

He immediately noticed the length of damp towelling in her hand. 'Should you be doing that on your wedding day? he asked, a twinkle in his eye.

She smiled. 'The others are enjoying themselves and I don't mind.'

He handed her a small parcel. 'A little something from me and Norma. It's a cruet set. I hope you like it.'

'Oh, just what we need,' she said, genuinely delighted at his thoughtfulness but declining to tell him that they had been given four sets already. 'Thanks ever so much. Look, Alec, I'm sorry . . .'

'Hey, don't worry, Kelly,' he gently interrupted, knowing instinctively what was troubling her. 'I know things are tight. I didn't expect an invite.' Especially not, he thought, with things the way they were between himself and Mickey. He glanced her up and down admiringly. 'You look nice.'

She smiled at the compliment. 'Thank you. Can I get yer anything?'

'No, I won't stop. I'm meeting Norma from work and taking her to the pictures. A little surprise for her. I just wanted to wish you the best, and also to tell you that she made enquiries and there's a couple of posts going if yer want to apply. One's in the stock room, the other behind the sweet counter. She says she'll put in a good word.'

For a moment Kelly felt disappointed then quickly chided herself. 'Thank Norma for me but it doesn't matter now.'

'Oh, yer going to stick with Lewis's, are you?'

'No, I'm going to be staying at home. Well, makes

154

sense really. Someone will have to look after the house and do the cooking, and I'm the obvious one.'

'Is that what you want, Kelly?'

'Yes,' she replied with conviction. 'Yes, it is.'

He was not entirely convinced but nodded all the same. 'Then I'm glad for you.'

A sudden loud good-humoured commotion erupted and Mickey's voice could be heard clearly above all the rest.

At the sound of it Alec realised he ought to be going. The last thing he wanted was for Mickey to discover he was here and cause a scene, not on Kelly's wedding day. He leaned over and pecked her lightly on the cheek. 'I'd better be off. Take care.'

She smiled. 'Yeah, you too, Alec.'

As she watched him depart she knew she would not be seeing so much of him in future. And with sadness it suddenly struck her that the occasional dropping in after work for a cuppa would stop now she was a married woman. That would not be the done thing, people would talk. And if Alec wanted to see Frank he could do that easily enough without coming to the house.

But she would miss their chats and knew Alec would too.

In the other room Glenda was in her element. Her dearest wish had come true. The wedding had been nothing like the one she had hoped for, but what did it matter? She was now Mrs Michael McCallan. She was so happy she felt she would burst.

Without warning a sharp stabbing pain shot through her stomach and she winced at its intensity. Fear suddenly seized her. Oh, God, her mind screamed. No, it can't be. Her monthly wasn't due for another couple of weeks. A familiar gnawing ache began to spread and she knew she was not mistaken. It was the excitement of it all, it had to be, that had brought her on early.

She had considered herself so clever, the way she had hidden her last period from her mother's beady eyes. That had taken careful planning and execution and she had hoped to do exactly the same thing again. But how on earth was she going to hide this from Mickey, on her wedding night, and she supposed to be pregnant?

'You all right, Glenda? Only yer've gone pale.'

She absently turned to face the woman addressing her. 'Yeah, yeah, I'm fine,' she replied just a shade too brightly. Her mind whirled frantically. She had to think of something, and quick, and couldn't do it surrounded by cackling women. 'I've got a headache coming, that's all. I think I'll go and get some fresh air.'

Stacking plates, Kelly noticed a clearly preoccupied Glenda disappearing out of the back door. Something was bothering her sister-in-law and Kelly was concerned for her.

She caught up with her leaning against the side of the outside privy. 'You okay?' she asked, laying a hand on Glenda's arm.

'Oh, it's nothing. Just a headache.'

Kelly knew by her worried expression that it was more than a headache. 'Don't lie to me, Glenda. Now what on earth is it?'

Glenda froze. She had no explanation ready. She hadn't expected this to happen just now. Then suddenly the solution came to her. It was blindingly simple and something that would gain her every sympathy, especially with it happening on such a momentous day. She turned slowly to face her sister-in-law.

'Oh, Kelly,' she whispered in a soft, distressed voice. 'Something's happening. I've got this terrible pain . . . I think I'm losing the baby!'

Chapter Fifteen

Mouth full of dolly pegs, arms filled with wet washing, Kelly fought against the strong breeze to pin the patched winceyette sheet to the line. It was the beginning of May and thankfully the weather was warming after a wet March and chilly April. Today promised to be a good drying one and she had set to extra early to tackle the ever-present pile of washing, hopeful that for once she would not have to cram it all to dry on the two ancient cradles spanning the kitchen ceiling, suffering the constant damp and condensation it created.

Then of course she had her other daily tasks to fit in plus the weekly washing of the windows and Cardinal polishing of the front door step, which if left undone for even a day or two would become the gossip of the neighbourhood. She sighed. Where did her day go to? She had assumed her role as full-time housewife, not now having to rush out to her job at the shop, would have meant she would have a little time left to herself, but she had been badly mistaken. Looking after a house and five adults – with all that entailed – was no easy matter. And not one of them lifted a finger to help her, not even Glenda.

The general consensus was that they all went out to work, bringing money into the house, and she didn't. It was only fair that all the housework should fall to her – as her contribution. She supposed in a way they were right, but it wouldn't have hurt for them to give her a hand, just now and again. Even making a cup of tea would be appreciated.

Why wasn't married life anything like the way it was portrayed in the bundles of tatty magazines Mickey, Rod or her father sometimes brought home? Housewives pictured in the articles or advertisement always looked as though they had just stepped out of the hairdresser's, perfectly made up, their fashionable clothes immaculate. Sometimes they wore tiny floral aprons that Kelly knew would offer nothing by way of protection when scrambling around in the coal house hoping to find some hidden lumps in the pile of slack. The women pictured never looked as though they tackled any chores of that nature, and judging by the happy, serene expression on their faces they never had any personal problems to deal with either.

Not like Kelly herself had.

She sighed heavily. She had realised immediately after her wedding that starting married life this way had been a mistake. Going out with someone was totally different from living with them. Getting used to Rod's ways and building firm foundations for a happy life together was nigh on impossible when sharing a house with another newly wed couple who barely spoke, the atmosphere between them so strained that one wrong word, a look or a gesture, had tempers erupting like a bomb going off. Added to which the estrangement between her father and Mickey showed no sign of healing.

Rod and she had no privacy except in the bedroom and even then she was terribly conscious of the presence of the others through the thin walls, which was putting a strain on their lovemaking.

She stopped what she was doing for a moment and stared absently into space. The act itself was not the thrilling, close experience she had thought it would be, and after just four weeks had settled into a routine of every Saturday night after they returned from the club – her weekly outing. Their wedding night had been a complete let down for her. Rod had been so drunk he hadn't even managed to make it to their bedroom before he had passed out, and when she had finally managed to get him to bed she had spent the night listening to his drunken snores. But then, she thought, she had hardly been in a receptive mood. Not after Glenda's bombshell.

All the women had flocked to her assistance when the announcement she was losing her baby had been made, and sympathy in abundance had been thrust upon her. The doctor had been called and she had been put to bed and had remained there, wallowing in her misery for three days. The men had attacked the beer barrel and when that had dried up, pockets had been emptied and another fetched from the pub. The whole episode had been a terrible strain to cope with, and not just because of the day it had happened on. It was Mickey's reaction that had been the worst thing.

When Kelly had pulled him aside and explained what was happening he had looked shocked but the relief that had also crossed his face had been unmistakable. Admittedly, she knew Mickey had not wanted this baby but all the same she felt his reaction was unforgivable, considering what his new wife was going through. And then openly to accuse her of never having been pregnant in the first place was inexcusable, especially when what had happened to Glenda was not uncommon, as the doctor had matter-of-factly told them. But worst of all to Kelly was that Mickey had spoken out in front of all at the wedding and it had been gossiped over ever since. Only now was the scandal just beginning to die down. But memories were long around these streets so it would never be totally forgotten.

Mickey's outburst had been put down to the shock

and his consumption of drink, but on reflection, when all the fuss had died down and Kelly had had time to think, she secretly wondered if her brother was right and Glenda had never been pregnant in the first place. Not that she had any concrete evidence, just little things that Glenda had said before they had married which now gradually filtered back to mind. But she thought better of pursuing these suspicions. The situation was bad enough as it was. She felt if she voiced her own doubts then the situation was bound to explode and there was no telling how Mickey would react.

The matter was best left alone. The only person who knew the truth was Glenda and she was sticking firmly to her own version of events no matter what.

Kelly mentally shook herself, realising she was standing in the middle of the yard, arms full of wet washing, a vacant look on her face. She hadn't the time for daydreams and hurriedly continued with her task. Regardless, her thoughts still whirled.

Would her relationship with Rod get better, she thought, when they managed to secure a house for themselves? She hoped so. Not that she was unhappy, just finding it hard to cope with all that was going on around her. Rod, though, seemed content enough. But then little had changed for him. He still went down the pub two or three evenings; Saturday night, after going to the football match, he would take her to the working-men's club on the Beatrice Road. All his mother had done for him, Kelly now tackled. The only change for Rod, apart from his address, was that Kelly now shared his bed. But then she supposed that was what it was like for all men. It was the women who had the biggest change to contend with.

Her thoughts were interrupted by a shout from over the wall. 'Oi, Kelly, me duck, can yer spare a drop of milk? Just 'til I get down the shop.'

Kelly parted the wet sheets to acknowledge her neighbour's request, hiding a smile at the comical picture Avril Mullins presented. A tiny woman, she was visible only from her chin upwards over the crumbling boundary wall. Her sparse head of mousy brown hair, which Kelly knew would be in dire need of a wash, was encased in a hurriedly tied turban-style scarf, three crooked pink rollers poking out of the front with long strands of hair springing up from them. Her face, prematurely aged from worry, was gazing at Kelly hopefully, awaiting her response.

She suddenly felt guilty for being disgruntled about her own situation. Compared to Avril's, her life was an easy one.

Despite being perfectly capable Avril's husband was hardly ever in work, and when he was any money earned went over the counter of the Charles Napier pub. Avril spent her whole life dodging people to whom she owed money and more times than not only managed to feed and clothe her children through the good nature of her neighbours.

Should Mickey and Rod ever find out just how much Kelly helped Avril out, all hell would break loose. But that prospect did not deter her. Avril was not a bad sort. Despite her lot she tried her best and her six children, whose boisterous cries now rang inside the house, were by no means the worst in the neighbourhood.

'I can only spare a drop . . .'

'Oh, that'll do,' Avril quickly cut in. 'It's just for the baby. As I said, it's only 'til I manage to go down the shop. And d'yer think I could push me sheets through yer mangle? That's if yer've finished using it yerself, 'a course.'

Kelly nodded. She knew Avril only washed the huge squares of thick calico when the weather meant they would dry the same day. She had nothing spare. Avril

161

did not have much at all, not even a bed. That had disappeared down the pawn, the same as most of her belongings had over a period of time, and she had never managed to get the money together to redeem them. They slept on an assortment of lumpy old mattresses that had been donated by the Salvation Army after hearing of their plight.

'Just let me finish pegging the washing out, Avril, then I'll get you the milk. And help yerself to the mangle. But be careful. I don't think it's in a very good mood today, it nearly took me hand off.'

Avril grinned. 'You wanna warn it, Kelly. Tell it in future that if it don't behave itself, you'll tek it up the rag and bone yard.'

'And I'd do just that,' Kelly laughingly replied, 'only what I'd make on the rusty old thing wouldn't be worth the effort of pushing it up there.'

Having finished pegging the washing, propping it up with a rotting wooden pole, she stood for a moment surveying her handiwork flapping wildly in the breeze, feeling an immense amount of pleasure that her whites were a blue-white and not the dingy grey that some lines held. She was just about to make her way back inside the house to fulfil Avril's request when the back gate opened.

'Glenda?' she exclaimed, astonished. 'What on earth are you doing home at this time?'

Standing just inside the gate, her bottom lip quivering, Glenda stared at her for several moments before bursting into a torrent of tears.

Kelly rushed over to her and put her arms around her. 'Come inside,' she ordered. 'I'll mash a cuppa.'

'I don't want a cuppa! Every time there's a crisis your bloody answer is to make a cuppa.' She noticed the hurt expression cloud Kelly's eyes. 'I'm sorry, I didn't mean that.'

Once seated at the table Kelly eyed Glenda worriedly. Her sister-in-law was still sobbing noisily into her handkerchief. 'What's happened?' asked Kelly.

She slowly raised her head. 'They sent me home 'cos I don't feel well.'

Kelly's face filled with concern. 'You do look pale. Where does it hurt?'

Glenda sniffed. 'Here,' she said, putting her hand on her heart. 'Me bloody heart's breaking, Kelly, that's what's wrong with me.'

She sighed. She didn't need to ask why. It was all due to the situation with Mickey.

'You can't carry on like this, Glenda. That's the third time yer've been sent home. They're only being lenient with you 'cos you've worked there so long, but if you ain't careful, you'll get the sack.'

'I don't care.'

'You won't be saying that when you've no money coming in. And I can't manage on less. I'm only just getting by on the housekeeping as it is. And getting another job when you've been given the sack wouldn't be easy.'

'Well, I'll bloody starve then. I don't care.'

Kelly shook her head. 'I'm sure you do.'

Glenda sniffed miserably. 'No, I don't.'

At this moment in time Glenda looked as if she wouldn't care if she were suddenly struck dead. She looked a mess. Her clothes, usually so neat and tidy, were crumpled; her fair hair lank. Despite recognising the possibility that Glenda had brought much of this on herself, Kelly did feel sorry for her. 'Look . . . er . . . have you tried . . .'

'I've tried everything, Kelly!' she erupted. 'Being sexy, crying, acting as though I ain't bothered. What else can I do?'

'Have you tried talking to him?'

163

'Talking! How the hell can you talk to someone who won't even look at yer? You've seen what he's like, Kelly. He can't even bear to be in the same room as me. We only sleep in the same bed 'cos there ain't nowhere else for him. Oh,' she wailed, 'what am I gonna do? I can't bear it, Kelly. I love him. I love him so much.'

She sighed. 'I know you do. Maybe too much.'

Glenda's eyes flashed. 'Wadda yer mean by that?'

Enough to trick him into marriage, thought Kelly. 'Nothing, Glenda, nothing. Look . . . the way I see it you'll just have to wait 'til our Mickey comes to his senses. And I'm sure he will, in time.' Though, she thought, how long that would be was anyone's guess. With a rift as wide as that between them, Kelly privately doubted whether Mickey and Glenda would ever sort themselves out.

Her sister-in-law sniffed, wiping her eyes. 'You think he will?'

She nodded, hoping she looked more positive than she felt.

'You won't tell Mickey that I was sent home, will yer?'

''Course I won't.'

Glenda smiled gratefully and got to her feet.

'Where are you going?'

'I dunno. Just out. I might go for a walk around the town.'

'Oh, I thought you might give me a hand here?'

Glenda grimaced. 'What, with the housework? You are unfeeling sometimes, Kelly. Here's me with all I've got on my plate, and you think scrubbing floors is going to make me feel better!'

Kelly stared at her, then shrugged her shoulders. 'It was just a thought.'

Glenda left, slamming the back door behind her.

It was only several moments after she had left that Kelly suddenly remembered she needed her weekly

164

supply of vegetables from the market which her sister-in-law could have collected, saving her the trip. She supposed she could shop at the local greengrocer's, but vegetables were slightly cheaper from the market as were butter and sugar at Lipton's or the Home and Colonial.

Like everyone else, Kelly had to watch the pennies. She would be glad when rationing finally came to an end, though when that would be was anyone's guess. The war had been over for more than three years and there was still no sign of rationing easing on many everyday items. When it was, though, she would have a lot more food to choose from and use to make tastier meals. Maybe then the lot she cooked for might cease their criticising. Not her father, though. He seemed content with whatever she put before him.

An hour or so later, weighed down by her load, Kelly ploughed her way through the crowds of other shoppers to stand on the pavement outside the Turkish Cafe in order to gather her thoughts, work out if she had everything she needed before she made her way home. A rich, aromatic aroma of fresh coffee filled her nostrils and she breathed deeply in appreciation, her mouth watering. She was hungry, not having taken time to make herself any lunch. She turned and gazed into the window at all the cakes and delicacies laid out invitingly in order to entice people in, then turned away abruptly, knowing she hadn't the spare money for even a cup of tea.

Having decided that if she hadn't purchased all she had set out to then it didn't matter anyway as she had not the strength to carry more, she eased the bags more comfortably and made to set off. As she did so she collided with somebody coming the other way.

'I'm very sorry,' she apologised.

'You should watch where you're going!'

The male voice was harsh. Kelly felt unjustly so. She

turned, frowning, to see who it had come from.

A man was entering the Turkish Cafe, his arm around a woman's waist, guiding her inside. Tall and erect, he was very smartly dressed and although she could only see his profile, Kelly could tell by the way he held his head how arrogant he was. Automatically her glance fell to the woman by his side, just catching sight of her as she disappeared through the door.

Kelly's mouth fell open. It was Norma Alderman, Alec's wife. She frowned, perturbed. There was nothing really wrong in a married woman going for a bite to eat in a busy cafe with a man. After all, he could be anyone. A work colleague. Just a male friend. What caused Kelly's concern was the way the man's arm had encircled Norma's waist. It had not been just to guide her, it had been an intimate, proprietorial gesture. Kelly did know the difference.

Distributing her heavy bags more evenly, she pushed the incident from her mind and plodded her way home.

Chapter Sixteen

Mickey was consumed with anger and bitterness. He felt cheated and trapped, having been forced into a marriage he had not wanted. And the reason for it all no longer applied – if it ever had in the first place, which he gravely doubted. At this moment he hated Glenda, the sight of her, even the thought of her. He couldn't bear to touch her. She had lied to him. Despite her vehement denials, he knew in his guts she had. But he had no proof.

Throwing down the stub of his Player's full-strength he slammed his boot against it, then reached inside his shabby donkey jacket, pulled out a packet and took another. He lit it while shielding his hand from the wind, afterwards flicking the match into the gutter. Fuelling his anger further was the fact that six weeks had gone by since their meeting and he still had not had word from Isaac Greenbaum, and that above all else was causing him worry. What if the man had changed his mind? What if he had decided not to take the risk of using Mickey? What if he never got another chance like this again? He sighed with frustration. One thing was for certain: if something did not happen in that direction soon he would crack under the strain.

Lounging back against the wall, he eyed the activity around him. For once his five colleagues were rushing around absorbed in their work – something for which he had no inclination or desire. If truth be told he wouldn't give a monkey's if Smiggy himself arrived and gave him the sack. But then, he could not afford to let that happen. His paltry wage was the only thing keeping him solvent and that was only by stringent management.

Thank God Glenda was earning! He dreaded to think how his financial status would be at the moment if he had to keep her as well as himself. And Rod was driving him mad. The man was like a leech, sticking to him like glue, constantly wanting to know what he was doing and where he was going, always dropping into the conversation the fact that he was now 'family', and should therefore be included in everything. It was bad enough working with him; there was no escaping him at all now they lived in the same house. If he did not back off, Mickey knew he would not be able to control his temper for much longer. To him, Rod had outlived his usefulness. There was no place for him where Mickey was headed.

A great urge to pay a visit to Latimer Street and relieve his pent up frustration swamped him. But he knew he couldn't. For six long weeks he had lived on his nerves, constantly peering over his shoulder for fear Isaac Greenbaum was keeping an eye on him, checking if he was doing as he'd been warned, seeing if he came up to scratch. Ever conscious of that he dare not put a foot wrong for fear of the consequences.

'Oi, Mickey!'

The shout made him jump.

'What the fuck you playing at?' Shouting across at him was Jim Bains, or 'Izabout' as the men called him behind his back because his favourite saying was: 'Izabout time you lot realised that yer paid ter do a job. This ain't a holiday camp, yer know.'

Izabout, a heavily built, squat man, with sparse grey-ing hair, long strands of which were plastered down over the top of his bald pate, was the Cody, the man in charge of the gang. The harassed man certainly had his work cut out trying to supervise the motley crew he felt he had been lumbered with; a crew who moaned continuously, threatening to cause strikes over their pay, the length of their tea breaks, dinner break, the weight of the bins, the dangerous stuff people put in them with no thought for the harm it could cause, the weather . . . anything in fact that was worth grumbling about, especially the attitudes of the Council hierarchy. But at the end of the day it was all hot air. They were afraid to carry out their threats in case it resulted in the loss of their livelihood. But loss of livelihood or not, like all the other bin men their main priority was not doing what they were paid for but scrabbling instead for what pickings were to be had on the side.

At night Izabout would profusely thank the Lord if he had managed to get through the day without any incidents, which did not very often apply.

As he ran over to Mickey, a village idiot would have had no trouble discerning from his expression that he was not a happy man.

Mickey nonchalantly righted himself. 'I was just having a fag,' he said defensively.

'You only had a break half an hour ago. It's about time you . . .'

'Yeah, yeah,' Mickey cut in '. . . realise I'm being paid to do a job.'

'Cheeky sod! One of these days your gob'll be the undoing of you. Now look, Smiggy's on the war path. I'm expecting him ter sneak up on us any minute. I've heard he's got a new Cody with 'im, showing him the ropes. And a fine kettle of fish it'd be, if he caught you idling.'

Mickey grunted. 'Who's the new Cody then?'

Izabout shrugged his shoulders. 'Dunno. I think it's

one of the bin men from one of the other gangs that's been made up. Anyway, one thing's fer sure – that'll never happen to you, will it? Not the way you carry on.'

'What's that supposed ter mean?'

'You know fine well. Apart from everything else, I can't remember the last time I saw you empty a bin.'

Mickey couldn't remember either and decided it would be better to get off that subject. 'What's he on the war path for this time?'

'Huh, well . . .' Izabout puffed out his barrel chest. 'Rumour has it that he's bin told by the Council officials he's to lose some bodies. The depot's overmanned apparently, though God knows how they worked that out. I can hardly manage with the men I've got to cover the number of collections I'm s'posed ter handle. I'd never manage with any less. Bloody officials! They should try doing our job. I'd bet a month's wages they'd not last a day.' He paused thoughtfully and eyed Mickey. 'You must be due your National Service? Rod Collins an' all by my reckoning. Yer must both be nudging twenty-one.'

Mickey grunted. 'I can't speak fer Rod, but you ain't getting rid of me that easy.'

'Oh! I know yer a slippery customer, Mickey McCallan, but I can't see yer getting out of that one. Better than you have tried and failed.'

'Wanna bet?'

Izabout's eyes narrowed interestedly. 'How much?'

'Five bob.'

He pondered a moment. 'Nah,' he said finally. 'Five shillin' is a lot of money to me. And I know you, McCallan. You've probably got it all worked out down to the last full stop. Come on then, tell me yer grand scheme?'

Mickey smiled secretively. 'Sorry, I didn't hear yer?'

'I said . . .' His eyes suddenly widened, impressed.

'Why, yer cocky bugger! I see what you're up to. Playing it deaf, ain't yer?'

Mickey's smile broadened. 'Doctor's sick of giving me drops. He reckons I must have burst me ear-drum. Deaf as a door post, I am, in one ear. And I wouldn't be surprised if me other ain't going either, by the pain it causes me.'

Izabout shook his head. 'I give up wi' you. When He dished out the cunning, He gave you the lot.'

'Well, if Alderman can do it, why can't I?'

'Alderman? Alec, yer mean? But he's summat genuinely wrong wi' him. Summat ter do wi' his heart as far as I remember.'

'Huh! Does he look sick to you?'

'I know it ain't exactly life threatening but it wa' enough to get him turned down. But that ain't the point, Mickey. I know for a fact Alderman wanted to do his bit. It was the officials that turned him down.' Izabout narrowed his eyes. 'Just what is it you have against that man, anyway?'

'That's my business,' hissed Mickey.

Indignantly, Izabout thrust out his chest. 'Well, clearing the bins in this street is mine. Now, you might not be bothered about yer job but I am. Get over to the cart and rake down the coals before the next bins are emptied.'

Mickey scowled indignantly. 'Eh? That ain't my bloody job. That's Little Harry's.'

'Now you listen here. I'm the Cody, and if I tell yer to do it, I mean it. Little Harry is doing what you should be and that's collecting bins. Or don't you want this bloody job?'

Mickey's lips tightened and he sniffed disdainfully. No, in truth he didn't want this bloody job, but at the moment he couldn't afford to lose it.

'Right,' said Izabout. 'I'm off to lend the others a

hand. I wa' supposed to be paying the boss of that factory down the road a visit as he's asked me to price shifting some scrap iron, but I ain't gonna tek the chance today. It'd be just my luck for Smiggy to catch me.' He smirked at the look on Mickey's face. 'See, you ain't that clever, a' yer, 'cos yer missed that one. Fair bit of money, I reckon, to be made in the scrap he's got hoarded in his yard.' Grinning from ear to ear, he ran back across the road.

Mickey's mood turned even uglier. All he could think of was what that scrap might have been worth to him. But there was no point in getting angry over missing out. He was supposed to be keeping himself on the straight and narrow. He had done it this long; he had no choice but to stick it out for the duration now.

'A' you McCallan?'

He jumped for the second time that morning and spun round to find a nattily dressed man standing behind him. His thick black wavy hair was plastered down with Brylcreem. Under his sharp pointed nose was a pencil-thin moustache. From the corner of his mouth hung a hand-rolled cigarette. His skin was pale and pitted with acne marks. His small grey eyes shifty and constantly darting.

Mickey did not like the look of him. 'Who wants to know?' he snapped warily.

The shifty eyes narrowed in annoyance. 'Don't piss me about. A' you McCallan or not?'

His arrogance had no effect on Mickey who nonchalantly leaned back against the wall and folded his arms. 'And I asked who wanted to know?'

The newcomer quickly realised that the man before him was not easily intimidated and he hadn't the time to mess about. He'd been told by his boss to be sharp, and when his boss gave an order it was meant to be obeyed. 'Look, I've a message for him, so if you ain't him can yer tell me where I can find him?'

'A message? Who from?' He scowled menacingly and grabbed the man by his lapels, yanking him close. 'Now who's pissing who about! I asked who from? Answer me or else.'

The little man looked terrified. 'Mr Greenbaum,' he stuttered.

Mickey's heart thumped wildly. He thrust the man from him. About bloody time, he thought. 'I'm McCallan so gimme the message.'

The man curled his lip. 'Why didn't you just effing say so in the first place? Mr Greenbaum wants ter speak to yer.'

'When?'

'Now. He's in the car parked round the corner.'

Mickey drew several deep breaths to calm and prepare himself, then brushed himself down – which since he was covered in a fine coating of ashes from the heaps thrown in the 'fryer' was a total waste of time – raised his head, then with a purposeful stride set off in the direction he'd been directed.

The black, shiny car was waiting as indicated. Mickey scowled, impressed and outclassed. It was a Daimler. He'd have one of those when he was rich. In fact, he'd have two. As he approached it the door opened. Sauntering now, not wishing to appear anxious, he took his cue and slipped inside.

Disdainfully Isaac looked him up and down. Mickey was fully aware the great man was not pleased by the state of his attire which threatened to soil the leather seats of his immaculate car.

'I am at work,' Mickey said defensively.

Isaac gave no response. Long moments passed as he slowly lit a cigar. Only when satisfied it was firmly alight did he turn his attention back to his guest. 'Still interested?'

Mickey nodded. 'Yeah, I'm still interested,' he said casually. 'Just need to know when.'

'Tomorrow night.'

'Eh!' Mickey gulped, his eyes wide. 'Bit sudden, if yer don't mind me saying so, Mr Greenbaum?'

'Sudden? How long do you want? You've had six weeks to think about it. A' you trying to tell me you haven't got a plan?'

'Oh, no, not at all, Mr Greenbaum,' he lied. Every moment of the last six weeks, all his thoughts had centred on the money he was going to earn, how he was going to spend it and what he'd do after that. Thoughts of making a plan had not even entered his head since he'd presumed he would have time to formulate one after the next meeting. 'I just expected a bit more warning, that's all.'

Isaac's face flamed angrily. 'For fuck's sake, boy, you're torching a bloody factory, not planning a bank robbery. Any idiot can strike a match. All you need to know is where to fling the bloody thing. If you don't want this job say so, I've others who'd jump at the chance for what I'm prepared to pay.' He scrutinised Mickey scathingly. 'Maybe I made a mistake with you, boy? Maybe you just ain't got what it takes after all.'

Mickey felt the heat of embarrassment creeping up his neck, beads of sweat forming on his brow and beginning to run from his armpits. Suddenly the enormity of what he was about to undertake overwhelmed him. He was scared. Terrified, in fact. But there was no turning back now. He could not, for any reason, lose face with the likes of Isaac Greenbaum. He would become a laughing stock and never get another chance like this to move in the circles he wished to enter.

Isaac's influence spread far and should Mickey let him down, no one else would consider him. All he could ever hope to do was spend the rest of his life selling his bits and pieces in the hope that what money he made would finance a few extra pints at the pub, a shilling or two for a bet on the dogs, or a new suit now and again. No, he had dreamed and planned too long now to settle for that way of life.

Besides, the money from this job was already spent in his mind. And added to that was the fact that Isaac would want his fifty pounds back if the job didn't go ahead and the likelihood of Mickey's coming up with that was zero. He did not relish in the slightest the thought of what would happen to him should he back out now. He couldn't see Greenbaum smiling as he waved him goodbye. No, he had no choice in this matter. He was in over his head and had been from the moment he had walked into that snooker club six weeks before.

He took a deep breath, conscious of Isaac's eyes upon him and the fact that the two men sitting in the front of the car were witnessing every word, one of them being that nasty little termite who had delivered the message.

'Just tell me where,' said Mickey gruffly.

Greenbaum smirked. 'I knew you wouldn't let me down, lad. Bradwick's. You know where that is?'

Mickey knew. Bradwick's was a big hosiery factory which backed on to the canal, only streets away from where he lived. Glenda worked there. It was a bit too close to home for Mickey's liking, the night watchman being the father of one of the mates he drank with down the pub. But he did not let this concern show. 'I know where it is.'

Isaac nodded. 'There's a door round the back of the loading bay. It won't be locked properly. That's your entry point. The rest is up to you. Just make sure you gut the main building. Understand?'

Mickey nodded. 'When do I get me money?'

Isaac's lip curled. 'You'll get what's due when the job's

done.' He signalled his driver who had been watching the proceedings closely through the mirror. The man leaped out of the car, rushed around and opened the door.

Mickey got out.

The driver returned to his seat and the car sped away, leaving him staring after it, thoughts whirling. A loud shout erupted behind him. He jumped, ears pricked. The voice had been Izabout's. More voices rang out. One was Rod's, the other a voice he could not immediately recognise. Despite his confusion Mickey sensed something was terribly wrong. He spun on his heel and belted back around the corner. He froze at the sight that met him. Thick, grey smoke was billowing from the 'fish fryer'.

Izabout roughly grabbed his arm. 'Where the hell a' you bin? This is all your fault. I told you to rake down the ashes. A dozen or more bins 'ave been emptied inside.' His eyes blazed angrily. 'I'll . . .'

'What's going on?'

Izabout and Mickey spun round. Pedalling furiously towards them on his Corporation issue push bike was Smiggy; several yards behind him another man came running. Mickey squinted hard then frowned his recognition. It was Alec Alderman. What the devil was he doing here? He had no time to think further as Smiggy arrived, leaping off his bike which fell to the ground with a crash. He stared disbelievingly at the dustcart, glared at Izabout, then at Mickey, back to the dustcart, then back to Izabout. 'Who . . . what . . . how . . .' he stuttered, flailing his arms wildly.

A breathless Alec arrived. He hurriedly sized up the situation and, realising Smiggy was in a complete flap, quickly took charge. 'Organise some water,' he demanded of Mickey. 'Knock on doors. Get buckets. I'll round up the men. We'll form a chain and . . .'

The mere presence of Alec Alderman was enough to incense Mickey. Alec ordering him about ignited instant fury. He pushed him hard on the shoulder. 'Just who the hell d'yer think you are? I don't tek orders from you.'

Alec stiffened. 'There ain't time for this, Mickey. If we don't get that fire out, the cart could explode. There's gasoline in the engine. Don't stand there like an idiot, man, do as I say!'

Mickey pushed him again, harder this time. Alec stumbled backwards. 'Like hell I'll take orders from you! Just who the fuck d'you think you are?'

Alec's fists clenched tightly. 'For God's sake, man, if it makes any difference, I've just been promoted to a Cody. Now this ain't the time to be airing grudges,' he warned, 'we need to get that fire out.'

Mickey stared. '*You! You're* the new Cody? And just who did yer bribe to get that job?'

Knuckles white with strain now, Alec fought to keep calm. 'The water, Mickey.'

Flames were shooting from the sides of the cart, black smoke pouring, fanned by the wind. Stunned residents emerged from houses, babies screamed, passers-by congregated. The rest of the gang, returning with their loads, looked on in horror. Bins were dropped, contents scattering, as they all raced over, shouting in confusion. The disorderly gang stared stupefied at the cart.

Smiggy suddenly regained his senses. 'Do as he says,' he spat at Mickey, then spun round to Izabout. 'Get down the telephone box and ring the fire brigade. Quick, man, quick!'

Izabout ran.

Smiggy rushed across the road to usher the crowd back to a safe distance.

Alec made to run across and organise the men but realised Mickey was still glaring at him. 'Fer Christ's sake, man, will yer move it?' he shouted. 'The cart is right next to some houses, it could set fire to them any minute.'

But Mickey was too incensed to consider all the possible dangers connected with the fire; or the fact that his carelessness had been the cause of it. All his thoughts were centred on the man before him, the one with the audacity to give him orders. A man he'd sooner spit on than look at. His fury erupted. Before Alec could defend himself, Mickey flung back his arm and smashed him hard on the chin.

Blood spurting from a deep gouge on his lip, Alec reeled backwards. Another blow caught him on his cheek. Provoked beyond endurance, despite himself Alec's temper flared and he leaped at Mickey. They toppled to the pavement, rolling over and over.

In the distance a fire engine was audible. It skidded around the corner, screeched to a halt. Firemen spilled out. Hoses were connected.

With the fire under control, the crowd's attention was drawn to the two men rolling in the gutter. In seconds a ring had formed and loud cheers spurred them on.

A bloody-faced Mickey, having overpowered Alec, sat astride him and had one fist raised ready to strike again when he was roughly grabbed by his shoulders and dragged backwards. A face that was purple with rage was pushed close to his. It was Smiggy. 'Yer sacked! Now get outta me sight.'

Struggling free from two of his mates off the round, Mickey stumbled upright. 'He fucking started it!' he cried, pointing at Alec still prostrate in the road.

Shaking now, Smiggy wagged a finger. 'Yer sacked, I said. You . . . you, McCallan, have bin n'ote but trouble since the first day yer started. I've just bin waiting fer a chance like this. Now clear off. You can collect yer cards on Friday.'

Suddenly Mickey wanted to laugh. It was ironic. Here

he was, getting the sack for innocently starting a fire. Tomorrow he was being paid handsomely for starting one on purpose. Sneering, he threw back his head. 'You can stuff yer poxy job right up yer arse! But if yer sack me, yer sack him too.'

Rod grabbed his arm. 'Come on, Mickey, leave it be.'

Mickey turned on him. 'Fuck off out of it!' He spun back to face Smiggy. 'Well?'

Smiggy's fury boiled over. 'Get him out of here,' he screeched to the men. 'Before I do for 'im.'

'Come on, Mickey,' Izabout coaxed. 'You've done enough damage today. Get off home before there's a murder committed.'

'I'm going,' Mickey spat. 'But I tell yer now,' he cried, wagging a fist at Smiggy, 'if he ain't sacked too, then you'll know what trouble is. And,' he snarled, 'that's no warning, it's a threat.'

Pushing Rod aside, he turned sharply on his heel and stalked off, his head held high.

Several hours later, nursing a painful black eye, swollen grazed chin and several tender bruises on his upper torso, Alec sat facing Smiggy across his desk in the small site hut at the back of the depot.

'I'm sorry, Alderman, but I've got no choice. Fighting is fighting, no matter what the circumstances. It's against the rules.' Smiggy sniffed loudly. 'It's a sorry day. I had high hopes for you. My job could've bin yours when I retired. But as it is . . . well, I just want yer to know I did try.'

Alec nodded solemnly. 'I appreciate that, Mr Smith.' He rose, holding out a bruised, swollen hand which Smiggy accepted.

Without another word, Alec took his leave.

Leaning back in his chair, a troubled Ernest Smith clasped his hands. He was not a sentimental man.

179

Normally the welfare of the men under his charge gave him no sleepless nights. But he was actually sorry to see Alec go. He was one of only a handful of loyal, trustworthy men employed on the bins. A reliable sort. It was a crying shame that something like this should have happened to him. Still, he had no time to dwell on it. Smiggy himself had other problems to deal with. He was still fighting to keep his own job. In charge overall meant he was ultimately responsible for any incident that happened on the bin rounds, big or small, and the blame rested with him.

A reluctant smirk twitched at the corners of his mouth. But one thing he was glad about: at long last he had gotten rid of that smarmy, good for nothing McCallan. And if anything could compensate him for all that had happened, and the possible consequences for himself, then it was getting rid of Mickey.

Chapter Seventeen

Rod opened the bedroom door and looked across at Kelly, sitting on their bed gazing absently out of the window. She turned her head, smiling wearily.

'I wondered where you were,' he said, advancing towards her. 'I'm famished. I fancy a sandwich.'

And you're expecting me to make it for you, she thought. She took a deep breath. 'There's bread in the bin and cheese in the larder. And if yer mashing a cuppa, I wouldn't say no to one.'

He eyed her in surprise. 'Oh,' he muttered. 'Oh, well, in that case I might pop out for a pint.' He looked concerned. 'Why are you sitting up here on your own?'

'I can't stand the atmosphere, that's why.'

'What atmosphere?'

Kelly's eyes flashed. 'Oh, come on, Rod, are you deaf and blind or summat? Our Mickey is unbearable. He's ready to explode. It's just like waiting for a volcano to erupt.'

'Well,' Rod said defensively, 'we have to make allowances. He has lost his job.'

'And whose fault was that?'

'It weren't just Mickey's. It takes two to make a fight.'

She shook her head. 'And you're trying to tell me it was Alec that started it? That I won't believe. Anyway, it was Mickey's fault the cart caught fire. Negligence like that could have got him sacked, without the fight.'

Rod sighed deeply. Kelly was right.

'Anyway, why are you defending him? You always side with our Mickey. You could witness him committing a murder and still plead his innocence. Why d'you do that, Rod?'

He shrugged his shoulders. 'He's me mate.'

Kelly shook her head, exasperated. 'I give up,' she uttered. Secretly, though, she admired her husband's loyalty, even though she felt it was misplaced. 'I'm just worried what he's gonna do for a job now. All he's ever known is the bins. Still I'm sure he'll come up with summat. I've never known him stuck on 'ote for long. Look, I'll be down in a minute to make you your supper. Has me dad come back from the allotment yet?'

He shook his head.

'Good. At least he ain't daft. He obviously knows it's best to stay out. What about Glenda?'

'Still round me mam's, I think.'

'Ah, well, that means there's only me and you to pussy foot around Mickey. But I tell you, I'm getting sick of his moods. The sooner we get a house of our own the better. You have put our names down, haven't you?'

Rod sheepishly lowered his head.

'Oh, Rod. You promised me you would.'

'I just ain't found the time. But anyway, what's all the rush? We're happy here, ain't we?'

'Apart from our Mickey, yes. But all married couples need a place of their own.'

'Me mam never had when she got married. She lived with me gran and grandad 'til they passed away.'

'People did that in the olden days. I want a place of our own, Rod. I want to make it a nice home to bring up our kids. Is that too much to ask?'

He shrugged. 'No, I suppose not. But I still don't see what all the rush is about.'

'Putting our names down is only a start. Getting

allocated a house will take months. Look, I'll go up the housing meself. After all, I've got plenty of time, ain't I?' She sighed. 'I'm sorry, I didn't mean to be sarcastic, but it seems I have to do everything. I thought married life was sharing things?'

He sat down on the bed next to her. 'It is. We do. Look, I'll go up the housing tomorrow after work.'

'You will?'

'I promise.'

She smiled tenderly. 'Thanks,' she said, planting a warm kiss on his cheek. She got to her feet. 'I'll make you that sandwich. But if you'd sooner go for a pint, I don't mind.'

'You don't?'

She shook her head. 'I've some socks to darn. You'll find a couple a' bob in me purse on the mantel.' She had been going to use it to get her hair cut but didn't begrudge giving it to Rod. Pat a few doors up would trim her hair if Kelly asked her nicely. It wouldn't be an expert job but it would tidy her up.

Downstairs, for the umpteenth time, Mickey fixed his eyes on the tin clock ticking merrily on the mantel. It was ten minutes to eight. Hours to go yet. The strain of waiting was driving him mad, as well as the increasing fear building inside him. He paced the room again, stopped by the table, picked up his tin of Old Holborn and rolled himself a cigarette, finding the task a welcome break from thoughts of the one he was about to undertake.

Everything was ready. Well, there wasn't much to prepare. Just a two-gallon container of paraffin he had hidden in a thick clump of bushes alongside the canal not far from Bradwick's and a box of matches, household size just to be on the safe side. Dry rags to get the fire going would be in plentiful supply, it being a hosiery factory. And a change of clothes so he could get rid of the ones he wore to do the job, just in case they should reveal any evidence.

He drew deeply on his cigarette. He could make an immensely profitable living from arson. Outlays were minimal. Enter the factory, spread the paraffin around, light a match, leave the same way you came in. He smirked. Piece of cake. All he wished was that the hours would hurry by until it was time for him to go.

At twenty past eleven he made his way up the stairs and lay still in the darkness, listening to the sound of Glenda's gentle snores. She had been at her mother's all night and on arriving had gone straight to bed. He was glad of that. At least he hadn't had to contend with her reproachful glances all night while he concentrated on the task in hand.

Bile rose within him. How he had come to hate the woman lying on the very edge of the bed beside him! Even in sleep she was careful not to touch him accidentally, fearful of annoying him. She, like the others, thought that in time everything would die down and things would return to the way they were before. But matters could never be as they had been. Especially not after tonight.

As soon as he received his money he was leaving. He would rent a little flat on the other side of town. Start living life as it was meant to be lived. He couldn't wait.

At just gone twelve he rose stealthily, careful not to make a sound. Several floorboards creaked. He froze, listening. Nothing stirred. Not even Glenda. He smiled as he let himself out of the bedroom, easing shut the door.

As she heard the door click shut, Glenda opened her eyes, lifted her head and stared across the room. Where was Mickey off to? What was he up to? Sighing softly, she lay down again and closed her eyes. But she did not sleep. She just lay waiting for his return.

In the room next door, Rod yawned loudly and eased his arm from around Kelly's waist. He was too restless to sleep. He knew why. He was worried about money. His dire lack of it. Before he turned over he gazed at his sleeping wife, smiling tenderly. Married life wasn't so bad, he thought. Kelly moaned a bit but then, according to his mates at the pub and the lads at work, all wives grumbled, it was a woman's trait. Especially Sniffy Eddie's wife, she sounded a right nagging bitch. To be honest, Kelly had right on her side.

He should really give her a hand now and again. But not with the dishes or the cleaning up or the shopping or the clothes washing. That was woman's work. He could offer to make her a cup of tea now and again. He wouldn't mind that so long as he didn't let it slip at work, not fancying the resulting ridicule. And he supposed he could take her out more often. Not on a Monday. Monday was darts night. And Wednesday was snooker. That only left Friday, because he took her to the club on Saturday for a game of bingo. But Friday was out really because that was the night kept free for jobs, or had been. But while Mickey had been in his recent frame of mind, Rod had gone out with his mates. He was back where he started. Ah, well, he thought. Kelly seemed happy enough so why change his routine?

He sighed contentedly. He'd made a good choice in marrying her. No raving beauty but she was pretty enough for him. He knew other men envied him. Her cooking was improving, if not yet quite as good as his mother's. She kept the house clean, and his clothes washed and ironed. But best of all it was nice to share his bed with her and he especially enjoyed their love-making on a Saturday night after they returned from the club. His smile broadened. Yes, things could be worse.

The only thing that bothered him was that he still had not become Mickey's right hand man as he had hoped. If anything that prospect looked more remote. And just lately Mickey hadn't, to his knowledge, done any jobs which puzzled Rod. It was quite out of character for Mickey. Rod had known him now for nearly five years and never during that time had he known Mickey not to be planning or executing some job or other. This was something to which he couldn't fathom the answer. If he didn't know better, he would have said Mickey was keeping a low profile, just like hoodlums did in films. No, he was letting his thoughts run away with him. Being stupid. Real life wasn't like that. Not in these streets at any rate.

Still, that state of affairs was bound to change now Mickey had lost his job. He would need money. Rod would approach him tomorrow, ask him very casually what he intended to do next. Drop gentle hints. Yes, that sounded good. Prompt him to tackle another church roof or similar. Rod desperately needed money himself. Payment was overdue on his suit and he hadn't the money. He sighed. If Mickey wouldn't do it with him, he'd have to do a job by himself. He had been on enough now with Mickey to know what to do. As he explored this possibility he smiled slowly. Maybe that was the answer? Go it alone. That way he wouldn't be so reliant on his brother-in-law. A surge of hope flooded through him and he smiled. One way or another his fortunes would soon change for the better.

Feeling more optimistic he bent over, kissed Kelly lightly on the cheek and snuggled back down, pulling her close, moulding his body against hers.

He was just about to drift off when a sound reached him. Half sitting up, he frowned. It had sounded like the back door shutting. Was it someone coming in or going out? It could be Frank returning. He had still been out when they had gone to bed. Rod strained harder to hear. Surely that was the back gate opening? He leaped out of bed and stepped across to the window, tweaking aside the yellowing paper blind. He peered into the darkness. There was someone by the back gate. They were opening it now. It was Mickey! Where was he going at this time of night. Rod grimaced. There was only one way to satisfy his curiosity. He would follow him.

Dressed only in his underpants, he snatched up his shirt and trousers, discarded earlier on the chair, grabbed his shoes on the way out and was standing the other side of the gate in less than a minute. Breathing hard, he peered up and down the jitty and just caught sight of Mickey disappearing around the corner.

Dressing on the move, keeping a safe distance, Rodney proceeded to follow him.

Frank had not realised he had fallen asleep until he toppled forward out of the old wicker chair. Having finished his tasks for the night, he had only sat down in the allotment shed to while away the time until he felt it safe to return home. It was a sad state of affairs, he thought, when the moods of your son dictated the way you lived. If he'd known what was in store he would never have agreed they should all live, for however long, in the tiny house in Tewkesbury Street; a house that had once been a happy one, ringing with laughter, filled with joy. But that was before . . .

He sighed sadly as he righted himself, rubbing his head which was smarting from the bump it had received as he had hit the rotting floorboards. If only Flora was still here. Her wisdom was what was needed to sort out this dreadful mess. She would have known how to tackle Mickey, find the right words, make him see reason and put matters right. But Flora wasn't here. The task fell to Frank now.

Humiliation swept through him. What a disaster he had made of it all. What he should have done was insisted Mickey listen to him, and thrashed out the problem straight away. Instead he had retreated, waited for his son to come to his senses. He thought he had been right to handle it this way. But he hadn't. His inaction had only resulted in a widening of the void, and a worsening of the situation. Now Mickey controlled them all. He was making all their lives a misery. Frank knew this situation couldn't go on. There was Kelly and Rod and Glenda to consider too.

He grimaced hard. It was about time he resumed his role as head of the house. Over the last weeks he had taken great steps towards dealing with his grief and was holding down a job, something he had thought he'd never achieve again. Mr Bundy had told him several times how pleased he was with him. Tackling Mickey would be hard but it shouldn't be beyond him now. All he had to do was work out what he was going to say and be firm about it, stand no nonsense. Sighing, he rubbed his hand back and forth across the stubble on his chin. But first he had to build up his courage.

He rose stiffly, felt his way to the door, opened it and looked out. The night was a dark one, no moon showing through the thick bank of clouds. It was late, near on twelve, he deduced. He took several deep breaths to clear his head. He needed to go home, get some proper sleep. He had a job he needed to rise for at six in the morning.

Securing the shed door behind him, he turned up the collar of his jacket, dug his hands into his pockets and slowly began the walk home.

Mickey found the door just as Isaac had told him he would. But it hadn't been easy to open. It had not been locked but was swollen from damp and disuse. In the

188

blackness of the night he'd had to hunt round for a discarded strip of metal, painstakingly wedge it into the gap and lever it open. He was not concerned about being discovered by the night-watchman. Mickey had already checked on him, relieved to see the man slumped in a chair sound asleep inside his hut, two empty beer bottles lying by his feet on the floor.

From a safe distance Rod had watched, anger mounting as a realisation struck him of just what Mickey was up to. He was robbing a factory! He could have told Rod. Brought him in on the deal. Mickey knew how much he needed the money. But what perplexed Rod most was what could possibly be in the container Mickey had carried through the door. In the darkness Rod could not tell what it held. As soon as he felt it safe he tiptoed across to the door and slipped inside after his brother-in-law.

Mickey stared around him. Although his eyes had become accustomed to the dark he was still having difficulty getting his bearings. He had entered the main workshop and before him, disappearing off into the distance, stretched five long rows of sewing, overlocking, button and embroidery machines, long metal rods holding cones of cottons protruding eerily. Beside each machine was a metal wagon filled with assorted cut outs in varying stages of completion. The small windows of the old Victorian factory were at ceiling height and all the walls were shelved and filled with rolls of fabric and boxes containing all manner of buttons, zips, hooks, eyes and press studs.

Mickey smiled. Ideal conditions to fuel a fire.

But where best to start it?

He stood for a moment and pondered.

Rod meanwhile, thinking he was trailing Mickey, had taken a wrong turning and found himself inside a well-filled stock room. His eyes ranged around and immediately his instinct for thievery took over, all thoughts of Mickey and what he was doing here dispelled. Soon a pile of items was building on the floor – jumpers, dresses, trousers and skirts. As many as he thought he could carry. He was overcome with excitement. There would be no shortage of buyers for any of this quality stuff.

Searching around, Mickey found the materials store. It was right next to the main workshop. He sized it up and nodded. This was the place. He turned to fetch over the container of paraffin, then paused and frowned. Something was bothering him but he wasn't sure what. He rubbed his chin. Something didn't add up somehow. Then it struck him. If he was the owner of this factory and had arranged to have it torched, then he would have sold off some of his stock, moved out a few machines, got as much cash as he could. If the owner was devious enough to pay for an arson attack then he was clever enough to flannel the insurance investigators, surely?

He shrugged his shoulders. It wasn't his place to reason why. He was being extremely well paid to do a job and the sooner he got it over with, the sooner he'd get his money.

After soaking a pile of rags with the paraffin he laid several interlocking trails, all ending in different locations, in order to achieve the maximum effect. The paraffin that was left he sloshed around. Making sure he had covered every detail, he stood well back and lit a match.

Frank hurried along the tow path that ran alongside the canal. He was tired and cold and all he wanted to do was get home and climb into bed. As he turned into the narrow muddy lane that ran down the side of the Bradwick's building he collided with another man coming the other way.

Both simultaneously expressed their apologies and side stepped out of each other's way to continue on their journey.

The taller of the two men hesitated. 'Er . . . it's Mr McCallan, isn't it? We're not personally acquainted, but you were pointed out to me the other day by one of my parishioners. I visited your sick wife.' He held out his hand. 'I'm Reverend Billings. Please accept my condolences. Mrs McCallan was a brave woman.'

'Yes, yes she was.' Frank took the reverend's hand and shook it firmly. 'My Flora appreciated yer visit, vicar. And so did I.' He hesitated, wanting to get home but not wanting to appear rude to the kindly minister. 'I'm surprised ter see a man of the cloth round these parts at this time of night.'

'Yes, it's a trifle late even for me. I've been visiting an old friend of mine who hasn't been too well lately and we got to talking over the old days and, well, you know how it is. Time flies. I must admit he's rather an interesting old gentleman and we got to discussing the classics . . .' Algernon's voice trailed off as he realised that a man of Frank's ilk probably wouldn't know a classic if he held one in his hand. He meant no disparagement by this, just knew the lower orders only received a basic education, which to his mind was barely enough to equip them to earn a menial living. 'I did mean to come and check how you were getting on. It seems trite of me to say that time is something I don't seem to have much of these days.'

'That's all right, Vicar, I understand. Anyway it's not as if I'm one of your parishioners,' Frank replied good-naturedly. 'I can't say it's bin easy, but I'm getting there.

I've got a job now,' he said proudly.

'Have you? Well, that is good news. Night-watchman?'

'Eh? Oh, no, no. I'm a road sweeper. I'm out this late 'cos . . .' He gave a laugh. 'To be honest, Vicar, I was up me allotment and I sat down to take a breather and must have fell asleep. When you do things like that it makes you realise you're getting old.'

Algernon laughed too. 'Indeed it does. I'm always doing it. Only have to see a comfy armchair and my eyelids start drooping. Well, my good man I'll let you get off home to your bed.' He laid a hand on Frank's arm. 'Remember, you are always welcome at my church.'

Frank smiled gratefully. 'I'll remember that, Vicar. Good-night.'

'Good-night.'

As Frank continued his journey he thought what a good man Reverend Billings was considering he was a clergyman. The others he had come into contact with all breathed fire and brimstone, their talk peppered with words such as 'hell' and 'damnation'. This one, unusually, seemed almost human.

Maybe he would pay a visit to the church sometime, he thought. Before the war he'd regularly gone to Sunday service, something Flora had always enjoyed. Suddenly a thought struck and a warm glow filled him. Maybe bumping into the Vicar and the resulting memory of the times he had accompanying his beloved wife to church was Flora's way of letting him know she was watching over him. The thought, silly or not, gave him comfort.

As he strode past the tall iron gates enclosing Bradwick's courtyard he happened to glance inside. Movement across the far side by the loading bay door caught his eye. A man was emerging, shutting the door firmly behind him. Automatically Frank's hand went up, his mouth opening ready to call a greeting. He had assumed the man to be Cyril Owen, the night-watchman, doing his rounds. But something struck him and he hesitated. Cyril was a small tubby man. This man was tall, and seemed to Frank to be acting strangely. Why had he looked all around before he had started to cross the yard towards the gates?

Although he didn't seem like a burglar, he was carrying no bag, the man was obviously up to no good. Without a thought for his own safety Frank began to climb the gates. 'Oi, you,' he bellowed. 'Stop where you are. The . . . the police are on the way,' he lied.

The very last thing Mickey was expecting as he crossed the wide yard was to be caught in the act, so full of conceit was he at his own cleverness. The job had been easy. Shortly the creeping flames would reach their destination and the fire would erupt. All he had to do now was climb over the gates and make his way home with no one the wiser as to who the culprit was.

The shout froze him rigid, the threat that the police were on their way shocking him senseless. Instinctively he shrank back into the dark shadows and for several long seconds stood rooted to the spot. His mind whirled into action. His eyes darted frantically, desperately seeking an escape route. The man was blocking his only way out. Then he saw it. Near the far end of the building a rusty iron ladder ran up the wall to the roof. He would have to cross over the roof and jump into the canal at the other side. Although it was the last thing he wanted to do, it was the only way. He ran the twenty or so yards over to the ladder and began to climb, all the time conscious that the man was getting nearer and time was of the essence.

Mickey was nearing the top when Frank reached the ladder and began to scale it after him.

Time spent pushing the heavy handcart and sweeping long strokes with his brush had strengthened Frank's arms, giving him an advantage, and by the time Mickey had reached the top and pulled himself over the ridge, Frank was almost on him. Gasping for breath, Mickey made a dive for the slippery roof tiles and began to claw his way upwards.

Behind him now, Frank made a sideways dive over the top of the ridge and, seizing his chance, made a grab for Mickey's ankle. He caught it, gripping with all his might and pulling him back down.

'Got yer, yer swine!' he cried triumphantly.

Kicking frantically to free his leg, Mickey half turned to lash out with the other when he caught sight of the face of his captor. 'You!' he exclaimed in astonishment.

Eyes wide, Frank gasped, 'Mickey?' With the shock of discovery, his grip slackened. 'Mickey?' he repeated. 'Oh, my God. No . . . I don't believe it. What in God's name are yer doing here?'

Freed from his father's grasp, Mickey shuffled back and stood up, awkwardly, fighting to keep his balance on the narrow space between the rising roof tiles and the protective raised parapet. He sneered down at his father. 'What I'm doing here is none of your business.' He started to push past Frank to get to the ladder. 'Get outta me way.'

He made another grab for Mickey's leg. 'No, yer don't,' he cried. 'You ain't going anywhere 'til yer tell me what you're up to.'

Mickey kicked out, catching him in the chest. 'And you're gonna stop me, a' yer?' he sneered sarcastically. 'Fuck off, will yer?'

Enraged by his son's callous disregard for him, and without a thought for his own safety, Frank reared up, grabbed Mickey by the shoulders and forced him down against the roof. 'I've had enough of you, my lad. Yer moods, the way yer treat people. It's about time yer grew up and learned some respect.'

'Respect?' spat Mickey. 'Respect? For you? Why, you make me sick!' His temper exploded. With all the strength he could muster, he forced his father over, pinning him flat. 'You'll never get that from me! Never, do you hear? How the hell can a son have any respect for a father that's n'ote but a coward?'

Incensed now, Mickey's long nursed resentment against him exploded. 'She begged you, didn't she? She begged you to do it. But you couldn't. She was screaming in pain but you'd sooner she'd suffered than put her out of her misery. You're gutless, that's what you are! N'ote but a bloody worthless coward. And you ask *me* to respect you? I *hate* you. D'you hear me? I fucking hate your guts.'

Frank gasped, the shock of Mickey's violent outburst forcing the breath from his body. 'I . . . I don't understand. Why . . .' he stuttered. 'Why . . .' Suddenly the truth hit him like a bolt of lightning. 'It was you,' he uttered. 'You killed her, didn't yer, Mickey?'

His son's face contorted with bitterness. 'I didn't kill her,' he hissed. 'I did what you should have. I ended her suffering. But it was you that made me do it. It was you she begged. But you couldn't. You couldn't do it, could you?'

'I loved her, Mickey. I couldn't do it 'cos I loved her.'

Outraged Mickey reared back, eyes ablaze with hatred. 'Love! You don't know the meaning of the word. I did it 'cos I loved her!'

Utterly devastated by this shocking revelation, Frank's whole body slumped. 'Oh, my God,' he gasped. 'Oh, Mickey, Mickey, what have you done?' Suddenly his head lifted and he sniffed. 'Smoke! I smell smoke. Christ!' he cried, scrambling upright. 'The bloody building's on fire. How the . . .' Another dreadful realisation suddenly struck him. In disbelieving horror he stared at his son. 'It was you? You've set fire to the factory. Why . . .'

The shrill sound of police whistles rent the air. Mickey spun round. From his vantage point he could just make out two shadowy figures running down the street leading to the factory. He jerked back to face his father. 'You called the rozzers?' he spat accusingly.

'No! No, Mickey, I didn't.'

Beyond reasoning now, he aimed a punch at his father. 'Don't lie, you bastard!'

The unexpected blow caught Frank unawares and he lost his balance. As he plummeted over the edge his cry of shock streamed forth. Desperately he made a grab for the ridge. Clinging precariously to the slippery coping tiles, a terrified Frank gazed down at the fifty-foot drop to the concrete surface below. His vision swam. Then a new terror seized him as he felt his hands beginning to lose their grip. Jerking his head back he locked eyes with his son. 'Mickey,' he pleaded. 'Help me, Mickey. Please, son, help me.'

One of the policemen had reached the ladder now and was halfway up it. The other was running across the yard, whistle still blaring. In the distance a siren sounded urgently and a car skidded to a halt.

Mickey froze. Time was running out. He looked down at his father, eyes cold and emotionless. He shook his head. 'It's you or me. Sorry, you lose.'

Spinning around, he made a dive for the roof and scrambled his way upward, negotiated the peak, slithered down the other side, stepped on to the ridge and without hesitation jumped into the canal.

Glenda stiffened as she felt Mickey climb in beside her to lie stiffly on the edge of the bed. She had heard him enter the bedroom, strip off his clothes, noticed how heavy his breathing was, as though he'd been running and had wondered why. Where had he been? What had he been doing? But, most importantly, with whom? Not that she hoped to receive an answer to any of her questions. Even to wish him good-night would incite further hostilities, and that she could not cope with. But regardless of all the emotions racing through her, at least he was home now, in bed with her. She decided not to think about who he had been with for the last hour or so.

As he had climbed into bed she had caught a whiff of something, but hadn't known what. Now it suddenly came to her. It had been a faint smell of paraffin. But how could it be? What would Mickey be needing with paraffin at this time of night? She decided she must have been mistaken, turned over and went to sleep.

Chapter Eighteen

'Believe me, that bastard is in on this business up to his neck.' Sergeant Little slammed his huge fist down on the table. The noise echoed around the small, sparsely furnished room deep inside police headquarters on Charles Street. The big florid man scowled furiously. 'I know I'm right, I just know I am.'

Fresh-faced Constable Plant, who had only recently joined the Constabulary in Leicester and, according to his junior colleagues, had drawn the short straw in being put under the charge of Sergeant Little, eyed his superior in awe. Despite his reputation for being stickler for the rules and a hard taskmaster, there was much to be learned from this seasoned policeman. Sergeant Little's instincts were legendary in the force, and something to be taken notice of.

'What makes you suspect him, Sarge? I mean, why not the brother-in-law? He could have set the fire himself and got trapped when he went back for the stuff.'

'No. I've thought long and hard about all this and it didn't happen like that. If Collins had bin the one to set it, he would've got the spoils out first before he struck the match. Believe me, Mickey McCallan is the guilty one. I knew it the first time I set eyes on him. Oh, he put on a good act all right, one that'd fool many, but not me. No, not on your nelly. It was hearing about his brother-in-law that gave him away. That was more of a shock to him than it was even to the others. What clinched it for me was when I very innocently remarked that whoever set that fire was guilty of murder. I thought he was gonna mess himself.'

'But the wife says Mickey was with her all night and couldn't have gone out without her knowing.'

'And she's lying. He went out all right and she knows he did. She couldn't look me in the eye.' Reg Little eyed the young policeman sharply. 'Constable, yer gonna have ter start watching people a bit more closely if you're ever going to catch criminals. Never believe what anyone says 'til yer've sifted through the facts.' His eyes twinkled wickedly. 'Then you add a bit, take a bit away, mix it all up, and if yer a good copper you come up with the truth.'

Kevin Plant looked bewildered. 'And how do you acquire the knack of doing that, Sarge?'

'Stick wi' me, lad. Listen and learn. 'Cause yer've got to have a copper's nose, which yer either born with or yer not. A natural talent, so to speak.' He leaned over and scrutinised Kevin's nose. 'We've yet to see whether you have it or not. D'yer get that from yer mother's side or yer dad's? It's a fair-sized hooter yer've got there, me lad.'

Rubbing the object in question, Kevin eyed his superior for a moment, unsure whether he was being jested with or not. 'Do you . . . er . . . think they're all lying in this case, Sarge?'

'Well, they can't be all lying, Constable, can they? We've got one dead man and one who's in severe shock and ain't uttered one word since Constable Jeffers saved his skin. Bloody lucky an' all. Another second and he'd definitely been a gonner. There's only one person who ain't lying and that's the dead man's wife. What's her name now?'

'Kelly, Sarge. Kelly Collins.'

'Ah, I see she made an impression on you too. You might make a copper yet. I thought meself she came across as the decent type.' He ignored the tide of embarrassment flooding the young constable's face, feeling he'd given him enough of a ribbing for the time being. 'She's told the truth. She knew nothing whatsoever about this business. She went to bed with her husband just after ten-thirty and the first she knew of this was when we banged on her door and woke her up just after three.

'I know Glenda McCallan is lying. I'm not saying she knew 'ote about the factory business. She's covering up for Mickey, silly fool. Her loyalty's misguided, though, 'cos if yer ask me, Mickey McCallan don't give two hoots for that wife of his. Anyway a wife can't testify for her husband so her statement is of no importance.' He sniffed disdainfully.

'McCallan, though, he's a different kettle of fish. A right cocky bugger and a born liar if ever I've met one. He's the one behind all this, mark my words. But nailing him is gonna be another matter.' He exhaled sharply. 'If only we had an eyewitness.'

Constable Plant scratched his head. 'Sarge, most of this business doesn't make sense to me. Are you sure the father couldn't have had anything to do with it? It seems a coincidence, him being on the roof.'

'Yes, it does, but sometimes coincidences happen. I would have thought like you if it hadn't have been for Reverend Billings. Can't get a more cast iron alibi than one from a Vicar. I know the Reverend personally. He's as straight as they come.' He sighed heavily. 'I've got to make a report out of all this claptrap and it ain't the only case we're working on. Let's go over the facts again, but first put the kettle on, there's a good lad.'

Ten minutes later, two steaming mugs of tea and a plate of doorstep-sized cheese sandwiches by the side of them, the two policemen got down to business.

Taking a huge bite from a sandwich, Reg Little raised his eyes from the statement he had been studying and leaned back in his chair, plonking his size eleven boots on the table. His face was stern. 'Right, what have we got to go on? One man dead from smoke inhalation. Another in such a state of shock he's no more than a zombie. A man who swears blind he was in bed at the time, and a wife who backs that claim. A factory owner who sez he can't think of anyone with enough of a grudge to try and burn down the place. And a night-watchman that slept through the whole lot. He's bin sacked, and quite rightly so. To my mind the most important fact in all this is the two anonymous tele-phone calls, one to us, the other to the fire brigade.'

Plant frowned thoughtfully. 'Do you believe Bradwick, Sarge?'

Little shook his head. 'No. I think he knows exactly who's behind it. And that ain't Mickey McCallan.'

'It isn't?'

Reg snorted, shaking his head. 'You country coppers haven't a clue what goes on in the city, have yer, eh? I bet the nearest you ever got to real crime was who nicked Farmer Giles's pig. Ever heard of protection, lad?'

Plant shuffled uncomfortably. ''Course I have. And you ain't being fair, Sarge. We had our fair share of crime to deal with, only not on the scale you have here. We had a murder once.'

'Oh, really?' Little mouthed sarcastically. 'And the murderer's still at large, I warrant?' Despite what Plant said he still felt country policemen had it easy. 'I think Mickey McCallan was being paid to do this job,' he announced.

Plant looked surprised. 'You do?'

Little nodded. 'It was the telephone calls that give the

game away. Ask yerself why anyone would set fire to a factory for no gain. Jeffers swears that the man that jumped over the roof was empty-handed.'

'Well, he was escaping, Sarge.'

'I'm well aware of that, Constable. But nothing was found lying around that he could have dropped while escaping.'

'Mmmm. Well, maybe McCallan's the one with the grudge.'

'Why would he have a grudge against the man who pays his wife's wages? Bradwick said he'd never met McCallan and I believe him. And there was definitely no hanky-panky going on between Bradwick and the wife. I checked with the secretary. Take heed, Constable, secretaries know everything about their bosses, even down to what colour underhose they wear. Well, maybe that's stretching it a bit far but they know more about 'em than their wives do. Bradwick's a happily married man and as straight as a die. He built that business up from scratch and ain't about to have it burn down in the hope of collecting the insurance money. Anyway, this shows all the hallmarks of Isaac Greenbaum, the slimy toe rag!'

Plant frowned. 'Who's he?'

'Local Al Capone, or likes to think he is. He came up from London during the war, running away from whatever, and I expect he found the pickings easier here and stayed. He's got the east of Leicester City in his pocket and it seems to me he's after expanding his territory, hence the factory. Notice the parade of shops nearby? Recently one had a fire and several were burgled. And if you'd done yer homework you'd have known all this already.'

Plant shuffled in his seat uncomfortably. 'I don't see the connection.'

'Don't yer? If you'd studied the reports properly you might. In all three no serious damage was done, and on each occasion anonymous calls were received by us and the fire brigade. A regular pattern which adds up to scare tactics so the owners'll pay up.'

'Oh, I see. And . . . er . . . you reckon this Greenbaum was behind them?'

'Them and many more, Constable, but like everything else he has his sticky fat fingers in, we can't prove it. No one dare talk, see. That's the bugger. If only one would show an ounce of guts we could coax the rest out from their rabbit holes. As it is . . . Anyway, this ain't getting what facts we have in order. Where were we? Oh, yeah, now the way I see it is that Bradwick wouldn't pay protection money so Isaac Greenbaum decided to give him the usual warning. That's where Mickey McCallan comes in. Isaac had probably been keeping an eye on him. 'Til recently he was a dustman by trade and from what we've found out did the usual thing of buying and selling on the side. Well, there's no law against that. But now he's been brought to our attention and we've had a chance to see what he's like, I know he's been up to no good in the past. Just lucky he ain't bin caught, that's all.'

'In what way do you think he's been up to no good, Sarge?'

'Just a guess. Small-time thievery – that sort of thing. When I dug back there was an incident of shop-lifting. Got caught fair and square but escaped borstal, the lucky little sod, 'cos the charge was dropped at the last minute. Anyway, apart from that juvenile incident he's no police record and the last person we'd think of questioning in connection with something like this. And we wouldn't have done if it hadn't all gone wrong. That's why Greenbaum picked him. Clever so and so he is.'

Little slid his legs off the table, leaned forward and rummaged through the sheaf of papers scattered across the desk. 'Where's Mickey's bloody statement? Ah.' He leaned back again and scanned through it. 'He swears he never left the house at all on Friday night and went to bed around eleven o'clock.' He fixed his eyes on the young constable. 'Wadda yer make of that?'

'Er? In what way?'

'Well, don't yer think that's unusual?'

'Er . . . should I, Sarge?'

Little leaned forward. 'How old are you, lad?'

'Twenty-two.'

'Wadda you do on a Friday night when you ain't on duty?'

'Meet me mates for a pint down the pub.'

'Exactly. And that's what the lot we questioned swear McCallan did most Friday nights. In at opening time, not leaving 'til they shut. Though I wouldn't believe any of 'em to tell the truth even if it was. But even so, why didn't Mickey go this particular Friday?'

Plant pouted thoughtful. 'He's married, Sarge. Maybe his wife kicked up a stink.'

''A' you married, Constable?'

'No, Sarge.'

'I didn't think so. Look, lad, a pint on a Friday night with yer mates is tradition for the likes of Mickey McCallan, wife or no wife, so why not this Friday? His brother-in-law still went. He only had a couple of pints. He told who was it now . . .' He leaned forward and picked up another piece of paper. 'Oh, yeah, a Paul Cross that he was broke and hadn't enough to buy a round. This Paul Cross said Rod Collins didn't seem his usual self. Seemed worried about something.'

'And what do you reckon that was, Sarge?'

Little shrugged his shoulders. 'I dunno. Could have been anything.'

'Do you think he knew what McCallan was planning?'

'Could have. According to their mates they were close.

But somehow I don't think it was that. I think McCallan played this close to his chest, wanted to keep whatever Greenbaum offered all for himself. How Collins came to be in that stock room we'll probably never know, but there's one thing I *do* know – if he'd been in on the plan to fire the place he would never have pratted around in that stock room. No man in his right mind would have.'

He took a breath. 'The father, now, I believe it was as stated. He'd been to the allotment – several witnesses have confirmed they saw and spoke to him there. Reverend Billings bumped into him at the turning into the lane running down the side of the factory on his way home. It was about quarter past twelve. They nattered for a minute or two and then both went their separate ways. I think McCallan Senior saw something as he passed by the factory gates. He'd have to pass by them, it's the only way. Maybe he saw his son coming out of the factory or perhaps somebody or something else, I dunno, anything that roused his suspicions. But the result was he gave chase and they ended up on the roof. Jeffers and Smith swear blind there were two men on that roof.

'It's a pity it was so dark that night or we might have managed some sort of description. But I know it was Mickey and one day I'll nail the bastard. I tell you, though, Frank McCallan is the luckiest man alive. If Jeffers had been a second later he'd have been a gonner fer sure.' Little frowned thoughtfully. 'It's his mental state that doesn't seem quite right to me.'

'Oh, come on, Sarge. The doctor said it was understandable. McCallan had been a prisoner of war and was ill for two years after he came home. His wife had not long died. Then, if it was his son he recognised on that roof . . .'

'It was his son all right.'

'Well, in that case, Sarge, after going through all that, wouldn't *you* be in shock?'

The sergeant slowly nodded. 'Yes, I warrant I would, but shock's one thing – losing yer marbles is another. And that man has definitely lost his marbles. But all the same . . .'

'All the same what, Sarge?'

'All the same . . . me gut instincts tell me there's summat else here, summat we don't know . . .'

'Like what?'

'Summat not connected with the torching of the factory. Several neighbours have said that father and son were on bad terms. When I questioned Collins's wife she confirmed this, saying it started over a silly argument after the mother died. But I think it was something a bit more than a silly argument.' Gathering up the sheets of paper, Reg Little put them inside a file and slapped it closed. 'As my old grandmother used to say, "It'll all come out in the wash." Frank McCallan is the key to solving all this. There's n'ote we can do 'til he snaps out of this so-called shock and we can question him.'

'So is that it then, Sarge?'

'Fer now, lad. But have patience. Just like Isaac Greenbaum, one day we'll get Mickey. If not for this crime, then another. And when we do, if yer've been a good boy, I'll give you the honour of reading him his rights.' He pushed across his mug. 'Now get us another cuppa.'

Chapter Nineteen

'Mr Greenbaum is busy.' The voice was harsh, dismissive.

'But I need to see him.'

'What about?'

Mickey's temper snapped. Over the last week his nerves had frayed to breaking point. Not only had the job on which he had pinned such high hopes gone horribly wrong but he was convinced the police suspected the extent of his involvement and that one wrong move on his part, a slip of the tongue even, would have them pouncing. He was taking a chance paying a visit to the snooker club but he desperately needed his money and as he had not received one word from Isaac Greenbaum, felt he had no choice. With money in his pocket he planned to escape as far away as possible from the town of his birth and start afresh elsewhere. At this moment he did not care where.

For the last week, apart from time spent being questioned extensively down at the police station, he had been cooped up inside the house, playing the part of the bereaved brother-in-law, acting as bewildered as the rest as to what had happened, his great fear being that his father would snap out of whatever mental condition possessed him and the truth would out before he could get away. Oh, why, he had vehemently wished, could it not have been his father who had perished that night instead of Rod?

He genuinely grieved for Rod. Despite becoming a hindrance of late, Rod had been his friend and in that respect Mickey missed him. He could only guess that Rod had had the misfortune to follow him that fateful night, not for a moment realising what he was up to. But Mickey did not see the death as anything other than a tragic accident, attaching no blame to himself. Why should he? Rod should not have followed him. What had happened was his own fault.

So consumed with worry for himself was he that whatever few words of comfort he offered his sister for her tragic loss were minimal, and for all the comfort they gave hardly worth the effort. For his father, Mickey felt nothing at all.

Now, despite the immense size of the doorman before him, a frenzied Mickey grabbed the lapels of his suit jacket and yanked him close. 'I need to see Greenbaum and I need to see him now,' he spat. 'Tell him Mickey McCallan is here.'

Eyeing him with contempt, the man thrust Mickey from him and nonchalantly brushed himself down. 'You're McCallan, are yer? Well, I've a message for you.' He thrust a menacing face into Mickey's. 'Mr Greenbaum sez the next time yer dare show yer ugly mug round 'ere, you'll get what's coming ter yer. Now fuck off.'

The man gave Mickey an almighty shove. Totally unprepared for this kind of response, he tumbled back on to the pavement, just managing to keep his balance. 'Now look here,' he hissed, 'you've got the wrong man. I did a job for Mr Greenbaum and I've come to collect me money – and I'm not going anywhere 'til I get it.'

The man stepped forward. With one massive hand he grabbed the front of Mickey's jacket and lifted him up bodily, Mickey's feet leaving the ground. 'If you've got any sense you'll get back inside the 'ole yer crawled out of and stay there.' He threw back his head and laughed. 'Yer don't get it, do yer? You've bin used, pal. Bradwick needed a warning and you're the one that gave it. Mr Greenbaum knew you hadn't got it in yer to do the job proper. If he'd wanted the place razed 'e'd 'ave called in an expert, not a poxy little bin man like you.

'Now tek a warning, pal. If you don't want witnesses suddenly appearing, claiming they seen what yer done, I'd keep well out of Mr Greenbaum's way. And don't forget your brother-in-law died in that fire and it wouldn't tek much to point the scuffers in the direction that you were both in it together and you left him to die. Mr Greenbaum's got connections and he's owed favours. Getting you charged with murder would be easy enough for him.'

Mickey paled alarmingly. 'Murder?' he gulped.

Without warning a clenched fist smacked straight into his face and he plunged to the ground. Then the toe of a boot slammed into his side so savagely it lifted his whole body. As he landed in the gutter he screamed aloud in pain.

A group of passers-by stared first at Mickey, writhing in agony, then across at the doorman who shrugged his shoulders. 'I told 'im it were members only but 'e wouldn't 'ave it.' Rubbing his hands, a smirk on his face, he turned and disappeared inside the club.

It took Mickey two gruelling hours to make his way home. Exhausted and clutching his injured ribs, he stumbled through the back gate and into the outside privy, easing himself down on to the seat. Gradually the pain in his side subsided and it was a relief to realise that the damage he had received was not as serious as he had first thought. He had feared that several ribs were broken at least.

In utter defeat he slumped back against the dank

privy wall and closed his eyes. He should have known better than to trust a man like Isaac Greenbaum. Through this one stupid act his whole life lay in ruins. He had no job, no money, in fact as matters stood, no prospects at all; his best friend was dead and there was still the threat that he could be charged with Rod's murder. And to cap it all, he was saddled by law with a woman he detested.

Mickey shuddered. At this moment there was only one thing he was sure of which was that nothing could induce him to go back inside that house. For the last seven weeks those four walls had been his prison, the people inside his jailers. For six of those weeks he had had to watch his every move because of Isaac Greenbaum. He was still in fear of the man, but now that fear had turned to terror. Greenbaum only had to click his fingers and Mickey's life would be over. The beating he had received from the doorman had been a warning, and now there was the police to consider also. Mickey wasn't stupid. He knew that Sergeant Little had his measure.

He would have to get away until the heat died down. What he would do or where he would go he hadn't a clue, but it had to be a long way from here.

As his mind filled with pictures of his vanished dreams a surge of acute misery filled him. Mickey bowed his head and for the first time in many a long year he wept.

Chapter Twenty

'Haven't you finished fixing those wireless sets yet?' Norma Alderman's pretty face looked cross as she stared at her husband, beavering away oblivious at the table. 'The dinner's ready. Though,' she said sharply, 'if you can call what I'm dishing up a meal is another matter. You have to get a better paid job soon, Alec. The money you're bringing in hardly goes anywhere. It's a good job I'm working, that's all I can say, else we'd starve. And what about my mother? She relied on the money we paid her. She doesn't half miss it, Alec. Alec – are you listening to me?'

He raised his head. 'Yes, I'm listening, Norma. I just wanted to finish welding this wire.' He laid down the soldering iron, stood up and circled his hands around his wife's trim waist. He pulled her close and looked into her big blue eyes, his own unashamedly revealing every ounce of the love he felt for this woman.

'I know this is hard for you,' he said tenderly. 'But, please, just bear with it. I know this job doesn't seem much but one day Raggy'll have to start taking things easier. He must be nudging eighty – could be over that, it's hard to tell – and he's no family. As I work for him I should get the first chance to take the place over or else he might consider making me a partner. I can make it into a little gold mine, Norma, I know I can.'

'How the hell can you ever expect to make money out

of a poky little rag and bone yard? Alec, really!'

'It might be a poky little rag and bone yard to you, Norma, but it does a reasonable amount of business and it'll do even better now Raggy has me there with him. There's a lot of money to be made from rubbish. Me years on the bins have served me in good stead in that department and I've already learned so much more from Raggy himself. People might poke fun at him, but deep down he's a decent bloke.'

'But you said this job were only temporary, Alec, 'til you got something better?'

He gnawed his bottom lip, guiltily. 'Yeah, I know, but this could turn out to be summat better in the long run.'

'Huh,' she mouthed, unconvinced. 'Okay, say he does retire and hand it all over to you – businesses cost money to buy or have you forgotten that?'

'No, I realise that. But . . . well, I'm hoping to strike some sort of deal.'

She frowned, perplexed. 'Deal? What sort of deal?'

'Well, he might let me work off the debt. Pay it in instalments.'

She pulled away from him, plucked up the bottom of her apron and wrung it agitatedly. 'People like Raggy, Alec, don't retire. They carry on 'til they die.' Her pretty face twisted angrily. 'Oh, stop daydreaming, Alec, and get a decent job. In a factory or something.'

'I wouldn't last five minutes cooped up inside a factory, Norma, you know I wouldn't. I've been an outside man all my working life.'

'But you could give it a try. You might like it.'

'But why should I when I enjoy the job I've got? I know the money ain't that good but it's not that much less than I was getting.'

'That was before you got promoted. You would have been getting ten shilling a week more for being a Cody. Oh, Alec!' she cried. 'How could you get the sack on your first day for fighting? And as if that wasn't bad enough, it had to be with Mickey McCallan of all people. Why didn't you just turn your back on him and walk away?'

He sighed. 'What's done is done, Norma. Can't you forget it? I have. Anyway, I feel McCallan did me a favour.'

'Favour! How on earth d'yer come to that conclusion?'

'I'm looking to the future, Norma. I was lucky to get this job, and if I'd still been working on the bins I wouldn't have had a chance at it. Raggy's never had anyone working with him before and it was him that asked me, don't forget that. He trusts me, Norma, and with a man like Raggy, believe me, that's an honour.'

She shook her head in disbelief. 'An honour! How could you think that way? I thought this job was just a stop gap. I never dreamed for one minute you'd want to keep it.' Her eyes filled with tears. 'Do you know what it's like for me? Do you know how embarrassing it is to tell people when they ask that my husband works at a rag and bone yard? And that you got excused doing National Service because you have a dicky heart.'

He stared at her, astounded. 'A dicky heart? Norma, for God's sake, the doctor found an irregularity in my heartbeat. That ain't a dicky heart. And besides, you were glad when I didn't have ter go.'

'Yes, I know. But . . . but you don't know how it is for me! All the girls talk about what their men got up to while they were away and I can't, can I? They all think I'm married to an invalid.'

He gasped. 'Oh, Norma,' he whispered.

'Don't look at me like that. You're like a wounded dog when you pull that sorrowful face. For goodness' sake, Alec, I'm a supervisor on the cosmetics counter at Woolworth's. I have a position in life. It was humiliating enough for me when you were a bin man. Now . . . now I'm . . . I'm . . . so ashamed.'

He stared at her aghast. 'Ashamed? You're ashamed of me? I never realised you felt like that.'

'Well . . . now you do.'

Angrily she cleared a space on the table, then flounced back to the kitchen. Moments later she returned carrying a plate and cutlery which she slammed down. Untying her apron, she screwed it into a ball and threw it into the worn leather armchair by the fireplace.

Alec stared bewilderedly at her, many questions about his wife's uncharacteristic behaviour whirling in his brain, but all he managed was, 'Aren't you eating?'

'No. I'm not hungry. I've a headache. I thought I'd go for a walk.'

'Oh! Well, if you'll just give me a few minutes to eat my dinner, I'll come with you. We can talk . . .'

'No,' she erupted. 'I'm not in the mood for talking. I thought you wanted to finish fixing those sets? You ought to finish fixing them, Alec, we need the money and you've been working on them long enough to have fixed ten.'

He glanced at the two wireless sets in pieces on the table, then back to her. 'You're being unfair. Don't forget I've also redecorated the house from top to bottom. I could hardly do that *and* fix the sets. Anyway, it'll be dark soon. I'll worry about you if you're out alone in the dark.'

'I'm a grown woman, Alec. Quite capable of taking a walk by meself. Look, just eat your dinner, will you, before it gets cold,' she snapped.

Spinning on her heel, she left the room and he listened to her footsteps pounding up the stairs. Sighing, he sat down, picked up his knife and fork and looked down at his plate. Sausage and mash. Norma's description was wrong. The meal on his plate was a decent meal by anyone's standards. There were people he knew of who would give anything to be sitting down to such an offering. But all the same, still stunned by her words, his appetite had left him and he absently pushed his food around the plate.

Minutes later she returned. He looked at her in surprise. She was wearing her best coat and shoes, and had tidied her hair. 'You look nice,' he said. 'I thought you were just going for a walk?'

She picked up her handbag, which was hanging on the back of a chair, unclipped it and started rummaging through. 'I've changed me mind. I thought I'd pop and see Janet.'

'Janet?'

Eyes still glued to the contents of her handbag, she pulled out her gloves. 'Janet Berry. One of the girls I work with. I've told you about her. She lives with her parents in a lovely house off King Richard's Road. That's why I've changed. I couldn't go visiting a nice house like that looking like a tramp.'

'You hardly looked like a tramp, Norma.'

She raised her head and looked at him sullenly. 'By your standards, Alec, maybe I didn't. But I felt I did.'

He laid down his knife and fork. 'Don't go out,' he pleaded. 'We do need to talk. Let me tell you the plans I have for the yard. Maybe then you'll see what . . .'

'Alec!' she yelled. 'A rag and bone yard is a rag and bone yard, and to my mind the people who run 'em are no better than tinkers. And how the hell can you expect ever to make a decent living out of other people's worthless rubbish?'

'But . . .'

'Look, I told you, I have a headache. We'll . . . we'll talk another night. Are you going to eat that meal I cooked you or not?'

He glanced briefly down at the plate then back to her.

'Yes, 'course I am.' He frowned in concern. 'Norma, what's wrong? I know summat is. This ain't like you at all.'

'Then maybe you don't really know me.' She stared at him for a moment then her shoulders slumped and she sighed heavily. 'I'm sorry, Alec. There's nothing wrong really. It's just that I wanted so much for us. I wanted us to have a nice home in a decent area. Somewhere we'd be proud to invite friends to.'

He raised his eyebrows questioningly. 'You're ashamed to bring your friends back here?'

'Yes . . . no . . . not exactly.' She inhaled deeply. 'Is it wrong to want something better for yourself?' she asked defensively.

'No, there's n'ote wrong in that, and we will, Norma, I promise yer.'

Her blue eyes flashed. 'When, Alec? I'll tell yer – when the cows come home, that's when. And if you carry on with this stupid idea of making a fortune out of the rag and bone yard, never.' Her eyes darted to the tin clock on the mantel. 'I'm going before it gets too late for visiting.'

Before he could say another word she had left the room and seconds later the front door slammed behind her.

Shocked and deeply puzzled, he sat back down at the table. Alec had never heard his wife speak out like this before. Never had she given him cause to suspect she was unhappy with her lot. He had thought she liked living in this house, which he himself thought so homely and far nicer than most of the others adjoining. Admittedly the furniture was second hand, but it was good second hand, the best they had been able to afford when they had excitedly scoured the shops for items to furnish their home.

Alec's face puckered. His wife's words had wounded

him deeply and he felt perplexed as to the reason why she should suddenly feel like this. She had known of his job when they had first met, and with what money he earned he had striven hard to give her all she wanted. The paper for redecorating the rooms had not been cheap, neither had the paint, and the money spent could have been put to much better use as the rooms had not needed to be done. But he had been happy to do it because Norma had wanted it.

Unlike other wives who worked, she kept money from her wage for herself. Alec had never begrudged her that. He felt it was his job to provide a roof and food for them. A woman needed money of her own. That was where, he felt, many men went wrong. They spent what they liked at the pub or betting shop, but begrudged paying for rent and food. A little for their wives was something that never even entered their heads.

Stroking his chin, he sighed. Norma was right about the yard. He was living in a fool's paradise thinking that Raggy would retire. Men like him didn't stop working. They were carried off the premises in a box. Raggy was old but he could still live for years and Alec hoped he did as he had grown quite fond of the cantankerous character.

He sighed again. He knew he should really look for something else, something with more of a future, something that would pay enough to provide all Norma hoped for. But then, he did love his new job and to give it up would be hard for him to do.

Just about every poor soul who came into the yard was desperate for money. A visit to the rag and bone yard with their bundles and bags, filled with items they could ill afford to part with, was a last desperate measure and the few coppers received made the difference in many cases between life and death. Alec smiled. In many cases, when he had known the situation to be particularly dire, he had slipped across an extra couple of pennies and seeing the delight on their faces gave him so much pleasure. Raggy still made a profit and if anything this act brought in more business as word spread that a fair deal could be struck at Raggy Harris's.

He pushed away his plate, appetite completely gone as the painful truth hit home. He had been deluding himself. As matters stood, all he was ever going to be was Raggy's hired help and Alec knew that that was not enough for him. He was twenty-five years old and time was slipping away. If he was ever going to make a better life, he had to do something about it and soon. What he would really like to do was have his own yard. But businesses such as the one Raggy owned were old established concerns and took years in the making.

His thoughts were interrupted by a knock on the back door. A tiny, plump woman entered, wearing a stained floral wrapround apron over her shabby black skirt and blouse. She nodded on spotting Alec, moving a strand of her sparse iron grey hair out of her eyes. 'I just popped in to see if our Norma fancies coming through for a cuppa.'

'Sorry, Mrs Quick, she's out.'

'Out?'

'Yeah, gone visiting a friend.'

'Friend! What friend?' she demanded, most put out.

'A Janet something or other from work.'

'Oh.'

Alec looked at her sympathetically. Iris Quick was a lonely woman who relied heavily on Norma and himself for company and support. She wasn't easy to get along with, had not to his knowledge any friends apart from her neighbours, who as most neighbours did, tolerated the people who lived next door to them. Alec suspected her husband, who had been dead for nearly fifteen years, had not had an easy time of it. 'I think you might find some dregs in the pot, if you fancy?' he offered politely. 'Though you'll have to excuse me, I must get on with fixing these wirelesses.'

'About time an' all, if yer ask me. Those sets'll be out of fashion by the time you come to sell 'em.'

Alec declined to answer. He wasn't in the mood for a confrontation with his mother-in-law, and besides, he really felt he should not have to justify himself to her. But out of respect for his wife's mother he always kept such thoughts to himself.

She noticed his plate, the food still on it. 'Warra waste of good food,' she said accusingly. 'Don't yer like my Norma's cooking or summat?'

He rose, picking up his plate. 'There's nothing wrong with Norma's cooking, Mrs Quick. I just wasn't hungry, that's all. Look, why don't you sit down and I'll mash you a fresh pot?' he said, going off into the kitchen.

She tugged out a chair and settled herself down. 'I thought you were never going to offer,' she mumbled. 'Now, young man,' she said, raising her voice so Alec could hear her. 'Ain't it about time you got yerself a proper job?'

Placing the kettle on the stove, he sighed. Whether he liked it or not he was about to receive a lecture from his mother-in-law and mentally steeled himself.

Chapter Twenty-One

'Come on, Dad,' Kelly coaxed. 'Take hold of this. Watch it now, it's hot.' Gently she took hold of his hand, placed the mug of weak tea inside and wrapped his fingers around the handle. She stood back and stared at his pathetic figure, huddled in the armchair. 'Oh, Dad,' she whispered, distraught.

The doctor had told her a week or so ago that there was nothing more he could do for Frank. He had retreated into a world of his own and no medicine the doctor knew of would bring him back until he was ready. That could happen tomorrow, or it could take years. As a last resort, he recommended Kelly consign her father to a mental institution, something she had baulked at. No matter what state he was in, she would never turn her back and put him into a place like that.

Her father was not mad, he did not rant and rave, did not run the streets naked and blaspheming, was no danger to society. In truth, he did not do anything. Once Kelly had got him up of a morning, washed, dressed and seen to his ablutions, something she found degrading for both him and herself, she would sit him in his chair. Apart from taking him to the lavatory, that was where she had to leave him until she put him to bed at night. During all that time not one word would he utter. He just sat staring, eyes lifeless, as if his very soul had been stripped from him.

The events of that dreadful night had caused terrible repercussions, which Kelly was still finding hard to bear. It wouldn't be so bad, she felt, if answers to her many questions could be given. Then maybe she could make sense of it all. But as it was, it was incomprehensible to her. She had gone happily to bed that night with her husband and fallen asleep – only to be rudely awakened a few hours later to find her whole life destroyed. Even after two months had passed, she still found that pain hard to endure.

Not for the first time she wondered if there was a God and this whole episode was penance He'd exacted, a price she had to pay for whatever wrongs she had committed in the past. If it was, then it was a terrible price.

She sensed a presence other than her father's and spun around to see Glenda framed in the doorway, her face the picture of misery.

'Glenda . . . why ain't you at work?'

Her whole body sagged despairingly as she stepped towards the table, dragged out a chair and slumped down, burying her face in her hands. 'I can't go on no more, Kelly. I . . . I . . . I gotta tell you the truth.' She raised her head, fixing sorrowful eyes on her sister-in-law. 'I got the push,' she blurted out.

Stupefied, Kelly's mouth fell open. 'The push?'

Glenda buried her face in her hands again. 'Two weeks ago. I couldn't tell yer, I just couldn't.'

'Two weeks ago?' Kelly whispered in disbelief.

Raising her head, her sister-in-law sniffed and nodded. 'It were awful, Kelly. You can't begin to imagine what I've had to put up with. They all think it was Mickey. That he set fire to the factory and that I was in on it. And they blame me fer the time they lost while the factory was put straight.' Tears rolled down her face. 'Oh, Kelly,' she wailed, 'they sent me to Coventry. No one spoke ter me for weeks, not one word. They knocked into me, spilt tea over me, and no one 'ud sit on the same table as me in the canteen. I got all the rotten work to do too. I tried to tell 'em Mickey had nothing ter do with it but no one would believe me. The boss said he had no choice but to let me go else he'd have a strike on his hands.'

Ashen-faced, Kelly wrung her hands. 'Glenda, please tell me this ain't true?' she pleaded.

Her sister-in-law's head drooped.

'Oh, my God!' Kelly's hand went to her mouth. 'Please don't tell me yer've no wage coming in this week?'

Glenda's head shot up. 'Is that all you can think of? My husband's disappeared, I've bin treated like scum and all you care about is me wage? Well, it's not fair! It's not fair that I've got all that burden.'

'Fair! You talk about what's fair?' Kelly erupted. 'Is it fair that my husband died? Is it fair that my dad's like that,' she cried, pointing a finger towards him. 'Is it fair that my brother, your so-called husband, upped and abandoned us without a second thought?'

She stabbed a finger to her own chest. 'I'm hurting, Glenda, more than you'll ever realise, but I can't just curl up and die. Though, believe me, right now that's just what I'd like to do.' She slammed her hands flat on the table, eyes ablaze. 'The money you earned was the only thing we had coming in. I know that ain't right, Glenda, but n'ote about any of this situation is right. I'd happily go to work, but how the hell can I and leave me dad like this? And however much I tried, I couldn't earn what you did. Now the rent's due tomorrow. You tell me how I'm gonna pay that to keep a roof over our heads without your wage?

'So you've bin treated rotten. In light of everything else, so what? You got the sack two weeks ago, you could have got another job by now.'

Glenda glared at her. 'You're unfeeling, you are. I've no idea where my husband is and . . .'

'At least you've still got one.'

Glenda flinched, Kelly's words rendering her speechless, and for several long moments the two women stared at each other.

Glenda gnawed her bottom lip, ashamed. 'Oh, Kelly, I'm sorry. I'm so sorry. I miss my brother too.' A gush of remorseful tears flooded down her cheeks.

Sighing deeply, Kelly sank down on a chair. 'Arguing and feeling sorry for ourselves will get us nowhere. What the hell are we gonna do?'

Glenda sniffed. 'I dunno.'

'No, neither do I.'

Her sister-in-law wiped the back of her hand under her nose. 'Why us, Kelly? Why did all this have to happen to us? And where's Mickey? Where the hell can he be?'

'I wish I knew.'

'It's the police's fault.'

'And how d'yer make that out?'

'All but accused him of doing it. That's why he's scarpered. He couldn't take it no more.'

Kelly silently shook her head. Surely Glenda did not believe what she had just said? She knew herself that her brother was made of much sterner stuff; he was more than able to withstand any amount of interrogation by the police. The reason for his sudden disappearance had to be something else. In fact she suspected that the police were now convinced he was guilty because he had disappeared. But Mickey's guilt was something she herself could not countenance. If he had set fire to that factory then he was ultimately to blame for her husband's death, and that thought did not bear thinking about.

She glanced at her sister-in-law from under her lashes. She suspected Glenda knew more than she was saying. Something about that terrible night that she was not divulging . . . Kelly had no evidence, just gut instinct. But no matter how hard the police had probed or she herself had casually questioned, Glenda was sticking firmly to her story.

Kelly turned her head and looked across at her father who was still sitting staring blankly at the wall opposite, the untouched cup of tea wedged in his hand. Something dreadful must have transpired on that factory roof, far worse than a confrontation with the arsonist, to send him into such a state. But what? It seemed only her father knew and at the moment he wasn't in a fit state to give any sort of clue. Maybe when he finally was, the truth behind this dreadful mess would be known.

A vision suddenly rose before her and she shut her eyes tightly, fighting to rid herself of a picture of Rod in that stock room, slowly choking to death. It was awful, terrible, to think of him meeting his end in such a way, and regardless of the fact that he should not have been in there, doing whatever he was doing, she wondered if the horror of it all would ever leave her.

How she missed her husband! They had been together such a very short time, still in the honeymoon stage of their marriage, just starting life together. In the light of that, how could Glenda talk of fairness?

Kelly took a deep breath and with all the strength she could muster, forced all thoughts of that terrible night to the back of her mind. At the moment the only thing they had left in the world, this house and its few bits and pieces, was in grave jeopardy. Saving it was what she must concentrate on.

She laid her left hand in the palm of her right. With tears pricking the backs of her eyes, she studied the thin gold band on her finger, the one Rod had clumsily pushed on only weeks ago. What she was about to suggest pained her greatly, but, she reminded herself, at a time like this it was no good being sentimental. She raised her head and looked across at Glenda. 'We'll have ter pawn our wedding rings.'

'Eh?'

'You heard me right.'

'Oh, I can't do that, Kelly. I won't.'

'Well, can you suggest anything else?'

Glenda gulped, stared at her for several long moments, then shook her head.

'I don't like the thought either, but I don't see that we have any choice. It's not as though we've 'ote else of value to pawn. Though I doubt we'll get much for them. We might just cover the rent if we're lucky. What we'll do for food, coal and whatnot is another matter. The insurances will have to be cancelled, and I still have to find two and six towards Rod's suit. But at least with the rent paid we'll have somewhere to live for another week.'

Glenda stared at her horrified. The direness of their situation was just beginning to sink in. 'And what do we do after that?'

'After? Glenda, I daren't think that far. I'm just worried about this week. But one thing *you* can do is start looking for another job first thing tomorrow.'

It wasn't strictly speaking fair that she should have to shoulder financial responsibility for them all, but then what other option did they have?

Suddenly a thought struck Kelly. There was another option for Glenda and it was only right that Kelly should voice it even though she felt surprised her sister-in-law hadn't thought of it herself. She took a deep breath. 'You're right, it ain't fair you should work to keep me and Dad. You . . . you could always go back to your own mam and dad's?'

Glenda didn't need to ponder that suggestion. She

had already thought of it immediately after Mickey's abrupt departure, when the truth hit home that she was now the sole bread-winner. Handing over all her wages had been a struggle but when she had weighed everything up, her decision had been easy.

Things might be dire in this house but it was still a better prospect than returning to her parents' cluttered, dusty one; putting up with her father's drunken ravings and her mother's constant whining. Handing over her wages was a small price to pay to live in relative peace. Besides, she had no intention of leaving, she wanted to be here when Mickey returned to welcome him back. She didn't care where he'd been or what he had been up to. His return was all Glenda prayed for.

'I couldn't leave yer, Kelly. Me conscience wouldn't let me,' she lied. 'You're me family now, and as such it's my duty to stand by yer.'

Surprised by her response, Kelly leaned across and laid a hand on hers. 'Thanks. You don't know how much of a comfort it is to hear you say that.'

Glenda forced herself to meet Kelly's eyes. 'It's the least I can do.' She desperately wanted to change the subject. 'Kelly, d'yer think there's any chance Ada Adcock 'ud take you back on?'

She shook her head. 'Not a hope. As far as I can gather the arrangement with her sister is working out very well. I feel awful to be thinking it, but it's a shame that it is because if I could have had me job back it would have bin ideal. I could have kept popping back to check on Dad. I can't leave him for long periods though, Glenda. He can't do anything for himself. You know, he won't even drink that tea 'til I coax him to. So how can I leave him for ten hours a day?'

Looking thoughtfully across at Frank, Glenda nodded. 'He's like one of them slot machines at the fun fair, ain't he?'

'Eh?'

'Yer know, when someone puts a penny in the slot, the light comes on and the machine starts up. When the penny runs out, the light goes off and the machine stops. That's just like yer dad. Like someone winds him up and he mechanically goes into action, then stops just as quickly.'

'Oh, Glenda, that's a terrible thing ter say,' said Kelly crossly, then fought to control her emotions. 'But I have to admit, if it weren't me dad you were saying it about, I'd find it quite funny.'

Glenda fought with herself to stifle the mirth that threatened, but failed miserably. She choked, then exploded into a gale of hysterical laughter which was so infectious Kelly could not help but join in. Finally wiping her eyes, she gnawed her bottom lip, ashamed. 'You're awful, you are. But yer right, it is just like that. Oh, God,' she groaned despairingly, wringing her hands together. ''Til Dad makes some sort of improvement, I don't see no solution to our problem.'

Both women jumped in alarm at a knock on the front door.

'Who the hell can that be?' Kelly said, frowning. 'I hope it ain't no one wanting money 'cos they've no chance.'

She rose and made her way down the dingy passage to open the door. A timid-looking woman, dressed in a brown coat, with a brown felt beret pulled right down over her head, stared back at her. She was carrying a huge brown bag, which appeared to be empty or if it wasn't there wasn't much in it.

Her own worries still very much to the forefront of her mind, Kelly snapped, 'Yes?'

The woman smiled brightly. 'I'm collecting for St Augustine's Church jumble.'

'Oh,' Kelly answered abruptly. 'That's nice of yer. When is it?'

230

'A week on Saturday.'

'Thank you.'

The woman stared at her, bemused.

Kelly frowned. 'Was there summat else?'

'Well . . . yes. Would you like to give anything?'

'Give anything?' Then the penny dropped. 'I'm sorry ter say that if yer looking for stuff from the folks in this street, then you'll have a long wait. We buy from jumbles, not donate to 'em.'

The woman looked embarrassed. 'Oh! Sorry. I'm . . . well . . . I'm new to this area, you see, and . . .'

'That explains it. Look, yer best bet would be to knock on the doors a few streets over that way,' said Kelly, pointing. 'They're a bit better off than us down here. Now please excuse me, I'm busy.'

'Who was that?' queried Glenda when she returned.

'Some woman collecting for a church jumble.'

Glenda tutted disdainfully. 'I hope you told her we could do with some donations ourselves?'

'I did more or less, but I've got to admit I feel terrible now. I was quite rude to her. She wasn't to know all of us round here haven't two ha'pennies to rub together. She said she was new to the area.' Kelly suddenly remembered her father and that he had not drunk his tea. She stepped across and knelt before him, placing her hand under his wrist. 'Drink this up, Dad, it's nearly cold,' she coaxed, guiding him.

She watched forlornly as he raised his arm and sipped the tea. It was just as Glenda had described, only she was wrong on one point. There was no 'light' that came on to indicate any life, just slow mechanical actions. When the mug was emptied she prised it from his grasp and returned to the table. 'Glenda, there's still time today to go job hunting. Why don't you try that hosiery factory on the bottom of Beatrice Road? You might be lucky and get summat, and they could start you straight

231

away. You'll have a short week money wise but anything you get would be better than n'ote. I'm positive they'd snap up someone with your experience.'

Glenda eyed her in alarm. 'Oh, Kelly, not today. I'll go tomorrow. I look a mess . . . I don't feel well . . . I . . .'

'Glenda, we need the money!'

Glenda sighed knowing resistance was futile. 'Yeah, okay,' she agreed reluctantly. 'I might as well.'

Kelly smiled reassuringly. 'You'll feel much better when you've swilled yer face and brushed your hair.'

'D'yer reckon?'

'Come on, Glenda, buck yerself up,' she said sternly. 'If we don't get some money coming in soon, we'll all be out on the street.' Her face softened. 'I will try and get summat meself. I don't know what, but there must be something I can do that'd fit in around Dad.' She turned and looked across at him. She hoped she sounded more convinced than she felt, because as matters stood her situation seemed hopeless.

Chapter Twenty-Two

The door clanged loudly as Kelly left the shop. She hesitated for a moment before putting down the brown carrier bag holding a small loaf, a quarter pound of Stork margarine, some potatoes and carrots. She opened her hand and studied the few coins in her palm, all she had left.

She frowned. It wouldn't go far. She calculated she had just about enough to pay the milkman what was owed and buy a small bag of coal. The milk would have to be cancelled. For the foreseeable future she would have to buy daily. At least that way she wouldn't be facing another bill at the end of each week, and she would start taking her tea without until their financial situation improved. Instead of mostly burning coal, she would have to see about getting some slack and wood.

The timber merchant's on the Woodgate sold their off cuts and, if you were lucky, sometimes old railway sleepers. A base of coal, heaped with slack then several chunks of hard wood, topped off with vegetable waste, gave out a generous heat and actually burned for longer than using just coal on its own. She could cut down on the amount of gas they used too by not turning on the mantles until absolutely necessary. She would save maybe a couple of shillings a week by doing that.

Kelly pursed her lips. There wasn't much else she could cut back on. They were living hand to mouth as it was. At least, she thought, with food still being on ration and talk of further cuts on cheese from two ounces to one and a half a week, she had been spared embarrassment over the small amounts she had bought.

She sighed forlornly, eyes travelling over her old brown skirt and cream jumper. She had stood staring longingly at a lovely costume in the window of Rene's Fashions on her way to town the other week. Pale blue it had been. A fitted jacket, belted at the waist to flare just above the hips, and a straight skirt to match, ending just above the calves. It was a dream of an outfit. Peep-toed shoes and a matching bag would just complete it. Wearing that, she would have felt like royalty. It was ironic that she had enough coupons to buy probably two such suits but no resources. Still, it was no use hankering after something she had no hope of having. Even someone else's cast-offs were out of her reach at the moment.

She was so fed up with making do and mend, having to worry over every penny spent, or where in fact that penny was coming from. Who was it, she thought, who had said that once the war was over a bright future would be had by all? Who had they been trying to kid?

If anything, things were worse now, and not just in her own household. You only had to look around. The houses they lived in were for the most part no better than slums, but regardless the rent was not cheap. Her gaze fell on a little lad sitting in the gutter. He looked pale and undernourished, clothes not far off ragged. Kelly knew his mother, knew she had lost her husband in the war, knew she did her best, against the odds, to care for her family. Like herself and many, many more, that woman was fighting a losing battle. But what could they do about it? How did you claw your way out of the poverty trap when every conceivable obstacle seemed to be blocking your way? How she wished she had the answer.

Forcing her eyes away from the child, she sighed again. She hoped Glenda was lucky with her job hunting. They both needed a stroke of luck to lift their low spirits.

'Kelly, are you all right?' a deep voice demanded.

She jumped. 'Oh, God, Alec, you did give me a jolt. Yeah, yeah, I'm fine. Why?'

'You looked worried.'

'Oh, er . . .' She would have liked nothing more than to spill all her worries out but Alec had done enough for her already. He had been a pillar of support and strength during the aftermath of that dreadful night, and looking back, she often wondered how she would have come through it without his help.

Shock and grief had rendered her practically useless. Unknown to Mickey, who for hours on end was down at the station being questioned by the police, Alec had dealt with all the legalities and formalities of Rod's funeral, leaving Kelly to tackle only what she felt capable of. He had also accompanied Frank home from the hospital, taking instructions on his care from the doctor. All this and more he had done while still fitting in his job and looking after his wife.

Glenda, during all this, had been virtually useless, too wrapped up in her own grief over her brother's death then Mickey's disappearance to have time for anything else. Kelly would be forever grateful to Alec for seeing them through such a difficult period. Even now he still popped in whenever time allowed to check that all was well, and would patiently sit and chatter to Frank in the hope it might do some good.

But there came a moment, Kelly felt, when enough was enough. Alec was a friend of long standing who, in time of tragedy, had shown Kelly just what the word truly meant. For herself, the friendship had deepened to something very special. But Alec was a married man with his own responsibilities. Hers she must now manage herself.

She smiled warmly at him. 'I was just wondering what to do for the dinner, that's all.'

'Are you sure that was all it was?'

'Stop fussing, Alec. You're a married man so you must know that us women always have a hundred and one things to worry about.' She frowned quizzically at the look that flashed across his face, not quite fathoming it. There seemed to be a mixture of hurt, confusion and something else in it. 'Have I said summat I shouldn't?' she ventured.

'Eh? Oh, no, Kelly. Everything's fine, ta. Couldn't be better,' he answered briskly.

Tilting her head, her eyebrows rose and she studied him for a moment. For whatever reason she knew Alec was not being honest with her. Something was bothering him deeply. She knew him well enough to know that. But it was no good probing, men did not easily unburden themselves and especially not outside Ada Adcock's corner shop. They were strange creatures, she thought. They did not readily admit to having problems of any sort, felt it somehow undermined their masculinity.

Not like women. Most women with a problem would seek out another trusted female and discuss, dissect, listen to advice then act upon it in the best way they saw fit. They wouldn't pretend a problem didn't exist, hoping that whatever it was, whatever had caused it, would miraculously disappear. Not that Kelly herself was an expert on men, but if her observations of her brother, father and Rod were anything to go by, then most of them acted the same way. As a member of the male species, Alec would be no different. Whatever was bothering him would have to be coaxed from him gently, and any advice given carefully worded so as not to appear intrusive.

Despite all she had on her mind at the moment, she felt she owed Alec her help. But how to go about it?

'If you say so,' she answered him matter-of-factly.

He frowned. 'And what d'yer mean by that remark?'

She shrugged her shoulders. 'Nothing. Have yer time for a cuppa?'

'Not really, Kelly. I've got the lorry parked round the side. I just stopped to get some bits from Ada's. I'm on me way to collect a wash tub from an old gel that can't get out and I've a pile of scrap to sort out back at the yard.'

Her face fell in disappointment. 'Oh, all right. Maybe soon then, eh?'

He pursed his lips, eyeing her thoughtfully. Kelly was worried about something. Her offer of a cup of tea when she knew he was working was a sure sign that she needed to talk. He didn't like the thought that something was bothering her, something that maybe he could help with. At her tender age she had already suffered more than some people did in a whole lifetime.

'Look, maybe I can spare a few minutes for a quick cup,' he said.

She smiled, hooking an arm through his in friendly fashion. 'We'd best hurry then.'

Kelly placed a mug of steaming tea before Alec and sat down opposite him at the kitchen table. 'I've no sugar,' she said apologetically. 'I . . . er . . . forgot to get some.' She didn't want to tell him of her financial troubles, not when she suspected he had worries of his own. Besides, he would want to help. It was in his nature to offer it whether he could afford to or not and she did not want to take advantage of that. She felt she had already demanded more than her fair share of Alec's attention.

He grinned as he picked up his mug. 'I was cutting down anyway.' He patted his flat stomach. 'I'm getting fat.'

She laughed. 'If you get any thinner we won't see yer when you turn sideways.' She took a sip of her tea then casually asked, 'So, mended those wirelesses yet?'

He nodded. 'Got one working as good as new, the other's just about there. Needs a couple of valves and a bit of soldering. Then hopefully I can sell 'em for a decent price.'

'Oh, you will, Alec,' she said with conviction before picking up her mug again and sipping her tea, her mind whirling. How did she get round to asking what was bothering him without seeming downright nosy? If she didn't get to it soon, it would be time for him to go.

Alec cradled his mug between his hands, eyeing her thoughtfully. Whatever was troubling her, she was not going to let it slip easily. He was suddenly conscious that time was moving on, he needed to get back to work, hadn't time for small talk. There was nothing else for it, he would just have to ask her outright and no messing. Putting down the mug, he looked straight into her eyes. 'What's the matter, Kelly?'

'Eh?' She frowned. 'With me, you mean? But . . .'

He leaned over and laid his hand on hers. 'Kelly, we're friends. You know you can trust me and I'll help if I can. Now what is it?'

She stared at him. How did he know she was troubled when she had taken such care to hide it from him? Her eyes locked with his and she saw the tenderness and sincerity shining from them. Before she could stop herself, tears welled up in her own eyes and splashed down her cheeks, and it all came tumbling out.

'I'm so worried,' she sobbed. 'Glenda got the sack two weeks ago and we've no money coming in. She's out now looking for a job and I just hope she gets one or we're done for. All I've got is a few clothing coupons I could sell.' She sniffed, wiping the back of her hand under her nose. 'I have ter get a job, I have to do summat, but what, with Dad the way he is? And he's not getting any better. He just sits there. If I didn't know better, I'd think he was dead. Oh, Alec, it's all so hopeless and I don't know what to do.'

Silently he rose, picked up the piece of threadbare towelling draped over the sink and handed it to her.

Taking it, she smiled gratefully and wiped her face. 'I'm so sorry,' she hiccuped. 'I didn't mean for this to happen, honest I didn't.'

He sat down again, leaned over and placed his hand on hers. 'Don't apologise, Kelly. You don't ever need to apologise to me. As I said, we're friends.'

'I know, but you done so much for us already and I don't want to tek advantage of yer.'

'That's what friends are for, to be there when yer need 'em. For as long as you need me, I'll do my best to be there for yer. Now, first things first. Have you enough to pay this week's rent?'

She didn't want to tell him of her plan to pawn her own and Glenda's wedding rings, so although she wasn't sure what could be raised against them she said, 'Yes.' A statement she hoped was true.

'Good.' He patted her hand, then sat back. 'See, things ain't so bad 'cos it would've been worse if you'd said you couldn't. Now I know this might seem a daft question but, apart from yer coupons, have you anything you could sell?'

She sighed, shaking her head. 'That was a daft question, Alec. You know we ain't.'

'No, not so daft.'

She frowned, looking at him quizzically from red-rimmed eyes. 'It ain't?'

He shook his head. 'You have a mangle and a wash

tub. You could manage without those for the time being. Do yer washing in the sink and hand wring. Other people do. And I'm sure if you look there's quite a few bits and pieces out the back and in the shed that you could bring down the yard. Anything metal we'll take and in whatever condition as long as it ain't too rusty. You won't get much but it all helps, Kelly. All you need do is make enough to cover things 'til Glenda gets her first pay.'

She looked at him. He was right. The rubbish that had been cluttering the yard and shed for years could be turned into money. There was that old bike of Mickey's. The wheels were long gone but the frame was intact. Then there was a rusty wheelbarrow; an old meat-mincing machine that had originally belonged to her grandmother; and hopefully there were other things her father had scavenged years back while working on the bins which could be worth a little in scrap value.

She nodded thoughtfully. 'I'll have a clear out and gather as much as I can together.'

'That's the spirit, gel. See, yer not as destitute as yer thought.' He paused for a moment, knowing what he was going to suggest next was going to hurt her but her situation was dire and therefore he felt he had no alternative but to bring it to her attention. The choice was hers. 'Kelly, we take clothes,' he said gently.

'Clothes? But I haven't got that much to start with. Probably a jumper I could manage without but even I know I wouldn't get anything at all for an old jumper. You need bagfuls to make it worthwhile.'

'I didn't mean *your* clothes.'

'Well, whose did yer . . .' Her voice trailed off and she eyed him in alarm. 'You mean me mam's and Rod's? Oh, Alec, I couldn't.'

'Kelly, be sensible. Whatever money you could make on them, you need. Come on. What good is it letting the

240

moths eat them? I can't speak for Rod, but I know your mother wouldn't want you to starve for the sake of keeping what's of no use to her any longer. I knew her well enough to know that. You can't be sentimental at a time like this, Kelly.'

She sighed. Again he was right. She had made the difficult decision to pawn her wedding ring, bullied Glenda into agreeing likewise, but always knowing that there was a possibility of redeeming them. The thought of bundling up her mother's and Rod's clothing, it being sold for others to wear, was something she could barely countenance. 'I'll think about it,' she whispered, swallowing hard to remove the lump forming in her throat.

He gazed at her kindly. 'Kelly, whatever you bring down that you really don't want to part with, just tell me and I'll put it aside. I'll let you have it back when you get the money. But that's just between ourselves, all right?'

'You'd risk yer job, doing that for me?'

He nodded. 'Yes. Anyway, it's not as though Raggy'll lose anything by it.'

'But what about his profit?'

He leaned over again and patted her hand reassuringly. 'Don't you worry about his profit. Just concentrate on getting enough things together.' The profit Raggy would have made Alec would pay out of his own pocket. For Kelly he would do that. But he would not tell her; he knew she would refuse his offer if he did.

Fresh tears filled her eyes. 'Oh, Alec, how grateful I am to have a friend like you! Norma is a lucky woman.' She frowned at the look that momentarily crossed his face. 'Alec, what is it? What did I say?'

'Nothing,' he said abruptly, and scraped back his chair. 'Have to get going. You'll probably need a hand getting the stuff down the yard. I'll bring the barrow around early tomorrow morning. I'll just say cheerio to yer dad now.'

Before Kelly could say another word he had walked into the back room and was addressing her father.

'Sorry I ain't time for a chat today, Frank. Hopefully tomorrow. Yer looking better, I must say . . .'

As he chatted on, Kelly stood in the doorway observing him. Anyone overhearing would have thought Alec to be having a normal two-way conversation. This was the way she herself talked to her father, telling him everything that was going on, keeping nothing back. Despite his mental state, he was after all family and, whether he really heard or not, deserved to be told what was happening.

How many men, she thought, especially busy ones like Alec and not even related, would take the time and perseverance to bother doing what he did? To all intents and purposes it appeared to have no effect, to be an utter waste of time. A warm glow filled her. Only a man like Alec. She suddenly realised, and with a guilty feeling for having such thoughts, that her own husband would not have acted in this way, and most definitely not her own brother.

After Alec had said his goodbyes Kelly leaned against the sink, deep in thought. It wasn't her own problems she was thinking of but Alec's. He was worried about something, she was convinced of it now. And whatever it was, it had something to do with Norma. But he obviously did not want to talk about it and until he did, if ever, there was nothing she could do, because one thing was for certain: she did not want to jeopardise their friendship by poking her nose in uninvited.

She turned her head as the back door opened and Glenda entered. Any hope of good news was instantly dispelled by the stricken look on her face.

'I take it there was nothing going?' Kelly prompted, hoping somehow she was reading Glenda's expression wrong.

'I tried three places. They were all taking on, all right. Had several jobs on the board outside. I could have done them standing on me head.'

Kelly frowned, bewildered. 'Why didn't they take you on then?'

''Cos I'm branded, that's why.'

'Branded? What d'yer mean, branded?'

Loosening her coat, Glenda moved across to the chair Alec had not long vacated and slumped down, hanging her head. 'As soon as I said me name, I was shown the door.'

'But why?'

'Word spreads, don't it, Kelly? This town ain't that big, and don't forget the story with names and everything was splashed all over the *Leicester Mercury* for several days.' She sighed forlornly. 'I can't get a job for the same reason I was let go from me last one.' She gave a great choking sob. 'Remember when you said I was acting like a gangster's moll? Well, that's what they think I am – and they think my Mickey's the gangster.' She shuddered violently. 'Oh, Kelly, what the hell am I gonna do? Oh, where is Mickey?' she wailed. 'Why doesn't he come home?'

Dumbstruck, Kelly stared at her. This was the last news she had expected to hear. She had been pinning all her hopes on Glenda's getting some sort of job. Kelly had no doubt she would eventually, when people's memory faded, but time they did not have. They needed money now.

A vision of them traipsing the streets, sleeping huddled together under arches or in derelict buildings, swam before her.

But whatever fate lay in store for herself and Glenda was not important. What became of her father was. At this moment in time he was helpless, not capable of controlling his destiny, and the thought of him reduced to such a squalid existence was more than she could bear. Utter hopelessness and desolation filled her being and she fought the tears that threatened. She had not envisaged matters could get any worse. How wrong she had been.

Suddenly a surge of anger ripped through her. She, Glenda and her father were guilty of nothing, but they were being punished as if they were. That wasn't justice. She marched across to the table, laid her hands flat on top of it, and with her chin raised determinedly, announced, 'I tell yer what we're gonna do, Glenda. We're gonna show 'em all, that's what we're gonna do.'

Her sister-in-law sniffed loudly. 'How?' she asked sulkily.

'I dunno. But we will. The first thing we're gonna do is stop feeling sorry for ourselves. Now, whether you like it or not, Mickey's abandoned us. Don't look at me like that. I don't care what reason he had for going, he shouldn't have done it. We're his family. Yer don't run out on yer family. Even if you hadn't lost yer job, he knew we'd be struggling. He's selfish, Glenda. He's only ever cared about himself and I shall bloody tell him so an' all if I'm unfortunate enough ever to clap eyes on him again.

'As for Rod . . . I'm not saying he deserved to get himself killed, but he shouldn't have been in that factory. Whichever way you look at it, he was stealing from that stock room. There can't have been any other reason for him being in there, and we can't ignore the fact that all those clothes were piled near his body.' She shuddered, wringing her hands, voice hoarse with emotion. 'I know I ain't bin no angel in the past, but I've learned me lesson, Glenda. From now on I do things honestly. That way at least I can hold me head up and I ain't in fear of who's the other side of the door whenever there's a knock.'

244

She took a deep breath, grasped her wedding ring and wrenched it off, slamming it down on the table. 'Now wipe yer face 'cos you're going down the pawn to see what you can get for our rings.'

'I ain't up to it, Kelly,' Glenda pleaded. 'Can't you go?'

Her eyes narrowed and her mouth set grimly. 'Okay, I'll go to the pawn. You can go down the rag and bone yard.'

'Eh?'

'You heard me. I saw Alec today and . . . well, I told him about our predicament. He suggested we get as much as we can together, take it down Raggy Harris's and see what we can get for it. I think he'll do us a good deal.'

Glenda snorted disdainfully. 'You only get a few pennies for a whole bag of rags. We'd need a mountain of stuff to pay for a week's groceries. Anyway, I wouldn't be seen dead in a rag and bone yard.'

Kelly scowled in annoyance, folding her arms under her bosom. 'Don't try and lie to me that you've never been to Raggy's before when I know for a fact that yer mam used ter send you regular when you were a kid with bags of rags. Rod told me. And better than you have been seen in places like that, Glenda. You ain't n'ote special. When yer desperate yer'll do anything to keep body and soul together. And we're desperate.' Her eyes flashed a warning. 'Now, if you wanna stay in this house you'll muck in and we'll fight this through together. If you can't face that then pack yer things and leave now.'

Glenda looked shocked. 'Yer don't mean that?'

'I do. I can manage without yer, Glenda, if I have to.'

'Oh!'

'So what's it to be? The pawn or Raggy's?'

'Th-the pawn.'

Kelly passed over her ring. 'Go to the one on Applegate Street. I've heard he's fair. Stick out for as much as you can. I'll make a start out the back.'

Glenda picked up Kelly's ring, pushed back her chair and left.

She returned just over an hour later and she shut the back gate behind her, stared in surprise at Kelly, emerging from the outhouse. 'What's the wash tub and the mangle doing in the yard? Surely you ain't gonna tek them down Raggy's yard? How's the washing gonna get done?'

'By hand in the sink. We've no choice, Glenda. The tub and mangle are about the only things I found worth any money. There's me granny's old meat mincer, but that's as rusty as hell. Maybe if I cleaned it up first we might get more for it. As for the frame on Mickey's old bike . . .'

'But you could hardly get in the outhouse. There must have been summat else, surely?'

Kelly shook her head. 'I thought there was too but there was only stuff that should have been thrown out years ago. Empty distemper tins, a couple of rotting clippy rugs, an enamel jug without a bottom, some bits of old toys of me and Mickey's, that kinda thing. They were all under a pile of sacks. I did find some wood we can burn. But that's about it.'

Glenda pulled a face. 'Well, so much for that idea. What do we do now?'

Rubbing her aching back, Kelly sighed. 'I dunno. Apart from your bedroom, I've bin round the house just in case there was summat I'd forgotten about. I suppose we could part with the sofa and one of the armchairs. I'll need to keep the one Dad sits in. There's the table and chairs in the front room.' Her voice faltered at a memory of her mother lovingly polishing her pride and joy. She forced it away. 'The back of one of the chairs is broken but the table's not in bad condition considering its age. Someone might be glad of it.'

'And what are we supposed to sit on and eat off?' Glenda asked, dismayed.

Kelly scowled as anger erupted again. 'You could try your bum on the floor! I am doing me best, Glenda. What good is a sofa if there's no house to put it in, or a table when there's no food on it? You tell me that. Look . . .' Her voice lowered to a whisper. 'The main thing is that we pay the rent. We can always get some more furniture when things get better. Now, about Mickey's good suit . . .'

Glenda frowned. 'What about it?'

'You could sell it.'

'I couldn't!' she cried. 'I couldn't sell his suit. He'll need that when he comes back.'

'Glenda, if you don't, I will. Mickey can always get another suit – *if* he comes back. You could get a couple of quid for it. That suit was expensive. It cost him at least a fiver, I'd stake me life on that. And he never bought it on tick. Paid cash.'

'A fiver! Cash? I know the suit's a good 'un but Mickey would never have had that kinda money to lay out.'

Kelly shook her head. 'It seems to me there's a lot you don't know about my brother. Or maybe you do but don't want to see it.' She ran her fingers through her hair, suddenly realising she was expecting Glenda to do something she couldn't and that wasn't fair of her. 'Don't worry, I wouldn't sell it behind yer back. I couldn't do that to yer. But be warned, if things get any worse, we ain't gonna have any choice. Now did he leave anything else?'

'Whadda you mean? Such as?'

'Glenda, stop acting stupid. You know what I mean. Any bits and pieces. He used to keep what he had in a box under his bed.'

'The box is empty.'

'Oh. I was hoping there might be something still in there.' Kelly looked at her expectantly. 'By the way, how much did you get for the rings? You did go, didn't you?'

'Yes, I went,' she replied defensively, 'and I got five bob each.' She pulled a ten-shilling note from her pocket.

Kelly's face fell. 'Five bob? Is that all?'

'It's more than he offered at first. Eight shillin' was all he was going to give me but I gave him such a cock and bull story about me six starving kids the man was nearly in tears. I think he gave me the extra two bob to get rid of me.'

Kelly took the money and the pawn ticket to put away for safekeeping. 'You should have bin an actress, Glenda. If we ever get 'ote else to pawn, you can go and do the business.'

She smiled proudly. 'Actually, I quite enjoyed meself.'

Kelly settled her gaze on the mangle. 'I wonder how much we'll get for that and the wash tub? We need another half crown towards the rent and then at least a pound for food. It's a pity your mam never got round to giving us that stuff she promised. I know it wouldn't be right, parting with anything that was a present, but I'm sure she'd have understood in the circumstances.'

Glenda grimaced. 'What stuff?'

'It was at our wedding. She said she'd sort out a few bits and pieces to brighten up our house. She mentioned a standard lamp and some brass ornaments.'

'Eh? A standard lamp? The only standard lamp I remember is one me dad brought home a couple of years ago. He was on the round off London Road. Yer know, them posh houses? It was a bloody awful-looking thing. Ancient it was. Wrought iron, I think. One of its feet was broken and it had no shade. What he brought it home for is beyond me. And as for some ornaments . . . Oh!'

'What? What is it, Glenda?'

She grinned. 'I've got an idea. What time is it?'

'Time? Er . . . somewhere around three, I think. Why?'

'Me dad'll still be at work and me mam'll be round me granny's. She always goes to me gran's on a Thursday afternoon,' Glenda said excitedly as she turned and hurried towards the gate. 'I won't be long.'

An hour later she struggled back carrying an enormous, overflowing wooden fruit crate.

Kelly, who in the meantime had been straightening up the mess she had created while emptying the outhouse, in between popping in and out to check on her father, stared across at her, bemused. 'What on earth have yer got there?'

Glenda kicked shut the gate behind her and gratefully put down the heavy box. 'The ornaments me mam promised,' she said breathlessly.

'Pardon?'

'Well, she did say she would give them to us. Only don't get yer hopes up. They ain't exactly heirlooms, but we might get summat for 'em.' She bent down and rummaged inside the box, pulling out two eight-day carriage clocks. 'These were in a box full of other stuff in the corner of the landing. There were loads of newspapers and old magazines piled on top. I doubt me mam or dad even remember they were there. They don't work. This one's a bit battered, but this one's not too bad. Maybe the brass cases might be worth a bit?' she said hopefully.

Kelly took hold of the clocks and examined them. 'These ain't brass, Glenda.'

'They ain't?' she said, frowning. 'What are they then?'

'I'm sure they're gilt. But I wonder . . .'

'Wonder what?'

'If Alec might be able to do summat with them. Maybe he could fix them. He's good at fixing things. We could split any profit he makes.' Kelly sighed. 'But I still don't feel right about it. I made a promise to meself that everything I did in future was going to be honest. You took this stuff without asking, and that ain't honest.'

'You mek me sound like a bleeding criminal,' Glenda fumed. 'I've only took what I reckon's mine. I paid me board. Let's be honest,' she said, hurt. 'If I'd had a proper mam and dad like yours were then they'd have give us this stuff to help us out, wouldn't they? They know we've bin struggling. Now I realise they ain't got much themselves but they could have come just to see us, check how we were. But no, they ain't bin near nor by since Rod's funeral. Well, sod 'em both, that's what I say.'

She raised her chin defiantly. 'Look, if it makes yer feel any better, Kelly, think on all this as my inheritance. Only instead of waiting 'til me folks kick the bucket, I'm having it now. I'm telling yer, they won't even notice it's gone.' Her face fell. 'I was only trying to help. I thought you'd be pleased.'

Kelly thought about it. Glenda was right. The Collinses had blatantly disowned them since the news of Rod's death had broken. Even at the funeral the only acknowledgement to herself had been brisk nods of the head. She had been far too grieved at the time and too preoccupied with her worries since to have paid much attention. But the fact was glaring now. And it wasn't fair that they should treat Glenda, their daughter, in this way. Even if they thought the two young women guilty of complicity that night, they had no business to be acting in such a self-righteous way when it was a known fact that Neville Collins was far from a saint himself.

And Glenda was also right about their not noticing

anything amiss in their own house. Even Dad had remarked that the Collinses' house was full of useless junk. If Kelly was honest, she was in no position to turn down this offer. It was doubtful a fortune could be made, but anything at all would be a Godsend. 'What else did you get?' she asked, squatting down eagerly.

Glenda knelt beside her and emptied the box. There were several carpenter's tools in surprisingly good condition; a metal darning mushroom; a wooden box that when Kelly opened it revealed a hundred or more assorted buttons; an aluminium teapot with a wobbling spout; two tin mugs; a blue and white enamel colander, well used but still intact; an old coach lamp which might be brass; three penknives; a pack of cards for the child's game of Snap; three brown bakelite ashtrays; a model of a fisherman – a souvenir from Skegness; two outside wall push bells; a flat iron; nearly a complete set of iron ring weights – the two-pound size missing; a small spirit stove and a cast-iron lemon squeezer.

'Wadda you think?' asked Glenda.

'Well . . . Alec might give us a couple of quid. We can hope. It's a pity one of the weights is missing. I know for a fact a new set costs about four pounds because Ada Adcock was moaning about the price when she bought another for the shop while I was working there. The penknives are in good condition. This one,' said Kelly, picking it up, 'has a mother-of-pearl handle. It might be worth a little more than . . .' She stopped, lifting her head as she heard her name being called.

'Cooee, is that you I can 'ear, Kelly?'

'Yes, it's me, Mrs Chivers. Hang on.' She scrambled up to address her neighbour, a short, thin woman with a pair of metal-rimmed spectacles perched on the end of her nose, who lived on the other side to Avril.

'I've a drop of soup left from 'Orace's dinner,' Mabel Chivers said, stretching over the crumbling wall between

251

them to hand Kelly an enamel bowl. 'Thought it might do yer dad good.'

Kelly accepted the offering. 'That's very kind of yer, Mrs Chivers. I'll give it him later.'

Mabel beamed. 'My pleasure. How is he? Any change?'

Kelly shook her head. 'Just the same, but I keep hoping.'

Mabel grimaced sympathetically. 'Such a shame. A nice man, yer dad. I'm sure he'll get better come time. I said as much to my 'Orace last night. "Such a shame about Frank. Couldn't have happened to a nicer bloke." Still, me duck, God moves in mysterious ways. I'll say this, though, yer coping well, what with all that's happened to yer.'

Kelly smiled wanly. 'I'm trying me best.'

'Yes, but it can't be easy for yer, gel, to be widowed at your age and only having bin married five minutes. Still, yer young enough to find someone else.' Her eyes glinted keenly. 'Did . . . er . . . did you ever find out what went off on that roof? 'Cos summat must have, mustn't it? I mean, a bloke like yer dad doesn't go doolally fer no reason.'

'My father is not doolally. He's . . .'

'Call it what yer like, me duck, but when it all comes down to it he ain't right in the head, now is he? He weren't right after he came back from the war. And what happened on that roof set it all off again, only worse. Me and 'Orace reckon him and Rod must have disturbed whoever set the fire. Rod must have got himself stuck in the stock room and yer dad gave chase. That's how he came to be on the roof. Well, meks sense. Mind you, it does seem strange your Mickey disappearing like that. Still . . .'

'My Mickey ain't disappeared, I'll thank you to know,' wailed Glenda, angrily, jumping up to stand by Kelly.

'He's . . . he's gone up North to find work.'

'Oh, really?' Mabel replied, unconvinced. 'Let's hope he's lucky then 'cos he's left you two in a right pickle, ain't he?' She suddenly peered across Kelly's shoulder. 'What's yer mangle doing in the yard?' She strained even harder to get a better view. 'Oh, and is that a colander? You ain't chucking it out, are yer? If you are, I'll have it 'cos mine's broke.'

'We're not chucking out. We're . . . we're having a clear out, that's all. I've two colanders,' fibbed Kelly to save face. 'What you see is all for sale,' she said matter-of-factly. 'As yer probably know, we need the money.' She felt a sharp nudge in her ribs and turned her face to Glenda's scowling one.

'Why d'yer tell her that for?' she hissed. 'It's humiliating.'

'It's the truth, humiliating or not.'

'Hang on,' said Mabel. 'I'm coming round.'

Seconds later she entered by the gate. 'How much d'yer want for the colander, then?' she asked, picking it up and inspecting it.

'Three shilling,' Kelly replied without thinking.

'Three shilling! I can get a new 'un fer that.'

'Oh, er . . . maybe . . .'

'All right,' interrupted Glenda. 'If you can get one for three bob then go and get one, 'cos you ain't having this one for any less.'

'Glenda?' Kelly whispered, pulling her aside. 'We should be glad of anything we could get for it.'

'Yer've got to haggle the price, Kelly, that's one thing I did learn from Mickey.'

'Two bob and that's me last offer,' Mabel said.

'Two and six,' responded Glenda. 'Tek it or leave it.'

'Huh . . . I suppose I could manage that. I'll pay yer at the end of the week.'

Glenda stepped forward and retrieved the colander

from her clutches. 'We'll put this aside 'til then.'

'Oh, but . . .'

'We don't give credit, Mrs Chivers.'

Kelly quashed an urge to burst into laughter at the look on her neighbour's face.

'Huh! Well, make sure yer do,' snapped Mabel, straightening her turban which had slipped forward. She folded her arms and asked directly, 'What d'yer want for the mangle? Phyllis Crag told me just this morning she was looking for a second-hand one 'cos one of her rollers is broke. Ripped her best twill sheet straight through. Fuming she is. She went down to Raggy's but he ain't got any in.'

A surge of excitement shot through Kelly. 'How much d'yer reckon we should ask for it?' she whispered to Glenda. 'I don't want to sell it for less than it's worth. I know, I'll ask Alec.' She addressed Mabel. 'Tell Mrs Crag to come and see it for herself tomorrow. We'll discuss a price if she's interested.'

Glenda stared at her, impressed.

Mabel stared in surprise. 'Oh, okay. Right little businesswoman, ain't yer?'

'Did I hear someone's selling things?' a voice boomed out from the jitty. 'Oi, Nell, the McCallans are 'aving a sale. Go and tell the others.' A head appeared enquiringly around the gate. 'What yer got then?'

'So how much did we make?'

Kelly sat back and eyed the pile of coins before her. 'I can't believe what happened, Glenda.'

'No, neither can I. But it did.'

'Yeah, but who'd have thought we'd have sold any of that stuff? I mean, what does Mrs Wills want with a lemon squeezer?'

'Lemon squeezer? Was that what it was. I told her it were an old-fashioned tea strainer, the sort they have in posh houses. Anyway she went away happy, so what does it matter? We got a tanner and that's all that counts.'

Kelly nodded. 'Yes, yer right. You do realise that me and you will have to share your bed, being's you sold the mattress off mine?'

Glenda pressed her lips together, suddenly seeing the incident as funny. 'I got carried away. Mrs Shish asked if we'd a mattress going and I said yes. Got a decent price though, didn't I?' she added hopefully to justify her actions.

'I suppose, considering . . . it was as old as the hills and as lumpy as hell. You should have sold her the bed and have done with it, it's no good to me without a mattress.'

'Oh, maybe I could have . . .'

'I was joking, Glenda. I don't intend to sleep with you forever. As soon as I can afford it, I'm getting another mattress.'

'Well, I'm not the only one who got carried away,' she responded haughtily. 'You sold nearly all the stuff we had in the kitchen. We've only got two plates and one saucepan left.'

Kelly smiled sheepishly. 'I know. I can't believe what I did. I just remember thinking we might as well make the most of it. If people wanted to buy, who were we to refuse? And I've just remembered about all those salt and pepper sets I got for wedding presents. Maybe we could have sold those too.' But not the set that Alec had bought. Somehow she couldn't bear the thought of parting with that particular one. 'It was fun, wasn't it?'

Glenda nodded. 'Yeah, it was. Well, come on then,' she urged. 'How much did we make?'

'Just under four pounds. Three pounds eighteen shillings and three farthing to be exact. And that's not including the mangle or the table and chairs.'

'Really! That much? Why, that's more than I earned in a whole week on piece work.'

Kelly stared blankly at her, rubbing her chin.

Glenda folded her arms and leaned on the table. 'What yer thinking? Kelly, what's on yer mind?'

'I'm just thinking it's a pity we couldn't make our living this way. I mean, it'd be ideal. We could do it from here and that way I'd still be on hand to see to Dad.' The first stirrings of excitement were building inside Kelly. Her mind was racing frantically, eyes shining brightly. 'I mean, think of it, Glenda. Look how quickly people came round when they heard we had stuff to sell. Some of them bought things they would never use. As you said, we made more in a couple of hours than you did all week at work.'

'Yeah, but apart from a few things, we sold nearly all we own. We ain't got n'ote else to sell, Kelly. 'Cept the mangle and the furniture.'

'Yes, and I don't intend to sell them if I can help it.' She stared around thoughtfully. 'There must be a way of getting hold of more things. Of course, only ones we'd make a profit on.'

'There's still the clothes. Lots of people asked if we'd got any clothes.'

'Yes,' Kelly said abruptly. 'I know they did. And I know that you're thinking of me mam's and Rod's stuff. I'll have to part with them soon, but not yet, Glenda. I don't know how I'd feel if I saw someone walking down the street in something I recognised. Anyway, I didn't hear you offer to sell anything of Mickey's.'

'You mean his suit, don't yer? I've already told you, he'll need that when he comes home. And don't say he ain't coming home. He is, Kelly. I know one day he will, and his suit and me will be waiting for him.' Glenda watched Kelly's mouth open, knew instinctively that she was going to tell her not to build up her hopes and hurriedly decided to change the subject before a full-scale argument broke out between them. Upsetting Kelly had never mattered to her before but for some reason it did now, Glenda didn't know why. 'I could always get some more things from me mam and dad's,' she offered.

'No.'

'But, Kelly, they'll never . . .'

'They will sooner or later, and I wouldn't like to be on the end of yer dad's temper then.'

'Mmmm.' Glenda nodded in agreement, not relishing the prospect either. 'What we need,' she murmured, 'is a miracle.'

'And that ain't likely to happen. What we need to do is think. Think of a way we can get lots and lots of things for practically nothing. What we don't sell, we can sort out and take down to Raggy's.'

'Like the totters and rag and bone men, do yer mean?'

Kelly stared at her. 'Why, yes, Glenda, that's exactly what I do mean.'

Glenda nearly choked. 'Listen here, if you think I'm traipsing the streets with 'oss and cart, shouting "Any old iron", then you can take a running jump.'

'But why not? People make a living out of doing that. Why shouldn't we?'

The very thought appalled Glenda. ''Cos . . . 'cos we ain't got a 'orse for a start.'

'Oh . . . yes, yer right, and even if we had we'd have nowhere to keep it.'

'You were serious, weren't you?'

'I was. I'll consider anything at the moment.' Kelly gnawed her bottom lip thoughtfully. 'There's got to be another way. There's just got to be.'

They sat in silence for several long minutes.

'Have yer thought of anything yet?' Glenda ventured hopefully at last.

'I'd have told you if I had. But I have thought of someone who just might be able to point us in the right direction.'

'Who?'

'Alec.'

Chapter Twenty-Three

With great difficulty Kelly unlatched the back gate to the house and manoeuvred herself and the heavy box she was carrying through. The gate slammed loudly behind her and she grimaced, hoping that although it was early evening she had not disturbed any of the neighbour's children. But, she thought, judging by the number who dodged by, squealing and squabbling playfully, she doubted any were in bed. And who was she to blame them or the parents for allowing them to stay out on such a lovely early-summer evening?

Hitching the box more comfortably, she began to make her way down the path to Alec's house. Halfway down she stopped abruptly, mouth dropping open. Several feet away was the sashed window of the back room. Through that window she could see Alec sitting at the table. Across it were bits and pieces from the wireless sets. But Alec was not working on them. He was sitting with shoulders slumped, his bowed head cradled in his hands. He appeared to be deeply distressed.

The picture he created upset Kelly greatly and she shivered, feeling mortified for witnessing her friend in such an intimate moment and also guilty for invading his privacy.

She knew Alec was alone. It was too early for Norma to have arrived home from work yet. Kelly had purposely timed her visit so she would not disturb their evening.

She hesitated, unsure what to do. Should she leave or pretend she had not seen him and knock on the door? In a dire situation like this appeared to be, it would be his wife he would want to comfort him. But Norma would not be home for at least another hour yet. And he did look so upset. It was something serious that was bothering him, she had no doubt of that. Kelly decided to take the risk. Alec had been there for her in her time of need, this was the least she could do for him.

Putting the box down by the door, she turned her back to the window and knocked loudly, shouting: 'Alec! Alec, it's me – Kelly.' She turned to face the window then, smiling broadly, and tapped on it, waving a friendly greeting.

Alec was sitting erect now, staring at her. After what seemed like an age he nodded and smiled. It was a forced smile.

She watched him rise and disappear out of view. Seconds later the back door opened.

'Hello, Alec,' she said breezily, purposely avoiding his eyes. She knew he had been crying and didn't want to have to comment on the fact. 'I ain't called at an inconvenient time, have I? Yer not about to have yer dinner or 'ote?'

'No . . . er . . .'

'Oh, good,' she cut in. 'I've got some stuff I wanted yer opinion on.'

'Oh . . . does it have to be now?'

'Well, I suppose it could wait, if yer busy?' she said, implying otherwise.

He stared at her for a moment. 'No, I ain't busy. Come in,' he said, standing aside.

She sighed with relief and stepped inside. At least there she had some hope of finding out what was troubling him and offering her help. 'Oh, I forgot me box.'

'Box?'

'Yeah, it's just by the door. Can you get it, please? Only me arms are about dropping off.'

'Yeah, 'course. Go through and sit down.'

He followed her carrying the box, the contents of which Kelly had covered with old newspapers, and set it down by the table.

Scratching his chin, he stared at it. 'What on earth have yer got in here, Kelly? It's no light weight, is it?'

'You'll see,' she said cagily.

'All sounds very mysterious. Would you like a cuppa?'

'I'd love one if it's no trouble?'

'It's no trouble.' He gazed at the table, raking a hand through his hair distractedly. 'I'm sorry about the mess.'

'But you have to make a mess when yer working, Alec, don't apologise for that.' Looking at the assortment of bits on the table, she frowned. 'I thought you'd finished fixing the sets, or are these another lot?'

'No, they're the same ones,' he said flatly, then turned and headed for the kitchen. 'I won't be a minute with the tea.'

A deep furrow creased her brow. A strange reply considering he had already told her one wireless was ready for sale, the other not far off, and rather abruptly given, she thought. Which wasn't at all like him.

As she waited she took a glance around.

Despite the littered table, this was a lovely room. The walls were covered with a pretty flowered paper which must have been expensive, Kelly thought. Despite the war being three years over, paper such as this was not readily available. And all the woodwork was painted cream, not the usual depressing brown.

Comfortable armchairs stood to either side of the hearth. Between them lay a red half-moon rug. Not a

261

clippy mat, a woollen rug. Probably the only woollen rug in this street. Only the best for Norma, she thought. The mantel was adorned with two brass candlesticks and spaced strategically between were several inexpensive but tasteful ornaments. Above hung an oval, wooden-framed mirror. The table they sat at was placed by the window. Underneath the protective covering Alec had thrown over it while he worked was a good quality green chenille tasselled cloth. The drop leaf table was of solid dark oak, the matching high-backed chairs sturdy but comfortable.

The rest of the rooms, she knew, would be just as nice as this one. For a moment she felt envious. It was exactly the kind of home she had hoped to make for herself and Rod. But envious was the wrong way to feel. Alec and Norma, but especially Alec, had worked extremely hard to get their home just as they wanted it.

The little two up, two down terraced house was in a long row, one of several identical parallel rows, running between the Hinckley Road and Glenfield Road. On the Hinckley Road side was a parade of assorted shops which catered for just about every need. Lane's the butcher's, Greasley the baker's, The Three Sisters clothes and haberdashery, a hairdresser's, barber's, chemist's, greengrocer's, bike shop and bank, meant the residents did not have to venture into town unless they felt it necessary.

It was a pleasant place in which to live and the residents felt themselves definitely a cut above the people in Kelly's area half a mile or so away at the town end of the Hinckley Road.

When Alec returned with the tea, she smiled. 'I was just admiring this room. It is lovely.'

He looked around for a moment. 'Oh, you haven't seen it since we moved in, have yer?' He sighed. 'Took a lot of work, but yes, I think it's nice too.' He frowned, eyeing her searchingly. 'Why haven't you ever visited us since the wedding, Kelly?'

She shuffled uncomfortably in her seat. How could she tell Alec that she had never felt welcome? Norma had made it perfectly clear at the wedding – which Kelly had attended with her mother – that anyone who came to her house would be invited. She did not care for people just dropping by, friends of Alec's or not, she had said then. Kelly shrugged her shoulders. 'Well, yer know how it was. With Mam being ill and everything.' She smiled. 'Anyway, you've both done yerself proud.'

'Mmmm. I'll . . . just get the rest of the tea things.'

She frowned. He was definitely not his usual self.

When he returned, she tried a different tactic. 'Didn't they work then?'

He looked at her, confused. 'Pardon?'

'The wirelesses. Didn't they work? Well, they're all in bits so I presume they didn't and you're fixing them again?'

'Oh, I see. Yes, they worked.'

'They did? Well, why . . .'

Her question was cut short by the back door opening. A woman entered. She stopped dead in the doorway on spotting Kelly. 'Oh! I heard voices and thought . . .'

'This is Kelly, Mrs Quick,' Alec said, rising. 'You remember Kelly McCallan – sorry, Kelly Collins as she is now.'

Fixing frosty grey eyes on Kelly, Iris Quick folded her arms aggressively. 'No, can't say as I do.'

Kelly rose politely and held out her hand. 'I met you at the wedding, Mrs Quick.'

She blatantly ignored the gesture. 'I can't be expected to remember every face from three years back, now can I?' She turned her attention to Alec. 'When I 'eard voices, I thought it wa' . . .'

He took her arm and ushered her back into the

kitchen. 'Please don't think me rude, Mrs Quick, but Kelly is an old friend of mine and she wants some advice.'

His mother-in-law tried to pull away from him and return to the back room. 'Oh, advice, is it? Well, I'm just the one to help then.'

He barred her way. 'It's private. She wants to talk to me.'

'Private?' Her eyes flashed angrily. ''T'int right.'

'What's not right?'

'You being in 'ere on yer own wi' 'er. 'T'int right.'

Alec fought to keep his temper. 'For goodness' sake, Mrs Quick, Kelly is a friend. I've known her for years. I worked with her father.'

'Is she married?'

His thoughts whirled. He did not want his mother-in-law to realise that Kelly was the wife of the man who had died in suspicious circumstances in that factory fire. People were still raking over the scandal. It wouldn't take long for his mother-in-law to put two and two together and he didn't want Kelly to bear the brunt of her opinion when she did. The only reason she hadn't immediately made the connection was that she had a more important matter on her mind. 'She's widowed,' he said.

'Oh, shame, and her so young. But all the same, my Norma . . .'

'Your Norma,' Alec said bluntly, 'ain't here. So it doesn't matter what she thinks, now does it?'

Iris's face turned the colour of beetroot. 'Well!' she spat. 'I see. Like that, is it? 'Cos my Norma's not 'ere, *I'm* not wanted either.'

He sighed heavily. 'It's not a case of that, Mrs Quick, and you know it.'

'Oh, do I? Do I indeed? I shall mek sure my Norma hears about this carry on. As soon as I see her,' she added hurriedly. She yanked the door open, stepped through and slammed it shut behind her.

'I'm sorry about that,' Alec apologised to Kelly on his return. He folded his arms and leaned against the table. 'Now, what's this advice yer wanted?'

Kelly stared back at him. The man before her was struggling hard to make it seem that everything was normal when it was blatantly obvious to her that it was not. 'I ain't daft, Alec.'

He looked at her quizzically. 'Eh?'

'I said, I ain't daft.' She took a deep breath. 'I know summat's wrong. Summat's bin wrong for a while, ain't it?'

He shook his head, face innocent. 'Nothing's wrong,' he said lightly. 'Whatever gave yer that idea?'

She reached across, laying her hand on his arm. 'I saw yer, Alec. I saw yer through the window. You were crying. And just look at yer. In all the years I've known you, I've never seen you look such a mess. When was the last time you had a proper shave? Now tell me to mind me own business. Tell me to bugger off. But don't insult me by telling me there's n'ote wrong.' Her voice lowered to a whisper. 'I thought we were friends, Alec.'

He stared at her for several long moments, then his face suddenly crumpled and tears ran down his cheeks. 'Oh, Kelly, yer right. Something is wrong. It's bin dreadful. I . . . I . . . still can't take it in.'

'What, Alec?' she murmured, his obvious pain distressing her greatly.

He gulped. 'It's . . . it's Norma,' he faltered. Reaching inside his trouser pocket, he pulled out a handkerchief and blew his nose noisily.

'What about her?' she coaxed, fear building inside her. Was Alec about to tell her that Norma was seriously ill with something terminal like her own mother had had? 'Is she ill, is that it?'

265

'Ill? No, it's nothing like that. It's terrible to say it but I wish that's what it was.' He swallowed back a sob. 'She's . . . she's left me, Kelly.'

She was astounded. 'What? Norma has left you! Oh, Alec, I'm so sorry. I . . . I can't believe it. But you two . . . well, you were so happy.'

'I thought so too.' He wiped his eyes again and blew his nose. 'But Norma wasn't.'

'But why wasn't she? Why, Alec? You did so much for her. Look at this house. She got everything a woman could ever want. And,' Kelly said softly, 'she had you, Alec.'

He took a shuddering breath. 'That's just it, Kelly. It's me she doesn't want.'

Speechless, Kelly stared at him. After several long moments, she said, 'What brought all this about? D'yer want to talk about it? I'll understand if yer don't.'

He sighed deeply, his head bowed. 'It ain't fair to burden you with my problems, Kelly, you have enough of yer own.'

'How can you say that to me?' she said softly. 'When you sat in my kitchen today, helping me, and all the time you were troubled yerself? Friendship ain't one-sided, yer know, Alec.'

He raised his head and looked at her. 'Yes, yer right. And I would like to talk about it, and you're the only one I would want to confide in.' He sniffed and took several deep breaths. 'It all came out of the blue. I'd no idea Norma was unhappy. Or maybe I did, but I just didn't want to see it. Anyway, about six weeks ago she came home one night and said she wanted to talk to me. She said she'd got promoted at work. I was so glad for her, Kelly. She worked hard and deserved what was being offered her. I said as much and told her I would do all I could to help. She said, that was just it, she didn't want my help. In fact, she didn't want *me*.' His voice faltered.

'She told me she didn't love me any more.'

'Oh, Alec,' Kelly whispered.

He lifted his head, the deep pain he was suffering etched across his face. This baring of his soul, Kelly knew, was not easy for him. 'I begged her, Kelly. Begged her to give me another chance. But she wouldn't. She said it was too late. She said she had given me all the chances she was going to.'

'What did she mean by that?'

'She . . . she was ashamed of me job. She'd been asking me to do something about it for a while. She hated this house and the area we lived in.'

Kelly stared at him, astounded. 'Really? But she grew up here. Her mother lives next door. And as for being ashamed of yer job, it's an honest living yer make, Alec. And you love it, don't yer?'

He nodded. 'Yes, I do, much more than being on the bins. But I should have got something better. Something with a better future. Something that'd pay enough for me to provide properly for her.'

'Provide properly?' Kelly's brow furrowed crossly. 'I'm sorry, Alec, think what you like of me for saying it, but you've only got ter look round to see you provided for her properly. For God's sake, just what did she want?' She tightened her lips, ashamed. 'I'm sorry. I shouldn't speak about Norma like that. She is your wife.' Suddenly a memory came to mind. She saw Norma entering the coffee house with a man, his arm clasped intimately around her. 'Look . . . er . . . are you sure it's not summat else?'

He eyed her questioningly. 'What d'yer mean?'

She swallowed hard. 'Another man?' she said tentatively.

He shook his head savagely. 'No. Norma might not love me any more but she'd never do that to me. It crossed me mind, 'course it did, and I asked her. She was really angry that I'd even think it.'

Kelly declined to comment further. She had her own feelings on the matter. Why would any woman want to give up all that Norma had, and more importantly a doting husband, even if she were dissatisfied with her lot? No, it didn't make sense. Kelly felt she was no expert on such matters but knew that if there was no other man, then there was something else Norma hadn't told Alec. 'So she just left then, did she?'

'Not quite. It was a week before she finally went. It was awful, Kelly. I kept hoping she'd change her mind. Every night when she came home I'd hope she'd tell me she was just going through a phase and that . . .' He shrugged his shoulders. 'I dunno, she'd got over it and we could go back to how it was before.' He exhaled forlornly. 'But she never.'

'Where's she gone?'

'Staying with a friend, she said. She won't give me the address in case I go round and cause trouble. As though I would, Kelly,' he said, hurt. 'I'd never do 'ote like that.'

'I know you wouldn't,' she whispered. And, she thought, Norma knew her husband well enough to know that too. So why wouldn't she give him her address? What was she hiding? 'Have you seen her since she left?'

He nodded. 'For the first couple of weeks she came round several times. Just called in to see I was all right. Said she was worried I'd do summat stupid.'

'Like what, Alec?'

'Top meself, I expect.'

In the light of what she had done to her husband, it was nice of her to be so considerate, Kelly thought scathingly, but kept her thoughts to herself.

'But though she said she was coming to check on me, I got the feeling it was the house she was really checking on. Yer know, making sure I hadn't got rid of anything.' He exhaled loudly, running a hand through his hair.

'Oh, maybe I'm imagining that. I asked her to stop in the end. Every time she came round I'd start thinking she'd decided to return. But she still came calling. She'd wander round the house, collect a few things, then go again.'

Kelly clasped her hands tightly. She was at a loss as to what to say to give her friend any comfort or hope. But how cruel of Norma to treat him in this way! She knew the man loved her, knew what she had done had devastated him. Why did she keep visiting like that? Did she not realise how much more pain she was causing him?

'She . . . she came again last night.'

'She did?'

'Yes. Gave me a list of the things she wanted from the house. And asked me for money. I gave her what I could.'

Kelly was shocked. 'Asked you for money? But she has a good wage, Alec. Surely she can manage without asking you? You still have all the bills to pay for this house and to eat and keep yerself warm.'

'Norma was never any good with money. She's never paid a bill since we got married. I don't think she'd know how. But that's my fault, Kelly. I wanted her to have her own money, to be able to buy what she wanted. I felt it was my job to keep her. She worked hard, she was entitled.'

Kelly could not believe what she was hearing. 'But you work hard too. Marriage is all about sharing, ain't it? It's not my business to ask but did Norma not put any of her money into the house at all?'

'At first she did, yeah. But . . . well, I don't know when it stopped really. It just sort of happened. She used her money to buy things for herself. She did buy the odd thing for the house. She bought the rug,' he said, inclining his head towards the red rug by the hearth.

'And she said she'd pay for the paper for this room?'

'And did she?'

'Er . . . no. I ended up doing it. I had no choice.'

'Oh?'

He eyed her sharply. 'Do you think it was wrong of me to treat her like this? To show I cared for her. I just wanted her to be happy.'

Kelly eyed him tenderly. 'Maybe you showed you cared for her too much, Alec.'

'What d'yer mean by that?'

'Just that some people are never happy, whatever you do for them. The more you do, the more they want.'

He stared at her thoughtfully. 'I have to admit that Norma never seemed to be totally happy. Even when summat good happened, she'd find something to moan about. It's funny but I've only just realised that.' He narrowed his eyes. 'Maybe I should have beaten her now and again,' he said scathingly. 'Gone down the pub every night and come home drunk. Maybe she wouldn't have left me then. Wadda you think, Kelly, eh?'

She shook her head. 'You couldn't hurt a fly, Alec, let alone take your belt to yer wife.' She took a deep breath. 'Look, what's happened has happened, for whatever reason. You have to stop going over the whys and wherefores. It doesn't get you anywhere. I should know. I've gone over everything that happened the night Rod died, wondering if summat I'd said or done was behind it. And you certainly have to stop blaming yerself. There's two in a marriage and sometimes it does happen that one doesn't want what the other does. You never know, Alec. In time Norma might realise what a dreadful mistake she's made and come back. I know it ain't easy to do but you have to put it all behind you and start living. Just take each day at a time. It will get easier. Believe me, I know.'

He sat deep in thought for a moment, then tilted his head and smiled at her. 'How old are yer, Kelly? Nineteen. Well, for someone your age you have a lot of wisdom.'

His smile was returned. 'At the moment I feel like a woman of ninety. But if I have any wisdom at all then it's me mam I've to thank. We spent a lot of time together, 'specially near the end. She talked to me about things I expect she wouldn't have 'til I were older. If she'd had a choice. But she knew, didn't she? She knew she wouldn't be around then.'

'Your mother was a lovely woman, Kelly. She was special.'

Her eyes misted over. 'Yeah, she was. But what about Norma's mother? What's she have ter say about all this? I expect she's upset?'

'Upset ain't a strong enough word. Her daughter can't do n'ote wrong in Iris's eyes.'

Kelly grimaced knowingly. 'Oh, I see. She blames you, does she?'

He nodded. 'Yes, she does, and she's made no bones about it. Said I failed her daughter. Said if I hadn't have got meself the sack in the first place, then didn't seem to bother about getting meself another proper job, none of this would have happened. She said she couldn't blame Norma for what she'd done.'

'Silly woman! You've bin good to her. Not many sons-in-law would have taken her on board. Take no notice of her.'

'It's hard not to when she lives next door and comes round all the time, wanting to know what's going on. I don't understand what's going on meself so how can I tell her?'

'Does she know where Norma's living?'

'If she does, she's not saying. It makes things harder for me though. Whenever I think I'm beginning to pick up a bit, she comes barging in and ruins it all and I'm back to square one.'

'You'll have to speak to her, Alec. Make her see your side of things.'

'I can't, Kelly. She's an old lady and apart from Norma I'm all she's got.'

'Oh, Alec. You're such a thoughtful, kind man. I think Norma's crackers to do what's she's done. Still, as I said before, there's nothing else you can do but accept all this and get on with yer life. I know it's easy to say, but what you're going through . . . I would imagine it's like a bereavement. You've lost someone you loved very much. The pain'll ease, yer know, come time.'

'Will it?' he said, unconvinced.

'You have to work at it.'

'I'm trying, Kelly. I'm trying really hard. But I can't shift this feeling of being such a failure. I can't help wondering where it was I went wrong. Maybe if I did understand then I could get over it easier. It's the not knowing, yer see. I must have done summat wrong, Kelly, or she'd still be with me, wouldn't she?' He paused for a moment. 'She did tell me I tried to please her too much.' He eyed Kelly questioningly. 'Do yer think that's it? That's where I went wrong?'

'Oh, come on, Alec, how can it be wrong to want to please someone you love? I know I'd have bin ecstatic if Rod had done things just to please me.'

'He didn't?'

Kelly stared at him. 'Well . . . to be truthful, I don't think he did. But then, Rod was different from you.' Her eyes filled with sadness. 'We weren't married long enough to get to know each other properly. And things were pretty hard for us when we got married.'

'Yes, I suppose they were,' he said and gazed at her searchingly. 'Do you still miss him, Kelly?'

'Yes, 'course I do, but not so bad as when it first

happened. It really hurts when people say I'm young enough to get someone else. I know they mean well. But all the same, I wish they'd keep thoughts like that to themselves.' She sighed heavily. 'I do feel guilty.'

'Guilty? Why in God's name do you feel guilty? Whatever for?'

'I . . . I feel awful for admitting it but I wasn't ready to marry Rod, Alec, not just then. I'd just lost me mother and me dad wasn't coping very well and there was the trouble between Mickey and him. I felt the time wasn't right. Oh, I loved him. I did really. But I felt that we only got married because of circumstances, that's all. Everybody said it was for the best and I couldn't find the heart to say no. But I was really looking forward to going to work and meeting different people. Then I couldn't, could I? Someone had to look after the house.

'I suppose that's why I felt more like Rod's mother than his wife. It wasn't like we did anything very different from when we were courting. He still had his nights down the pub. And the football. He wouldn't miss a match when Leicester were at home. I didn't begrudge him, not at all I didn't, but . . . well, I had hoped we'd do more things together. Me mam and dad always did things together, before the war that was and everything changed.

'I just feel guilty for thinking these things. Rod was Rod. I knew what he was like and it's not that I expected to change him, but I suppose I hoped he *would* change.' She shrugged her shoulders. 'Then again, as I've said, we never got long together.' She suddenly paused, looking surprised. 'I've never spoke to anyone about me feelings like this before. You do that to me, Alec. You have this way of putting me at me ease. I do feel better for it.'

'Yes, so do I. Thank you, Kelly.'

She folded her arms and leaned on the table. 'It's you I should be thanking, for all you did when Rod died. I wouldn't have come through it all without your help.'

'It was my pleasure, Kelly. All we need now is for yer dad to recover.'

'Yeah, and that day will be the best of me life.'

He leaned back in his chair, rubbing the back of his neck. 'All this talking has fair tired me out and made me parched. Would you like some more tea?'

She looked down at her cup. 'I haven't drank this one yet. Too much gassing. I wouldn't say no to a hot one, though.'

She rose and followed him into the kitchen, leaning against the sink as she watched him going about the mashing of a fresh pot of tea. 'So,' she asked, 'what do you intend doing?'

He turned to face her. 'In what way?'

'Are you going to try and win Norma back?'

Filling the teapot with boiling water, he gave a deep sigh. 'I've already tried all I can and she's made it clear how she feels. You're right, Kelly. I have to get on with my life. It ain't gonna be easy. I still care for her so much. I can't help worrying about her too. But I have to stop doing that too, don't I?'

'In the meantime, yes. And what about yer job?'

'I love me job, Kelly. At the moment I don't see any reason to leave it.'

'Good, and neither should you. Here,' she said, taking the teapot from him, 'I'll carry that through.'

Back at the table, she said, 'There was summat I wanted to ask . . .'

'Oh, what's that?'

'The wireless sets. Why did you take them to pieces again?'

He picked up a large glass valve and studied it. 'One night last week I got so low I took them apart for summat to do, then I couldn't find the heart to put them back together again.'

'But you will now, won't you, Alec?'

Laying the valve back down, he nodded. 'Yes, I will, then I'll sell the bloody things.'

She grinned. 'As you would say to me – that's the spirit. Now have you eaten?'

'Eh! Oh, er . . . I'll have something later.'

She scanned her eyes over him. He was definitely getting thinner, his face quite gaunt. 'When was the last time you ate, Alec?' she asked in concern.

He looked at her sheepishly.

She pushed back her chair. 'Come on,' she ordered. 'It's only veggie soup and bread.'

'Oh, but I couldn't impose . . .'

'Do as yer told,' she commanded. 'I won't be able to sleep tonight, knowing you ain't eaten, so unless you want me having a sleepless night on yer conscience, you'd better come.'

He smiled. 'All right. Oh, but what about the advice yer came to see me about? And I want to know what's in that box.'

'You can give me the advice I need just as good in my house as in this one. And as for what's in the box, it's just some bits I wanted you to look at.' She laughed. 'But I'd be even more grateful if you'd carry it back, I don't think me arms'll stand up to it again.'

Chapter Twenty-Four

'You've some decent stuff here,' Alec said later that evening. After his soul-searching talk with Kelly, he'd enjoyed a delicious bowl of soup, the only hot meal he'd had for days. In friendly company, for the first time in weeks he felt he could begin to look forward. Unburdening himself to Kelly had been surprisingly easy, but why had that fact surprised him? If there was anyone in this world he trusted and respected it was his friend Kelly Collins, and if he couldn't be honest and truthful about his innermost emotions to her, then who could he confide in?

Glenda and Kelly were busy emptying the contents of the box on to the table and for a moment Alec looked at Kelly in a way he'd never done before. As any man would. She was blossoming. A woman now, no longer the girl he always pictured her as. And an attractive woman at that, albeit her clothes were shabby, her hair scraped back untidily at the base of her long slender neck and secured with a piece of elastic. But despite that there was a presence about her he had not noticed before. He didn't know what it was but it was something that made you sit up and take notice.

Kelly had never been anyone's fool, had always had spirit, never been afraid to say what was on her mind. It was as if all that had happened to her over the last few months had softened her somehow, brought hidden qualities to the surface. He smiled. People were right. She would have no trouble finding someone else. Alec, although not wishing ill of the dead, just hoped it was someone more worthy of her than Rodney Collins had been.

He leaned over the table and picked up the clocks. 'These are gilt as you said, Kelly, but I reckon I could make one reasonable one out of the two. I can't promise, I ain't no clockmaker, but I'll have a go. The spout on the teapot I can weld back. Someone might buy the weights even though one is missing. I'll take this lot back home with me and start working tomorrow night. Then we'll take it from there.'

'Thanks, Alec,' she said gratefully.

'How much money d'yer think we'll make?' asked Glenda.

He frowned. 'Hard to say at the moment.' He smiled at both women across the table. 'I'll fix 'em up the best I can and get a good price. I won't do yer down.'

'I know yer won't,' Kelly responded with conviction. 'We appreciate what yer doing and we'll go halves on the money, Alec.'

'We'll see. Now what was this advice you wanted?' he asked.

Folding her arms, she leaned on the table. 'I want to know how we can get hold of stuff for next to n'ote to sell on? The sort of stuff people round here need, 'specially old clothes.'

Taken aback by her unexpected question, he stared at her for a moment then leaned back in his chair and laughed. 'We'd all like to know the answer to that one, Kelly. If I did, I'd be rich, I can tell yer.' Her face fell and he quickly spotted it. 'I wasn't laughing at you, Kelly,' he said hurriedly. 'I can see how yer mind's working.'

'Yes, well,' she said defensively. 'We made as much in

an hour with the bits and pieces we sold as Glenda would earn all week in the factory, and I just thought . . .'

'Why not make yer living that way?' he cut in. 'And yes, why not, Kelly? Many do. It ain't a great living. But all the same it's a living.' He scratched his head. 'The only people who get 'ote for n'ote are ones collecting for church jumbles, charities and such like. As for getting stuff cheap, rag and bone men and totters, as you know, go around with lorries or carts. They're prepared to take anything, Kelly, and it's damn' hard work. Yer know that, don't yer?' He eyed her worriedly. 'Are you prepared to do that? All the heavy lifting involved. Out in all weathers. And some people don't treat you very nice either. Somedays you don't get anything that's worth your trouble.'

She sighed, seeing her plan rapidly disappear. 'It was just a thought,' she said forlornly.

'It was a good one, Kelly.'

'And there's no other way, Alec, none at all?' Glenda asked, suddenly realising that this meant she would have to muster all the courage she could summon and resume the task of finding a job. With this idea in tatters there was no other choice. Or was there?

'Kelly, you could go job hunting and I'll stay at home and look after yer dad?' she suggested.

Kelly turned sharply to face her. 'We've bin through this before, Glenda. You know I won't earn as much as you could, not enough to keep us at any rate. We were scraping by on what you brought in as it was. You could always go back home . . .'

The other woman shuddered. 'As if I could, and leave you in this mess.'

Kelly turned her attention back to Alec. 'I suppose it was a brainless idea anyway. Oh, but it would have bin the answer to all our problems if we could have made it work!' She rose and went over to her father. Kneeling down, she took his hands in hers, stroking them tenderly. She stared up into his face. His eyes were seemingly sightless, staring, hardly blinking. 'Never mind, Dad, summat'll turn up, eh? Now how about a cuppa for you? Yes. Okay,' she said, resting his hands back in his lap and giving them a gentle pat. 'I'll be back in a minute. Then, when you've drank yer tea, I'll take you to the lavvy and get you ready and tucked into bed.'

She had gone as far as the kitchen door when something Alec had said suddenly struck her and she turned back. 'Church jumbles?'

'What about them?' he asked, eyeing her in confusion.

'Scouts and Brownies and others like that have jumbles too, don't they?'

He nodded. 'Yes. So?'

'Do they always sell everything?'

Unsure where this conversation was heading, he frowned, but before he could reply Glenda asked, 'Why a' yer asking that?'

Eyes shining excitedly she sprang back to the table and sat down. Clasping her hands, she said, 'I just want to know what's done with the stuff that's not sold when the jumble's over?'

'Well, 'course, there's different kinds of jumbles,' said Alec.

'There is? What d'yer mean by different?'

'I know what he means,' piped up Glenda. 'Posh jumbles and our kind. I've got a couple of nice outfits from posh jumbles.'

Kelly flashed her a scathing look. 'I thought you said you wouldn't be seen dead in places like that?' she said accusingly.

Glenda glared back. 'I said rag and bone yards, Kelly. You can't compare a rag and bone yard to a posh jumble, now can yer?' She raised her head haughtily.

'Some of the best people buy their clothes from posh jumbles, so why shouldn't I?'

'So my place ain't good enough for you then, Glenda?' Alec said with a twinkle in his eye.

She nearly choked. 'I . . . I . . .'

He laughed. 'Don't swallow yer tongue. I understand, don't worry.' He turned to Kelly, eyeing her keenly. 'As far as I know what's left gets stored to bring out again at the next jumble – that's if there's somewhere to keep it. Or the ones that can be bothered collect it all up and bring it down to us or one of the other yards. We give the going rate. Now come on, gel, you've got me all intrigued. Just how is your mind working?'

The idea Kelly had begun to formulate was running away with her, all sorts of things flashing through her mind. She was hardly able to contain herself. 'Well, what if we could buy what was left? We could . . .'

'How can we buy anything when we ain't got any money?'

'Oh, shut up, Glenda,' Kelly erupted. 'Let me finish.'

'Yeah, be fair,' Alec said. 'Carry on, Kelly,' he urged.

'I was going to say, we could buy it all up. At a reasonable price of course. And we could sort it out. Keep back what we could sell and bring the rest down to you. I mean, organising jumbles and sales is all done voluntary. By the time the jumble's over people are fed up, ain't they? They just want to get home. They might be glad of someone going in and clearing what's left, as you said, Alec. Saving them the trouble.'

He looked impressed. 'It's a cracking idea, Kelly.'

Her eyes sparkled. 'You think so?'

'Yeah,' he said thoughtfully. He clasped his hands and leaned over the table. 'I know it sounds morbid but have yer thought also about people who've died?'

'Eh!' both women said in unison.

He laughed. 'Oh, you should see your faces! What I

281

mean is that dealers scan the papers for death notices. Then they go round to the address and offer to buy anything that's not wanted. And it's not much they offer either. The deceased usually has something.' He lowered his voice. 'Clothes. In cases where the person lived alone there's also furniture, a cooker of sorts, wash tub, that sort of thing. Depending on the area, it's mostly not in that good a condition but sometimes yer get lucky.'

'I hate to put a blight on all this,' Glenda piped up. 'I mean, it's all well and good talking about buying stuff, but what about money? And of course we ain't any transport to lug the stuff in if we did get it.'

Kelly sighed, a look of acute disappointment spreading across her face. 'Yeah, you've a point, Glenda. Maybe I was just getting carried away. But we could still do the jumbles. So what if we have to make several trips?' She narrowed her eyes. 'Do yer think I *want* to do this, Glenda? Don't yer think I'd sooner get a proper paying job? I need to look after me dad and if this is the only way I can do it, then that's what I'll do. And let's face it, you ain't in no position to turn down anything that'll make money.'

The thought of several trips backwards and forwards with heavy boxes and bags did not appeal to Glenda at all, but was still better than the prospect of both returning to her parents' home and having the humiliation of applying for jobs and the resulting knockbacks.

Still, there was always the hope that Mickey would return and rescue her from all this. That was all she dreamed of. And she knew he would. She just prayed it was sooner rather than later. She realised Kelly was talking to her. 'Eh? Sorry, I missed that.'

'I was just saying that I could always deal with that side of things if you really don't feel you could do it. It wouldn't bother me.'

'What side of things?'

'Buying and collecting the stuff. You could be the one to sort it out and organise our sales. Put the word round. We never had any trouble with our first sale. Okay, I admit that might have bin a fluke. But somehow I don't think so. People always need things, and folk round here ain't got the money to care whether it's new or not. Think about it, Glenda,' Kelly said excitedly. 'We could do this, I know we could. And we could have fun. It was fun, wasn't it?'

'Mmmm. Yeah, it was.' Glenda nodded. 'Okay, I'm in. But as I said before, don't expect me to go round the streets knocking on doors, 'cos I won't.'

Kelly couldn't contemplate any of this without Glenda alongside and gratefully grasped her arm. 'Thanks. And I promise not to send you door knocking.' She added with a twinkle in her eye, 'Not straight away at any rate.' Then turned her attention back to Alec and frowned at the sight of him slumped back in his chair, deep in thought. 'What is it?' she asked worriedly. 'Alec?'

'Oh! Er . . . I was just thinking.' He pulled himself up. 'I'd have to speak to Raggy about it first, but maybe I could help on the transport front.'

'You could?'

'Don't get yer hopes up, Kelly. As I said, it depends on Raggy, but I don't see why not as we already collect anyway. But you'd have to promise just to use our yard to sell your stuff on.'

'Of course,' she said, hurt. 'Who else's would I use?'

He grinned. 'There's no need to get uppity. But to put to Raggy what I intend putting to him, then I'd need summat as a bargaining factor. And as fer money to get you started . . . I might be able to help there.'

Kelly gazed at him. 'I wouldn't expect you to do that. Anyway, you ain't exactly rich, Alec, so how can yer?'

'No disrespect, Kelly, but I'm better off than you.'

'Me neighbour next door who's got all her stuff in the

pawn is better off than me at the moment, Alec. What I meant was that you hardly have money to throw around.' She grimaced. 'How much d'yer reckon we'd need to get started?' Thinking of the nearly four pounds they had already made, trying to work out how little they could manage on, but in truth knowing that all the money she possessed at the moment was already spoken for twice over.

'Not too much. About a fiver.'

Her mouth fell open. 'Is that all? Regardless, though, five pounds was a fortune at this moment and something she had no hope of finding even in dribs and drabs. 'Might as well be a hundred as a fiver, I've no hope of getting that amount together.'

'I could. I could fix those bloody wirelesses and sell 'em, and with the stuff you already have here, I should just about raise that figure.'

'But I couldn't let you do that.'

'Why not? We're friends, ain't we?'

'Yes, I know, but . . .'

'No buts, Kelly. I want to do this. Please let me.' He rose. 'Can I talk to you in the kitchen for a minute?' He looked at Glenda apologetically. 'Nothing against you, it's just kinda personal.'

She sniffed. 'Don't mind me.'

In the kitchen he took Kelly's hand. 'Let me do this. I need summat to occupy me mind. Fixing those wirelesses and the other stuff will give me a purpose. As for the money, if it makes you feel better, you can pay me back when you make your first hundred.'

She looked into his eyes. Pride notwithstanding she had no choice but to accept this offer. 'Oh, Alec, thank you.'

He leaned over and gave her a friendly peck on the cheek. 'You'll make this work, Kelly, I know you will. Just don't forget me when you buy your first mansion.'

She laughed, with a mixture of excitement, enthusiasm, but more than all of those – hope. 'As if I could.' She grasped his arm. 'Oh, Alec, for the first time in ages I feel good about summat. Come on, we'd better get back or Glenda'll think we're talking about her.'

'A word about her, Kelly.'

'Oh?'

'Just watch her. Make sure she pulls her weight. I've nothing against her but . . .' She was Mickey's wife, and Mickey he did not trust. But how could he voice his fears to Mickey's sister?

'But what?'

'Look, what I'm getting at is that she's the type who'd just sit back and let you do all the work if you let her.'

Kelly smiled knowingly. 'I have Glenda's measure, Alec, don't worry. I shall be keeping me eye on her.' She paused for a moment, thoughtfully. 'She's changed, yer know, Alec, since all the trouble. I can't put me finger on it exactly. But she ain't quite so . . .'

'Selfish?'

'I don't know whether selfish is the word. I suppose I mean she used to be out for herself. If that's selfish, then yes. She's still like that, and who can really blame her, Alec? But she ain't quite so bad, if that makes sense. I ain't no fool, though. I know the main reason she won't go back home is to do with Mickey. She wants to be here if he comes back. And to be honest, I need her. I can't manage without her, Alec, and I ain't ashamed to admit that.' She smiled. 'I didn't really used to like Glenda, but I'm getting to.'

'Good, 'cos there's got to be a lot of trust between yer if you're going to try and earn a living together.'

'Yes, I know.'

He patted her arm. 'Well, just keep yer wits about you, that's all I'm trying ter say.'

A warm glow filled her at the thought that he should

be so concerned for her welfare. But then friends, good friends, did concern themselves with such matters. Wasn't she the same about him? 'I will, Alec, don't worry.'

Back at the table, he began to put all the stuff back in the box. 'I'll get off and make a start.'

'Not tonight, Alec. It's late,' Kelly said.

'Sooner I get started the better.' He picked up the box. 'And both of you could make a start too. I suggest you take a walk round tomorrow.'

'What for?' asked Glenda.

'Churches, libraries, post offices, those kinda places. They all carry advertisements when jumbles are on. Oh, and I know it's a good trek but it'd be worth one of you going around Clarendon Park, and there's a good few churches further up the London Road. One or two of them are bound to be having a jumble for some good cause or another and the stuff donated around those areas will be good quality.'

Kelly smiled gratefully. 'Thanks, Alec. I can't go too far 'cos of Dad, but there's a good area around here I can cover. Glenda could go further, couldn't you, Glenda?'

Her eyes flashed. 'I suppose,' she said grudgingly.

She was still sitting at the table when Kelly returned after seeing Alec out.

'Shame about him, ain't it?' Glenda said matter-of-factly.

Collecting the dirty mugs together, Kelly stopped what she was doing and looked at her. 'Wadda yer mean? Shame about what?'

'About Norma leaving him.'

'How d'you know that?'

'Everyone knows.' She grimaced at Kelly as though she was stupid. 'You can't keep secrets like that round here, Kelly, you should know that.' She folded her arms

286

and leaned on the table. 'I never liked her meself,' she said icily.

'I didn't realise you knew her?'

'Not all that well, I didn't. She's much older than me. At least three years. Selfish cow she is and always has been. Thinks 'cos she works at Woolies she's better than anyone else. I never used to think much of Alec, but I'm quite getting to like him now I know him better. But there's one thing I am sure of and that's that he deserves better than Norma.'

'That's an unkind thing to say.'

'It's the truth though,' snapped Glenda. 'It's a man. Well, it's gotta be.'

'Pardon?'

'The reason she's left him. There's a man behind it, mark my words.'

Mugs still clutched in her hand, eyes glued to Glenda, Kelly sat down. 'Alec challenged her about that and she denied it.'

Glenda tilted her head, tightening her lips knowingly. 'She can deny all she likes. I'd bet a week's wages it's a man. Come on, Kelly, what woman in their right mind 'ud leave behind what she has for any other reason? Alec doted on her. Whatever she whinged for she got. Even if she was fed up with her lot, she'd never have upped sticks to go and fend for herself. Not without somewhere to go, she wouldn't.'

Kelly frowned. 'Well . . .'

'Yeah, exactly. There's another man behind all this, believe me.' She stuck out her chin knowingly. 'Ada Adcock thinks so too.'

Kelly gawped. 'Ada? You were discussing Alec's business with Ada? In the shop?'

Glenda looked surprised. 'Why not?'

''Cos it's not right, that's why not. Was anyone else there at the time?'

Glenda nonchalantly shrugged her shoulders. 'Might have bin.'

'So there was! And I suppose they put their penn'orth in too?'

Glenda eyed her sheepishly. 'But people talked about us and what happened, and still do for that matter, so why not about Alec?'

'Because . . .'

'Because what?'

'Because Alec is a friend, Glenda. No, he's more than a friend.'

She snorted. 'To you maybe.'

Kelly's eyes flashed in annoyance. 'To you as well. How can you think anything else after all he's done for us? He didn't have to. He could have left us to get on with it like everyone else did. And, don't forget, he was going through hell himself at the time and still is.' She scraped back her chair and rose abruptly as it suddenly struck her that she didn't like the fact that anyone was discussing Alec's business, and she felt disloyal for doing so herself. She slammed the mugs back down on the table.

'Just think next time you decide to have a good gossip, Glenda. Think how you felt when Mickey was the topic. You didn't like it, did you? Now I'm gonna get Dad ready for bed,' she said frostily. 'You can clear up in here. And don't leave the pots in the sink like you normally do. Wash up.'

'Just a friend, eh?' Glenda muttered as she rose to begin her task. 'She might be kidding herself but she ain't kidding me.'

Chapter Twenty-Five

Glenda stopped her traipsing for a moment to rest against a wall. Idly she turned round to view the house behind her. It was big, with nice curtains – no, not curtains, they were pieces of cheap material drawn over windows in houses like the ones she lived in. Against these leaded panes were drapes and, if she wasn't mistaken, made of velvet. The front door was newly varnished with not a speck of grime to be seen. Kept clean by a maid, she presumed. And the walled garden, which was filled with summer growth and neatly kept, was tended by a gardener. Probably a doctor's or lawyer's residence, she thought. Definitely not a bin man's. She turned back, running her eyes casually along the well-kept, tree-lined avenue somewhere near Victoria Park, off the main London Road. She wasn't quite sure where she was, she had long since lost her bearings.

She hadn't enjoyed her morning. It was hardly her idea of fun, walking the streets taking notes of dates and times when jumbles were being held. Not that it was likely in this area, but she hoped no one she knew saw her, and asked what she was doing. It would be humiliating to have to explain. But then she wouldn't do that if challenged anyway, she would just make up some plausible lie.

As she had walked around she had found her mind going over what Kelly and she were undertaking, and the more she had considered it, the more it appealed. The success they had achieved at their first sale had clinched it for her. As Kelly had pointed out, it had been fun. In fact there was no comparison between it and having to clock in and out, eight and a half hours a day, head bent over a machine scratting for a miserly living.

Although she did miss the company of the other girls and the gossip they had shared, but then on reflection they were nearly all two-faced anyway and whatever you said always got spread around. And neither would she forgive any of them for the way she had been treated after the factory fire. Whether Mickey was guilty of anything or not, Glenda felt she did not deserve the repercussions she had suffered.

Yes, when weighed up properly, working for yourself had to be far better than working for someone else. Glenda was no fool, she had no illusions that it was going to be easy. This morning had proved that. It had sounded simple. A walk around taking notes. But to get those notes she had walked miles to find the places first. Still, she supposed, someone had to do it. Though why Kelly couldn't have left her father on his own for a few hours . . . It wasn't as though he was going anywhere. Still, she supposed she was being unkind, having thoughts like that, and she really shouldn't give Kelly such a hard time over it with everything else she had to worry over. He was her father and whichever way you looked at it, a sick one.

Glenda frowned as a thought struck. Normally it wouldn't have bothered her, having thoughts like that. They were mild in comparison to some she had. Why? Why should she suddenly feel bothered? Then, with a sense of shock, it suddenly struck her why she was feeling remorseful. She was beginning to care about Kelly, actually beginning to like her and admire the way she was rising above the traumas and problems she had suffered. In fact was still suffering. And during all this time she had never once excluded Glenda when she could very easily have done so.

Kelly was becoming more to her than just Mickey's sister, someone to be tolerated, act friendly to. She was Glenda's real friend. No, more than that, considering all they had gone through. It was like Kelly had tried to explain about Alec; Glenda was beginning to understand what she had meant now. A sense of unaccustomed warmth flooded through her. Kelly needed her but she also needed Kelly. They were in this together.

Since Mickey had left her all Glenda's energy and thoughts had centred on his return, his coming back to reclaim her. It was something she still longed for, but somehow it didn't seem quite so important as making a success of this venture with his sister.

Suddenly she wanted to get home, share her findings and plan their next move. It was suddenly important to her that Kelly should see that she was pulling her weight. Oh, my God, she thought worriedly, what's happening to me? I must be having a change of personality. Thrusting her hand inside her pocket, she pulled out the crumpled scrap of paper, smoothed it out and studied it. Alec had been right. Two churches and a branch of the Women's Royal Institute whose notice she had seen pinned up outside the parish rooms were holding jumbles in the next few weeks, and judging from the way people were dressed in this area then the stuff they would have for sale would be of far better quality than nearer home. They just had to hope that not all of it was bought and would then be let go of cheaply.

Carefully folding the paper, she put it back in her pocket and glanced up and down the street. She had no idea in which direction home lay. She stood for a moment deliberating and had just decided to risk trying right, hoping that would take her to the main London

Road, when round the corner came a woman. Glenda eyed her for a moment. She was odd-looking, wearing an old-fashioned brown coat almost down to her ankles, brown beret pulled over her head leaving hardly any hair showing, a pair of round metal glasses slipping down her long sharp nose. Still, she did look as though she knew where she was going.

'Excuse me,' Glenda said as, eyes seemingly glued to the pavement, the woman arrived abreast of her.

She stopped abruptly, lifted her head and looked at Glenda blankly. 'Yes? Oh, there you are,' she exclaimed with such joy Glenda thought for a moment the woman was going to embrace her. 'I've been looking all over. I did say for them to tell you to wait on the corner of Holmfield Road. Oh, but never mind, you're here now.' She suddenly stopped her flow, eyeing Glenda up and down. 'But you're a woman?'

Bemused by the whole conversation, Glenda's eyebrows rose. 'For me sins.'

'But I did ask for a man. I mean, how are you going to manage?'

'Manage?'

'Yes. It's very heavy or I'd have done it myself. Come on, I'll show you.' She began to walk back around the corner, expecting Glenda to follow. She did, just out of curiosity. 'I never hoped to get anything near what I have,' she was babbling. 'People have been so kind.' Turning another corner she pointed to a large high-sided hand cart standing by a red-brick garden wall. It was piled to overflowing with all sorts of different things.

Standing by the side of the cart, amazed, Glenda ran her eyes over its contents. 'What's all this stuff for?' she asked, confused.

The woman turned to her, frowning. 'Why, the needy, of course. Look, I'd like nothing more than to chat but I've so much more to collect today. Are you sure you can manage? Only you don't look all that strong. I did ask for a man. It wasn't fair of them to send you.'

Glenda's mind was running ahead of her. 'Eh? Oh, yes, I'm stronger than I look. Where have I to take this cart to?'

'The Red Cross Depot near the railway station. Didn't Mrs Mountmaston tell you anything?'

'No,' Glenda said truthfully, then added a lie. 'She just sent me along to help. There weren't anyone else available.'

The odd-looking woman patted her arm. 'It's very good of you, my dear. If the likes of us didn't give up our time, I sometimes wonder who would.' She smiled warmly. 'It's so heartening to see someone so young giving up their time for such a good cause.

'My pleasure,' Glenda mumbled. 'You did say all this was for the needy?' she clarified.

The woman eyed her strangely. 'Yes.'

She beamed broadly. 'Oh, that's all right then.' And added to placate the woman, 'I just didn't want to be giving all me effort for anything else.'

'Bless you, my child. The Lord in His way will reward you, you'll see.'

I doubt He will, thought Glenda, when He realises what I've got in mind! The woman had said this stuff was for the needy, and who was more needy at this moment than Glenda and Kelly?

'I'll leave you to it,' the woman twittered. 'I've so much more to do today and while people seem in such a benevolent mood I don't want to waste another moment. 'Bye for now. Hopefully I'll catch up with you back at the depot and we can have a cup of tea together.'

I don't think you will, thought Glenda. ''Bye,' she said, waving.

Several hours later an exhausted Glenda finally arrived home. She hadn't found it too bad guiding the cart downhill, all she'd had to worry about then was finding the strength to stop it running away from her. The problem had been on the inclines. The slightest rise in the road she was travelling along caused her problems. Luckily, several obliging males had come to her rescue. The cart was now parked askew in the jitty by the back gate, Kelly staring at it astounded.

Dragging her eyes off the pile of stuff she turned to Glenda. 'None of this makes sense. A woman gave this to you? Just gave it?'

Glenda nodded. 'Yeah, honest she did. Said it was for the needy.'

Kelly scanned her up and down. 'We're needy, Glenda, but I wouldn't say you looked that bad. Not enough for someone to stop you in the street. You've yer best coat on. She was posh though, was she?'

Glenda nodded.

'Well, I suppose in that case you could look needy to her.' Kelly turned her attention back to the cart. 'She gave you that an' all?'

Glenda nodded again. 'Look, Kelly, I'm bloody knackered. I've told yer what happened. I know it sounds fishy but, well . . .' She shrugged her shoulders. 'I happened to be in the right place at the right time. She did say the Lord has a way of thanking people.'

Kelly frowned. 'Oh, for God's sake, Glenda, His way is more loaves and fishes.'

Glenda grimaced. 'Ah, but this woman was kinda odd. Maybe she thought a cartful of stuff 'ud be more use than half a dozen stale loaves and a bunch of smelly fish? Anyway, what does it bloody matter?' she said, annoyed. 'This is the miracle you were on about never happening. Maybe,' she prompted in all seriousness, 'this is the Lord's way of showing He exists?'

'D'yer really think so, Glenda?'

'To be honest, Kelly, at this moment I couldn't give a

monkey's. I just want to get this stuff unloaded and put me feet up. If we leave it out here, in two minutes flat it'll be nicked.'

'Yes, yer right. You did get this woman's address?'

'Er, no, why?'

'I'd like to go round and thank her, Glenda. It's the least I can do.'

'Well, I didn't,' she said hurriedly. 'So you can't.' Reaching over with difficulty, she pulled a large sack off the cart. It fell to the floor with a dull thud. 'Help me drag this in,' she ordered.

An hour later, the contents of the cart strewn about the small back room, Kelly stared around in disbelief. 'Oh, Glenda, I can't take this in. Why, if you hadn't told me yerself, I would never have believed it.' She glanced across at her father. 'Wadda you think, eh, Dad? Some bloody miracle all this, ain't it?' She scanned her eyes around, not quite knowing just what to focus them on, there were so many different items.

'Would yer just look at these clothes? We'll get a good price down the second-hand shop for the dresses. There's no point trying to sell those round here. Too posh by half. But the skirts and jumpers we can.' She laughed. 'Look at these whale-bone corsets,' she said, grabbing them and holding them out. 'I've never seen anything like 'em. I wonder if they're the kind your mother wears?' She giggled at the thought.

Easing her aching body off the chair, Glenda picked her way over to join her. 'I do like this skirt,' she said, picking it up and holding it against herself. 'It's my size, and this blouse 'ud go lovely with it.'

'Put them down, Glenda,' Kelly commanded. 'We need to make as much money as we can, and we won't do that by keeping the stuff ourselves.'

'Ah, just a couple of things wouldn't hurt, Kelly. You could do with a few things yerself. How about this?' she said, picking up another skirt. It was of good wool and blue in colour, similar to the skirt of the costume she had drooled over in the shop window only the other day. 'Looks just your size and I'm sure you've more than a good selection of blouses here to go with it.

'And what about yer dad? He might sit there all day in dreamland,' Glenda said, inclining her head towards him, 'but he still needs summat to wear. Go on, Kelly,' she coaxed. 'Just one outfit each, eh? Anyway,' she said, scowling, 'as it were me that got given the stuff, I don't really need to be asking you if I can have anything, do I?'

Kelly took the skirt from her. It was nice, of a quality which would normally be beyond her pocket, and it did look her size. Her decision was easy. 'A couple of things each then, the rest is for sale.'

Glenda beamed. 'Good on yer, Kelly.'

Both their heads jerked as they heard a knock, then the back door opened and seconds later a head popped round the door leading from the kitchen.

Alec's eyes bulged at the sight that met them. 'What the . . .' he exclaimed.

Delighted to see him, Kelly jumped up, ran over to him and grabbed his arm. 'Come and look,' she urged.

'But where did it all come from? Surely you never collected all this today?'

'Glenda did,' she said, and proceeded to tell him the story Glenda had related. 'Wadda you think?' she asked him when she had finished.

He scratched his chin, stunned. 'Ours not to reason why, Kelly. Just thank God this odd woman accosted Glenda and not anyone else. It's . . . well, it's the answer to a prayer, ain't it? It's all you need to get started.' He bent down and rummaged through some of the clothes, then sifted through a pile of boots and shoes, eyed the large pile of bedding items, and picked up an ornament – one of many – to examine it. 'I don't know who in their right mind would give this away but I'd say you'd get at least . . . oh . . . three or four pounds from an antique dealer. Mind you,' he added, 'I ain't no expert. But this is no cheap ornament from the likes of Woolies.'

Kelly was amazed. 'Four pounds? That much? Really?'

He nodded. 'It's Royal Derby.'

She frowned. 'Royal what? What's that when it's at home?'

He smiled. 'Summat you'll have ter learn about, Kelly, if yer serious about this kinda business.' He knelt down. 'Now let's have a proper look through this lot and sort it out.'

She suddenly remembered something. 'Did you get any dates for jumbles?' she asked Glenda.

'I did. I've scribbled them on a piece of paper. It's in me pocket.'

Kelly rubbed her hands together. 'Good, and so did I. There's three being held round here over the next three weeks.'

Alec lifted his head. 'And I asked Raggy about using the lorry to collect any stuff you might get. He thought about it hard before he agreed. It's like I thought. He's no objection so long as you only use his yard afterwards, and of course don't abuse it. Oh, and we need to get hold of some petrol. We only just about manage on the amount we're allowed as it is.'

'Petrol. Can we do that?' asked Kelly.

'There's always someone who's got black market contacts as long as you have the money to pay. And going by this lot, that shouldn't be any trouble.' He stood up, smiling. 'Looks ter me like yer on yer way, Kelly.'

She grinned excitedly. 'Yes, it looks as if we are.'

Chapter Twenty-Six

Kelly shivered, the sharp November wind cutting right through her. It was nearly the yard's closing time and she was last in the queue. She smiled to herself. She couldn't believe that it was over six months ago she had first stepped into Raggy's yard to do business. It seemed such a long time ago. The place felt familiar to her now, almost a second home. Raggy, who at first had acted almost aggressively towards her, though Alec had assured her it was just his way, was now almost friendly. She had grown quite attached to the gnarled old man. And Alec was right. Despite his great age Raggy was still an astute businessman, knowing as much as there was to know about the trade he was in, and mostly fair in his dealings.

The only people he did treat severely were the dealers. He did not like them in any shape or form, had a complete distrust of them, even the odd ones he knew to be honest. He didn't like the huge profits they made on the items they sold, knowing that they had mainly obtained their stuff from the unsuspecting public who in their innocence would accept a dealer's word on what their precious possessions were worth. Raggy didn't hold with this practice even though it was commonly used. 'That's why I ain't rich like some of them bastards,' he had once told Kelly. 'But at least I sleep easy at night.'

Getting started had not been without its problems.

Knowing just what to charge for the items they had for sale, proved, in some cases, to be a costly business. Items they could have got several shillings for were let go for pennies. And then there was the buying of the stock. They very quickly learned that no one gave anything away for nothing, even the worst things left over from the poorest areas' jumbles that were useful for no more than bagging up to take down the yard. Haggling over a price soon became an art they were familiar with.

Another thing Kelly had learned was that she did not dress in her decent clothes when she went out on business. The shabbier she looked, the more pity was taken upon her and the cheaper she got her 'job lots'. She felt somewhat guilty for doing this but, as Alec told her, business was business, and in order to make an honest living, if it meant she looked no better than a bag lady, then so be it.

Despite Glenda's experience on the day she had first traipsed the street taking notes on jumbles, it took her far longer to become accustomed to her new line of work. It was months before she could actually attend a jumble and bring herself to negotiate for anything left, and then only because there were two good ones being held on the same day and Kelly baulked at the idea of having to miss out on one. Leaving Glenda with no choice but to go.

Even then, and considering that although they were earning reasonable money it did not stretch to dress shop clothes, Glenda's dressing down for the occasion was not achieved without a verbal fight and a good deal of sulking. But at least she had gone, and since that first time had done so on several other occasions, surprised to find she actually enjoyed herself.

Through Alec and Raggy, Kelly had learned so much more as well. How they went about sorting the scrap and how, when enough bulk was collected, it was sent off to the different foundries. All scrap materials had their uses. Much to Kelly's amazement, for instance, she found out that all woollen items were sent up to factories in Dewsbury where they were shredded and turned into carpets.

'No carpets, even the best quality, are made from new wool. It's all old stuff,' Raggy had laughed, in his dry, aged cackle. 'D'int know that, did yer?' he had added proudly, and then proceeded to tell her that rags were sorted and where possible sold as oilcloths and machine cleaning wipes to all sorts of companies. He warned her whenever she accepted filled bags of anything to take the time to check the contents. People, even the most honest-looking, would try all sorts of tricks to make more money. Wool weighed more when wet, and bags of anything weighed far more when half filled with earth or ashes.

So much she had learned in such a relatively short space of time. Despite the fact there was still a lot more, Kelly now knew she was well able to earn a good living. They all ate decently and did not have to worry about the rent.

The business was still run from her own back room, under the blank gaze of her father, whose condition had not improved, much to Kelly's distress, though she lived in hope. People from all around her area – and word was continually spreading – came to her door with their precious belongings, knowing that they would get a just price. True to her word, all her business was put down to Raggy's yard and now that business was growing also. He didn't appear to mind how much they used the old Ford lorry. In fact he didn't say anything much, apart from give his usual grunt, when he saw her in the yard, showing that he was happy enough with the state of affairs.

The wind whipped through Kelly again and she

shuddered, stamping her feet. One thing about this line of work she'd never get used to was how much time was spent outside, especially in the winter. Chilblains were a nightmare on her hands and feet, despite the two pairs of fishermen's socks she wore under her sturdy, fleece-lined boots and the thick gloves on her hands.

Raggy's yard was situated between two factories and entered via a pair of huge wooden doors, which were opened each morning for business and closed and pad-locked from the inside at night. A smaller door cut into one of the bigger ones allowed him access in and out at other times.

Once inside the gates, past huge disorderly heaps of all manner of things, in a clearing near the front of the yard, to the right, side on, stood a ramshackle old wooden, open-backed lean-to, propped up by four thick railway sleepers. Kelly could not see him from her place in the queue but she knew Alec would be inside the lean-to, inspecting or weighing whatever was brought in on the large flat floor-scale by his feet, then negotiating a price. The money duly paid, the weighed bags would then be thrown behind him and anything else into a box at the side, to be sorted out later in quiet moments.

She smiled distractedly. Quieter moments! Alec didn't seem to get any of those. He always seemed to be working. But then, she knew it was his way of coping with his hurt over Norma. He hardly talked of her now and Kelly knew he hadn't seen or heard from her for over three months. Terrible of her though it was, Kelly was secretly glad of that and hoped the woman stayed away permanently.

Glenda had been right. Alec was better off without her. Gradually they had seen the sparkle come back into his eye. He was enjoying life more than before. Without his ever realising it, Norma's constant desire for a lifestyle beyond their means had been the one thing holding him back, not the other way round. Would the woman ever realise just what she'd given up? Kelly hoped not. That might mean she'd come back. And how would Kelly herself feel if that did happen?

Dear Alec, she thought. For her the biggest joy of this job was her daily contact with him. She knew by the way he acted that he held her in very high regard, but she knew too that the feelings she was harbouring for him now were much more than friendship. It had been no gradual thing or something suddenly sprung to life. Somehow she knew her love for him had always been there from when she was young and had first noticed how different he was from the other boys she knew. If Rod had not died and Norma not left Alec, maybe she would never have realised her true feelings. But now they were both free she had.

She loved so many things about Alec. His kindness, his caring, his honesty, the way he made her feel comfortable and safe. Just the joy of being near him for even a few minutes was enough to make her day. Kelly sighed. If only he could feel the same about her. But would he ever love again after what Norma had put him through?

The queue moved up and more of the yard came into view. For a moment she watched the antics of several shabby adults and children, sifting through varying piles searching for whatever they needed.

She looked around for Raggy, knowing he would be either in the dilapidated shed at the back of the large muddy yard immersed in repairs on items they had bought hoping to sell, or dismantling obsolete vehicle or machine parts ready for when they had enough to warrant a trip to the foundries. Either way he'd be covered in oil and rust.

The creases in Raggy's face were permanently black from years of this practice. Where he had a bath or if indeed he ever had one was a mystery as the work shed was also his home and there was no tin bath that Kelly had ever seen amongst the rest of the junk that filled it, although he had access to many rusty ones coming and going through the yard. Water was collected from a tap, the pipe protruding from the ground which froze solid in winter. A spirit stove, an ancient flock mattress, one threadbare armchair, were his only creature comforts. On realising his lifestyle and worried for his welfare, Kelly had taken it upon herself to see that he did at least eat.

She had never seen him in any other clothes than the same filthy pair of trousers, indeterminately coloured collarless shirt and heavy hand-knitted cardigan, which was in huge ragged holes all over. During cold weather he wore an aged, moth-eaten, evil-smelling sheepskin. From his head sprang a thick mop of wild shoulder-length wiry grey hair, from his chin a profuse chest-length beard. A roll up cigarette hung permanently from the corner of his toothless mouth. This was Raggy's choice of lifestyle, one he'd lived since everyone could remember, and he seemed happy in it, much to Kelly's amazement.

The queue moved up again. Sighing with relief and grabbing the handles of her hand cart, she moved up also. In front of her now only two rather suspect-looking gypsy types remained, standing to either side and holding on to the bridle of a tired, underfed horse. The large dray cart it was pulling was in such a bad state of repair it looked hardly capable of carrying a fraction of its haphazardly piled contents. She was used to seeing characters like these down at the yard, and standing behind them, even though they had sized up both her and her laden hand cart several times, she was not unduly concerned. One step out of line and she'd only have to scream and Alec would come running.

She watched as the unsavoury-looking characters started to unload their cart. A dozen or so filled sacks were dumped by the scales. Alec began his task of checking and weighing, logging the entry in the receipt book, then chucking the sacks backward. The cart was cleared of sacks, then came the metal. Long bits, short bits, old tools, two mangle tops, several rusty radiators and a garden roller that looked pre-First World War were thrown by the scales. Kelly leaned wearily against her hand cart. Her wait, she decided, was going to be longer than she had first thought.

She had had a long day, productive but still tiring. Having limited storage space meant that most days a trip down to the yard was called for and usually she was the one to do it, Glenda being kept busy back at the house sorting through their new acquisitions and hopefully putting on something for dinner as well. This was the bit Kelly disliked the most. The waiting. She knew she could go and sit by Alec and wait her turn, or even seek out Raggy in the hope of a mash of tea, but she didn't feel it was fair to any of the other patrons to abuse her friendship with the proprietor or his helper. The other patrons never got a seat or a mash while they waited so why should she?

She suddenly realised that one of the men had disappeared. A minute or so passed then she saw him sidle furtively from the side of the lean-to, dragging a filled sack. He skirted round the far side of the cart and heaved it on. The other man then unloaded the sack and put it before Alec. Kelly watched, bemused. This happened several times before curiosity as to where the man was getting the filled sacks got the better of her, her view being blocked by the back end of their high-sided cart.

Leaving her own cart unattended, she walked casually away until the back of the lean-to came within view. Then she realised what the men were up to. One man was keeping Alec talking while the other was nipping around the back, grabbing a sack that had already been weighed and logged and putting it back on the cart, thus by Kelly's reckoning seeming to treble what they had in fact brought.

She was astounded, her anger mounting to see them so blatantly cheating Raggy and Alec. Running back, she went straight up to Alec, in her haste almost knocking into the gypsy he was principally dealing with. 'Alec,' she cried urgently.

Without lifting his eyes or stopping his task, he replied, 'Not now, Kelly, I'm busy. I'll be with you in a minute.'

His tone was unexpectedly abrupt and she flinched.

'But, Alec, there's something . . .'

He lifted his head, eyeing her sharply. 'I said, not now, Kelly. Please wait yer turn.'

The man nearest her sneered, 'You heard the young fellow, get back in der queue.' His Irish accent was thick, eyes menacing.

Undeterred she tried again. 'Alec, please . . .'

'Kelly,' he snapped, raising his hand, palm outward in warning.

There was a look in his eye, one she had never seen before. It frightened her. She stepped slowly backwards, not stopping until she came to her cart. And there she stayed, watching the proceedings tight-lipped.

Finally, Alec finished totting up and announced their payout.

The men erupted. ''T'aint right, so it's not.'

'What's not?' he asked calmly.

'The money. Should be much more.'

Alec grimaced. 'Okay, I'll add it up again if you like.'

The men nodded and stood side by side, glances riveted on him while he went over his figures again. 'Same total,' he said.

There was instant verbal abuse from the men.

Alec shrugged his shoulders. 'That's the amount, fair and square. You watched me weigh and log it, so take it or leave it. If yer think I'm cheating yer, then I'll have the police fetched and let them sort it out.'

One of the men snatched the other's arm and yanked him aside. They whispered between them. Then one stepped forward, face contorted in fury, his hand outstretched, while the other grabbed their horse's bridle, turned the cart around and started to lead it away through the gates.

Silently Alec counted out the money due, ripped out a receipt and slapped it into the man's palm. 'Nice doing business, call again.'

He gave a furious snarl then turned and ran.

Kelly leaped over to the lean-to. 'Alec!' she cried. 'They were cheating you. They were . . .'

She stopped talking as she realised with a sense of shock that Alec was holding her protectively in his arms. 'Oh, Kelly, never do that again! You had me terrified witless. Oh my God, you had me so worried.'

She stared up at him, eyes wide with bewilderment. 'I did?'

'They were dangerous, both had knives. Did you not see them in their belts?'

She shook her head. 'No.'

He let out a sigh of anguish. 'Oh, Kelly, you are so innocent. I've got a jemmy I keep for protection but if one of them had attacked you, I couldn't have got to you quick enough.' His arms tightened round her and she felt him shudder.

'But all the same, Alec, they were . . .' Belatedly realisation struck. 'You knew, didn't you? You knew what they were up to?'

He dropped his arms, nodding. 'It's an old trick. What they didn't know was that I had me foot under the scales. Whatever was put on weighed only a quarter of what it should have. I reckon we ended up about equal.'

'But what if they come back? What if . . .'

'They won't, Kelly, not today. Threatening 'em with the coppers is usually deterrent enough. I get types like that in most days. I'm used to dealing with 'em. That's what I meant when I said you need yer wits about you all the time.'

She exhaled thoughtfully. She had experienced several cases of verbal abuse when people were not happy with what she was prepared to offer them. Thankfully she had not as yet been bodily attacked. She had handled those experiences just as Alec had instructed: 'If they aren't happy, tell them to try somewhere else then walk away or shut her door.' Usually they then ungraciously accepted what was being offered, knowing it was the best they would get. But the thought of Alec in this danger-ous situation daily did not sit easy with her. How could she express this without giving away her true feelings? Something he might not welcome.

'I was so angry,' she said. 'I thought they were diddling you and you hadn't a clue.'

'I couldn't say anything. One word to the wise and they'd have turned nasty.' Fear of anything happening to Kelly filled him again and without thinking he grabbed her by the arms, his eyes filled with tenderness. 'I'm sorry I was so sharp with yer, but I couldn't risk that, Kelly. I couldn't risk them harming a hair of your head.' His face filled with horror as it dawned on him he had spoken to her in an intimate manner. Hurriedly releas-ing her, he took several steps away. 'Come on, show me what you've got. Did you have a good day?' he asked lightly.

She stood staring at him. 'You . . . you care about me, don't you?' she whispered boldly.

He stopped, turned to face her and for several moments they stood facing each other, their hearts pounding.

Finally he answered.

'Yes, Kelly, I do. Very much.'

Her whole body sagged. 'Oh, Alec, I care for you too. More than friends do. Much more than that.'

He stood stunned, her words the last he'd ever expected to hear. Before he could stop himself his arms were around her, pulling her close. 'Me too. Oh, Kelly, me too. I've always liked you, always, but I knew it was more than just liking the day you came to my house and we talked. From then on it's just grown.'

She pulled away fractionally, looking up into his eyes. 'But what about Norma?'

He sighed. 'I still care for her, Kelly. Worry about her. That she's doing all right. If I knew she was then maybe I wouldn't worry so much. That's just me, I can't help how I am. But I don't love her any more. That's died, gone.' He felt her sag with relief. 'It's you I love now, Kelly.'

'You do? You really love me?'

'Oh, yes,' he announced. 'There are so many things I love about you, and it's a different love from the kind I felt for Norma.' He sighed. 'The love I had for her was . . .'

'What, Alec?'

He sighed again, deeply, sadly. 'Like that of a father for a child. Does that make sense? I didn't realise it 'til recently, but I feel she only married me because she knew I'd look after her. She was like a child in many ways. And she was right, I did everything for her.' He smiled down at Kelly. 'But you – oh, Kelly, you're so different. There are so many things that I love about you. Your strength, your loyalty, the way we can talk so openly together, your . . .'

'Eh up,' she cut in, smiling. 'Are yer sure it's me you're talking about, Alec?'

'Oh, yes, Kelly, yes. And the love I feel for you is no fatherly love, believe me. Me stomach turns over whenever I see you. And when I touch you, even by accident . . . oh, Kelly, I want to grab you in my arms and . . .'

Tilting her head, her eyes narrowed knowingly. 'And what, Alec?'

He smiled. 'You know, don't you, Kelly?'

She nodded. 'Yes, I do.' He wanted to whisk her off to his bed and make passionate love to her. 'I feel like that for you too,' she confessed.

His arms crushed her fiercely against him. 'I never dared hope that you'd feel the same way. Never. It's like a dream.'

'But why?'

He laughed ironically. 'You, Kelly, are a lovely woman. And me, well . . . Rod was such a good-looking man.'

Her eyes narrowed in annoyance. 'Alec,' she scolded, 'I can't deny Rod was handsome, but he'd none of your qualities. I loved him, yes, but it was a sweetheart's kind of love I felt for him. First love. And Rod loved me too, in his own way. If he hadn't died we'd probably have bin married forever, just muddling along like some couples do.' She gazed deep into his eyes. 'But then I'd never have known what real love is, would I?' Her voice lowered emotionally. 'Just as you wouldn't have if Norma hadn't left yer.'

He smiled down at her, a broad smile, eyes filled with love. 'Oh, Kelly. I promise I'll never hurt you, never leave you.'

'That you can't, Alec. I wish you could, but no one can promise things like that. Let's just promise to be honest with each other.'

He sighed. 'For someone so young, you're very wise.

What a lucky man I am.' His face suddenly filled with worry. 'I can't offer you much, Kelly. Me earnings, well, they ain't no fortune, and more importantly, I'm still married, ain't I? But I do want to be with you so much. I'll sort it out, I promise, and ask yer properly as soon . . .'

'Yes,' she soothed, 'I know you will. When yer good and ready, Alec. It's not easy having to face things like that. I just want to concentrate on us at the moment, not things like that. And as for what you can offer me – just yerself is enough. I don't care what you earn, or what we have to go without. As long as the rent's paid and we have summat to eat, that's enough for me.'

'Oh, Kelly,' he uttered, then feeling a tug on his arm he released his hold on her. Standing beside him was an aged, wizened filthy creature, dirt-engrained hands clasping the handles of an equally filthy pram. So engrossed in each other were they, they hadn't heard anyone approach. 'Got some stuff,' the creature mumbled.

'Oh, right,' said Alec, flashing an apologetic glance at Kelly. 'Bring it over here and let's have a look what yer've got. If you want to leave your stuff with me, Kelly, I'll go through it when I've finished with this lady.' He glanced kindly at the filthy creature beside him. Despite their state, Alec always addressed everyone with equal courtesy. 'I'll bring the cart back tonight, if you like, along with yer dues.'

Kelly smiled. She knew all her worldly goods were safe in Alec's trustworthy hands. And he knew she was tired, but more importantly wanted to get back to check her father. Glenda looked out for Frank, but not in the same way as his daughter did. 'I'd like that. Will you stay and have some dinner?' she tentatively asked.

Alec nodded, delighted. 'I'd like that.'

Her whole being filled with happiness. 'Yes, me too.'

311

Chapter Twenty-Seven

A dozing Mickey, long legs hanging over the end of the antique Chesterfield settee, nearly jumped out of his skin as the door to the living room of the flat crashed open and an agitated woman burst in. Despite his sleep-induced dullness the appearance of the woman, regardless of her obvious anxiety, had its usual effect. His heart thumped painfully, his whole being soared joyfully. For the first time in his life Mickey was seriously in love and had been from the instant he literally collided with Mitzi, lost, broke and alone in the middle of Newcastle, a month after he had fled from Leicester.

He had hitched a lift on a lorry heading north. At the time he had not cared where it was going. Newcastle to him was as good a place as any to get lost in and far enough away from Leicester not to be found.

It had been nearly midnight. Desperate for money to buy food and lodging, he'd been trailing a prosperous-looking man, ready to relieve him of whatever valuables he was carrying as soon as he saw his chance. So preoccupied was he, he hadn't seen the woman emerge from the door of the Pink Flamingo club until the very last second. He tried to dodge her and in doing so fell smack into a gas lamp, nearly knocking himself out.

Sprawled on the pavement, rubbing his badly cut head, his eyes had fixed on her red leather court shoes. Slowly they travelled up the length of long shapely legs, encased in expensive sheer nylons, passed by the hem of her calf-length tightly fitting red silk dress to the mink stole draped casually around creamy shoulders. At the base of her long slender neck hung a necklace he knew to be of diamonds, and matching stones dangled from her ears. Eventually his eyes had fixed on her face. And what a face! It was stunning. A mirror image of Elizabeth Taylor's.

She had bent to help him up and brushed him down, apologising profusely for her lack of concentration, insisting the accident had been entirely her fault. Who was Mickey to argue? Her voice was musical and thickly accented. Later he found out she was German, having fled from the Nazis during the war. That night she offered to take him home and bathe his cuts.

Despite his total confidence in his looks and magnetism, even Mickey sometimes had trouble believing that nine months later he was still here, that such a woman could want him.

Swinging his legs to the floor and sitting upright, he gazed up at Mitzi now standing before him, her beautiful face contorted in terror. 'What's happened?' he asked anxiously.

'You have to go, Mickey,' she cried.

'Go!' He was shocked by her unexpected response. 'Wadda yer mean, go? Go where?'

'Just go. I don't care. Look, darlink, I'm scared. He knows.'

'Don't be daft, 'course he doesn't. Too busy with his business to bother what you're up to.'

'That's where you're wrong. He loves me, Mickey. He wants me to marry him.'

Mickey's eyes flashed with worry, his brow creased. 'And do you want to marry him?'

'No, I don't. I love you. But I'm scared of him, Mickey. I've told you what he's like. He'll murder us both.'

He jumped up, grabbing her in his arms. 'Come with me, Mitzi. I can't – won't – leave without yer.'

She pulled away. 'And live on what? We've no money.'

'I'll work. I'll get a job.'

'Mickey, a job? Down a pit?'

He scowled 'Don't be so sarky.'

She frowned. 'Sarky? What's that?'

He ignored her question. 'I'll look after yer, Mitzi. I told you about my business. It's just a matter of time.'

She swung her arms wide, encompassing the expensively furnished room, then fingered the gold necklace she wore. 'Like this, Mickey? You'll look after me like this?'

'Yes, I will. Another few months, that's all I need. Just let me lie low here for another few . . .'

'No, Mickey, you can't,' she cried. 'He's coming round.'

He eyed her questioningly. 'He's never come in all the time I've bin here. Why now?'

'I stopped him before, Mickey. Made excuses. But he is tonight. He's due any minute. Now. You have to go *now*.'

Face hardening, fists clenching, he breathed in deeply. 'I'll face him, Mitzi. Tell him about us. He doesn't scare me.'

'No!' she cried, then her voice softened. 'I'm scared for you. If anything happened to you, I'd die. You know I'd die. I need to keep him sweet for a while, Mickey. You know he pays for everything. I have no money of my own. He's kept both of us since you came.' She moved closer to him, rubbing her thighs against his, hands running seductively up and down his chest. She felt his body stiffen. Despite their dire situation he could not control his lust for her. She felt the excitement of her power over him. It gave her such pleasure. 'Look, Mickey,' she coaxed. 'Go home. Sort out your business like you told me you would. All the fuss will have died down by now, surely? Your fine policemen will have other fish to fry, eh? Then send for me.'

'You'll come?'

She smiled. 'Running.'

He stared at her. What lies he had told the woman he adored! How easily they had poured out as they had sat together on her couch on the evening of their accidental meeting, Mitzi gently bathing his wounds. Despite knowing she was attracted by his looks, he realised a woman like her would never have entertained an out of work bin man. So he had played the part of Isaac Greenbaum, a hoodlum with the east side of Leicester in his control. He told her a job had gone wrong and he'd had to flee and lie low. He had money, plenty of it, but while he was out of the city it was inaccessible. In his absence his men were looking after his business interests.

His story was full of holes big enough to fall through, but Mitzi had seemed satisfied and after a while, as he embroidered on his lies, even Mickey began to believe them.

For nine months he had lived the high life. She had bought him tailored suits, silk shirts, leather shoes. Food and wine that he had only ever heard of, and much more that he hadn't, had been bought for him in classy restaurants. They had frequented a casino. A maid cleaned the flat. The grimy streets of Leicester faded rapidly from Mickey's mind. And now here she was, telling him to go home. He had nothing to return to. He had tasted an expensive way of life and baulked at the idea of leaving it. And the thought of leaving her behind sickened his stomach. He searched frantically for a plan that could bring him wealth enough to cover the lies he had told and keep a woman like Mitzi happy.

Someone pounded loudly on the door. Mitzi jumped. 'It's him, Mickey,' she cried fearfully. 'The window!'

His face turned ashen. 'But we're three floors up. And what about my clothes? And I've no money.'

She made a grab for her bag, wrenched open the gold serpent clasp, thrust her hand inside and pulled out a crisp white five-pound note, which she shoved at him. 'Take this.'

'That won't get me far.'

'It's enough for your train fare. Now go, Mickey. *Go*.'

'But what about me clothes?'

German blasphemies rang out. Rushing across to the wardrobe, she yanked open the door and grabbed a large bag which had been stuffed at the bottom of it. She ran back, pushing the bag at him. 'The ones that you came in.'

'But . . .'

Someone pounded on the door again.

'Mickey, please,' she begged.

He grabbed her and kissed her fiercely. 'You'll come when I send for yer? It might take me a while to sort everything out.'

Her voice was husky. 'I'll wait.'

He made a dive for the window, opened it and looked out. Running close to it was a drainpipe.

More pounding on the door.

'For God's sake, Mickey, he'll break it down if I don't answer soon.' Her hand went to her mouth. 'I hope he hasn't brought his gun.'

'Gun!' That threat was enough for Mickey. He threw the bag of clothes out of the window and scrambled out on to the narrow ledge. Then, his heart in his mouth, swinging his legs, he made a lunge for the pipe. By the skin of his teeth he just managed to grasp it and hung there, gasping heavily.

Mitzi leaned out of the window. She blew him a kiss and waved. '*Auf Wiedersehen*, my sweet. Till we meet again.'

317

She slammed the window shut.

Heart pounding painfully, Mickey shinned down the pipe. On reaching the ground he snatched up his bag and without a backward glance raced off down the street.

Mitzi strolled leisurely down the wide, plush-carpeted hallway and opened the door.

The immaculately dressed woman who entered looked at her enquiringly. 'Well, did it work?' she asked lazily, sucking hard on the end of her cigarette holder.

With the woman following, Mitzi sauntered back to the living room and sank down on the couch. Lounging back, she crossed her shapely legs, reached inside her handbag and drew out a packet of cigarettes and a gold lighter. With deliberately slow movements she lit one and blew a plume of smoke in the air. 'Like a dream, darlink,' she said finally.

Her visitor laughed.

Mitzi exhaled. 'Oh, what a relief! I thought I'd never be rid of him. It was fun, though.'

'And you like your fun, don't you, Mitzi dear? But you kept him around for longer than the rest. What did he have that the others didn't?'

Mitzi leaned forward, uncrossing her legs, eyes shining wickedly. 'I had good reason to keep this one around. He was common, darlink. Rough. Ate like a pig and snored like one too. He was *such* a liar. He really thought I believed he was a great man in the place where he lived – the one with such a peculiar name. What was it now?' She waved one delicate hand. 'It doesn't matter. But, oh, Rita darlink, he was an animal in bed!' She leaned back, recrossing her legs, smiling secretly. 'Reason enough to keep him, don't you think?' She tilted her head. 'I shall miss him.' Then she added with a laugh, 'Maybe.'

Rita Rachelle, or Elsie Ramsbottom as she was known to her mother, raised one finely arched eyebrow. 'And Albie?'

'What about him?'

'Are you sure he doesn't mind?'

'About my young men, darlink?' Mitzi pouted, child-like. 'Of course not. Why should he? He might have money and power but he can't satisfy me, can he? He knows the only way I'll stay with him is if he allows me my young men.' Lounging back again, she draped one arm over the back of the couch. 'I could leave him any time, get anyone else I wanted. He needs me to grace his arm at all those dreadful functions, and he likes to show me off. But in bed . . . phuff! He's no good, darlink.' She rose. 'Come, I take a bath and you can tell me where we're going tonight.' She giggled. 'Somewhere with young men, I hope. And I want one a teeny bit more refined this time.'

The lorry slowed down. It shuddered and shook, loose rusty exhaust emitting a loud, smoky explosion before it came to a final grating halt. A head with an unruly mop of greasy hair popped out of the glassless driver's window. 'Where yer headed, mate?'

Before answering Mickey dubiously glanced the length of the dilapidated vehicle, wondering if it was capable of moving off again let alone arriving anywhere.

He knew exactly where he was going. There was only one place he could go to do what he had in mind – and that was home. His decision had been made the moment he'd had time to gather his thoughts as he sat huddled in the freezing waiting room of the railway station after his brush with death. He was now a man with a mission, that mission being to make money. Mounds of it. He needed enough to keep his woman in the way to which she was accustomed. And he knew exactly how he would do it.

He had hated every minute of his job on the bins but the one thing it had afforded him was a knowledge of every street in the city of his birth. He knew the poorer areas too well but he also knew where the wealthy lived. He knew the back alleys, hidden walkways, quickest routes from one place to another. In fact, he was an expert on them. This knowledge would stand him in good stead.

He was going to rob the city blind, take as much as he could lay his hands on in as little time as possible. In order to do so he was going to have to lie and cheat, find even more cunning and conniving ways than he'd done before. The result would be worth it though. Mitzi.

'I'm going to Leicester,' he said.

'Where?'

'I said Leicester.'

The man grimaced. 'Never 'eard on it. Where is it?'

'South.'

'I'm off to London, that's south.' The driver screwed up his face. 'I think.'

Mickey scanned the vehicle again. He aimed to get to Leicester in one piece and doubted that would be achieved in this contraption.

The man misinterpreted this for admiration. He put his arm out of the window and affectionately patted the rusty dented door. 'Nice, ain't she? Only cost me a tenner.'

'You were done, pal.'

The man scowled. 'Well, if that's your attitude, you can bloody well walk.' He put his head back inside the cab and slammed one foot against the accelerator, revving hard. The engine screamed, agonisingly. The lorry lurched off.

Mickey flashed a glance up and down the deserted road. He could wait for hours for another chance like

320

this. He would be chancing his life, he knew, but it was cheaper than the train. 'Hold on, mate,' he shouted. 'Just a joke, honest.'

The brakes were applied and the head popped out of the window again. 'Joke, eh? It 'ad better have been,' the man warned. 'All right,' he relented. 'Get in.'

Chapter Twenty-Eight

Glenda sat back wearily on her haunches and stared around disdainfully as she rubbed her aching back. The pile of rags and woollens they were sorting through didn't appear to be diminishing. This was the part of the job she disliked the most. Some of the items they handled were grubby to say the least, their previous owners' total lack of hygiene only too obvious. The sour stench emanating from them clung to her hair and clothes, and despite her nightly ritual of a thorough scrub down she never felt she was quite free of it.

She would be so glad when they could employ a couple more women besides Avril to do this job, and free her from it. But at least Kelly never asked her to visit the yard. Despite their business centring around it, that was still the one thing Glenda couldn't bring herself to do and silently she blessed Kelly's sensitivity. But if she was sensitive on that one issue she wasn't on anything else. Kelly expected Glenda to pull her weight in every other area and the slightest reluctance was cheerfully bullied out of her.

Glenda sighed again. And today Kelly had given herself the whole day off! It wasn't fair. Well, she grudgingly conceded, Kelly had worked herself into the ground over the last few months and in that respect maybe she did deserve a break. But then, so had Glenda herself and Alec hadn't offered to take *her* for a ride in the country, even if it was supposedly a business trip.

Then despite herself she smiled. It was nice to see Kelly happy again, and Alec for that matter. The pair of them were so well suited. She was being mean, begrudging them some time on their own. And in fairness to Kelly, she had said that Alec would take Glenda the next time he had business out of the city. She just hoped that wasn't a long time coming. She had never been to the countryside before. In fact, until they had started this business she had never had cause to venture much further than the area in which she lived.

For a moment a vision of Kelly and Alec rose before her. She saw them sitting close together on the long front seat of the ramshackle old Ford lorry, lost in their own world. Suddenly the vision changed and instead of Kelly and Alec it was herself and Mickey.

Glenda sighed forlornly. She couldn't imagine Mickey actually taking her on a trip like that. The cinema and local dance halls were the extent of their outings.

A great sadness filled her. Despite knowing what she did about Mickey and his lack of love for her, she could not rid herself of deep feelings for him and wondered, as she had since the day he had left, where he was? What was he doing? Was he all right? What did the woman he was with now look like? And as always these thoughts caused a dreadful gnawing pain, starting low in her stomach and rapidly spreading to fill her very being.

She turned abruptly towards Avril, intending to tell her to mash a pot of tea. It was past the time that Kelly usually gave Frank his mid-morning cuppa. Instead she frowned, annoyed. 'Oi,' she exclaimed. 'Rag bag fer that.'

Avril stopped what she was doing and grimaced. 'But it ain't so bad, Glenda,' she said, holding the ragged jumper against herself. 'It's still got some life left in it. I'd wear it,' she said, placing it against herself and casting her eyes over it admiringly. 'In fact, it ain't bad at all. Can I have it then?'

Glenda tutted. In her own opinion the jumper in question wasn't fit even to unpick and rewind, and sell the resulting wool. 'If yer want it that bad, yer can have it fer tuppence. I'll dock it from yer wages.'

Avril gasped. 'Eh, yer a bloody hard woman, Glenda McCallan, so yer are.'

'Yer might be a neighbour, Avril, but this is a business we're running, not a bloody charity. If yer want the jumper, yer pay for it. If not, put it where it belongs, in the sack for the yard.'

A miffed Avril did as she was told, ramming the offending item inside. Tuppence out of her wages was tuppence too much considering her financial status. This job was a Godsend and she needed every penny she earned from it. 'Kelly wouldn't 'ave made me pay,' she mumbled under her breath.

'What were that?'

She raised her head, eyes innocent. 'Er . . . n'ote, Glenda.'

'Well, fer your information I heard yer and Kelly's too soft by half. It's our living we're earning, Avril, and don't forget that. And if you ain't happy with yer working conditions then I'm sure someone else would be.'

Avril's face filled with alarm. 'Oh, I am 'appy, Glenda. Really, I couldn't be happier. Er . . . you look tired, let me mash a . . . Oh!'

At the astonished look that came over her face Glenda frowned. 'What's up now?' She realised Avril was staring over her shoulder and automatically turned her head. The sight that met her eyes shocked her senseless. Her mouth fell open and for several moments she stared, fighting to convince herself she was not seeing things. Finally she gasped, 'Mickey?' and rose slowly to her feet, clasping her hands so tightly her knuckles shone white. 'Mickey?' Her whole body sagged. 'Oh, Mickey,' she whispered.

Chapter Twenty-Nine

Eyes sparkling with happiness, Kelly scanned the view through the grimy windscreen of the old Ford lorry. She had never before seen the spectacular Leicestershire countryside in all its winter glory. Now it was unfolding before her, each bend in the road bringing with it a new delightful scene. Kelly thought it breathtaking. A wintry sun filtered down, its rays dancing on thick frost still clinging to bare branches and lying along trenches of furrowed earth. It was like a scene from a Christmas card.

'Happy?' Alec asked, allowing his attention to stray for a moment from the narrow road he was carefully negotiating. A warm glow flooded through him as it always did whenever he looked at her. How lucky he was to have her by his side. Kelly found pleasure in simple things and that knowledge gave him pleasure too.

Unintentionally, he suddenly found himself comparing her to Norma. If it had been his wife with him now, he knew she would not have taken joy in the scenery around her; she would have been complaining about the cold and asking how much longer they had to travel. In fact, Norma would not have wanted to accompany him on this journey, would have used any excuse to avoid doing so.

He mentally shook himself. He should not be comparing the two women. They were different people, with totally different characters, and although he had once loved Norma deeply, he was now relieved that she found happiness elsewhere. Not that he knew what she was doing exactly, having heard not so much as a word for months now, but he hoped she was faring well. At one time the thought of her with another man would have devastated him. Not now though, not when he had the love of the woman seated beside him. A woman who had shown him what it was like to have his love fully returned.

Kelly smiled at him. 'I'm very happy, Alec. Thank you so much for bringing me with you.' She pulled the old rug tighter around her knees. 'I'm sorry this trip ain't going to make the profit you'd hoped it would, though.' She eyed him hopefully. 'They wouldn't let you just have the lead bits, Alec, if you explained?'

He shook his head. 'The contract is for the complete batteries, Kelly, not just the lead. It's a shame it's all done by weights. They weigh the lorry when we arrive and again when we leave. The problem for us is the battery casings. Bakelite is heavy, and unfortunately, though it's worthless to us, we have to pay for it.' He shrugged his shoulders. 'Can't be helped. When I tendered for the contract, I cut it as fine as I dared 'cos I knew other yards were desperate for it. I never thought that meantime the price of lead would fall so dramatically. Hopefully we'll just about break even. It's Raggy I feel for. This would've made him a nice tidy sum otherwise.' He smiled. 'Never mind, though, these things happen. Look, we've another few miles to go before we get to the American airbase so do you want to stop for a drink or wait 'til we get there?'

'I'm happy to do what you want, Alec.'

He eyed her tenderly. 'I'm glad yer happy, Kelly. I want you to enjoy your day out. You deserve it after all you've bin through and how hard yer've worked to get your business off the ground. We'll push on then and have our sandwiches when we arrive, get on with the job and be off before it gets too dark. That suit you?'

'Suits me fine. Oh, look,' she exclaimed excitedly. 'It's a rabbit, Alec. Look at it run.'

Two hours later she carefully eased herself out of the lorry and stood staring in amazement at the huge pile of old spent batteries that had serviced the several hundred trucks housed on the large base in Cottesmore, Lincolnshire. Before he had gone off in search of some possible help, Alec had voiced deep concern that there was not room in their lorry to take a quarter of these batteries, let alone all of them. Much to his dismay he realised another couple of journeys would have to be made to fulfil their obligations.

Kelly ran her hand thoughtfully over her chin. Such a shame, she thought. All this backbreaking work for no return. Still, as Alec had said, it was the luck of the draw. Maybe the next time he'd be much more fortunate. For her, though, there had been a bonus – the trip to the country. She had never felt so happy, relaxed and contented. She wished the day could go on forever and knew without having to ask that Alec felt the same way too.

'Problem, ma'am?'

She spun round. So engrossed in her thoughts was she that she had not heard the approach of the troop lorry. A dozen uniformed men carrying assorted tools, obviously returning from some manual work detail, were standing in the back. The man addressing her through the open passenger window then opened the door and jumped out, coming briskly towards her.

'You look worried,' he said, respectfully removing his cap. 'Can I be of any assistance?'

She was acutely aware of all the men's eyes riveted upon her but especially those of the tall, blond American airman addressing her. She reddened. 'Well, I don't know,' she said, frowning. 'My friend . . .' She paused, turning to look in the direction that Alec had disappeared over ten minutes ago. There was no sign of him returning. She turned back to the airman. '. . . went off to see if he could get some help. We've got the contract to collect these batteries, only we didn't expect there to be so many and there's just the two of us.' She grimaced, realising he was looking at her in bemusement. 'What's the matter?' she asked.

He gave a disgusted grunt. 'I just love you British but I'll never understand British men. We Americans would never send women to do a man's job, especially not a pretty one like you?'

'Oh, but . . .'

'Don't you fret now, little missy,' he cut in, taking her arm. 'Uncle Sam's here. You need this lot loading, you say?' He paused, appraising the mountain of batteries and the carrying space on the back of the old Ford lorry. Letting go of her arm, he scratched his head. 'Can't see you having room for that lot. And can't see the truck standing the weight either. No, siree.'

'That's what we thought. It looks like we'll have ter come back, only it's such a long way from Leicester.' She sighed and said distractedly, 'And it's not like we really want the complete batteries, just the lead bits inside. We'd have plenty of room for just that. Still . . .'

'Just the lead? Well, in that case . . .' Turning to address the men on the back of the lorry, he bawled, 'You men, you heard the little lady. Let's get to it.'

'Ah, Lieutenant,' they protested.

'If you want to go to the dance Friday night then you'd better move it,' came the stern reply.

Kelly watched in astonishment as the men tumbled out of the back of the lorry, tools raised. Within seconds the batteries were smashed open, the valuable lead parts removed and thrown to an airman on the back of the old Ford. The lead was stacked neatly, the useless casing thrown in another rapidly mounting heap.

Worried, Kelly turned to the Lieutenant. 'Look, mister, there's something I'd better tell you . . .'

He smiled down at her. 'Wilbur, missy.' He held out his hand, eyes twinkling. 'Wilbur Crosby, no relation to Bing. Pleased to meet you.'

Automatically she held out her own hand. 'Kelly Collins. I'm pleased to meet you too. But there's something . . .'

'Any chance of you coming to the dance on Friday? I'd sure like it if you came.'

'Oh! Er . . . I . . . Well, it's such a long way.'

He was staring at her intently. 'They have coaches laid on from Leicester. Lots of pretty ladies like you come. You'll enjoy it, I'm sure. Bring your friend. D'you know how to jive?'

She did, loved all kinds of dancing, but felt it would be unwise to give this man any encouragement. 'Er, no.'

'Don't you worry none, I'll soon teach you. The dance starts at eight. Wadda you drink? Gin? I'll have one waiting.'

'I really don't . . .'

'Good. Be waiting by the doors.'

Kelly was far more concerned with what was going on around her than the fact that Wilbur Crosby was going to be a disappointed man come Friday night when she did not appear. 'Look, Lieutenant, please listen ter me. What you're doing is really great, but our contract is to take away all of the battery even though we only need the lead. So, you see, we could get into trouble.'

The Lieutenant stared at her, then his face creased into a broad grin. 'No problem. You only need the lead, so why bother with the rest?' He winked at her. 'I'll take care of it.'

'You will?'

'Yeah, no trouble. The incinerator will burn that lot up in no time and no one'll be any the wiser.'

Wide-eyed she asked, 'Are you sure?'

'Little lady,' he whispered close to her ear, 'that ain't nothing to what we got up to in the war. Doing this for you is peanuts by comparison. Now don't you worry your pretty little head. If I say I'll take care of it, I'll take care of it.'

Her eyes danced excitedly. All she could think of was Alec's delight when she explained what had happened. So thrilled was she, she wanted to hug the handsome American in gratitude, but decided it would be best not to. He was coming on strong enough without her doing anything to encourage him. 'Thank you. Thank you very much,' was all she said.

Wilbur took her arm. 'Come on, I'll take you over to the canteen and get you a hot drink. Then we'll see if we can locate that friend of yours. Shorty,' he shouted across to a huge man who reminded Kelly of Bluto in the cartoons of Popeye the Sailor Man. 'When you're finished loading, take the truck over to the weigh station. We'll pick it up there. And that,' he said, inclining his head towards the mound of dismembered battery cases, 'you can lose in the incinerators. And be sharp about it. Keep a look out for the Colonel,' he added.

Shorty nodded. 'Sure thing, Lieutenant.'

On the way across the parade ground heading towards the canteen building, Wilbur asked, 'This friend of yours, what's she look like? Blonde? Brunette? Is she as pretty as you?'

Kelly inwardly froze as it suddenly occurred to her that maybe the kindly Lieutenant might not have been quite so obliging if he had realised from the off that her friend was a man. Her mind sought frantically for a way to address this awkward situation without causing any bad feeling. She was saved from answering when an airman came running up to them.

They all stopped and the men saluted each other.

'Lieutenant,' said the newcomer breathlessly, nodding a greeting at Kelly. 'Excuse me ma'am,' he said, taking off his cap. 'The Colonel's wanting to see you, sir?'

Wilbur groaned. 'Now?'

'Now, sir. About the visit of the British dignitaries.'

Wilbur turned to Kelly. 'You'll excuse me?'

She smiled, hiding her relief. 'Yes, of course. I'll find me friend around here somewhere. Thanks for yer help.'

'My pleasure. See you Friday, then?'

She held out her hand. 'Goodbye, Lieutenant. And once again, thank you.'

Once they were back in the truck Alec couldn't stop laughing. He was laughing so much tears rolled down his cheeks, blurring his vision so that he had momentarily to bring the truck to a halt while he calmed down enough to resume the journey.

'I don't believe it, Kelly. All the time I was sitting in that office, waiting for an interview with the man in charge to see about some help, I was worried to death about you. I . . .' He stopped abruptly, suddenly realising that he had been about to reveal that his worry had encompassed a certain amount of jealousy towards the handsome uniformed airmen wandering the base. He trusted Kelly implicitly but she was an attractive woman and a likely target for any normal red-blooded male, let alone Americans whose reputations with the ladies was legendary. 'I . . . er . . . well, I was worried about you being left alone in a strange place. Worried too that we'd never get the truck loaded and be off before dark.'

Kelly grinned. 'It was very nice of the Lieutenant, wasn't it?' she said, tongue in cheek.

A deep crease furrowed Alec's brow. 'You liked this Lieutenant then, did you? Good-looking, was he?'

Kelly tilted her head, eyes narrowed. 'Why, Alec Alderman, I do believe you're jealous.'

'I'm not. Of course not,' he denied, then sheepishly grinned. 'Well, yes, I might be, just a little.' He leaned over and smacked a noisy kiss on her cheek. 'You're a good-looking woman, Kelly McCallan. Of course I was jealous.'

She laughed. 'Well, yer've no need ter be. I only have eyes for you. Now give me a proper kiss,' she demanded.

Their kiss was long and lingering and full of passion. It was several minutes before they pulled apart.

Gazing tenderly at her, Alec smiled. 'It's a pity I never got to meet that Lieutenant and thank him myself. The profit we'll make is all down to him. I know Raggy'll be grunting happily when I tell him.'

'Happily enough to give you a share, you reckon? You deserve it.'

'I don't know about deserve, Kelly. I know what happened was none of our doing but it weren't exactly honest. Someone's lost out at our expense.'

'Yes, the American Airforce. They owned the batteries. But if we went back and came clean, the Lieutenant would get into serious trouble. There's nothing you can do, Alec. By the time I managed to explain about our contract it was too late. What's done is done and for once we're the winners.'

He looked at her closely. 'Yeah, yer right. For once we are, ain't we, and it makes a nice change.' He put his foot down and revved the engine. 'We're going to celebrate, Kelly. I'm going to find us a fish and chip shop on the way home, and if you behave yourself I might even treat you to a bottle of Vimto.'

She smiled, turning her attention to the road ahead. 'Sounds wonderful.'

Looking thoughtfully at her, he momentarily slowed the truck. 'Kelly?'

She turned her head. 'Yes, Alec?'

'If . . . if Raggy does pay me a bonus, I'm going to use it to get a divorce.'

Her face softened tenderly. There was no need for her to answer. This was Alec's way of telling her he wanted to marry her. She knew he would never formally propose until he was a free man. And she knew without a doubt what her answer would be when he finally did.

Chapter Thirty

A tired but happy Kelly, mentally reliving every moment of the day she had just spent with Alec, walked into the house later that evening totally unprepared for the shock that was awaiting her.

She jumped in surprise when Glenda pounced on her as she entered the back door.

'Had a good day, Kelly?' she blurted.

There was something about her tone of voice, something odd about her manner, an uncertain look in her eye, that struck Kelly immediately. She was certainly on edge about something. 'Yes, I had a wonderful day, ta,' she said, shutting the door. 'I've so much to tell yer but I'll mash a cuppa first.'

'I'll do it, Kelly. You take yer coat off and go through for a warm.'

She eyed her sister-in-law quizzically. 'Is . . . is everything all right?' She froze suddenly. 'Dad! There's n'ote happened to me dad, 'as there?'

'No, yer dad's fine,' Glenda answered, placing the kettle on the stove. 'I've got him ter bed.'

'What, already? You know I don't usually bed him down 'til about ten.'

'Well, I thought it best.'

'Best? Wadda you mean?'

'Well, he . . . he was tired.'

'And he told yer that, did he?'

337

'No, you know he didn't, but he looked it,' she said defensively.

Kelly frowned. 'What's happened, Glenda?' she demanded. 'I know summat's not right. You're like one of them Mexican jumping beans you get free in a penny Lucky Bag. Now out with it before I throttle it out of yer.'

She gulped, gnawing her bottom lip anxiously. 'I don't know the best way to tell yer this, Kelly, but . . .' She took a breath. 'Mickey's home.'

Kelly stared at her, astounded, mouth opening and shutting like a fish. 'Mickey's home? Here?'

She nodded vigorously.

Kelly's whole body sagged. 'Oh, God,' she gasped, clasping a hand to her mouth. Mickey had come back. Of all the things she'd hoped would never happen that was top of her list. A feeling of utter dread filled her being and she stared at Glenda, horrified. 'Tell me yer joking, Glenda? Please?'

'No, I ain't. He's upstairs in bed.'

Kelly tightened her lips, eyes narrowed harshly. 'Good job we got a mattress to replace the one we sold, ain't it?'

Glenda grasped her arm. 'There's no need ter be like that, Kelly.'

'Ain't there? Glenda, for God's sake. Mickey might be my brother and your husband but him coming back here is the last thing we need. We were getting on just fine without him. Now . . .'

'Stop it, Kelly,' she pleaded. 'He's changed, honest.'

'Changed! Our Mickey? The Pope's got more chance of marrying a nun.'

'No, honest, Kelly, he has. Like you I was . . . well, it knocked the stuffing out of me, seeing him standing there. I thought me eyes were playing tricks. But they weren't. It really was him. I didn't know what to say. I didn't know what to do. I didn't know whether to be

338

happy or cut me throat. You know how he was treating me before he went off. Anyway, he went mad at first, Kelly. Asked what the hell was going on when he seen all the clothes and sacks. Asked what were we doing, turning his home into a pigsty.'

'And you say he's changed?'

'Hear me out, Kelly. When I explained it were our living, he said he was sorry. He was just tired after his journey and seeing the state of things gave him a shock, wondering what the hell was going on. Well, it would, Kelly, wouldn't it?'

'Pardon? My brother said sorry? I've never heard our Mickey say that word in all the years I've known him.'

'Yes, I thought I was hearing things 'til he said it again. But I believed him after he told me how he'd been living. And so will you.'

'You think so?' said Kelly harshly.

Glenda nodded. 'He's had a terrible time, Kelly. Couldn't get work, and if it hadn't have been for the likes of the Salvation Army he'd have died of starvation. He slept most of the time in shop doorways, getting moved on by the coppers all the time. He walked back, all the way from Manchester. It took him two weeks and it rained nearly all the way. Can you imagine it? Over a hundred odd miles in pouring rain.'

'Manchester? What on earth was he doing in Manchester?'

'He hitched a lift in a lorry and that's where it was heading. Oh, Kelly, it must have been dreadful. Up there all alone, no money, nowhere to live. He said it made him think, Kelly, made him realise how badly he'd treated us. Especially me . . .' Her voice trailed away. 'Over the baby and everything.' She grabbed Kelly's arm, eyes pleading. 'He wants us to forgive him.'

'Our Mickey wants us to forgive him?' Kelly raised her eyebrows. 'You sure you're talking about Mickey? You ain't bin drinking or 'ote, have yer, Glenda?'

'No,' she cried, voice rising angrily. 'Mickey says he won't come back unless we both want him to. I want him to, Kelly. I want to give him another chance. Why won't you believe that he's changed?'

Kelly sighed, her whole body sagging. 'I want ter believe yer, Glenda, really I do. But I know our Mickey, and I don't care what he's bin through, none of this rings true. You're his wife, you love him, you want to believe all this. Me, well . . . I just don't know what ter think.' She sighed again. 'I just hope this ain't all an act to get into our good books and worm his way back, then before we know it take over again. I can't face the atmosphere we had before, all his nastiness and his moods, and the way he treated Dad.' She shook her head. 'No, I can't go through that again. I can't.' A terrible thought suddenly occurred. Her eyes flashed. 'Does he know about me and Alec?'

'No. Not about what good friends you are though I did mention we had dealings with him through Raggy's yard when I was telling Mickey what we did.'

'And what did he say?'

'Nothing.'

'Nothing? What, nothing at all?'

Glenda shook her head.

'And yer don't find that odd, knowing how he feels about Alec?'

'I might have done before but not now, Kelly. You wait, neither will you when you see how he's changed.'

Kelly wrung her hands. She wanted to believe Glenda, wanted so much to believe some sort of miracle had worked its magic over her brother, but somehow she couldn't. She felt a desperate urge to see Alec, speak to him about all this, ask his advice on how to act. She knew that despite his personal feelings towards Mickey, his advice would be wise and impartial. But then, she thought, would it be fair of her to drag him into all this? She decided it wouldn't. This was a problem she had to sort out herself. She raised her head. 'What about me dad, Glenda? How was Mickey about him?'

'Concerned, really concerned. Asked all about him and seemed bothered about him getting better.'

'Bothered? In what way was he bothered?'

Glenda tutted. 'He asked if the doctors thought yer dad would ever recover enough to speak again. That kind of bothered. Oh, Kelly, for God's sake. Why don't yer ask him yerself? He asked me to wake him when you came in.'

'Why?' she asked, alarmed.

''Cos he wants to see yer. You're his sister.'

But I don't want to see him, she thought, not yet, not until I've had time to take this all in, decide how to handle things. 'Leave him sleeping, Glenda. I can see him in the morning, that'll be soon enough.'

Glenda cocked an ear. 'I don't think you have any choice. I can hear him coming down the stairs. I'll mash some tea,' she said matter-of-factly. 'Why don't you go into the back room and sit with him? The least you can do is hear what he has to say.'

Kelly's back stiffened. Glenda was right. The least she could do was greet her brother and listen to his story. Whether she believed what she heard was another matter. One thing was for certain: she wasn't going to let herself be so easily convinced as Glenda appeared to have been.

Hands tightly clasped, she braced herself and walked slowly from the kitchen.

A short while later Mickey took a deep sorrowful breath and eyed his sister pleadingly. Kelly's reaction was all important to him. Winning Glenda over had been easy, although he had nearly blown it before he'd even begun.

When he had first seen the state of the house, filled to bursting with what he saw as pile upon pile of stinking rubbish, his temper had got the better of him. It had come as such a shock after the last nine months of living in virtual luxury. After tasting that way of life, this hovel – for he no longer thought of it as his home – with its old, battered furniture and grimy walls, was totally alien to him. For the occupants, living their squalid hand-to-mouth existence, he had no feelings whatsoever, except a slight residual guilt for what had happened to his sister.

Kelly had never really done anything against him except make a stand over no longer wanting to take part in any jobs, and he could not blame her for that. But regardless he was not going to let what feelings he had for her stand in his way. He didn't belong here any more and the sooner he executed his plan and escaped a rich man the better. He could put all this behind him then as if it had never existed.

But to achieve his aim, Kelly's good opinion of the new Mickey was vital. He felt he'd played the part admirably, painted a thoroughly convincing picture of the way he hoped she believed he had survived, and of how his close encounter with death through starvation and lack of shelter had made him realise his mistakes and want to put them right, live a clean and honest life. But had he convinced her? That's what mattered.

'So, Kelly, will yer forgive me? I've said I'm sorry.' Begging her galled him but it had to be done. 'I've told yer I've no intention of ever going back to the way I was before. Just give me a chance to prove it.'

She stared at him. Everything he had said had sounded so convincing and of course she wanted to believe him and welcome him back. Despite what he'd done in the past – what she knew of, and what she didn't – he was her brother and as her flesh and blood she loved him.

She suddenly felt tired, emotionally drained and in no fit state to make any sort of decision. But Mickey and Glenda, in her way, were forcing her to do so.

Mickey sensed her hesitation with a growing fear that she was seeing right through him. 'I don't have ter ask you if I can come back,' he blurted. 'I have every right to walk back in whenever I want. But I didn't want to do that, Kelly. I don't want you having to watch me like a hawk, waiting for me to put a foot wrong. I don't want suspicion falling on me whenever anything unusual happens. I want to be the man I would have bin if the bloody war and everything hadn't turned me into the bastard I was. You've got to give me that chance. You've got to help me do it, Kelly. I can't do it without your support. Glenda's willing to give me another try so why won't you?'

Kelly was staring at him. He certainly had changed. Never had she expected to hear her brother talking like this. Now she realised just what Glenda had meant. He did deserve a chance and who was she to refuse him? Before she gave her approval, though, there were two questions to which she needed answers. 'What about Dad, Mickey?'

He pictured the motionless upright figure sitting silently in the chair by the fire when he'd first arrived. He remembered fighting the bile that rose in him, the intense hatred that had filled him, and braced himself to say the word he'd vowed never to say again. 'Dad?' He forced a semblance of remorse. 'I was hurting, Kelly, over Mam's death. It was wrong of me to treat him like I did. It's preyed on me mind a lot. I'd do anything to try and put that right.'

Her heart went out to him then, knowing what she had suffered herself. She could appreciate what he had gone through, despite feeling she'd never understand his reaction. Maybe that had been Mickey's way of handling his grief. His answer was enough for her. The only thing that bothered her now was her brother's possible reaction to her relationship with Alec. But that could wait. Enough had been said, too many emotions experienced for one night.

She smiled at him warmly. 'Welcome home, Mickey.'

His face flooded with relief. 'Thanks, Kelly. You'll not regret this, I promise.'

Those few words, so sincerely spoken, were by far the worst of all the lies he had told since he'd been home.

Chapter Thirty-One

An exhausted but exhilarated Alec unlatched the back gate and strode jauntily down the dark path towards the back door, memories of his delightful day still lingering. He was glad it was far too late for him to receive his nightly visit from Mrs Quick, although he knew she would know what time he had returned home. It wouldn't surprise him in the least to see her nose peeking round the bedroom curtain should he look up. Tomorrow he would receive the usual third degree about what he'd been up to.

He felt sorry for Norma's mother but her constant vigilance over him was beginning to get on his nerves, although he had not the heart to tell her so. For a brief moment he wondered how much the old lady knew of his relationship with Kelly. At this moment, though, he was too happy and too tired to care, although he knew he would have to tackle the subject with her sometime. It would not be fair for her to find out through gossip. After all, she was his estranged wife's mother and deserved the courtesy of learning his intentions from him.

He had just spent the last couple of hours unloading the lorry of its cargo of precious lead, feeling it would be unwise to leave the task until morning. Friday mornings were busy times at the yard. Penniless people facing the weekly payment of their bills joined the endless queue with whatever they could lay their hands on in the hope that their debts could be met this way. Chances were the lorry and its cargo would remain untouched until the following Monday as Saturdays were just as busy too. Despite his tiredness after such a long day. Alec felt it unwise to allow that. The yard was a constant target for unscrupulous people and a loaded lorry a huge temptation.

He had not minded the extra work and Raggy had been quite happy to let him get on with it, being already otherwise occupied with a screwdriver and hammer in his ramshackle shed. When Alec had told him the good news about the lead, Raggy just grunted. Alec took this as a sign that he was pleased or would be once the lead was sold on.

As he had laboured, all Alec's thoughts had centred on Kelly and how happy she made him. The future with her by his side stretched away rosily and he knew instinctively that Kelly felt the same way too.

He sighed contentedly as he stopped by the door and searched through his pockets for the key, thinking how nice it would be if she were here with him now and they were entering the house together. But then he thought, Not this house. Another. One with no ghosts, nothing left of the past. A new start. He wanted nothing to mar their future life together and felt Kelly deserved the best start he could possibly give her.

He found the key and inserted it into the lock. As he turned it he frowned. The door was not locked. But he distinctly remembered locking it when he had left that morning. He always double checked, it was a habit of his. Tentatively he pushed the door open and stepped through. He groped his way over to the stove and felt around for the box of matches he always kept there. Striking one, he lit the kitchen gas mantle and turned it to its fullest. Eerie flickering light flooded the small room. Still armed with the box of matches, he stepped across to the door to the back room, pushed it open and walked through.

He froze, shocked, as a ghostly figure sitting in the furthest armchair by the fireplace got to its feet.

'Hello, Alec. I thought you were never coming home.'

For several long moments he stood staring blankly. 'Norma!' he finally uttered. 'But . . . what are you doing here?'

She took two steps towards him, clasping her hands. 'I've come home.'

A terrible foreboding flooded through him. 'What d'yer mean, you've come home? I don't understand?'

'I made a mistake, Alec.'

'Mistake?'

'Yes, mistake. I . . . I was going through a bad time, I wasn't myself when I left. I shouldn't have gone, I realise that now, so I've come home.'

But you can't, he wanted to cry. I don't want you here, you don't belong here any more. But the words would not come.

'Is there any chance we can have some light on in here?' she asked agitatedly.

'Er . . . yes, of course.' Automatically he lit the two nearest wall mantles and turned to face her. She was smiling at him, looking quite unconcerned, as though nothing was wrong, as though the last year had never happened. As if she'd just gone away for a week to visit a relative.

'Look, why don't you sit down?' she offered. 'I'll make you a nice cup of tea.' She shuddered, rubbing her hands together. 'It's freezing in here, Alec, I had to keep my coat on. I could have lit the fire only you didn't leave it laid. We should really get one of those gas fires. Save a lot of trouble and mess.' She walked past him into the kitchen. 'I'll make enquiries at the gas

347

showroom tomorrow to see about getting one put in. Oh,' she called from the kitchen, 'can you take my bags up? I've left them by the front door.'

Stunned by her casualness, a confused Alec ran both hands slowly through his hair, his mind in turmoil. Why had his wife suddenly come back without so much as a warning? Taking a deep breath, he headed for the kitchen. 'Norma, I want ter know what's going on?'

She was searching through the pantry. 'We've no sugar, Alec. Oh, it's all right, I found it,' she announced, emerging holding the blue bag aloft. 'The sugar basin needs washing. I'll do it later.' She stopped and stared at him. 'Did you take my bags up?'

'Norma, stop it,' he said sharply. 'I want to know what's going on? You can't just come back like this. Just walk in like nothing has happened.'

Her face puckered, bottom lip trembling. 'Don't shout at me, Alec.'

'I wasn't shouting.'

'Yer were. You've no idea what I've gone through. It's been awful.' She sniffed back tears. 'I went away because of you. I've already told you that. You stifled me, sometimes I felt I couldn't breathe. You did everything I asked you to do. You were just like a lap dog. It was almost like living with a father. I had to get away. I couldn't stand it any more.'

'Then why didn't you tell me? At least give me the chance to do something about it.'

'I couldn't.'

'Why? Am I that much of an ogre?'

'No, 'course not.'

'Then why not talk to me about it?'

'Because I didn't want to hurt you.'

'Hurt me? For God's sake, Norma, what d'you think you did to me when you told me you were leaving? I was devastated. I felt like killing meself. Do you know how close I came to doing just that?'

'Oh, Alec, please stop shouting at me.'

'I'm not shouting. I'm trying to explain my side of things. Norma, all I ever wanted was to make you happy.'

'Well, you didn't,' she sniffed. 'You made me bloody miserable.'

He looked at her in shock.

'Don't look at me like that, Alec. It's true, all of it.'

'But how could I treat you like a woman when most of the time you acted like a little girl?'

It was her turn to stare. 'How dare you, Alec? How dare you say I acted like that? If I did then it's because you made me.'

'But all I did was love you, Norma,' he answered, distraught. 'I was only trying to look after you. I didn't want to be like some other husbands are to their wives. I could have beaten you, come home drunk most nights demanding me dinner, kept you short of money, not tried to help with the housework so you wouldn't have so much to do when you came home. Are you telling me that's what you wanted me to be like?'

'No,' she said sharply.

'Well what, then? I don't understand. You're saying I made you unhappy by being good to you, yet you didn't want me to treat you bad. You ain't making sense, Norma.'

'I know,' she cried. 'I'm so confused, Alec.' A torrent of tears spurted from her eyes. 'Please,' she begged. 'Let's just put all this behind us. Let's start again. I love you, Alec. I've been such a fool. I just want things to go back to what they were between us.'

She rushed towards him and flung her arms round his neck. 'I know you love me, Alec. I know I've hurt you dreadfully. But surely you can forgive me? I'll be a good wife in future. I won't complain. Really, I like the way you treated me. You made me feel safe. I didn't realise none of this 'til after I left. Alec, please don't send me away. We belong together. Norma and Alec. It's always been Norma and Alec. I need you, Alec. I can't manage without you.'

A dull feeling of doom spread from the pit of his stomach through his body. He didn't want this. He no longer loved the woman in his arms, her closeness felt so alien now. He cared for her still, worried for her welfare, but that was all. Yet how could he refuse to give their marriage another try after the way she had begged him? He remembered only too painfully the despair he himself had experienced when he had asked her to give him another chance and she had flatly refused. Knowing how much that had hurt, how could he put Norma through the same?

His conscience was pricking him. His heart, his soul, his very existence, now belonged to another. Kelly. The thought of never holding her in his arms again, never kissing her, his dreams of their life together going unfulfilled, overcame him with dread. Yet what about his loyalty to Norma? She was his wife, and according to her it was all his fault she had felt the need to go away. His burden of responsibility towards her was suddenly crushing and he knew his conscience would not permit him to abandon her just because he now loved another.

He took her arms from around his neck and stepped away. 'I have to know, Norma. Did you leave me for another man? I want to know the truth. If we're going to try again, I need to hear the truth.'

'Of course I didn't,' she cried, deeply offended. 'How could you even think such a thing? I went to stay with a girlfriend. I just needed time, I've told you. I've done nothing wrong, Alec, you have to believe me.'

'And what about my job? You said you were embarrassed about what I did?'

'Oh, that was stupid of me. I don't mind, really I don't. You love that job. It was wrong to expect you to give it up.' Her eyes lit up hopefully. 'You said Raggy might make you a partner. You'd be a businessman then, wouldn't you, and I'd be so proud. But,' she added hurriedly, 'I'm proud of you anyway.'

He eyed her for a moment. She was fighting hard, he could not deny that. She obviously desperately wanted to save their marriage. He took a deep breath. 'How do I know you won't just up and leave me again?'

She grabbed hold of his arm. 'Oh, Alec, I won't. I promise you I won't. Please trust me.'

But that was just it. He didn't trust her. The unquestioning love and trust he had once held for this woman had gone and it was something he doubted could ever be rekindled. Regardless, he knew he had no choice. Norma was his wife. Whatever she had done, his conscience told him she deserved the right to another chance, whether he liked it or not. How he was going to tell Kelly of this turn of events he did not know. The thought of the pain this would cause her broke his heart. He didn't want to think of the pain he himself would suffer.

Sighing deeply, he lifted his eyes to meet his wife's. 'I'll take your bags up.'

Norma waited until she heard Alec climbing the stairs before she dared allow herself to sigh with relief. That had been much harder than she had envisaged. She had taken it for granted that he would welcome her back with open arms. Surprisingly that had not happened.

The things her mother had told her about Kelly Collins must have been true then. Mum was an exasperating old woman who drove her to distraction. The biggest mistake Norma felt she'd ever made was moving next door to her. But for once her mother had served her purpose. Norma had not intended to come back just at this moment, implicitly believing that Alec would always be there for her, whenever she wanted him. Had she not received an inkling of his growing attachment to Kelly then she might well have left things just a little too late. Yes, she had acted just in time, thank goodness.

Her eyes glinted maliciously. What a fool Alec was to believe anything she had said. The only reason she was back now was because she had no choice. She thought of James Wilkinson then and, try as she might, she could not stop her heart from thumping wildly. How she loved that man still, despite the shameless way he had treated her.

He had been her manager at work and constant closeness had ignited their passion. Norma had given up everything for him just as he'd begged her. His promises had known no bounds. Promotion to supervisor; moving into a flat together in a good part of town; seaside holidays; the best food in smart restaurants; that they'd live happily ever after . . .

The promotion had come but Norma wasn't experienced enough to cope with the job and was soon out of her depth. Other staff began asking questions about why she had been chosen. The flat, although spacious and tastefully furnished, overlooked a factory whose huge chimney continually billowed black smoke. The rent wasn't cheap either. The fancy restaurants, visits to the theatre, and entertaining his boring friends proved very expensive, and he'd expected Norma to pay her share. He automatically saw her role as including taking care of him. As well as his bedmate she became his washer-woman, cook, cleaner and nursemaid, while he sat back and enjoyed all the attention she lavished upon him.

But still she loved him, clinging on in the hope that things would improve. Then rumours had reached her of his pursuit of another. A brunette, stunningly attractive, with a very wealthy father. Norma had been devastated and knew then that her time with James was rapidly running out. When her mother had told her the news about Alec and Kelly there was no decision for her to make. James was tiring of her, in truth her affair with him was over, very soon he would give her no choice but to leave. A demotion at work was imminent.

She wasn't equipped to fend for herself, having gone from a doting mother to a doting husband. Back in a lower paid job she could not afford to live alone, could not cope with the worry of bills. Going back to Alec was her only salvation. It had never entered her head that he might not want her. But whether he did or not, she intended to stay, safe, secure, protected, with solid, dependable, loyal Alec, while she recovered from her heartache and until something better came along.

She did not love him, had stopped loving her husband a long time ago, but it had shocked her greatly to realise that he no longer loved her. Well, she didn't care about that, she would turn a blind eye. She was back under his roof and that was all that mattered. Kelly could always have him back when Norma's need of him was over.

As he re-entered the kitchen, she ran towards him, wrapped her arms around him and laid her head on his shoulder. 'Oh, Alec,' she said with all the enthusiasm she could muster. 'It's so good to be home.'

Chapter Thirty-Two

Kelly was up and out of the house early the next morning. She wanted to catch Alec before he opened the yard for business. News of Mickey's return would spread rapidly and she did not want him to learn from the gossips, causing him to worry about any repercussions on their relationship. She wanted to tell him of Mickey's drastic change and of her hope that now her brother and Alec could finally settle their differences and become friends. She did not expect that state of affairs to take place overnight but hopefully it would one day.

She met up with him just as he was about to step through the door to the yard.

Immediately she looked at his face she knew something was terribly wrong. He was ashen and drawn, dark circles under his eyes, mouth set into a grim line.

'What on earth's wrong, Alec?' she asked, all thoughts of the reason for her own visit forgotten.

Shocked at her unexpected arrival, he stared at her without speaking. All night he had tossed and turned, trying to fathom a way to break this devastating news to the woman he adored. He had been up since four pacing the icy kitchen, and still had not found the right words to say to her. How did you tell someone you loved, and who loved you in return, that through no fault of theirs you would have to part?

Fear and trepidation were building inside Kelly. She

suddenly thought Alec must have heard of Mickey's return, but then realised it was not possible yet, and despite the bad feeling between Alec and her brother, Mickey's return would not be enough to cause the dismay Alec was obviously suffering. This was something else. By the look of him something catastrophic. 'Alec, please, tell me what's wrong? Has someone died or . . .'

'No, it's nothing like that. Look, Kelly, we can't speak here. People will be arriving soon. Can we meet up somewhere later? Somewhere private.'

'Private?' Her fear suddenly heightened. 'You're frightening me, Alec. I'm not leaving 'til you tell me what's bothering you?'

Shutting his eyes tightly, he nodded. 'Kelly, I'm sorry, I didn't mean to frighten you.' He took her arm. 'Come inside.'

Silently she followed him through the doorway and over to the lean-to. Inside its shelter, hands clasped tightly, he said the words that she had always dreaded.

'Norma's come back.'

An icy fear gripped her. 'Back?' she said. Mind whirling, she stared at him for several long moments. 'To . . . to collect some things from the house?' she asked tentatively.

He shook his head. 'No, Kelly. She's come back for good.'

'You . . . you mean as your wife?'

He nodded.

Her whole body stiffened. 'And what about you, Alec? Is that what you want?'

'No, Kelly, it's not.'

'Do you still love her?' she whispered.

'No,' he said without any hesitation. 'I've never lied to you about that, Kelly. I did once, but not now. I care for her, I'm worried for her, but that's all I feel.' Eyes filled

356

with deep pain settled on hers. 'You know I love you. God, how much I love you! The thought of what this'll do to us is tearing me apart. But I have no choice.'

'What d'yer mean, you have no choice,' she cried. ''Course you have. Tell her you don't want her back.'

'I can't, Kelly.'

'Why not?'

'Because me conscience won't let me, that's why. She begged me, she pleaded for another chance. I . . .' He sighed despairingly. 'I just couldn't tell her I didn't want her back as my wife. She's had an awful time. She's not her usual self. I can't break this to her while she's in this state. And I feel so responsible for what she's gone through. Maybe once she's stronger, I can tell her then.'

'And what about me, Alec? What am I expected to do? Do yer think I can just shut off my feelings?' A rush of tears filled her eyes and her voice faltered emotionally. 'I love you too, Alec,' she whispered. 'But I don't understand. How can you hurt me when you can't hurt Norma?'

His already ashen face turned whiter. He grabbed Kelly into his arms and crushed her to him. 'Oh, Kelly, I don't want to hurt you. The very last thing I want is to hurt you. I wish you could understand. I just feel so responsible for her and I know that if I told her the truth about my feelings for you and she did something stupid, I'd never be able to live with meself. She's not strong like you, Kelly, she can't cope. This is something I have to do.' He bent his head and kissed her tear-wet cheek. 'Oh, Kelly,' he moaned. 'I'm so sorry.'

'So am I,' she whispered. She pulled away from him then, wiping her wet face with her hands, took a deep breath and raised her chin. 'I wish you the best, Alec. I just want you to be happy, and I mean it when I say I hope you both will be.' Her eyes narrowed. 'But, by

357

God, if you ain't, I shall be bloody angry that we've both gone through so much pain for the sake of poor little Norma.'

She spun on her heel and left him there, staring after her.

Chapter Thirty-Three

Kneeling before her father, tears of distress pouring down her face, Kelly gently took hold of his hands. 'Oh, Dad,' she choked. 'What am I gonna do?' Through her tear-blurred vision she gazed deep into his blank eyes. What she would give to feel his arms around her in a comforting hug, hear his soothing voice issue fatherly words of advice. Despite all she had faced in her life before, she had never felt so much in need of the love, support and wisdom that her parents would have given her.

The pain of her mother's loss still cut deep; that death was something she knew she would never get over. Rod's too. Kelly had loved him in an innocent, immature way, and regardless of her feelings for Alec, still thought of Rod often with deep affection. But this pain she was now suffering was like a hand ripping out her heart, her very soul. How she could live through it she had no idea. At this moment the only solution she could think of was to curl up in bed and hopefully die.

Leaving the yard early that morning, Alec's words ringing loudly in her ears, she had wandered the streets, lost in her grief. Miles she had walked, going over and over what he had said, trying to understand his decision to stay with a wife he did not love, while fighting her own violent emotions. But despite the hard talking to she had given herself, the decision she had forced herself to make to bury her feelings and get on with her life, she still could not comprehend or accept the unexpected crushing blow he had delivered.

The fact that he would no longer hold her in his arms, that she would never witness in his eyes that tender look of love that was especially hers, that their unspoken understanding to cement their love in marriage would never materialise, was unthinkable to her. She sighed, a long, deep sigh filled with sorrow. How she would miss Alec. Life without him by her side stretched into dark oblivion.

In her emotional state the pressure applied to her hands was so slight she nearly missed it. Head jerking up, face wreathed in shocked surprise, she stared at her father. 'Dad, you squeezed me hands, I know you did. Do it again, Dad. Please. Try again,' she pleaded.

With bated breath, she waited and waited but nothing happened.

Sadly, laying his hands back in his lap, she tenderly patted them then stretched up to kiss him on his cheek. She knew she had not imagined what she had felt. She knew that deep within her father's fuddled mind he had heard her cry for help and struggled to reach out to her. That knowledge gave her comfort.

'Thank you, Dad,' she whispered. 'I know you understand how I'm feeling.' She smiled at him tenderly. 'I'll get through this, just like you did over Mam. But, Dad, please do summat for me? Please come back to us. Only when yer ready. We're all here waiting.'

'I can see you've bin busy today. Decided to take a holiday?'

The unexpected voice made her jump. She stood up awkwardly, looking guiltily over the piles of clothes and bric-a-brac she was supposed to have sorted. 'I . . . I . . .'

At the sight of her miserable blotched face, Glenda frowned in concern. 'What happened?' she demanded, then sighed knowingly. 'He's told yer then?' she said, stripping off her coat and hat and flinging them across the back of a chair.

'Told me?'

'Alec has, about her coming back,' she said matter-of-factly, then watched in horror as Kelly's face crumpled and her eyes filled with fresh tears.

'How do you know?' she choked.

Glenda grimaced. 'It's common knowledge.'

'What?' Kelly's body sagged. 'Oh, Ada and her cronies, I take it?'

'Yer can't stop gossip, Kelly. Anyway, madam came into the shop while I was in there this morning, bought a whole load of stuff and told Ada to put it on the slate and that Alec 'ud settle up at the end of the week. Before she left she looked right at me, said that she was going to cook Alec a big dinner 'cos he looked like he'd not eaten properly for months. Right cocky she was. She knows about you and Alec, yer know.'

Sniffing hard, Kelly frowned. 'I don't see how she can. Alec hasn't told her.'

Glenda's eyebrows rose. 'You ain't half innocent, gel. Her mother lives next door. I bet she knows just about everything – even how many times he's visited the lavvy since her precious daughter did a bunk.'

'Don't be nasty, Glenda. She told Alec she didn't know where Norma was. She could see what he was going through so wouldn't you think she would have put him out of his misery if she'd have known?'

Glenda shook her head. 'You're too trusting, you. If you believe that, you'll believe anything. Oh, fer God's sake, sit down, gel. I'll get you a cuppa and you and me can have a good talk.'

'I'm all right, Glenda, I don't want to talk about it. Anyway, what is there to talk about? Alec's back with his wife and that's all there is to it.'

Glenda stepped across to her and laid a hand on her arm. 'Kelly, I thought me and you were friends. Well, I hoped we were. I can't deny that I never used to care two hoots about yer, I kept in with yer just because you were Mickey's sister. But . . .' A pink colour tinged her cheeks. 'I do care about yer now. Look, I can't take yer pain away, gel, or make things any easier for yer, but I remember what I felt like when Mickey went away. I know you could have asked me ter leave but you didn't, did yer? I won't forget that, Kelly. Anyway, we're business partners and partners look out for each other, don't they?'

Miserably, Kelly nodded.

'Good. Now take the weight off yer legs, I won't be a minute.' She flashed a smile. 'Surprising what a natter over a cuppa can do for yer spirits. You taught me that.'

A few minutes later Glenda plonked two steaming mugs of tea on the table and pushed one towards Kelly. 'I put two heaped sugars in yours. You need the energy.' She took a sip from her own mug, put it down on the table and looked meaningfully at Kelly. 'So, what yer gonna do?'

'Do? In what way?'

'Well, you are gonna put up a fight, aren't you? I know I would.'

'Like tell him I'm pregnant, yer mean, and force him to leave Norma.' Kelly clasped her hand to her mouth. 'I'm sorry, Glenda. I . . .'

'It's okay,' she cut in. 'I thought that was my little secret. I underestimated you, didn't I?' She sighed. 'I learned to me cost that dirty tricks don't pay off. But that don't mean you can't go round and see Norma and demand ter know what she's up to.'

Kelly looked shocked at the very idea. 'I couldn't do that.'

'Why not? I would. And you've every right.'

'I have no rights, Glenda.'

'That's not how I see it. The man loves you. That fact's plain enough for anyone ter see. And you love him, don't yer? That's plain enough too.'

Kelly nodded.

'Well then, if that's not right enough, then I don't know what is. I don't bloody understand him, I don't. I mean, the woman just ups and leaves without a thought for what she's doing to him and then comes back without a by your leave. And you think she loves him?'

Part of Kelly didn't understand either, but this behaviour was typical of Alec. He was too caring sometimes for his own good.

'I know her little game,' Glenda hissed angrily. 'Bloody nerve she's got. She's only back 'cos that bloke didn't want her.'

Kelly stared at her, stunned. 'What bloke?'

'Remember I said when she first left that I bet she had a bloke? Well, it's true, she did. Everyone knows. 'Cept Alec, I expect. And, by the looks of it, you. Norma might have thought she was being clever but she wasn't, 'cos she was seen.'

This revelation had knocked the stuffing out of Kelly. 'Who by? Who saw her?'

'Mona, Ada's sister. After she left the shop today, Mona was full of it. "That's the snotty little madam that shacked herself up with her boss from Woolworth's, 'til he got tired of her and swopped her for someone else." Seems the flat they rented is part of a house that Mona used to clean years ago. She still visits the old lady who owns it. She lives in the flat underneath.' Glenda grinned. 'Small world, ain't it? So, are yer gonna tell Alec?'

Kelly stared at her blankly. After several moments she shook her head. 'No.'

'No? Why ever not?' said Glenda, aghast. 'Well, if you won't I will.'

'No, you won't,' Kelly ordered. 'Apart from the fact that this news would hurt him dreadfully, if he's to find out then he must do it for himself and not because we've interfered. Have yer got that, Glenda?'

Sulkily she nodded. 'I was only trying to help.'

Kelly sighed forlornly. 'I know yer were, and I'm grateful, but Alec has made his decision and whether or not I like it, I have to abide by that.' She took a deep breath. 'Glenda, walking away from this is the hardest thing I've ever had to do, but I know I must. I . . . I love him enough, you see,' she said softly.

Glenda pressed her lips together tightly. 'Suit yerself. So, what are yer gonna do?'

Kelly shrugged her shoulders. 'The only thing I can. Just get on with things. I only wish . . .'

'What?'

'That I could go down the doctor's and ask him to cut out this pain else give me a pill to cure it.'

Glenda smiled ironically. 'If only it were that simple, eh?'

'Yes, if only.' Kelly leaned across the table and laid a hand on her arm. 'I'm glad we're friends now.'

Glenda beamed. 'Yeah, so am I.'

Painfully, Kelly forced a smile to her face. 'So, how did you get on today? Did you get to see Reverend Billings?'

Glenda frowned. 'What was I going to see him for?'

Kelly shook her head. 'The usual. His church held a bazaar on Tuesday night. You were going to see about what was left.'

'Oh, yes, so I was. I forgot. To be honest, me mind's bin full of Mickey and his job hunting.' She looked sheepishly at Kelly. 'I spent most of the day wandering around the town, didn't get around to doing anything about work. I did see a nice costume in C & A, though.'

Kelly leaned over and gave her arm an affectionate pat. 'Seems both of us had a holiday today then, didn't we? Try not to worry, Glenda. Mickey'll get summat, I'm sure. If not today then there's always tomorrow. He does seem keen.'

'Yeah, he does.' Glenda's face suddenly lit up with a large bright smile. 'I don't care how long it takes him. The main thing ter me is that he's come back. And come back the Mickey I always dreamed of having.' She suddenly eyed Kelly anxiously. 'Kelly, you do believe that people can change, don't yer?'

She frowned. 'What makes you ask?'

What *had* made Glenda ask that? Nothing in particular that she could think of. In fairness Mickey had only been back a day and a half and during that time had not put a foot wrong. He had been attentive, caring towards her, very eager to please. The only thing that he hadn't done, which she wanted him to do very badly, was make love to her. But then he had been tired after his journey, still recovering from his ordeal while away. She couldn't expect everything to fall into place after such a long time apart. So what had made her ask that question?

She shrugged her shoulders. 'Oh, it was nothing, I'm just being silly. I suppose I'm having a job believing he's here after I willed it to happen so often.' She got to her feet. 'Come on, you make a start sorting those rags, while I get cracking on the dinner. I want to do something really nice for Mickey tonight. Faggots and peas. Oh, no – steak and kidney pie with loads of gravy. He loves that. If I hurry, I'll catch the butcher.' She grinned mischievously. 'And you can come with me tomorrow to visit the Reverend. I don't know what it is about that man but he gives me the willies. Always trying to turn me religious.'

'That's his job, Glenda.'

'Yeah, I suppose.'

'I think he's a nice man, personally. I know me mother liked him. Look, I'll go tomorrow, if you want?'

'You're just the kinda business partner I'm glad I've got.'

'And the only one you're gonna get.'

Both women smiled warmly at each other.

Chapter Thirty-Four

Lounging back against the crumbling red-brick wall, Mickey pulled up the collar of his jacket, dug his hand deep inside his pocket and pulled out a half-empty packet of cigarettes. He lit one and drew on it deeply, filling his lungs with smoke. As he exhaled sharply, the smoke and his breath spiralled away on the freezing night air. In the distance he heard a church clock strike the hour. One, two . . . it continued until seven. Seven o'clock. He had left the house at eight that morning and if truth be told would have done anything not to have to return. But return he must if an innocent cover for his true activities was to be maintained.

Taking another deep drag on his cigarette, he smirked. He had made a good start. His day had proved most productive. He had eyed up four smart detached villas at the top of the Narborough Road. Each was a burglar's dream.

To have a poke around he had adopted the guise of a gas man checking properties for possible gas leaks. To complete his cover he had purchased second hand a blue jacket, albeit a shabby bus driver's one which he'd hoped would not be spotted, peaked cap and a dusty black Gladstone bag. He'd had to use ten shillings of the money Mitzi had thrust at him. At not one of the houses had any of the maids who'd answered the door asked for any credentials. If they had he would just have said he had temporarily mislaid them and would call back later. In fact the maids had been very glad to leave a gratified Mickey to his own devices.

The houses were all identical in design. As he'd pretended to poke and prod inside, he'd quickly noted the well-stocked gardens, affording plenty of cover. Behind the garden wall ran a service lane, ideal as an escape route. The houses would be a doddle for him to enter, the aged french windows having just one lock which could be easily picked. With stealth, haste and Lady Luck on his side, all four could be relieved of valuables the same night. Sammy the Shammy, he knew from experience, would be only too delighted to pocket a few shillings by loaning out his window-cleaning barrow, and more importantly would ask no questions. For some unknown reason the authorities never bothered to stop, question or search a weary man pushing a window-cleaning barrow, regardless of the hour.

The only problem Mickey faced was finding a hiding place in which to stash his ill-gotten gains until he could dispose of them around several trusted fences he'd used in the past. It was a big problem, and one that would need careful consideration. He needed somewhere safe and secure, somewhere where no one would think to look if ever suspicion fell on him and a search was made. Until this problem was answered, he would have to put the jobs on hold. But in the meantime, there was plenty of planning to keep him occupied.

A vision of the whole reason for his existence suddenly danced provocatively before him. She was lying naked on a bed covered with pale blue satin sheets, her arms stretched welcomingly towards him. He felt a painful ache of longing rise in him and his eyes glinted darkly. 'Soon, Mitzi. Soon,' he whispered.

Throwing down his cigarette, he ground it out with

his boot, straightened up, hunched his shoulders and planted upon his face the most miserable look he could conjure up. Mentally he prepared a tale of a soul-destroying day, trailing around factories, warehouses and building sites with not one offer of work.

Chapter Thirty-Five

Steeling herself, Kelly manoeuvred the heavily laden hand cart into Raggy's yard. It was three weeks since Alec had broken the news of his reconciliation with Norma, three weeks since she had set eyes on him. During that time, Glenda had insisted that she would handle the daily visit to the yard. Kelly had been grateful for her sensitivity, especially so knowing how much her sister-in-law detested this part of their business. But that state of affairs, Kelly felt, could not go on forever. Sometime or other Alec and she would come face to face, if only because their daily lives had to be run in close proximity. Despite her evasive action, she was actually amazed that the inevitable meeting had not happened yet.

As she approached the lean-to and the top of his head became visible, she paused to calm her jangled nerves. The next few minutes while he dealt with her wares were going to be extremely painful but this had to be done.

Realising it was her standing before him, Alec caught his breath. 'Kelly,' he whispered, voice filled with emotion, eyes that had been filled with sadness suddenly sparkling. 'Oh, Kelly, how are yer?'

'I'm very well, thank you,' she replied stiltedly. 'And how are you?'

He knew by the false smile on her drawn face, the forced lightness in her voice, that all was not well with her. He wanted to leap over the counter, gather her up in his arms and crush her to him, telling her how much he was missing her, that life without her was torture, that returning home to Norma each night filled him with dread. But how could he? Apart from being conscious of the queue of people behind Kelly, several of them within earshot, he had no right to hold her in such an intimate way any more, or to tell her of his feelings. His decision to stay with Norma he already knew to be a wrong one. He had thought that nursing a broken heart would be easier than living with his conscience. He had been badly mistaken.

'I'm okay,' he said matter-of-factly. 'Ticking along.'

The dark circles under his eyes and the false bright-ness of his voice told her otherwise, but she felt it was no longer her place to make personal comments. She longed to speak of how much she'd missed him, tell him that her every waking minute and sleepless night were spent reliving memories of precious moments together; that her need of him, her want of him, her love for him, was as strong as ever.

Instead she said, 'I'm glad things are working out for you.' It was a lie. The last thing she wanted was for his marriage to work, but how guilty she felt for having such a thought. She should be pleased for Alec. Abruptly she turned towards her cart. 'We've picked up a couple of things that might interest yer, otherwise the sacks are filled with the usual rags and woollens. How's Raggy?'

'He's fine.'

'Good. Please tell him I was asking after him.'

Their business was concluded and both said a cheerful goodbye with a heavy heart.

Glenda caught up with Kelly later that afternoon as she was pushing the half-filled hand cart down the maze of streets at the back of the Royal Infirmary.

Kelly eyed her in surprise. 'What a' you doing here? N'ote wrong, is there?'

'No, everything's fine. I've left Avril to get on with it. She knows to keep an eye on yer dad and what time to give him a cuppa. She said she ain't tekking him to the lavvy, though, draws the line at that. So I took him before I left.' She exhaled noisily. 'I just had to get out of the house, Kelly. I was getting sick and tired of sorting rags so I said I'd give Avril a bit extra to stay and do my share. She jumped at it, brought her eldest in to help.'

A deep frown creased Glenda's face. 'I just couldn't keep me mind on things today. I'm worried about Mickey. Worried that if he don't get summat soon, he'll up and leave.'

'Oh, he'll get summat, Glenda. He's out every day and someone somewhere will give him a chance. They will, you'll see.'

'I wish I had your faith.' She checked up and down the street before moving closer to Kelly, eyes filled with worry. 'I know this ain't the place but can I talk to you, Kelly, personal like?'

'Er . . . yes, 'course yer can. What's on yer mind?'

'Well . . . it's to do with me and Mickey.'

'In what way?'

Glenda wrung her hands anxiously. 'It's kind of embarrassing. But, well, he . . . he doesn't touch me in that way, if you know what I mean. He hasn't made any effort. In fact, he hasn't made love to me once since we got married. I can't stand it, Kelly. He gets into bed every night, turns over and goes to sleep. But most times I know he ain't really, I know he's pretending. I can tell by the way he snores. I've tried everything to attract him. I bought a new nightie and a bottle of the latest Yardley eau de cologne. I even tried a new hair style. You know you said you liked me hair up in that french pleat.'

'Yes, I did, and I meant it.'

'Well, what am I doing wrong then, Kelly?'

'I . . . I don't think you're doing anything wrong.'

Miserable tears filled her sister-in-law's eyes. 'But I must be if he don't fancy me,' she sobbed. 'Before we married he couldn't keep his hands off me. I know the reason that stopped when we got married was because I lied about the baby. But he don't actually know the truth about that. Only you do.' Her eyes flashed in alarm. 'You ain't told him, have yer?'

'No, 'course I ain't. I can't say as I agree with what yer did but if ever Mickey is to find out the truth, it won't be from me.'

Glenda looked relieved. 'Well, what's up with him, Kelly? It was him that came back begging us to try again. So why is he being like this with me? I'm going to lose him again,' she choked. 'I know I am.'

Such obvious pain touched Kelly. Throwing her arms around Glenda, she pulled her close. 'No, you ain't,' she soothed. 'Mickey probably just needs time. And don't forget he doesn't like the fact that he ain't bringing any money into the house. We're keeping him, Glenda, and no man likes to be kept by a woman. You know what men are like. Once he gets a job it'll all be fine, you'll see.'

'D'yer really think so?' she uttered hopefully.

'I'm positive. Plus there's the fact that he could be worried the police are going to start hounding him again once they know he's back. They never did find the man who started the fire that killed Rod, did they? So, you see, he's a lot on his mind. But it'll all sort itself out.' Kelly put her hand in her coat pocket and pulled out a handkerchief. 'Here, wipe yer eyes and put a smile on your face. In a few weeks' time, when our Mickey's settled, you'll be walking bandy-legged and moaning to me that he won't leave you alone.'

Glenda chuckled. 'Oh, Kelly, d'yer reckon?'

She grinned. 'I know so.'

'Thanks, Kelly. Thanks for listening to me.'

'That's what friends and business partners are for. And talking of business, I've some more streets I want to have a go at this afternoon and you can give me a hand.'

Glenda gawped. 'Eh! Now, Kelly, I ain't knocking on doors.'

'Why not? I have to. This is our business, Glenda. Not everybody is gonna come to our door, so we have to go to theirs. You do know how many rag and bone carts go round these streets? I know of five that cover this area alone. We need to get in first. Look, why don't yer give it a try? After the first time it's easy. All you ask is if they've any clothes, rags or such like they want rid of, and tell 'em we pay cash – not give 'em a half dead goldfish.'

'I can't.'

'Yer can. Go on. Try that house over there. Number twelve.' She gave Glenda a push. 'Go on.'

'All right, I will.' With her chin raised, Glenda crossed the road and banged hard on the door of number twelve. Nothing happened so she rapped louder. From inside the house she heard a baby start to wail. The door was yanked open by an angry woman, wiping floury hands on her stained floral apron.

'What?' she spat.

'Have you anything you want rid of? We pay cash,' Glenda announced.

'Yeah, I bloody have. Three kids and a flipping useless husband. Now bugger off!'

The door was slammed shut.

An indignant Glenda spun on her heel and marched back across the road. 'See, I bloody told yer,' she erupted, wagging a finger angrily at Kelly. 'I'm warning yer, don't ask me to do that again. And stop laughing.'

Doubled up in mirth, Kelly spluttered. 'I can't. Oh, Glenda, that was so funny. You just picked a bad house, that's all. You get responses like that sometimes, but mostly people are really nice.'

'You can tell me what you like but it won't make no difference. Now I don't mind sorting the rags, I've got used to the stink now. I quite enjoy negotiating to buy what's left over from jumbles and bazaars. I don't even mind taking the cart down to the yard. But knocking on doors I ain't. Oh!'

'What is it?'

'I'm so sorry, Kelly, I forgot about yer visit down the yard today. I know yer weren't looking forward to it. How did it go? How did you feel, seeing Alec again?'

Kelly tightened her lips. 'It was hard, Glenda, I can't deny that. But I got through it.' She exhaled sharply. 'Alec looked terrible. He looked like he ain't slept a wink for weeks.'

'Well, he probably hasn't. He don't wanna be with Norma, does he? It's you he loves. It's you he wants to be with.'

'Then why is he doing this if it's making him so miserable?'

Glenda shrugged her shoulders. 'You tell me. I don't understand him at all. I mean, she bloody walked out on him in the first place so he's quite within his rights to tell her he don't want her any more. But he told you his conscience wouldn't let him. Conscience? Trust you to get a man with conscience. Any other man would tell her to sling her hook.'

She eyed Kelly thoughtfully. What she would really like to do was to go round to Alec's house and give him a piece of her mind. Let him know just how much pain his stupid conscience was causing her friend. But she couldn't do that. Kelly would not thank her for it. 'Take my advice, Kelly. What you need to do is forget Alec and . . .'

'Don't tell me to find someone else, Glenda. That's

what you were gonna say, weren't it? Well, I can't. I couldn't look at another man while I still feel like this for him.' She went to the hand cart and grabbed hold of the handles. 'Look, we must get on. I'm not happy about leaving Dad with Avril for too long. I'll knock on doors while you mind the cart. All right?'

Glenda nodded. 'Seems fair to me. Oh, Christ!'

'What is it?'

'Quick, that bloody Reverend has just come round the corner and he's bound to ask us to go to church. If we hurry we can hide.'

'Stop being silly, Glenda. We can hide us but what about the cart? If he does ask us to go to church, we say what I always say: that we will go when we can. Anyway it's too late now. Hello, Reverend Billings. All right, are yer?'

Algernon Billings approached them, respectfully lifting his hat. 'Hello, ladies. How's business?'

'Not bad,' Kelly replied, smiling. 'Could always be better though. Visiting the sick, are yer?'

He nodded. 'I'm looking for number fifteen. Poor lady just lost her husband. Or is it fourteen? Oh, dear, I can't quite remember.'

'So long as it ain't number twelve. Right old battleaxe she is,' muttered Glenda.

Kelly gave her a sharp nudge in the ribs as she eyed the old gentleman with concern. Despite the guilt she felt about their initial encounter, she had grown really fond of Reverend Billings through their business dealings and she would never forget how much kindness he'd shown her mother as she lay dying. 'You look tired, Reverend. Not overworking, I hope?'

'Pardon? Oh, no more than usual. I'll be retiring soon, plenty of time to rest then.'

'Oh, really? We'll miss dealing with yer, won't we, Glenda?'

'Mmmm,' she mouthed.

'Nice of you to say so.' He smiled at the two women. In the world he moved in, where it was all too easy for the poor to moan and grumble about their lot, showing no inclination to make any effort to better themselves, it was heartening to witness the way these two women had thrown themselves into earning a living. Especially Kelly, having to overcome all that she had suffered while still so young. He just wished more people were as enterprising and resourceful. His own job would be so much easier if they were. 'That idea of yours has served us both well, I must say. Buying up what was left from our jumbles. The extra money we make through you is allowing us to give the children better Christmas presents this year. Are you both looking forward to Christmas?'

Glenda didn't know whether she was or not, her happiness depended on Mickey. Kelly wasn't because of her heartache over Alec.

'Yes,' they both answered.

He sighed. 'I can't say I'm looking forward to it as much as I usually do. It'll be my last as Vicar of Holy Cross. I've been there thirty-five years,' he said proudly. 'Still, time marches on and there's nothing we can do to prevent that from happening. And that's my other problem,' he mused. 'I have a task to perform when I return to the Vicarage, and one that I'm not looking forward to.'

'Oh, and what's that, Reverend?' asked Kelly out of politeness.

'I have to retire Albert Flowers, my verger. Been with the church for . . . well, since a young man. I should have retired him a while ago but I just couldn't bring myself to do it. Well, I have no choice now. Found him asleep in a grave just as the mourners and I had gathered around it for the burial. Dreadful state of affairs. The

378

Bishop was fuming when he heard.'

Both women clamped their lips tightly shut to hide their mirth at the picture the kindly old clergyman was conjuring up.

'Well, I suppose he didn't do it on purpose,' said Kelly kindly.

'You think not?' replied Algernon. 'My dear, nothing Albert Flowers does should surprise me. There are stories about what he's got up to over the years that would make your hair curl. I remember once . . .'

'Well, we must be off, Reverend,' Glenda cut in, grabbing the cart's handles and starting to push it away. 'So much to do, you know.'

'Oh, quite, quite. I'll say my goodbyes. And don't forget . . .'

'Yes, we will, as soon as we get time,' called Glenda. 'Come on, Kelly,' she ordered. 'We'll make a start on the houses down there.'

'You were rude,' snapped Kelly as soon as Algernon was out of earshot.

'I was not. I was telling the truth. We *are* busy. And I thought we'd never get away from him.'

'Glenda, we hardly spent five minutes with him. If you were moaning about hours, I'd understand it.' She looked annoyed. 'It wouldn't hurt you to be a bit more Christian.'

'A bit more Christian! That's good coming from someone who used to rob church roofs of their lead.'

'Eh, we'll have less of that. That's all in the past. Summat I went along with when I didn't know any better. Anyway, I can talk to the old boy if I want. I quite like him. I don't expect he gets much chance to talk about what's bothering him. Too busy listening and trying to help with other people's problems.' Suddenly something he had told them struck her. She pulled the cart to a halt and grabbed Glenda's arm.

'What is it now?' she said, frowning at Kelly. 'Knicker 'lastic broke or summat?'

'Ho, ho,' Kelly mouthed sarcastically. 'Be serious and listen. The Reverend said he'd got to sack his verger.'

'Retire him,' corrected Glenda. 'So what?'

'He'll need another then, won't he? People won't stop dying 'cos the gravedigger's retired.'

'Yeah, but what's that . . . Oh! A job for Mickey,' she cried excitedly. 'D'yer think the Rev would give him a try?'

'There's only one way to find out,' said Kelly.

'But hold on. I mean, digging graves. Big come down, ain't it?'

'A come down from what? He ain't got anything to come down from unless he was lucky today.'

'Yer right, and Mickey did say he'd take anything.' Glenda grabbed her arm. 'Let's go and tackle the Rev now.'

Abandoning the cart, they ran back down the street and caught sight of Algernon just about to knock on the door of number twenty-five.

'Oi, Reverend,' Glenda shouted breathlessly. 'Just a minute.' They slowed down as they neared him. 'You do the talking, Kelly. You can handle him better than I can.'

Glenda happened to glance at the door number as they arrived. 'I thought you wanted number fifteen or fourteen, Reverend?'

He grinned sheepishly. 'Seems I was wrong about both. Age has finally caught up with me. Anyway, ladies, is something wrong?'

'Wrong? Oh, no, Reverend Billings,' Kelly assured him. 'I . . . we . . .' She looked at Glenda. 'Both of us were wanting to know what you're going to do about getting another gravedigger? Well, you'll have ter, won't yer, if yer gonna sack . . . retire . . . Albert?'

Eyeing her, perplexed, he nodded. 'Well, yes, I will.

Why are you so interested?' His large bushy eyebrows were raised in surprise. 'Not thinking of applying for the job yourself, are you?'

'No, Reverend. But then, if I was desperate I would. No, it's our Mickey.'

He frowned uneasily. 'Your Mickey?'

'Yes. He's desperate for a job. This would suit him down to the ground.'

Memories of a cocksure Mickey McCallan and the incident with the lead from his roof flashed to Algernon's mind. And that handing over of forty pounds, a very questionable sum from a man of his status. Algernon also remembered only too vividly rumours of Mickey's possible connection with the factory fire in which this young lady's husband had died. The father was still in a dreadful state of shock, apparently. It was looking doubtful whether he would ever recover his senses. Although any involvement by Mickey McCallan had never been proved, the thought of employing such a character made Algernon shudder in horror.

'I . . . I don't think this is in your brother's line,' he said diplomatically. 'It's really a job for someone older.'

'But why? Surely a young man is more able to tackle a job like that?'

'Yes, but it's not only the digging of the graves. The job also involves caretaking the church, cleaning the windows, all sorts of things like that.'

'Our Mickey could do that. Please, Reverend Billings, just give him a try. He's changed. He's not the man he used to be.'

'Changed?' Algernon asked dubiously. 'In what way has he changed?'

'Oh, he's much nicer now,' piped up Glenda. 'He's so ashamed of how he used to be. Me and Kelly have given him another chance and we ain't regretted it, have we, Kelly?'

'No. Oh, Reverend, he needs a job. No one'll give him a chance. They all remember the newspaper reports. But he wasn't involved. I know he wasn't.' Kelly's eyes flashed. 'Reverend, where's your charity?' she demanded.

In this case I don't think I have any, was his immediate reaction. But he fought with his conscience. Kelly was right. If he, a servant of the Lord, could not give this young man the benefit of the doubt, then all his years of preaching sermons had been a total waste of time. He just hoped he did not live to regret his decision.

'All right, ladies. I'm not making any promises, but ask him to come and see me and I'll have a talk with him.'

A delighted Kelly and Glenda flung themselves on him. 'Oh, thank you, Reverend. Thank you so much,' they both exclaimed.

Mickey could hardly contain his excitement. Unbeknown to the two women facing him, they had innocently handed him a solution to his big problem. A church. Who in their right mind would think to look for stolen property in a church? If they didn't both repel him so much, especially Glenda, he would have leaped over the table and hugged them both in gratitude, putting his show of emotion down to enthusiasm at the prospect of a job.

In his mind he pictured Mitzi. His pulse raced and a great rush of need and longing surged through him. Not long now, he thought, until he was back in her arms. The prospect of being united with her had been the only thing to keep him going during these past few weeks of pure living purgatory.

His list of promising houses had grown to twenty. He reckoned four weeks should be enough time to cover them. Added to that there was a factory that produced expensive clocks and dress watches. Wilf Wallace, a well-trusted fence, would jump in excitement to have those and pay handsomely.

But it was neither the contents of the houses nor the factory goods that was Mickey's main target. Something else was – something very lucrative. Something he hadn't thought of until very recently – though for the life of him he wondered why.

The dustmen's wages.

The route and the timing of the clerk who delivered them on his bicycle every Friday morning had gone unchanged since before Mickey had joined the gangs. All he had to do was don a balaclava, nab the unsuspecting clerk in a pre-determined quiet spot not too far from the depot – he wanted all the wages, not just some – relieve him of the packets before making his escape. So simple. He wondered why someone hadn't done it before. If they had, it hadn't taken place during the last few years. Time it did then, and what more deserving man to do it than one who felt he had been shabbily treated by Leicester Corporation?

Calculating the whole value of the jobs he was planning was hard but he reckoned by the time he had finished he should be richer to the tune of five thousand pounds. Enough to keep a woman like Mitzi happy until he got his idea for a business off the ground.

In fact he had plenty of ideas. Isaac Greenbaum's example had taught him a lot. The grudge he held against that man ran deep within him, but then in another sense he had a lot to thank him for. If Greenbaum hadn't so blatantly used him he would not have met Mitzi, who in turn had given him a push towards branching out on his own. Yes, he thought as he rose to leave the table, if ever he had the pleasure of Isaac's company again, he would shake his hand.

Through narrowed eyes he scrutinised his wife and his

sister. What fools they were! And what a shock they were both going to receive when all this came to light. He hid a sly smile. And how were they going to convince the police that they had no knowledge of what had been going on right under their noses? But it was no more than they deserved. Glenda had deceived him into marriage; Kelly, his own flesh and blood, a sister whom he had at one time loved and respected, had deceived him also. She did not realise that he now knew of her relationship with a man he detested. Oh, yes, he knew all right. Ada Adcock loved to gossip. What did it matter that Alec's wife was now back and the relationship was over? Kelly had still gone ahead, knowing how Mickey felt. Loyalty? Well, she obviously had none. So why should he?

If only, he thought, before he finally left he could somehow make Alec Alderman pay for the misdemeanours he'd committed against Mickey in the past. Well, there was still time. He would not write off that possibility just yet.

He flashed a secret glance across to the man he had once called his father. The score with him was settled, all debts of this man's paid in full. He vehemently hoped that whatever dark abyss Frank's mind had fallen into would keep it a prisoner until he died. He deserved no better for what he had made Mickey suffer.

He grabbed up his jacket from the back of the chair. 'I'll go and see the Reverend now,' he announced enthusiastically. 'I know it's past seven but no point in wasting time. Don't want anyone else getting in before me.'

They both smiled at him.

'Good luck,' said Kelly.

'Yeah, we'll keep our fingers crossed,' said Glenda.

No need, thought Mickey. The job is mine.

★ ★ ★

Further up the Hinckley Road, in her immaculate little terraced house, a bored Norma lounged in an armchair before a blazing fire, thumbing idly through a magazine. Momentarily lifting her eyes from the advert she was scanning, she flashed a disdainful glance at her husband who sat hunched over the table, fiddling with the intricate mechanism of a mantel clock. His face was twisted in concentration and he had no idea of the look of utter disgust his wife was giving him.

'Can't we go out, Alec?' she whined. 'Alec, did you hear me?'

His head jerked up and as it did a spring from the clock shot from his hand across the room to vanish behind the china cabinet. 'Oh, no,' he groaned. 'I just about had that in place. Never mind,' he said, rising to retrieve it. 'Sorry, Norma, what did you say?'

'I said, can't we go out? To the pictures or something?'

Sitting down again, he picked up his screwdriver. 'Tonight?'

'Yes, tonight.'

'Well, for one thing I'm busy trying to fix this clock, and for another I've no money for the pictures, Norma.'

'What do you mean, yer've no money? What about the bonus you got from Raggy over that business with the lead?'

'That's spent.'

'What, all of it?'

'Yes, all of it, on that gas fire you ordered. They're coming on Monday to put it in, remember? But if you want to treat both of us, I've no objection. Is there anything you had in mind you wanted ter see?'

Her mouth dropped open. He had no objection to her paying! Well, she had. It was Alec's job to keep her, not the other way round. Besides, she hadn't any money. All her wages since she had come back had been spent replenishing her toiletries and makeup, items she had

385

run down on and been unable to replace while living with James due to having to pay her own way. And Norma was not in the habit of matching her expenditure to what was in her purse. At the moment she had only four shillings and sixpence left over from her wages and it was still only Tuesday.

'There's nothing in particular I want to see,' she said sharply. 'Anyway, it's too late to go now.' Agitated, she slapped the magazine on the table. 'Have you spoke to Raggy about your partnership yet?'

He looked across at her. 'I never said I would, Norma. I said I hoped he would *offer* me a partnership.'

'You have to push these things, Alec. You're so . . . so backward when it comes to things like this. Make a stand, for God's sake. Tell him you want a partnership or else.'

'Or else what? Threaten to leave, yer mean? Norma, this is the man's business we're talking about. He's already upped me wages to show how pleased he is with me and I feel I earn what he pays me so we're square. If he intends offering me a partnership, he'll tell me when he's good and ready and we'll discuss terms. If he ever decides to retire I'll ask him if we can strike a deal for me to take over the yard. No, Norma, I've no intention of pushing things. If it were my business I wouldn't like someone pushing and threatening me into something I didn't want.'

'You're just weak,' she snapped. 'If you don't do something all you'll ever be is a . . . a . . .'

'A what, Norma?'

'I don't know. What's your job called?'

'Assistant. Runabout. General dogsbody. What does it matter?' He narrowed his eyes. 'Some people would give their eye teeth for a job like mine. A fancy title would be the last thing on their mind.' He stared at her searchingly. 'Is that how you see me, Norma? Weak? If that's the case, I'm sorry. I'd call it considerate myself. Now, I don't want to discuss this any more.'

She stared at him in shock. Alec had never spoken to her like this before. Anything she had ever wanted him to do, she had somehow manipulated him into. But it didn't really matter. If Alec wouldn't do anything about tackling Raggy, then she'd pay him a visit herself. She didn't intend being married to a rag and bone man's assistant for much longer. But a partner in a business was a different matter.

'Are you going to be working on that thing all night?' she asked.

He sighed. 'That thing, Norma, is an eight-day walnut-cased mantel clock, and if I can get it going I can make a pound, maybe a bit more.'

The clock could have been Cornish tin for all she cared. What made her take interest was the mention of the money. 'Oh, I see.' She rose and made a great show of inspecting it, which Alec actually found quite irritating since he knew it was only a pretence. At one time he would not have noticed a glaring fact like that, but not now he had wised up to her and his feelings had changed.

He suddenly imagined that it was Kelly instead of Norma by his side. Her interest would have been genuine. In fact, Kelly would have been sitting at the table with him. They would have been talking and laughing as he carried on with his work. But it was no good daydreaming about Kelly. All that achieved was added pain at thoughts of what might have been.

'Norma, please, you're blocking me light,' he said agitatedly, then sighed apologetically. 'I'm sorry, I didn't mean to snap. I'm just tired and I want to get this finished tonight, if I can.'

'You're always tired,' she complained unjustly, then thought that the sooner he got the confounded clock fixed, the sooner he'd make that pound. If she played it right she might wheedle it out of him to buy the dress she had spotted in Lewis's department store.

'Maybe it's better I leave you to it,' she said, leaning over to give him a light peck on the cheek. 'I'll pop round and sit with Mother for a bit.'

Sitting with her mother and listening to her complaining was actually the last thing Norma felt like doing, but it was a damned sight more interesting than sitting here watching Alec laboriously earn the money for her dress.

He raised his head momentarily as he heard the back door shut and the click of Norma's heels on the path outside. Then he laid down his tools and clasped his hands in his lap. He had never felt so miserable in all his life but the worst of it was that there was nothing he could do about it. He had allowed Norma to walk back into his life and could not go back on that decision now. An old saying sprang to mind. 'You've made your bed, now you must lie on it.' It was most appropriate in his case.

With a resigned sigh, he picked up his screwdriver and resumed his task.

Chapter Thirty-Six

Constable Kevin Plant breezed into the office carrying a wreath of holly, a hammer and a large nail.

Not a flicker of emotion on his face, Sergeant Reg Little picked up his pipe, leaned over to tap the bowl into the metal waste-paper basket, then righted himself. 'Who's died then, Constable?'

'Funny, Sarge. I thought this would make us feel Christmassy, that's all. They're selling 'em cheap on the market, being's it's Christmas Eve.'

'By the looks of it you should have got that for n'ote, lad. How much were cheap?'

Frowning at the object in question, Kevin answered, 'Two and a tanner, Sarge. They were five bob before.'

'Well, at that price you could have got me one for Mrs Little.'

'I could go back?'

'You needn't bother, I'll have that one.'

'Oh, but Sarge . . .'

'Put it down, lad. As I've said, it'll tek more than a bit of holly to brighten this place up. But it'll certainly help brighten up Mrs Little. I ain't told her I'm working tomorrow yet. By the way, I volunteered you too.'

PC Plant's face fell. 'Me?'

'You heard, lad. You're in the police force. If you expected an easy life you should have gone to work for Billy Butlin. Now make sure you bring plenty of turkey sandwiches 'cos the canteen'll be shut. I'll bring the playing cards and the whisky. Oh, and I like pickle on mine.'

Plant frowned, confused. 'On what, Sarge?'

'The bloody turkey sandwiches, what did yer think, yer daft sod? Now sit yerself down and let's go over yer notes from yesterday.'

For half an hour the two of them discussed the events of Plant's day.

'So I cautioned the lad . . .'

Little tutted sternly. 'Cautioned! Bloody borstal's where that evil sod ought to be. It's a wonder he didn't burn the whole school down.'

'Oh, hardly, Sarge. It was just a prank gone wrong.'

'Ah.' He leaned forward, eyeing the young constable shrewdly. 'They all start somewhere. Next thing yer know they're being paid to commit arson.'

'Yeah, I suppose, Sarge,' Plant agreed grudgingly. 'I'll keep me eye on the little bugger.'

Sergeant Little hid a smile. Plant was coming on just fine for a country copper, he was even learning the terminology. 'Bugger' had not figured in his vocabulary when he'd first arrived. There was hope for him yet.

'Oh, Sarge, that reminds me. It was that talk of arson. Mickey McCallan's back. Been back a few weeks by all accounts.'

Eyes sparkling keenly, Little leaned forward. 'Is he now? You've seen him, have yer?'

'I have, Sarge. He's the new gravedigger at Holy Cross. I meant to mention it before but it slipped me mind.'

'You having me on?' barked the sergeant.

'No, honestly, Sarge. That's my local church and I always take my landlady to the Sunday morning service when I'm not on duty. The old duck's getting on a bit and not so good on her legs. I saw McCallan last Sunday as we were leaving. He was sweeping the paths.'

'This isn't some sort of country yokel joke?'

'No, it ain't,' Plant replied, offended. 'I was surprised too, so I went back and spoke to the Vicar about him. Seems McCallan's turned over a new leaf.'

'That I don't believe.'

'True, Sarge. The Vicar's convinced. You told me you set great store by Reverend Billings.'

'So I do.'

'Well, he seems happy. Said he can't fault McCallan. Turns up when he should, gets on with his job, and up to now ain't put a foot wrong. Just to make sure, I checked the pubs he used before. No one had seen him. In fact, the crowd he used to mix with weren't even aware he was back.'

Reg grimaced. 'Don't like the sound of this. What's he up to, I wonder?'

Kevin shrugged his shoulders. 'Maybe he isn't up to anything? We could pull him in and question him.'

'About what?' the sergeant barked. 'We've no new leads on that factory fire and can't exactly question him on his motives for taking a job as gravedigger, now can we?' He exhaled thoughtfully, running a hand over his stubbly chin. 'There ain't much we *can* do. But at least we know he's back and anything that sounds like summat he could be involved in, we'll act on. In the meantime, just keep in with Reverend Billings. We can watch McCallan too that way.' He sat back in his chair. 'Well, better finish going over your notebook. Any more on that bogus gas man that's been going around?'

Kevin shook his head. 'No, no more reports. The houses he went to haven't had anything unusual happen. All the identifications were too sketchy to make anything of. Apart from the fact that the maids said the bloke was good-looking.' Kevin shrugged his shoulders. 'Could be anyone, Sarge. Probably just a lark.'

'Strange lark. Mind you, some bloody folk are strange. We had a bloke once that posed as a sanitary inspector. Seems he had a thing about lavatory brushes. We caught him red-handed with three up his jumper.' He sighed. 'Yer know, lad, sometimes I hate being a bloody copper. I reckon I should have bin a milkman. Eh, tek that wreath off the chair. Be just our luck for the Chief to wander in and sit on it. And while yer up, go and make a mash.'

Once Plant had left, a thoughtful Sergeant Little reached into his pocket for his tin of Mellow Virginia tobacco. Slowly and precisely he packed the barrel of his pipe then struck a match, puffing hard until he was satisfied that it was lit. Leaning back in his chair, he raised his legs and plonked his boots on the desk, eyes narrowed thoughtfully. Mickey McCallan a gravedigger? No, it didn't ring true.

One of the most important qualities a policeman could possess was patience. Where catching a criminal was concerned Reg had plenty. One day, in Mickey McCallan's case, that patience would pay off.

Chapter Thirty-Seven

'Ah, there you are, Mickey.' Algernon stood at the bottom of the rickety ladder and peered upwards. 'I hardly expected you to work on Christmas Day. You should be at home with your family.'

Mickey descended the ladder and stood facing him. 'I felt it only fair, being's you were working, Reverend.'

Algernon smiled. 'Maybe you're taking this job a little too seriously, my boy. Christmas Day is the most important day in the year of a clergyman, but cleaning gutters can be done any time. Now get off home.'

'I will when I've finished what I started. I'll give the aisle a mop over too, ready for the evening service.'

'There's no need, Mickey, really. It's quite dry today and Mrs Baker will be in tomorrow. If there's nothing for her to do, she'll accuse you of trying to have her out of her job.'

Mickey sighed forlornly. 'I was just trying to help, Reverend. To be truthful, I wanted to try and repay yer for showing yer faith in me and giving me this chance.'

If Mickey had been really truthful with Algernon he would have told him his reason for working on Christmas Day was because he couldn't stand the thought of being cooped up inside the house on Tewkesbury Street for a whole day with no chance of escape. Telling the women of Reverend Billings's automatic assumption he would work had worked a treat. Glenda and Kelly had been most sympathetic.

But even more pressing than his reluctance to be incarcerated inside the house was his dire need to get hold of the key to the church. Two minutes was all it would take to impress a copy on to the Plasticine he kept in readiness in his pocket.

He had found the perfect place to hide his spoils, somewhere even the Almighty Himself would never dream of looking. Mickey had been jubilant at his discovery. Now everything was in place, but he could not move without getting hold of that key. He had been trying for two weeks, using all sorts of ploys without success, and it had taken all Mickey's willpower to hold on to his temper. Algernon and his precious key were not going to part company easily.

The Reverend Billings laid a reassuring hand on his shoulder. 'My boy, you have more than repaid my faith in you. I admit I was rather reticent over employing you but I must say I'm glad I did. Now everything is all locked up and secure so please go home. Enjoy what is left of the day.'

'I'd like to finish unblocking the guttering, if you don't mind, Reverend. We're not having dinner 'til later anyway.'

Resigned, Algernon patted his arm. 'As you wish, Mickey. But I'll have to leave you to it as I am serving Christmas dinner at the Hillcrest Hospital. Mind you, some of the people there wouldn't know whether it was Christmas or Easter, poor old things, but the staff are glad of my help. Then I shall do the rounds at the Infirmary and hopefully have time to fit in some of my lonely parishioners before evening service.' He consulted his watch. 'Oh, dear, I am running late. Merry Christmas, Mickey.'

'Same to you, Reverend.' You stupid old bastard, he thought.

Mickey had already anticipated this reaction and had planned accordingly. Though if this scheme didn't work he'd just have to steal the damned key and be done with it. He waited several moments for Algernon to hurry off down the path. 'Oh, Reverend, I've left me coat in the Vestry,' he shouted, running after him. 'I know you're late, Reverend, so give me the key. I'll make sure the door's locked properly then slip it through the Vicarage letter box.' Mickey saw reluctance in the clergyman's eyes. 'Come on, Reverend. Do yer really think I'm gonna steal the church silver? If I was gonna do that, I'd have done it before now.'

Algernon shuffled his feet uncomfortably.

Mickey sighed. 'I can't say as I blame yer. I just wish you of all people'd believe that I had n'ote ter do with the factory fire and Rod's death. I never had 'ote ter do with pinching the lead off this church roof neither. I'm guilty in as much that I knew who did. That's why I handed over the money you wanted to replace it. Years and years it took me to save that. I was gonna buy a little house for me and Glenda. But it was a small price to pay.'

Algernon was staring at him, confused. 'Small price to pay for what?'

Mickey exhaled forlornly. 'I can see I'm gonna have ter tell yer. To cover up for me dad and Rod. It were them, you see. It were them that stole the lead off yer church roof. I'd bin out that night and I came back and found 'em trying to hide it in the old wash house. Shocked ain't the word for what I felt. Me dad hadn't bin right in the head since he came back from the war but I didn't know he'd turned to stealing. And worse even than that, he'd roped Rod into helping him too. I demanded they get rid of it and said if ever I caught 'em at 'ote like that again, I'd go to the police meself. That's when you must have seen us. I was giving them a hand loading it back on the cart.

'Knowing what I knew, I couldn't let you go to the police, could I? The truth would have come out, and what with me mam being so ill and our Kelly to think of . . . well, I had no choice. I'm not sure what went on over the factory business but it's my guess that Rod and a mate were robbing the place and it got out of hand. Unless me dad recovers we'll never know the truth. I can only pray he does then I can clear me name. That's why I went away. I couldn't stand the police swarming all over me. They were hell-bent on pinning it on me. I couldn't name me father and me sister's husband. Couldn't bring meself to do it. Well, now yer know the truth of it, Reverend.'

'Oh, dear.' A deeply shocked Algernon scratched his head. 'I didn't know your sister's husband but I can hardly believe this of your father. Seemed such a very pleasant man. But I know what the war did to people. You're a good son, Mickey, suffering for his misdeeds.'

'He's me father, Reverend. What else was I suppose ter do? Look, I don't mean ter hurry yer but those people at Hillcrest will be wanting their dinner.'

'Oh, yes, yes. I must be off.'

'And what about me coat?'

Algernon pulled the key from his pocket. 'You'll lock up properly?'

'Trust me, Reverend,' he replied, a wicked glint sparkling in his eye.

Chapter Thirty-Eight

Glenda eyed her husband hesitantly as he sat shovelling down his dinner. 'Would yer fancy going to the pictures tonight?'

His head jerked up. 'Eh?'

'Well, it was just a thought. We haven't been out since yer came back. And yer've done nothing but work, Mickey. I can't understand Reverend Billings, expecting you to do all the hours God sends for the wages yer get. 'Specially Christmas Day. It's criminal.' She glanced across at her sister-in-law. 'It is, ain't it, Kelly?'

As usual she had been thinking of Alec. She eyed Glenda distractedly. 'Pardon? Oh, I've got to agree, Mickey, yer do work long hours.'

Yes, he thought, I do, but not the kind of work you think I'm doing.

Getting out of the house at night had proved no problem. All he had done on the nights in question was ply both women with a couple of glasses of cheap port and they had slept like babies. Relieving the houses of their valuables had been easy. A quick, quiet jemmy of the lock, or forcing of a scullery window after the occupants had retired to bed, ten minutes inside grabbing as much as he could, then out again. Child's play.

The factory proved no more difficult, his only problem being the night-watchman, who for some reason on the particular night Mickey had chosen for his venture, seemed restless, as though he sensed something was about to take place. It was well past one in the morning before Mickey, from his hiding place behind the nightwatchman's hut, saw the man's eyelids droop and heard the sound of snoring. Half an hour it had taken him to get inside and grab as many watches and clocks as it would take to stock a couple of jeweller's shop windows. The fence and two unscrupulous jewellers had been delighted to buy his haul for a reasonable price. Not as much as Mickey had been hoping for, but he was in no position to haggle.

Tomorrow morning the unsuspecting wages clerk was going to be relieved of his delivery. The timing could not be better. The Reverend Billings had a burial to perform at eleven – precisely the time the clerk left the depot. The gravedigger always made himself scarce during that emotive time so his absence would not be questioned, it being taken for granted that he was busy elsewhere.

Although the strain of keeping up this pretence and executing his plans was telling on Mickey, he was feeling proud of his accomplishments too and would have liked nothing more than to have bragged of his achievement, but that was the last thing he could do. He had to keep this façade up for just a little longer, then he could turn his back and walk away, go to be with the one person he desired above everything, the whole reason he had been driven to tackle this immense undertaking: Mitzi. Even the thought of her sent a shiver down his spine. The thought of being reunited with her set him ablaze with longing.

Twenty-four hours more, that was all he needed. This time tomorrow he planned to be on his way back to Newcastle and it couldn't come soon enough for him.

Laying down his knife and fork, he pushed his plate away and looked across at the women regretfully while the accomplished lies spewed forth.

'It ain't the good old Vicar's fault I work all these hours.'

'It ain't?' Glenda frowned questioningly. 'Then whose is it?'

'It's mine.' He took a deep breath. 'I can't keep yer on the wage I get at the moment, Glenda. Yer see, I want to get a decent paying job, one to keep yer proper, like you deserve, and I thought if I worked me backside off in this and the Reverend Billings sees I'm genuine then he'd put in a good word on me reference.'

'Oh, Mickey,' Glenda whispered tenderly, eyes shining with love. 'Why didn't yer say? I've bin thinking all sorts of things.'

'Well, don't. I don't want you worrying about anything, Glenda. I'm going to start looking for another job again and when I get one everything will be all right between us. Trust me.'

Glenda blushed. She knew what he meant by his emphasis on the word 'everything'. He meant lovemaking. Her heart thumped wildly and in her mind's eye she pictured the house they would rent, the home she would make of it. Hopefully they could start a family. How happy they would be together – when Mickey regained his self-respect by getting another job.

'If you don't mind, I'm going to bed,' he said. 'I know it's early but I'm really tired. Unless there's anything yer want me to give you a hand with?'

Kelly shook her head. 'We're up to date with everything, thanks, Mickey. You go up and get a good sleep.'

With all that was on his mind, he hoped he could. He wanted to be fresh and alert tomorrow. But his main reason for retiring so early was that he could not bear to sit with them and the 'dummy' all evening.

He said his good-nights and departed.

Much later, when the household tasks had been dealt with and Frank made comfortable ready for Kelly to settle into bed, the two women sat down at the table over a pot of tea and a packet of gingernut biscuits.

'You look more cheerful than I've seen yer for a while,' Kelly observed of her sister-in-law.

'I am,' replied Glenda, pouring milk into the mugs. 'It's what Mickey said about why he's been doing all these hours and about him trying for another job. I wish he'd said before though 'cos then I might not have had such a bloody awful Christmas Day. Oh, I don't mean 'ote by that, Kelly. You worked hard to make the day. The dinner was lovely and it was nice those neighbours popping in and us having that sing-song. It was just that I missed Mickey.'

Kelly smiled knowingly. 'You don't have to explain to me. Of all the days I've had to get through without Alec, that was the hardest for me. I kept picturing him all happy with Norma and her mother.'

'You know that ain't what it's like at all.'

'No, I don't. He could be for all I know.'

'Don't be stupid, Kelly. The man looks like death warmed up. If he's happy then I'm a Dutch uncle's maiden aunt.' She tutted crossly. 'It's about time Alec Alderman stood up for what he wants.'

Kelly sighed despairingly.

'It ain't that easy, though, is it, Glenda? I wish it was.' She took a deep breath. 'Oh, I'll get over it in time,' she said optimistically, but knew it could take years. 'Pass us a couple of those gingernuts. On second thoughts, is there any of that port left? It helps me sleep. In fact, it knocks me out.'

'Me too. It's strong, ain't it? I think we're supposed to put lemonade in it. It were nice of Mickey getting it for us, though, weren't it? He would never have given us a thought like that before.' Glenda rose. 'I think there's a drop left in the bottle.' She retrieved it from the pantry and shared what was left between two tumblers.

'Enough to wet both our whistles,' she said, grinning. Returning to her seat, she looked at Kelly enquiringly. 'Stop thinking about him. Yer won't get over him that way.'

Kelly took a sip of her drink and shuddered as it hit the back of her throat. 'I wasn't thinking of Alec. Actually it was Mickey I was thinking about.'

'Mickey?'

'I was wondering if there was anything we could do for him.'

'In what way?'

She took a deep breath. 'Well, I still don't think he's going ter find it easy getting anything. Anything worthwhile that is. I'd hate to see him knocked back again, Glenda. If he is there's a risk he might go back to his old ways. So I was just thinking . . .'

'What? What were you thinking?'

'Of him working with us.' She eyed her sister-in-law sternly. 'Now don't get excited but I do have something in mind. We need to work it out and then discuss it with Mickey. He might not want to.'

'Oh, I'm sure he will,' she cried enthusiastically. 'Tell me what you were thinking of, please, Kelly?'

'Well.' She ran her eyes around the small back room. 'This place ain't ideal for our business any more. We're always falling over sacks and stepping over piles of clothes, and the place stinks, Glenda, despite all the disinfectant we use. It can't be doing Dad any good. This is our home but it could be Raggy's yard by the state it gets into.' She glanced across at her father, smiling tenderly. 'I should really get him into bed.'

'Yer dad's fine, finish telling me yer idea first.'

'Okay. I was thinking that if we worked our money out we could see if we could afford to rent some sort of lock-up and sort the rags and whatnot in there. We could get a little primus stove for Avril and Hilda. It'd be much better all round and we could get this house back to what it should be. But if we do go ahead with that idea, there's something you'll have ter think on.'

Glenda frowned worriedly. 'Oh, what's that?'

'Me dad. I'll not leave him on his own all day so it would mean taking turns collecting. That means you'd have to knock on doors, Glenda.'

'I'll think on it but I ain't promising.' Glenda grimaced quizzically. 'But where does Mickey fit in? I can't see him rummaging around in a lock-up all day, sorting rags with Avril and Hilda. That pair get on my nerves, let alone his.'

'Neither can I. The lock-up was just something I've been thinking about for a while. What I thought for Mickey was that we could go more into the scrap metal side of things. We've avoided that because it's too heavy for us to handle. But there's money to be made from scrap.' She grinned. 'And I'm sure he wouldn't mind shouting out "Any old iron". Don't look like that, Glenda. I'm just having a bit of fun. And there's other things we could do, like buying up some of the war surplus stuff the Government is auctioning off. Mickey could deal with that too. He's good at striking deals.'

Glenda was gazing at her in awe.

'What d'yer think of my ideas then?' Kelly asked.

'I . . . God, Kelly, I think they're just brilliant.'

She smiled. 'We do need to discuss them in a bit more detail but as a start tomorrow I'll check the rent on some lock-ups around here. Don't say anything to Mickey at the moment, Glenda. It wouldn't be fair to build his hopes up if we can't do it just now.'

'But why can't we?'

'Because we need to buy a 'oss and cart or a lorry or something and find somewhere to keep them at night. We don't know whether we can afford it 'til we check our books properly. We ain't made the books up for over a week 'cos we ain't had time. We've made money but I'm not sure how much profit by the time we've taken out our living expenses.'

'Oh, yes, I see. All right. But you must think we can afford it or else you wouldn't be suggesting it, would you?' she asked hopefully.

'I'm not committing meself 'til we've done the books.' Kelly paused. 'I should really go and talk to Alec. He'll put us right on whether he thinks it would be worth our while to go into the scrap metal side.'

Glenda tilted her head and her eyebrows rose. 'It'd be an excuse to go and see him.'

Kelly's eyes flashed. 'That's not my reason and you know it,' she said defensively. 'I value his opinion. I accept that he's back with his wife but he's still my friend and I trust him. Now, as I said, don't build yer hopes up 'til we look into this proper.'

'I won't, Kelly.' Nevertheless Glenda was filled with anticipation at the thought of Mickey working alongside them. A real family business it would be then.

Yawning, Kelly rose. 'That drop of port has worked wonders. I'm going to get Dad to bed then go meself.'

Glenda downed the last of hers. 'Me too,' she said, rising. 'I'll clear these pots away.'

It was a happy Glenda who climbed into bed beside her sleeping husband that night, confident that Kelly would have good news for her the next evening.

In her own room Kelly tossed and turned, wondering if her suggestion about Mickey joining them was a good one. She and Glenda had worked extremely hard building up their small business and dealing in just clothes. They had earned themselves a good reputation which was steadily growing. Her worry was that Mickey's joining them could in some way jeopardise all they had worked for.

She mentally chided herself. He had made great

403

efforts to prove to them how much he had changed. He was nothing like the man he used to be and had given no sign whatsoever of returning to his obnoxious ways. He'd even gone so far as cutting off all ties with old friends and as far as she was aware had not even made a visit to his former drinking haunts. So what further proof did she want? Her fears were groundless, she was just being silly.

Turning over, she snuggled more comfortably under the covers. As usual, as soon as she closed her eyes a vision of Alec rose before them, and as usual with a great effort she forced away all thoughts of him and tried to sleep.

Chapter Thirty-Nine

Kelly glanced up and down the deserted street. She guessed the time to be nearing five o'clock and already it was dark with a fine freezing drizzle beginning to fall. We must be insane, she thought, still to be out on such a dreadful night. She looked hard at the door she was just about to knock on, then turned to face Glenda, standing by the cart.

'We must be bloody mad,' she said. 'Who in their right minds would be knocking on doors at this time of night when they could be sitting by the fire? Come on, let's call it a day.'

'I thought you'd never suggest it,' Glenda mumbled, shivering. 'I curse the day we took on Hilda as well as Avril to do the sorting. If we hadn't I'd have been at home now, roasting by the fire.'

'Yeah, and you'd also be complaining of the stink from the clothes and yer aching back. Still, never mind. Hopefully if we can afford to take on one of those lock-ups we saw this morning, we won't have ter bother about the stink for much longer.' Kelly frowned thoughtfully. 'Five bob a week is a lot to pay for a falling down lean-to, though. We'll have to step up on our collecting to make it up. Mind, I suppose . . .'

'Kelly,' Glenda erupted, 'can we go or are you going to stand there all day talking to yerself?'

She grinned. 'You get off home and get the kettle on.

Oh, and you'll need to get some bread and tea from Ada's. I'll take these bits round to Raggy's and park the cart. As soon as we've cleared up after dinner we can make a start on the books.'

'Seems fair to me,' Glenda said happily. 'I'll see you in a bit then,' she called, making off down the road.

'Eh,' Kelly shouted after her. 'Not a word yet to our Mickey.'

'All right, all right,' came the disgruntled response. Kelly didn't realise what she was asking of Glenda, telling her not to divulge their plans to Mickey. She couldn't wait to see the delight on his face when they did.

Mickey hummed to himself as he stepped jauntily down the stairs, grabbing his coat from the end of the banister where he had discarded it earlier. Finally, he thought, as a thrill of satisfaction filled him, the time had come for him to leave this house and its occupants for good. The last few weeks had seemed an eternity. He thought of the money he had amassed, waiting for him to collect from its well-chosen hiding place before he began his journey to Newcastle, and he smirked. Every second of this purgatory had been worth it.

As he entered the back room he glanced at the tin clock ticking away merrily on the mantel. It was ten minutes past five. Glenda and Kelly would be in as usual at six. By that time he would be long gone with them none the wiser until he failed to come back, giving him plenty of time to make his escape.

He pulled on his shabby overcoat and buttoned it up, then stared down at it disdainfully. It was the last time he would be dressed like this. As soon as he reached Newcastle – by train this time – he planned to deck himself out in a smart outfit, one to match the others awaiting his return inside Mitzi's wardrobe. He wanted to arrive back in style, was anxious to see her admiring expression when she opened the door before she fell into his arms and their life together began. One far removed from life around these streets.

He patted his breast pocket just to make sure he was carrying the key to the church, then he took a final glance round to check he hadn't forgotten anything, before heading for the door. As he did so his eyes fell on his father and rested there. A sickening bile swirled in his stomach and before he could stop himself he was standing before the armchair, eyes burning with hatred. The words he had wanted to say to this man since he had stepped over the threshold several weeks previously poured out.

'You pathetic bag of bones,' he hissed. 'D'yer know what being in the same room as you made me feel? No?' he said sarcastically. 'Well, I'll tell yer. You made me skin crawl. You're no man, yer just a corpse. No, yer worse than a corpse. At least you can bury a corpse and be done with it. Why don't you do yerself and everyone a favour, eh, and die?'

Lips tight with malice, he took a deep breath, nostrils flaring. 'I used to admire you. When I was little I wanted to grow up to be just like you. Hah, what a laugh! Fancy wanting to turn into a pitiful creature that hadn't got the guts to put his own wife out of her misery.'

His eyes narrowed and he leaned over to jab his father hard in the shoulder. 'D'yer know what it's bin like for me having to live with what you made me do? D'yer know what it feels like to put a pillow over yer own mam's face and hear her breathe her last? No, yer wouldn't would yer, you selfish bastard? You'd sooner have seen her suffering day in, day out. I'll never forgive you. Never, do you hear? I hope you rot in hell for what you've put me through.'

Straightening up he made to turn away then stopped

as a great surge of desire to brag about his accomplishments filled him. After all, what better person to do it to than the man he most detested and one who could not repeat to anyone what he was about to hear.

Mickey reared back his head, eyes flashing with pride. 'D'yer want to hear what yer son's been up to? D'yer, eh? I don't care whether you do or don't 'cos I'm gonna tell you anyway.' He gave a low, menacing laugh. 'I've robbed this town clean, got the rozzers running ragged, and they ain't a clue it's me. And you'll never guess where I hid it before I sold it on? Shall I tell yer? All right. It's in the church. But I ain't telling yer where. Try and work it out with that empty mind of yours,' he said, his tone malicious.

'And that ain't all I've done,' he announced proudly. 'I've got me own back on good old Leicester Corporation. And d'yer want to know how? I took what was owed me and extra as compensation. My God, if those idiots knew it was Mickey McCallan who took the beer from their bellies and the food from their brats' mouths, there'd be a hanging. But they won't, will they? 'Cos you can't tell 'em.'

His laughter rang out. 'Yeah, it's hilarious, ain't it? Well now yer know.' He leaned forward and prodded his father hard in the chest several times. 'And d'yer wanna know summat else? I feel better for telling yer. Yeah, I do.'

He straightened up and patted both his pockets again, checking all was in order. Then for the last time he settled venomous eyes on Frank. 'Now I'm off. And where I'm going is a far cry from this hell-hole. And best of all I've got a woman there, a real woman, one who knows how to make a man feel good. She's waiting for me. Yeah, she's waiting for me, Mickey McCallan. And d'yer know what? We're gonna live the life of Riley, me and her. The money I've made up to now is just the beginning.'

His passion spent, he turned and made for the back door. Then he stopped, turning back. 'No more back doors for me,' he growled. 'I'm leaving by the front.' As he passed by Frank he gave a salute. 'So long then, Father. Give my best to that stupid wife and sister of mine. Don't bother to get up and see me out. I know the way.'

Making his way down the dingy passage Mickey missed the sight of his father's hands gripping the arms of his chair.

Kelly arrived at Raggy's yard to find the place securely locked. She stared at the doors, confused. Alec never closed the yard until six o'clock and she reckoned it was only about a quarter past five.

A shoddy woman struggling to carry a heavy sack waddled up to join her. Letting the sack fall to the ground, she too stared in dismay at the closed wooden doors.

A door opened in a house across the road and a woman emerged clad in winter attire and carrying a shopping bag. She looked across at them. 'He's gone,' she shouted. 'Stormed out of that yard like the devil wa' on 'is tail about twenty minutes ago. Slammed them doors shut so 'ard I thought they'd fall off. I was watching from me window.'

'Alec?' Kelly shouted back, frowning. 'You're talking about Alec?'

The woman came across to join them. 'Yeah,' she said, nodding. 'Nice man is Alec.' She frowned. 'Well, he weren't nice about 'af an 'our ago. Flaming mad he wa'. Still, I can't stand round 'ere all day. Tarra.'

'Tarra. And thank you,' said Kelly.

She gnawed her bottom lip anxiously as she wondered what on earth could have happened to cause him to get angry enough to shut the yard early. Knowing him as well as she did, it must be something catastrophic.

The woman carrying the sack grumbled, 'I can't feed me kids now.'

Momentarily forgetting her concern over Alec, Kelly turned to the woman. 'What's in yer sack?' she asked.

The woman grabbed hold of it protectively. 'Bloody cheek! Mind yer own business,' she spat.

'I was only asking so I could offer to buy what you had, that's all. I deal in rags and woollens meself.'

'Oh,' the woman replied sheepishly. She opened out the sack. The stench from the collection of filthy rags inside hit Kelly full force. 'How much you gimme then?' she asked, eyes sparking keenly.

Under normal circumstances Kelly wouldn't have touched them. She had her rules as to what she would handle. 'A shilling,' she offered, much more than their true value and purely out of kindness.

'D'yer take me for an idiot?' the woman retorted.

Kelly was cold, tired and hungry, desperate to get home where it was warm. 'A shilling. Take it or leave it,' she said agitatedly.

The woman scowled. 'I'd get more at Raggy's,' she snapped aggressively.

'You'd get less at Raggy's. A tanner at the most. Them rags ain't worth the sack they're in and you know it.' She held out a shilling. 'Now d'yer want this to help feed yer kids or not?'

Scowling, the shoddy woman snatched the money from Kelly's hand and waddled hurriedly away. Holding her breath, Kelly tied the sack back up and heaved it on her cart. She looked once more at the closed wooden doors before heading on her way.

'Snow soon, I reckon,' Ada Adcock remarked as Kelly passed by her shop.

'Oh, hello, Ada.' She pulled the cart to a halt and shuddered, looking skyward. 'Yeah, I reckon you could be right.'

Ada picked up a box of apples, part of the fruit and vegetable display from the trestle table by the shop window. 'Thought I might as well get this lot in. Can't see me getting much more custom tonight.' She eyed Kelly's cart. 'You don't usually bring that home with yer, do yer, ducky? Thought you left it overnight down Raggy's yard?'

'I do normally but Alec closed up early.'

'Did he? Not like him. Hope n'ote's wrong?'

So do I, she thought. 'Well, I must get on. I'll have ter leave the cart down the jitty tonight and just hope no one pinches it. Oh, did Glenda come in and get some bits on her way home?'

'Yeah. Mona served her. I think she bought bread and tea. Oh, and a bottle of port.'

'Oh, did she? Well, she needn't think that's coming out of the housekeeping. See yer soon, Ada,' she said, giving the cart a heave into motion.

'Yeah, good-night, gel. Oh, just a minute – have yer heard?'

Kelly pulled the cart to a halt. 'Heard what?'

'About the dustmen's wages.' Ada put down the box of apples, pulled her cardigan round her and folded her arms, looking important. 'Snatched they were about eleven this morning.'

'Never?'

'It's true. Poor lad's in the infirmary with a bump the size of an ostrich egg on his head. The dustmen are up in arms. Well, yer can imagine, can't yer? Them going home and no wage in their pocket. I bet the wives are hopping mad, I know I would be.' She sniffed loudly. ''Course if they ain't bin paid, I won't get paid either so my tick book will be full before tomorrow's out.'

'Do they know who did it?' asked Kelly, appalled.

'No. Coppers ain't got a clue as usual. But whoever did's got some nerve doing it in broad daylight.' She shook her head. 'We ain't safe in our beds. I blame the war.'

'How?'

'Well . . . it must have summat ter do with it.'

Kelly couldn't see the connection. 'Let's just hope they catch whoever it was. Good-night again, Ada.'

She picked up the box of apples. 'Yeah, tarra, me duck.'

Face contorted angrily Alec stormed through the back door and into the back room. Norma was toasting her feet on the hearth, her nose in a magazine, the wireless blaring popular music. As it was snapped off, Norma jumped, her face paling alarmingly when she saw the thunderous look on her husband's face.

She closed the magazine and laid it on the floor beside the armchair. 'You're home early,' she said non-committally. 'I haven't got the tea on yet.'

'Cut the pleasantries, Norma.'

'What?' She was shocked by his tone.

'Did you have a nice day off?'

'Eh? Oh, yes. Yes, I did.'

'And what did you do?'

'What do you mean?'

'I asked a question. I'd like an answer.'

She shifted uneasily. 'Well, I did some shopping. I cleaned up.'

'And what else?'

Her eyes narrowed. 'I can't remember,' she said cagily. 'Nothing else, I don't think.'

'Don't lie. How could you?' he uttered. 'How could you do it, Norma?'

Panic filled her and her heart thumped erratically. In all the years she had known Alec, never had she known him to lose his temper. Witnessing him now in such an obvious fury frightened her witless and she knew only too well the reason for this show of uncharacteristic emotion. Slowly she rose, clenching her hands tightly. 'I . . . I don't know what you're talking about,' she said, her voice and face the picture of innocence.

'Yes, you do. Stop lying, Norma. You went to see Raggy, didn't you? Waited 'til I was out collecting on the lorry. You told him I'd leave if he didn't make me a partner. You told him if he didn't, I would start up a yard meself in competition.'

'No, I didn't,' she snapped defensively. 'I just paid a visit as your wife to show an interest in your job.'

'Don't lie, Norma.'

'I'm not. It's Raggy that's lying.'

'Raggy doesn't lie. That's one thing I do know about him. But you do. Do you know what you've done?' Alec said icily. 'You've devastated that old man. That yard is his living. He built it up from nothing. He thinks I'm going to leave him and take all his custom. He was weeping, Norma. I hope you're proud of yerself?'

Her back stiffened and her head came up. 'I did it for you,' she declared.

'Me!' He shook his head. 'No, Norma, you did it for *you*. My job as a dustman wasn't good enough for you, was it? This job really shamed you.'

'Yes,' she cried. 'It did. You could easily have got something better, but would you? No, because you've no backbone, Alec Alderman.' Her face glowed red in temper. 'Oh, I wish I'd never come back.'

'Then why did you?'

Before she could control herself she screamed, 'Because I had no choice. James didn't want me any more and you're better than nothing. Besides, *she* wasn't going to get her hands on *my* house.' Her hand went immediately to her mouth. 'Oh, God,' she moaned, throwing herself at him. 'I . . . I . . . Oh, Alec, I never meant none of that. You . . . you made me say it. I was

413

just angry. Alec,' she beseeched, 'don't look at me like that.'

He pushed her from him. 'So, Norma,' he said icily, 'we finally get the truth.'

'Truth? No . . . none of what I said was true. Please believe me, I just wanted to hurt you. I . . . I . . .' Her voice trailed away in horror as she watched him turn from her and head for the door. 'Where are you going?' she demanded.

'What does it matter?'

'It matters to me. You're my husband.'

'Was, Norma.'

'What! You don't mean that, Alec.'

'Oh, I do, Norma.'

Her face darkened in fury. 'It's because of her. That's where you're going, to her. Well, she won't get you. I'll never divorce you, Alec, never.'

His eyes narrowed angrily. 'Her? She has a name. And Kelly's done nothing to you. I gave her up for you – and what a bloody fool I was.' He took a deep breath. 'I'm going to try and sort out this mess with Raggy and I hope to God I can. But don't expect me back, Norma.'

She looked alarmed. 'Where will you stay?'

'I don't know and at this moment I don't care. I'll collect all me stuff as soon as I can. You can have the house and everything in it. I'll pay the rent 'til the end of the month to help you out, but that's all I'll do. I wish you well, Norma, and hope you find someone who can give you the living and the happiness you feel you deserve.'

He spun on his heel and headed through the door.

For several moments Norma remained quite still, shocked by what had just happened and waiting for it to sink in. When it did a torrent of tears burst from her and she crumpled to the floor, weeping bitterly.

★ ★ ★

Algernon paced the threadbare Axminster carpet. He stopped by the hearth and leaned over, holding his hands towards the glowing coals for warmth. Sighing, he straightened up, eyes staring unblinkingly at the fire. He should be glad he was soon to be leaving this freezing mausoleum, but he wasn't. He would miss it terribly. Thirty-five years he had lived in this house, thirty-five years he had preached the gospel from the church close by. First thing tomorrow the new Vicar would be arriving. Two weeks after he had seen the new man settle in, this church and Vicarage would no longer be Algernon's.

The new Vicar was a young man, hardly out of his curacy. How would he handle the needs of the people who made up his congregation? Would he bother to help those who lived in the vicinity that didn't come to church? Algernon took a deep breath. He shouldn't be worried about that, but he was.

He looked up at the clock on the mantel. It was just after a quarter past six. An hour and forty-five minutes to go before he gave his last sermon as Vicar of this parish, and so sorrowful was he at the prospect of leaving he hadn't a clue what he was going to say. But somehow he didn't feel it mattered. The congregation knew him, knew all that he stood for, and if his last sermon was not of his usual standard, he felt sure they would understand.

He felt a sudden need to go to his church, to be on his own there and say his goodbyes. This would be his last chance. Collecting his coat from the stand in the hall, he slapped his hat on his head and left.

As he rounded the bend in the path, automatically ducking to avoid a stray branch of laurel, the church loomed silently before him. He stood for a moment and stared at it. It wasn't a magnificent building, quite plain in architectural terms. There was no bell tower. No ornate gargoyles or impish devils or sweet-faced cherubs adorning elaborate masonry. Just stray grass and clumps of rotting leaves overflowing the lead guttering. The moss-covered, dirty gravestones, some so old their inscriptions had worn away, stuck up like crooked teeth amid tufts of rough grasses.

Nevertheless this church and all it encompassed was beautiful to Algernon. He thought of all the joyous weddings he had blessed; the numerous babies he had christened; the sad occasions of burying the dead. All part of his job, but something which for him had been a true vocation.

He arrived at the huge wooden door, took hold of the dull brass handle, turned and pushed. The door did not budge. It was locked. He frowned. But it should be open for anyone to visit at this time of night. He patted his pocket. Thankfully it held the key which he must have forgotten to return to its hook in the Vicarage after opening up that morning. Sometimes his vagueness paid off.

Inserting the key in the lock, he pushed open the door and entered.

Entering the back door, the first thing that a weary Kelly noticed was that the kettle was not boiling merrily away on the stove, and neither were any preparations for dinner underway.

Her mouth set grimly, still unbuttoning her coat, she made her way into the back room. Her eyes went straight to Glenda who was sitting at the table, still dressed in her outdoor attire, something which Kelly did not immediately comment on. 'Glenda, why isn't the . . .' She stopped abruptly as the look of utter devastation on her sister-in-law's face registered. 'What on earth's happened?' Her eyes flew straight to her father's chair. It was empty. Her mouth dropped open in horror. 'Glenda!' she cried. 'Me dad? Where's me dad?'

416

She ran round the table, grabbed Glenda by her shoulders and shook hard. 'Me dad? Where's me dad?'

Her head slowly rose, vacant eyes looked into Kelly's. 'Church,' she uttered.

'What?'

'Church,' she repeated matter-of-factly. 'He's gone to the church?'

'Church!' cried Kelly, dumbfounded. 'My dad can't think for himself, Glenda. He's a sick man. He ain't walked further than the lavvy for God knows how long. You've let him go to church?'

'He didn't ask me, he just went.' Moving mechanically she stood and picked up her handbag. 'He's gone to get Mickey.' Walking past Kelly, she headed for the door.

Kelly pulled her back. 'No, you stay here in case me dad comes back. I'll go to the church.'

Glenda shook her head. 'I'm sorry I can't. I have to go somewhere.'

'But me dad . . .'

'I'm sorry, Kelly. As I said, I have somewhere I have to go.'

Seeming totally oblivious to anything else, Glenda walked sedately out of the house.

Kelly wondered for a moment just what was going on, then bolted after her.

As she hurtled round the corner leading on to the Hinckley Road she ran slap bang into Alec who was on his way to Raggy's. He grabbed her by the shoulders. 'Kelly, what's got into yer?'

She stared wildly at him, panting hard. 'Me dad. Alec, it's me dad. He's . . . Glenda's . . . I can't understand . . .'

Firmly he held her at arm's length. 'Calm down. Catch yer breath a minute. Now tell me?' he ordered.

'I . . . Oh, Alec, I got home, me dad was gone. Glenda . . . summat's wrong with Glenda. She's . . .

she's had a brain storm. All she said was that me dad had gone to church to get Mickey.'

'To get Mickey? Why would he want to go and get Mickey? Where's Glenda now?'

'I don't know.'

'None of this makes sense, Kelly. Your dad's not got out of that chair for months. He ain't got the strength to walk far by himself, let alone . . .'

'Alec,' she cried, 'there's no time for this. I've got to get to the church. If anything happens to me dad, I'll . . . I'll . . .'

'Okay.' He grabbed her by the arm. 'Come on.'

Engrossed in his desire to begin his journey to Newcastle, Mickey failed to hear Algernon's footsteps approaching down the darkened aisle. What he did hear was the 'Amen' the clergyman uttered as he finished a prayer. But it was too late. Mickey had already appeared from behind the altar.

They stared at each other in shock.

Regaining his wits first Algernon exclaimed: 'What a start you gave me, Mickey.' He took a deep breath, and patted his chest. 'Enough to give an old man a heart attack. I thought you'd gone home.' His smile faded and a frown appeared on his face as he noticed the canvas bag Mickey was carrying. 'What's in the bag?' he asked in bewilderment.

'Er . . .'

Mickey's faltering response caused Algernon concern and he eyed him suspiciously. 'Well, Mickey?' he asked gravely.

Sheer panic gripped him. He had no excuse prepared, the last thing he'd been expecting was to bump slap bang into the Reverend Billings. His instinct for self-protection reared and without a thought for what he was doing he made a grab for a pewter candlestick from the top of the altar and slammed it down hard on a surprised Algernon's head. He dropped unconscious to the stone-tiled floor, a deep wound on his forehead pouring blood.

Staring down at him, Mickey's anger flared. Blast the stupid old devil. This had not been in his plan. This was not supposed to happen. Kneeling down, he placed his ear next to Algernon's mouth. He was still breathing. At least Mickey wasn't going to be done for his murder. He jumped back, alarmed, when the old man groaned. He was regaining consciousness.

Springing to his feet, Mickey snatched up the bag and started to run down the aisle. He stopped suddenly, staring back, his mind whirling frantically. He couldn't leave the injured man there. The congregation would be arriving shortly. Once the Reverend Billings was discovered he would name his attacker and then everyone would be on the lookout for Mickey. As a consequence all he had striven for, all he had achieved, the life he'd planned with Mitzi, would be shattered. He would spend the rest of his days incarcerated in jail. Mickey's mouth tightened grimly. He had not laboured hard and suffered as he had for that to happen. It was not going to happen. All he needed was some time to make a safe getaway.

Frantically he stared around him, fighting to work out what to do. Then suddenly it came to him. He raced back behind the altar, throwing the bag to one side of him, and scrambled around until he found what he was looking for. Grasping an iron ring embedded in a large slab on the stone floor, he pulled hard. The slab inched upwards. Mickey grabbed the end and heaved it away from the entrance to the crypt, the very place where he had hidden all the spoils from his robberies. Jumping up, he grabbed hold of Algernon's legs and heaved him across to the hole in the floor. With an unceremonious shove he pushed the old man through. A dull thud echoed round the church as his body hit the dusty earth floor several feet below.

Mickey was just about to replace the slab when a hand grasped his shoulder. Shocked witless he shrieked in terror, scrambling backwards, eyes frantically seeking for whatever had attacked him. They settled on a grey shape swaying before him. Recognition struck and he froze momentarily. 'You!' he cried.

Exhausted from his journey and gasping hard for breath, Frank slumped for support against the back of the altar. His speech was laboured. 'I'm . . . taking . . . you . . . in, Mickey.'

'In? The police, you mean?' He smirked. 'What for?'

'You . . . know . . . what . . . for. I heard . . . all you . . . said.'

Mickey's sneer broadened. 'So what? And who the hell d'yer think is ever gonna take anything you say seriously when you ain't spoke a word for the last nine months?' With sarcastic emphasis he jabbed his finger several times against the side of his own head. 'Doolally, that's what they'll say you are.'

'They'll listen . . . Mickey. I'll make 'em listen. You're . . . bad. You have . . . to be stopped. You have to pay for what you've done.'

With all the strength Frank could muster, he righted himself and made a feeble attempt at a lunge for his son.

Mickey anticipated it and side-stepped out of his reach. But he need not have bothered, Frank had no hope of restraining him and they both knew it.

Mickey laughed. 'I ain't got time for this. I don't give a fuck what you heard. I don't give a fuck what you tell anybody. I won't be around to care. Now get outta me way.'

As he rushed past Frank, he swept his arm wide, catching him full in the chest.

Frank stumbled backwards, straight down into the dark abyss of the crypt.

At that moment a distraught Kelly, with Alec just behind, ran breathlessly into the church, coming to a halt by the first row of pews. 'Dad!' she cried, her eyes scanning frantically around. 'Dad, where are yer?'

Mickey froze. No, it couldn't be. He couldn't believe it. This was all he needed, his sister turning up at such an untimely moment, and it sounded very much as if she had someone with her. Once again his mind whirled frantically into action. Just how was he going to get out of this situation? But he would have to think of something. He had no intention of letting anything stop him now. Suddenly an idea struck him. Dropping his bag, he put it out of sight. 'Is that you, Kelly?' he called.

'Yes, it's me. Is Dad with you?'

'You'd better come here, and quick,' came the grave response. 'I'm behind the altar.'

Kelly looked at Alec. He grabbed her hand. 'Come on,' he ordered, running her down the aisle.

'Thank God yer here,' Mickey cried as they arrived, despite the instant hostility he felt when he spotted Alec. Quickly he hid an evil smile. He couldn't have wished for a better person to have accompanied his sister, considering what he had in mind. Mickey had waited years to settle this score. He had finally got his wish.

With a bewildered look on his face, he addressed his sister. 'It's dad – he was raving like a lunatic. He's attacked the Reverend Billings.'

'What?' Alec demanded. 'Frank attacked him? I don't believe it! Are you sure?'

Mickey held his breath, fighting to control an urge to respond with physical violence. 'I wouldn't have believed it neither but I saw him with me own eyes. I was in the vestry doing a job for the Reverend when I heard shouting. I wondered what the hell was going on. I

421

thought it were some ruffians wrecking the church. I was so shocked to see me dad. I couldn't believe it, Kelly. Him and the Reverend were arguing. Before I could do 'ote, me dad had grabbed hold of a candlestick from the altar and bashed the Rev over the head.'

'What?' they both cried, shocked.

'Where are they now?' Kelly demanded.

Mickey inclined his head, indicating a foot or so to the side of them. 'Down there. When me dad hit the Rev, the Rev made a grab for him and they both fell in. I think they're hurt bad. I was just going for help when I heard you shout.'

They both spun round and stepped across to peer into the blackness of the gaping hole below.

Kelly's hand went to her mouth. 'But none of this makes sense,' she said, confused. So many questions were flashing through her mind.

Taking charge, Alec grabbed her arm. 'Let's ask questions later, Kelly. We need to get down there and see what's happened.' He motioned to Mickey. 'Pass me that candlestick. Have you got any matches?'

Reaching up for it, Mickey nodded. 'In me pocket somewhere.'

The candle was lit, and leaning over the entry to the crypt they all looked down. The flickering light did not reach far enough for them to see the bottom.

'One of us will have ter go down,' said Mickey. 'You go,' he addressed Alec, 'while I run for help.'

Alec nodded. 'Hurry!'

Mickey ran off.

Handing the candlestick out to Kelly, Alec sat on the edge of the hole, searching with his feet for a rung of the rusty iron ladder that led down to the crypt.

'Quickly, Alec,' she urged, kneeling by the side of him.

Halfway down he reached up his hand. 'Pass me the candlestick and be careful you don't put the flame out.'

She did as he bade, then swung her legs over the side. 'What are you doing?'

'I'm coming down too.'

'Kelly, this isn't the place . . .'

'Can yer see me dad and the Reverend?' she interrupted as she began her descent.

Jumping down on to the earth floor, he held out the candle, peering round him. 'Yes. But things don't look good, Kelly.'

She stepped off the last rung and threw herself down by her father.

'Oh, Alec,' she said. 'He's bad.' She whipped off her coat and spread it across Frank. Her eyes flashed to the crumpled body of the Reverend Billings close by. 'So's the Rev. I hope Mickey isn't long.'

'Best not to touch them, Kelly, just in case,' ordered Alec. 'I'll go back up and see if I can find some blankets or something in the Vestry. I'll leave you the candle.'

Suddenly he noticed a brown envelope by Frank's head and automatically bent to pick it up. He held it towards the light and frowned in bewildered recognition. 'Why, this is . . .'

A movement from above startled them both and they looked up. They could just make out Mickey's face peering down at them.

Kelly's heart leaped. 'Oh, thank God, Mickey, that was quick.'

A sound alerted Alec and he suddenly frowned, the expression rapidly changing to one of sheer dread. 'Just what are yer playing at, Mickey?' he demanded savagely.

Kelly turned and eyed him, confused.

'Doing?' Mickey grinned. 'You wanted to be together, didn't yer? I'm just making sure you are. Goodbye, Kelly. And you,' he spat at Alec, 'this'll show it doesn't ever pay to cross Mickey McCallan.'

With horror Kelly suddenly realised just what Mickey

423

was up to. 'Mickey, don't!' she screamed.

Alec made a lunge for the iron ladder but he was too late. 'You bastard, McCallan!' he shrieked as the slab covering the entrance slammed into place with a dull echoing thud, the draught it sent blowing out the flame of their candle and plunging the crypt into pitch darkness and an eerie, deathly silence.

Kelly emitted a scream of sheer fright. 'Oh, my God,' she shrieked. 'Alec, we're shut in! We're going to die. He's left us to die.'

He was very afraid she was right. Despite his own rising terror, he gingerly stepped off the ladder and felt his way over to her, mindful of the prone bodies of Frank and the Reverend Billings. He put his arms round her, pulling her to him. 'Now then,' he soothed. 'We ain't going to die. Someone will find us.' He doubted that statement very much but the last thing he should do was to say anything to worsen her fears. 'Now come on,' he urged. 'Sit down, that's it.' Huddled on the cold earth floor, he rocked her gently in his arms. 'The congregation will be arriving soon. We'll make such a racket then they're bound to hear us.' He wiped her tears away tenderly with his fingers.

She raised her head and although she could not see him, looked into his face. 'Will they, Alec? We won't die then?'

He knew they could make all the noise they wanted but this place was airtight and possibly soundproof, the slab flooring above being at least three inches thick. 'We'll be out of this place before you know it.' He hoped he sounded positive, although it was the last thing he felt. He laid his cheek next to hers. 'Would I ever lie to you?' he whispered.

'No, Alec,' she sobbed. 'You'd never lie to me.' She sniffed hard as she pressed herself closer to him. 'This place smells horrible. What's it used for?'

He held his breath. Thank God she didn't know, oblivious to the rows of decaying bodies that lay along stone shelves cut into the walls. Thank God that she had been so concerned for the welfare of her father and the clergyman that she hadn't had time to take stock of her surroundings. 'It's . . . er . . . musty wine you can smell. It's where the altar wine is stored.' He forced a light-hearted chuckle. 'Probably a dead mouse or two as well.'

He felt her shudder and automatically tightened his arms round her protectively. For several long moments they lapsed into silence.

'Alec, it was Mickey, wasn't it? I don't know why, but I know it was him that did this to me dad and the Reverend. I just know it was. They weren't fighting, Mickey was lying. But what made me dad come here? What?'

'Hush, Kelly, hush. You'll drive yerself daft trying to work out what happened. We'll find out everything when we get them out of here.'

Alec thought he had a good idea of what had transpired. It had been Mickey who had stolen the dustmen's wages. The evidence of that was inside his pocket in the shape of a brown wage envelope. Somehow the Vicar must have found out and that had sealed his fate. And Frank? He still couldn't fathom how Frank, in his mental and physical condition, had found his way here. But at this particular time he did not feel it right to voice his worries to Kelly. She was distraught enough as it was.

'We will get out of here?' she pleaded.

'We'll get out, Kelly.'

They lapsed into silence again.

'Alec?'

His mind was fully concentrated on trying to find a way out of here, but the only way he knew of was securely barred to them. 'Mmmm?' he murmured.

'What did Mickey mean when he said you'd crossed

him? Is it something to do with why he hates you so much? Please tell me what happened. I need to know.'

'It was so long ago, Kelly. It was a misunderstanding of sorts. I was about fourteen at the time, Mickey about ten. I'd gone into Ada's shop for something for me mother. As I opened the door I saw her disappear into the back and as she did Mickey shot behind the counter and grabbed some packets of cigarettes. As he ran for the door he stopped when he saw me and just glared at me. It was a warning.

'As he ran out Ada came back and I remember thinking it was strange 'cos she never said a word, just asked me what I wanted, served me and I left. The thing that really struck me, Kelly, was that I instantly knew it wasn't the first time Mickey had done this.

'Anyway, next thing I knew Mickey was accusing me of splitting on him as the local copper had been round to see your dad. Mickey was going to be charged, Kelly, and that meant he would end up in borstal. He threatened me with all sorts. I must admit, though, I didn't let his threats bother me.'

'But Mickey never went to borstal, so what happened?'

'It was your dad's doing. He pleaded with Ada to drop the charge and paid for the cigarettes that were stolen. Worked long hours to make that extra money. Took him weeks. When yer dad found out Mickey was hell-bent on revenge against me, he came and explained what had really happened. He asked me not to tell anyone as Mickey had promised him it would never happen again.'

'If you didn't tell the police, then who did?'

'Ada. He'd been stealing from the shop for quite a while. She'd been trying to catch him red-handed for ages. It was her that pressed the charges.'

'Did he know it was Ada?'

'Later. But he still chose to believe I was involved in it somewhere.'

'So he's carried a grudge against you all this time for no reason?'

In the pitch darkness Alec nodded. 'But I suppose his grudge against me for getting him the sack from the bin rounds was justified in a way. And I should never have retaliated against him. Because I did, I was sacked too.'

'Oh, Alec,' she choked. 'This is all my fault. I know Mickey probably better than anyone. I had a good idea what he was capable of. But I never expected anything like this. When he came back I wanted to believe he'd changed, more for Glenda's sake than anything. I should have known he'd be up to something. It was too good to be true. That should have warned me. But it didn't, did it?'

'With the best will in the world, Kelly, if someone wants to fool you bad enough, they'll do it. I should know.'

'You? What d'yer mean?'

He took a despairing breath. 'Norma. She fooled me good and proper. And what a fool I was! I gave up you, whom I really loved, because I thought I had no choice but to take her back. I was so wrong to do that, Kelly. Will you ever forgive me?'

'Forgive you?' she murmured. Momentarily their dire situation and the possible consequences were forgotten as her heart burst with joy. 'Oh, Alec. I love you. There's nothing to forgive. You did what you felt was right and I admire yer for that.'

'You do?'

'Oh, yes. I can't lie and say it didn't bother me. The pain I suffered was terrible, but so long as I thought you were happy . . .'

'Happy? Oh, Kelly, I've never been so bloody miserable in all me life.' He held her even tighter. 'Will you still have me, Kelly?' he whispered emotionally.

'Alec, you know the answer to that.'

427

His lips sought hers. Their kiss was long, demanding, passionate.

Finally she broke away from him. Reaching up, her hand found his face and she tenderly stroked it. 'How long have we been here, Alec?'

It felt like hours but could only have been minutes. 'Not long.'

She sighed. 'I'm worried for me dad and the Reverend. We need to get help for them.' Her voice faltered. 'Oh, Alec, I ain't stupid, I know it's all hopeless. No one's gonna find us down here.' She lovingly kissed his cheek. 'I know this is selfish but I'm so glad you're with me. When . . . when the end comes . . .'

She paused, feeling him stiffen.

'There's going to be no end, not yet, Kelly. While I have breath left in me, I'll fight.' He released his hold on her. 'Stay here,' he ordered.

'Where a' you going?' she cried. 'Alec, don't leave me.'

'Leave you? Never again, Kelly. I'm going to get us out of here.'

Stumbling upright, he stood still for a moment to get his bearings, trying to remember which way Frank's feet had been facing when he had first set eyes on him on reaching the bottom of the ladder. Alec took a calculated guess, searched around until his hand touched Frank and felt along his body. Satisfied, he stepped gingerly across. His guess proved right. His hand scraped the metal side of the rusting ladder and he winced at the resulting graze which trickled blood.

Hunched nearly double at the top of the ladder, he pressed his back hard up against the entrance slab, his hands to either side, and with all the force he could muster heaved his weight against it, muttering, 'Sod you, McCallan, I ain't beaten yet.'

428

As the slab to the crypt thudded into place, Mickey breathed a deep sigh of relief. He was safe. Anyone who could stop him leaving was now dealt with. And dealing with Alec Alderman had given him such satisfaction. Thoughts of his sister and father incarcerated below he shoved aside. What had happened to them was their own doing. They should not have interfered. Although he did feel a stirring of guilt about the Reverend Billings. He was a nice old man and had done Mickey no harm. Still . . .

Retrieving the canvas bag from a secure place under the altar he swung it on to his shoulder and hurried down the aisle, his thoughts filled with his forthcoming journey and the woman who waited for him at the end of it.

'Going somewhere, Mickey?'

A man seated in a pew rose up and side-stepped into the aisle, blocking Mickey's route.

He gasped, mouth dropping open, eyes wide in alarm. 'Er . . . I'm . . .'

'What, Mickey?'

'Just on me way home. Bin doing a job for the Reverend.'

Grimacing, the man nodded. 'Taking work home with you, I see?'

'Eh?'

The man's voice deepened. 'What's in the bag, Mickey?'

'The bag?' He gulped. 'Oh, this bag. It's the Reverend's. He asked me to drop it in at the Vicarage on me way home.'

Smiling grimly, the man shook his head. 'I've met some liars in my time but you beat them hands down, McCallan.' He held out his hand. 'Pass it here.'

Unhooking the strap from his shoulder, Mickey clutched the bag to his chest. 'I said, it's the Reverend's, and if yer want to see inside it you'll have to ask him. It's private.'

'McCallan, pass it over.' This was not a request but a demand. 'Or are you afraid of what I'll find inside?'

Mickey threw back his head. 'Afraid? Me?' He shrugged his shoulders. 'Why should I be? I've told yer, this is the Reverend's bag.'

'And you're a liar. I know, Mickey. I know it all.'

'Know what? You know nothing.'

'Oh, but I do.'

He smirked. 'You've got n'ote on me.'

'Ah, but we have.'

'How?' he nonchalantly demanded, feeling positive that the only person who could have revealed anything was safely disposed of in the crypt.

From a pew further down the dimly lit aisle another figure rose. 'Because I told them, Mickey.'

He squinted hard in the dimness. As recognition dawned he froze, horrified. 'You?' he spat.

'Yes, me, Mickey. I've told them everything.'

'Huh! You know nothing.'

'Oh, but I do. I heard, you see. I heard every word you told yer dad.'

His jaw dropped, eyes bulged. 'But . . . but you couldn't possibly . . .'

'I was in the kitchen, Mickey. I'd come home early. I wanted to make you a nice dinner. Kelly and me had something to tell you. I was so excited.' Her voice lowered. 'I couldn't believe what I heard. How you bragged to your father about what you had done. You make me ashamed to remember that I was so in love with you. I was blind to what you really are. You're not fit to be walking the streets.' Glenda took a deep breath, and looked at him defiantly. 'The police know everything, even about the factory fire.'

'I had nothing to do with that!' he cried.

430

'Didn't you? Then how come I smelled paraffin on you when you came home that night? You can't lie and cheat yer way out of this one, Mickey.'

A sudden fury erupted inside him and he made to attack her but a forceful grip restrained him. 'Don't even think about it,' he was harshly warned.

'You bitch!' Mickey spat. 'How could you do this to me?'

'How could I, Mickey?' Her voice lowered to barely a whisper. 'You killed my brother. But d'yer want to know what really finished me? The knowledge that you've never loved me. All I was to you was something to be used. I loved you. You were me whole life, so much so I turned a blind eye to all you got up to. I would have crawled on me hands and knees to the ends of the earth for you. But not now. Let your other woman do that for you, if she ever gets the chance. And, Mickey, believe me, she's welcome. I just hope she realises what she's letting herself in for.'

Face devoid of emotion, Glenda turned and walked slowly down the aisle and out of the church.

'Charge him, Constable Plant,' Sergeant Little instructed the young constable who had been watching from the back of the church. 'And don't bother trying to make a run for it, McCallan. There's four policemen outside the door and that's the only way out.'

'That's him in the Black Maria, Sarge, so are yer coming?'

Seated once more in a pew, Reg eyed Constable Plant thoughtfully. 'I'm sure you can manage to deal with him down at the station. I think I'll stay here. It's kinda peaceful.' He picked up a Bible from the shelf in front of him and flicked through the leaves. 'The evening service starts soon. I might stay for that.'

'What, you, Sarge?'

Reg eyed him, offended. 'And why not? I'm not averse to a bit of religion, lad. Besides, it's Reverend Billings's last service. Done a lot of good in these parts has the Reverend, he'll be missed. I'd like to pay my respects. You've no objection, have yer, Constable?' he suddenly barked.

At his unexpected retort, Plant jumped. 'No, Sarge,' he replied hurriedly.

'Good. Off yer go then. And you can let the congregation come in now.' A sudden sound made him start. 'Just a minute, what's that?'

'What's what?'

The sergeant stood up. 'That noise. It's coming from . . . over there, back of the altar if I ain't mistaken.'

Both running down the aisle, they arrived behind the altar and looked around, listening.

A noise at his feet made Reg skip sideways. 'Down here, Constable. Quick, help me get this slab up.'

As the slab was raised a pair of eyes looked gratefully into his and a relieved Alec said, 'Am I glad to see you.'

Chapter Forty

'Kelly, for goodness' sake, what have I told yer about lifting heavy things?' Alec rushed over to his wife, took the box off her and put it on the counter. He slid one arm protectively round her waist and tenderly patted her swollen stomach, his face filling with pride. 'Please, Kelly, if anything should happen to you and the baby . . .'

'Stop fussing,' she interrupted him, eyes twinkling happily. 'The box was light, Alec. Anyway, I was only trying to help. You know I miss working.'

'I don't know how you can miss it. You're down here more than you're at home. You should be resting, Kelly.'

'Resting? Alec,' she gently scolded, 'I'm having a baby, I'm not ill.' At the look on his face she raised her hands in mock surrender. 'Okay, I give in. I'll rest. Well, I'll put my feet up for half an hour this afternoon. That suit you?'

He smiled. 'It's better than nothing, I suppose. I just . . .'

'I know,' she said, her eyes filling with love. 'You're just taking care of me. Well, don't ever stop. I like you fussing over me.'

'And our son?'

'Or daughter.'

'Oh, no, Kelly, the first one has to be a son. Alderman

and Son, Scrap Metal Dealers.' He grinned. 'Though I suppose Alderman and Daughter would look just as well on the sign.'

She slapped him playfully on his arm. 'I don't care what it is so long as it's healthy.'

'Neither do I. Now get home and put yer feet up.'

'In a minute. I want to pop and see me dad and Raggy first. I suppose they're both in the shed fixing things as usual?'

'I'm not sure what Raggy is fixing but yer dad is fiddling with a cuckoo clock.'

'A cuckoo clock?'

'Mmmm. It's lost its "cuck" though. It just goes "oo". He's hell-bent on mending it.'

They both burst into laughter.

Alec bent over and whispered in her ear, 'I'll let you into a secret. He wants to give it to you as a present when the baby's born.'

Her face lit up with delight. 'Oh, Alec,' she whispered.

He kissed her cheek. 'I'll see you later. If I don't get back to this queue of customers, I'll have a riot on me hands.'

She made to walk off then stopped. 'Oh, don't forget Glenda and Reverend Billings are coming for dinner tonight. Though he did say he might be late as he's some visits he wants to make.' She tutted. 'When will he realise that he's supposed to be retired?' She shook her head. 'Never, I expect. I'll ask Raggy to come to dinner too, shall I?'

'You can, but you know he won't.'

'One time he might surprise us. We can but hope. He'll enjoy the leftovers I bring down tomorrow, though.'

'He always does.' Alec wagged a finger. 'Now remember what I said.'

'I will. As soon as I've seen me dad and Raggy, I'll get

off home. Oh, but are you sure I shouldn't stay and help
Avril and Hilda . . .'

'Kelly!'

'All right, I'm going.'

A smiling, deeply contented Kelly weaved her way
steadily through and round the heaps of scrap metal and
sacks of rags and woollens towards the shed at the back
of the yard, nodding a greeting here and there to the
customers. For a moment she stopped and looked
around. Always when she took time to do this her heart
would fill with pride.

Alderman's Scrap Metal Dealers covered a large,
purposely enclosed area off the Braunstone Gate back-
ing on to the canal. It was the ideal location to attract
people from all areas. They had chosen this site well.

It did not seem possible that she and Alec had been
married for nearly two blissful years. Not possible that
nearly four had passed since that terrible episode in the
church and its aftermath: the slow healing of shattered
minds and dreadful bodily wounds. But they had come
through and now it was all beginning to fade into
memory.

Kelly and Alec lived in a roomy terraced house off
the Narborough Road, allowing a bedroom for herself
and Alec, one for her father and one for the baby when it
arrived. There was a little garden out the back which
Frank tended with loving care. Glenda rented a tiny flat
above a grocer's shop on the Hinckley Road not too far
away and visited often. Kelly and Glenda's friendship
had deepened considerably as each supported the other
after their terrible ordeal and for both women a life
without the other in it had become unthinkable.

Making the decision to open his own yard had not
been easy for Alec, his loyalty to Raggy weighing heavily.
It was the old man himself who had suggested it and
who had volunteered the money to finance it initially. He

was getting too old now, he had realised, to be running his own yard. Conditions had been stipulated though. He wanted to live on the premises, in his own shed, and he wanted Frank as his crony. These demands had been readily accepted.

All his old customers were happy to patronise the new yard and many others joined them. The business was doing well. The main thing that concerned Kelly was that Alec was happy.

She patted her swollen stomach. 'All this will be yours one day,' she whispered to her baby. 'But you'll have to promise that me and yer dad and yer grandad, Uncle Raggy and Auntie Glenda, can always be part of it 'cos yer see we all love it so much.'

'Talking to yerself?' a voice said behind her.

She spun round and smiled warmly in greeting. 'Hello, Glenda.'

'Hello, yerself. I thought you were supposed to be resting?'

Kelly eyed the laden hand cart. 'And I thought you said you'd never knock on doors?'

Glenda grinned. 'I don't, they come to me,' she playfully fibbed. 'About dinner, Kelly . . .'

'Oh, yer still coming, ain't yer?'

'Yes. But . . . is there room for another?'

'Another?' Her face lit up. 'You've a . . .'

'Friend,' Glenda cut in. 'But let's say it looks promising.' She pecked Kelly on the cheek. 'See you later.'

Eyes shining, Kelly watched as her friend pushed the cart away. This was the news she had waited so long to hear. It meant that finally Glenda was putting the past behind her. How her sister-in-law had suffered through Mickey. What torment she had gone through, her statement being the crucial information that had put him away. Despite knowing she was right in doing so, the guilt had lingered on.

This news that she was bringing a man to dinner was indeed a turning point and no one was more delighted than Kelly.

She walked towards the shed with an added spring in her step. Opening the door, she poked her head round. The sight that met her eyes sent a warm glow rushing through her. Two pairs of hands were busy fiddling with intricate bits and pieces, two pairs of shoulders hunched over the bench, two faces frowning deeply in concentration.

'Everything all right, you two?' she enquired.

'Mmmm,' mumbled Frank.

Raggy just grunted.

At The Toss of a Sixpence

Lynda Page

At eleven years of age, Albertina Listerman loses her parents in a terrible accident. Approaching her twenty-first birthday, she experiences further tragedy: her half-brother commits suicide, having squandered the family fortune, and Ally is no longer acceptable in the elegant Victorian society of her childhood.

Robbed of her very last penny, Ally is thrust into a world of hardship for which she is ill-prepared. Her only salvation comes from meeting Jack Fossett during one of the worst rainstorms in Leicestershire's history. Jack is a kind, caring young lad who takes pity on the beautiful, bedraggled girl, and he and his younger brother and sister welcome Ally into their hearts.

But Jack's mother, Flo, is deeply resentful of all gentlefolk. And time must pass and secrets must be revealed before Ally and Flo can see eye to eye – particularly when they discover that Ally is in fact not as destitute as she thought . . .

0 7472 5504 0

HEADLINE

And One For Luck

Lynda Page

Grace Wilkins and Bessie Rudney have been neighbours for over twenty years but it takes the outbreak of the Second World War for them to become friends. Bernard Wilkins doesn't like his wife or their daughter mixing with the Rudneys; and the more time Grace spends with Bessie, her six boisterous children and her loving husband Tom, the more she realises what has been missing from her own loveless marriage.

As the war takes it toll on Leicester, and one by one the menfolk leave to join the fighting, Grace finds comfort in helping others. First, Clara Smith, her reclusive neighbour with a tragic past, needs her support; then hundreds of evacuees come to town. Among them are Londoners Madge Cotting and her waiflike children Jessie and Tony, whose welfare causes Grace serious concern. Each day, as she takes on another new challenge, Grace realises that her daughter has been right all along – it's time to break out, really make something of her life, and possibly find true love, before it is too late . . .

0 7472 4855 9

HEADLINE